SILENCE PASS

SILENCE PASS

Liahona West

Blackbriar Press

ISBN 978-1-7368206-6-7 (paperback)
ISBN 978-1-7368206-5-0 (ebook)

Published in the United States of America.

liahonawestauthor.carrd.co

To my very own grump.

A Note to Readers

This book contains scenes with/mentioning/allusions to:

Grief
Emotional, verbal, and physical (minor) abuse
Violent death of a loved one
Sexually explicit scenes
Swearing
Violence
Traumatic death of a teenager
Kidnapping

Other Works

The Fade Series
Metallic Heart

Anthologies
Straighten Your Crown
Twisted Tales of Holiday Horror

Scan me to listen to

the book's playlist

Preface

Originally, *Silence Pass* was never planned...until Sibyl and Luke changed things. They were such a hit with the early beta readers of *Metallic Heart* that I knew I needed to explore a relationship between the two: Luke, the moody, reclusive hunter, and Sibyl, the woman who somehow knew exactly how to bring out more than just the grump. Who are they to each other? What are their hopes? Dreams? What challenges will they face within their story?

There was a few changes I needed to make to *Metallic Heart* before I could work in an unplanned book, but it was so worth it.

Creating these characters and writing them together was simple. They somehow just...fit. I knew there had to be a reason why, and so their past together was formed, taking a bit of inspiration from my real life husband to bring Luke to life. Maybe that's why they worked? Maybe, in using much of my husband's personality, I subconsciously saw myself in Sibyl? Whatever the reason, these two were such a joy to sit with for the six months it took to write this book. Enjoy!

- The Author

Part One

Reconnect

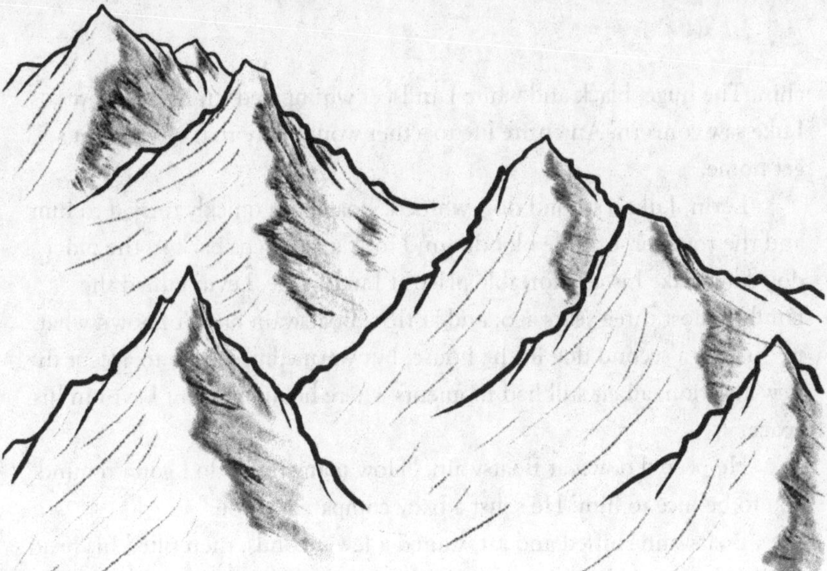

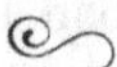

1 | LUKE

Dance among the poppies, the daffodils, and the wisteria.
Dance among the clouds. The sun. The moon.
It is there that you will find your soul,
a soul I shall cherish for eternity.

Luke leaned against his bow, hand stuffed underneath his thick coat to stop the blood oozing from the gash in his side, and blinked. He'd managed to climb out of the ravine, so what did it matter that he now had to find his way home without a trail to follow? He knew the way home well enough, even with the fine coating of snow growing thicker by the minute.

One of his dogs shoved his elbow and he cried out when the action shifted his torso. Again, he pressed his hand against the torn shirt underneath his coat, cursing his luck. He'd been seconds from bagging a deer that would set him and his dogs up for months when the ground gave way beneath him. Luke knew better than to stand so close to the edge of a ravine, but desperation drove him to make poor decisions. No meat for a month, all the while rationing his own food so his dogs wouldn't go hungry made him desperate.

"I know," Luke whispered as he scratched underneath Boatswain's chin. The huge, black and white Landseer whimpered. In his kind eyes, Luke saw concern. An entire life together would have that effect. "Let's get home."

Levin, Luke's second dog, whined. Boatswain quickly turned to him and the younger, brindle bloodhound took a few steps back so the older dog could take his comfortable place at Luke's side. Levin joined the family almost three years ago, and at first, Boatswain hadn't known what to do with a second dog in the house, but warmed up slowly to accept the new addition, albeit still had moments where he didn't want Levin in his space.

He peered down at Boatswain. "How many times do I gotta remind you to be nice to him? He's just a baby compared to you."

Boatswain sniffed and sat, waited a few seconds, then tilted his head back to look at Luke.

"You be nice," Luke reprimanded again, not convinced Boatswain would listen. He rubbed underneath the dog's fluffy chin. "You guys are brothers."

Boatswain groaned in response.

After a short sigh, Luke said, "Alright," and eyed the way back home again. His vision blurred then snapped back into focus. Dread took hold. If he didn't get back to his cabin soon, he'd have to start considering emergency field protocol and he regretfully didn't know as much about the plants in the area to know which ones would clot the blood and which ones would leave his dogs without their human.

Levin, in his ever unsatiated energy level, ran circles around Boatswain and Luke. He'd dash off into the brush, too-long-for-him-legs flying awkwardly every which way, and would return with various treasures: small sticks, a squirrel, leaves. At one point, Levin came back with a long branch, perfect for using as a walking stick if he snapped a few thin twigs off.

"Good boy," Luke said as he rubbed Levin's frozen jowls.

Luke couldn't reach over his head to secure his bow, so he groaned loudly as he bent over and tied it to Boatswain's pack. He didn't like leaving his weapon and lifeline strung, but he currently didn't have the strength.

It took far too long to reach the cabin. Luke stumbled and fell. Boatswain's search and rescue training snapped into gear and he released a high-pitched bark and licked Luke's cheek before going back to barking.

"I'm alright," Luke groaned and used Boatswain's pack to leverage himself to his feet. He groaned again, his eyes watering. It had taken a few years for him to adjust to the pain, but injuries like the one threatening to bleed him out were now minor inconveniences. Sure, they still fucking hurt, but he managed the pain so well, he worried if he had nerve damage somewhere.

Sweating and frozen from the weather, Luke stepped up to the crooked old door. He stared at it for a few moments, building up the mental cage for his pain receptors so he could ram his shoulder against the door and get it open.

"The only damn time I regret living here," Luke grumbled, pressed his bloody hand on the cold surface, and inhaled. He could do it. Just a quick one, two, slam, and he'd be in.

Boatswain panted beside him and when Luke glanced down, the dog put his nose against Luke's leg, a slight sliver of white visible in his eyes. He could always count on Boatswain to hint at the seriousness of an injury.

"Better take care of this quick then, huh?" Luke turned back to the door, closed his eyes once more, turned the knob, and slammed his shoulder against the wooden surface. Immediately, he wanted to cry as pain sledgehammered through his body. He yelped and stilled, fists balled, and waited for the pain to wane.

Boatswain whined and paced a hole in the ground.

"I'm sorry boy," Luke said as he prepared to hit the door again. "We have to get inside."

Twice more Luke hit the door and by the third, Boatswain let stress get the better of him, and growled and snapped at Levin who came over to investigate the commotion.

"One more time," Luke whispered, trying desperately to keep his emotions in check. The heat of his blood lingered on his pant's waistband now. He hated making Boatswain so worried.

Just get inside. Climb through the window if you have to.

"One more time." Luke shook his head to clear his vision. "One more time then I figure something else out."

He could go toward the Compound, and might actually make it, but if he passed out, Boatswain knew to use his nose to sniff out the birch bark a few select people carried on them.

With a fourth slam against the door, it swung open and Luke nearly toppled inside. Levin made a beeline for his bed, spun in circles, and laid down to watch Luke hobble inside. He tore his shirt and coat off and dumped them on the floor before gathering up supplies in the chest Boatswain nudged open with his nose.

First aid kit in hand, Luke crashed into the spare chair, fell into the other one, and with shaking hands tried to sew up the nasty gash right below his ribs.

"God fucking damn it!"

His body went rigid as soon as the needle touched his inflamed skin and right then and there Luke learned just how dull it had become after doubling as a clothing needle. Soora would probably have a conniption if she found out. At least he sanitized it after each use.

Luke tried again, biting down on his lower lip, eyes watering, and vision going all funny when he tried to force the needle. He'd pass out soon and still hadn't made the first stitch.

Levin perked up, ears forward, whip-like tail smacking the cabin wall. Boatswain did the same, but unlike Levin who jumped to his feet to greet the visitor Luke hadn't yet heard, Boatswain stayed by Luke's side.

Soora appeared in the open doorway, confusion falling as soon as she saw Luke's predicament. "What did you do now?" she reprimanded and immediately went into doctor mode. As soon as she inspected the wound, she tsked and looked up at him with her almost black eyes. "You've been acting a fool again, haven't you?"

Not in the mood, Luke glared down at her. "I haven't. We're all hungry, chachi. Can you blame me for getting reckless?"

He was as white as they came, but Soora had asked him to call her the Hindi word for auntie long ago and he gladly fell into using it.

She pulled her long hair free of her hood and set the tan animal fur coat on the back of her chair before digging in her doctor's bag to pull out a fresh bone needle and horse hair thread, and snatched his dull one away. "Don't do this." She waved it in front of his face and set it down on the table. "Honestly," Soora grumbled. "Have you retained nothing from my lessons?"

"No. I haven't. Because I'm currently bleeding out, one of my dogs is clueless, and the other is hovering like a mother hen about to implode from the stress I'm causing him. So, no, I'm not currently worried about your doctor stuff."

She groaned. "Hold still."

The bone needle burrowed into Luke's lacerated right side, shooting stinging pain into his armpit. He groaned through clenched teeth, tilted his head back, and forced his body to stay still despite the urge to scramble away clawing through his bones.

"Chachi," Luke yelped at his uncle's wife, white-knuckling his chair seat. "Sew *faster!*"

Soora huffed, her dark eyes flicking to him as she stabbed his tan skin again with the threaded needle. "You know, you remind me very much of a toddler—"

"Ow!"

"—who doesn't want to put on his shoes. If you keep squirming, I might—"

"Fuck!"

"—miss."

Luke stared up at the ceiling and his eyes caught the unmistakable movement of bugs crawling along through the rafters he'd just sealed last week and glowered. He counted five new webs. Luke kept the cabin as clean as he could but, with the colder temperature outdoors, the pests were relentlessly searching for warmth, and his house was, apparently and regrettably, the target.

Great, Luke grumbled internally as his skin crawled. *Why does it have to be spiders?*

He squirmed in his seat and decided to watch Soora work instead of contemplate spider deaths. She wiped quickly at some dried blood left over from his fruitless effort to fix his own problem and kept working.

Soora glanced at him, her dark eyes sharp daggers warning him to quit moving. Of her and Mason, Luke's blood uncle, she was the wilder one. The one with a tattooed sunflower on her half-shaved head, and eloped with a white military brat, much to her traditional parent's dismay. She studied medicine, never bore her parents any grandchildren, and spoke just a bit too blunt for their liking.

Luke adored her...Except when she stitched him up like a doll who'd lost its arm.

He grumbled, tired of sitting through pain. Each stab of the needle sent a shock across his chest.

"How much longer? I need to get back to my mischievous w...w-ways."

"Twelve stitches isn't quick work. Your so-called mischievous ways will have to wait."

Luke ground his teeth together and opted to stop talking.

The evening, autumn sun slipped into the cabin through the window, marking three hours since Soora had arrived. She'd finished a while ago, opting to stay for tea and monitor Luke's condition after watching him nearly pass out and picking up his blood-stained clothes from the floor.

"Your mother's birthday is in a few days." Soora glanced at him expectantly then set down her now empty cup. "Are you going to be there?"

Luke stood to take her dish to the sink, immediately slow to straighten fully, the burn of his freshly sewn skin forcing him to calculate his movements. "At her celebration?" he clarified. "No. I'll get her something though."

Soora clicked her tongue. "This is the fourth one you'll miss. Eventually, she's going to ask why."

"Then let her."

"I know you don't mean that."

They shared a glance, sizing each other up, two hard-headed bulls waiting for the other to charge.

Luke folded his arms. "I'm not going."

"That's not why you need to go. Your mom misses you, she rarely sees you – I know because she talks to me about it – and if you go, you'll shock everyone. Especially," Soora poked his chest, "if you speak."

Luke waved her hand away. "I don't see w...w-why she doesn't come here for a visit. Do I really have to go there?"

"Normally, I'd suggest that to her, but in your case, you need the push."

He absolutely didn't need the push, finally happy in his run-down cabin with his dogs and no nosy aunties taking it upon themselves to change his situation. It wasn't like he'd wanted to leave, but the bullying had gotten to be too much, too physical, and in order to find his own path, Luke had pulled away from everyone. Was it healthy? No, but he didn't have the physical strength back then to fight back and now, even after six years, he still didn't know if he had the mental bravery to confront those responsible.

Levin, his mastiff, named after the landowner in the book Anna

Karenina, pushed on Soora's hand until she rubbed his head.

Much like his dog, Luke held a general dislike for humans. They were loud, smiled too much, and enjoyed talking. Worst of all, their pointless questions drove him mad. But Levin sure adore Soora . Boatswain shouldered in on the scratches, his tongue soaking Soora's pants.

"I don't like talking," Luke mumbled in an almost-whisper.

"I know."

"People don't talk to listen. They talk to hear themselves."

"That's partly true."

"Are you coming? At least?"

Soora smiled apologetically. "I'm afraid not. The Compound is preparing to harvest what hasn't been killed off by the frost."

Soora and her husband, Mason Hodge, founded the Compound nine years ago along with Mason's best friend, Graham Whickman. Now a thriving community housed in an abandoned high school, all three original founders could enjoy their retirement, passing it down to Mason's protégé and her husband: Eloise and Bannack Owusu. Luke knew them through his ex, Sibyl Marchant, and had become fast friends with Bannack about three years ago when Luke had helped them escape a nasty storm.

Catching onto a potential subject change, Luke leaned forward. "How are things?"

"Not good. This early cold snap has us worried how we'll make it through the season. It's normally a stressful time. Especially now since we didn't have enough time to squirrel away enough food. We'll make it, by Bannack's projections, but barely. Mason came out of retirement to help manage everything." She released a bitter chuckle. "What a year to take over a community."

Luke nodded, unsure what to add, except, "I'm sure Mason trained them well. I know you guys will figure it out, and if you ever need more hands on deck, I'll gladly make the trek over."

"That's kind of you." Soora continued, "The Compounders are concerned, and rightfully so. Every day this week, we had to break a thick layer of ice with a rock to get water for the horses and lost our rabbit kits and many chickens to the weather. And the windows are freezing over."

He shook his head in disbelief. "That's horrible."

"It is." Soora looked at her hands. "An early winter hasn't happened since the Day of Ashes..."

Her words drifted away, and Luke didn't speak. Day of Ashes happened fourteen years ago when the radical terrorist group, Fade, kidnapped and murdered the president and her officials, and unleashed nuclear bombs on the six most dangerous fault lines in the United States. The resulting explosions decimating the country. Fires, earthquakes, and tsunamis came next, fracturing the bomb survivors. Terror led to mobs and civil wars broke out. Without good medical care, death tolls rose and disease spread, killing millions within the first year.

"Have you been practicing?" Soora asked after wiping at her eyes.

He gave Levin a scratch underneath his chin and the dog's leg smacked the floor like a woodpecker digging in a tree. "Not in a bit."

"Practicing before a big event like your mother's party has always helped words flow easier for you. Gets rid of the jitters, at least."

"I know." He gave her a sideways glance. "Still not leaving my cabin."

"And when are you going to give her an answer about her offer?"

Luke groaned and leaned back. His chair creaked loudly. "This again?"

"Yes. I'm going to keep asking about it until you understand how important it is to have goals and look forward to a future. Hiding away from your problems here won't make them go away, it just saves them for a later date, and they'll be worse."

"I have no intention of becoming clan leader." He turned away. "You hear it. My stutter. They'll think I'm an idiot."

"If you truly don't want to take over for your mom, then tell her. She'll be okay with your decision." Soora smiled at him. She tilted her head. "Do you want to take over? Honestly."

"I..." He leaned back in his chair. Living in the cabin had been the best years of his life but every time he returned to his parents' home and saw the work his mom performed with ease and grace, he craved that intimacy of knowing who he wanted to be, yet he couldn't shake the fear that he'd fuck it up somehow. He wanted to make her proud. He wanted his life to mean something, to help people. But he couldn't believe he was built for it, no matter how often people told him he'd do great. Something smaller, maybe? More...quiet. He couldn't take over his mom's legacy, could he? Why did it have to be him, anyway? Why not his dad?

"She has to name someone, you know that, right?"

"I do," Luke said and his heart fell a little at the idea of another person taking care of his mother's clan. "I'm w—" he paused, closed his eyes to find a different word so he wouldn't fumble through the original one, "frightened I'll ruin what she built."

"She needs to know. Tell her." Soora yanked hard on the crooked door, stumbling backward as it swung forcefully open. "She'll understand."

He rubbed his hands together as he glanced outside at the falling snow, grateful for the heat of his cabin, and stared at the floor. "Shit. I don't know if I can let her down like that."

"Let her down as in you don't want to do it or you do, but you're scared shitless?" Soora asked and let her words hang in the air for a second before continuing, "I will tell you one thing..." she approached and leaned against the back of the chair she'd sat in, "well, two. One, your mom will love you no matter what you decide. Two, the Compound is struggling with frost, then your mom's clan definitely is. They're farther north than we are. You may need to check in on her."

"Fine," Luke sighed and walked to the fireplace to toss another log in. "I'll go. But I'll be grumpy about it."

"I wouldn't expect any less from my favorite nephew," she said as she gathered her things and walked back to the door. "Be careful with your stitches, okay?"

Luke nodded. "Bye."

The slam of the crooked door made Luke flinch. Boatswain whined as if he understood Luke's woes. He glanced down at the Newfoundland. The dog smacked his lips then curled his head up at his master.

"You and Levin are the only company I need."

The dog sneezed in response and lifted his body off the dusty floor to rest his head in Luke's lap. The large dog's weight and warmth brought him comfort. He stroked the long, silken, black and white body of his dog, tufts of downy undercoat floating silently to the floor and mixing with the thin layer of dirt.

Can't forget to brush him out today.

Levin, in seeing the pets Boatswain enjoyed, shoved in on the action.

"For some reason, Soora's convinced I need to be around people." Luke grasped Boatswain's cheeks and inclined his head to look into his large, brown eyes. "Why are people so exhausting?"

Someone tapped on the door and Levin, still firmly attached to the trigger of a knock, rushed forward and released a menacing string of wall-shaking barks. A muffled yelp of surprise came from outside.

"I came out here to be alone," Luke grumbled, dreading the cold he'd subject his body to when he opened the door, "and people keep knocking on my damn door today."

He stood, grunting from the stitches pulling at his skin, stepped between the dog and the door with one finger raised, and stared at Levin while he walked forward. Levin tried to get around Luke, but he kept his body between the mastiff and the trigger. After a minute or two, Levin reluctantly boofed and sat.

"Good," Luke praised with an airy, happy tone and gave the dog a piece of leftover jerky. "Stay."

Levin lowered to the floor.

Luke opened the door for a young man holding a bundle of papers in his arms, cold air invading his warm bubble. The dark-skinned visitor covered in a generous layer of animal fur and crocheted clothing stared around Luke to look at Levin on the floor. "He's not gonna eat me, is he?"

"No. He's fine now." Luke patted Boatswain's head when the older dog nudged him. "Can I help you?"

"Yeah." The young man held out the papers, his breath leaving his mouth in puffs. "It's my sketch book. I'd like them bound."

Luke welcomed him into the cabin and gestured to the table in the middle of the room. "Your name?" Luke asked as he closed the door behind him.

"Maxwell, sir." The kid shed his furs, placed the bundle he'd been holding onto the table, and warmed up by the fire.

The formal title of "sir" made Luke want to frown. "Just Luke is fine." He picked up the papers and quickly rifled through them. Each handmade page stretched as long as his forearm, thicker than he was used to working with. "Make these yourself?"

Maxwell nodded then glanced down. "I know they're thick but I'm getting better at it."

"How many books ya requesting?"

"I was hoping maybe...five? With how thick the paper is and all." Maxwell glanced at Luke, shoulders raised as if he were cautiously protecting himself. "O-or not. I'm open to suggestions. I've gone to the others, but they all told me the paper's too thick."

Luke sighed. The others Maxwell spoke of were the three

bookbinders in the area. He'd met them before and quickly noticed with their gatekeeping and better-than-those-people behavior. They were picky, snobbish, turning away bright-eyed artists like Maxwell who only wanted to keep their papers in one place. Luke had received more service from those the other binders turned away than people who came to him via word of mouth.

"I can bind them for ya."

Maxwell beamed. "Really? They're not too thick?"

"No." He rubbed the paper. It had a good texture with beautiful flecks of tan, purple, blue, and green. "How did you make it?"

Maxwell scooted forward in his seat excitedly. "I got some tow from La Parfana – she had extra – then added some shredded old clothes and dried lavender – I like the smell – to get the flecks." He glanced up at Luke, hopeful. "What do you think?"

Something about the paper made it special. Luke could feel the imperfection, created through hands empty of callouses and scars, yet encapsulated his entire soul.

"Can I keep looking?" Luke asked as he lifted the corner of a page.

Maxwell nodded with a slight smile.

Bodies—muscle bound, clothed and unclothed, serpentine, elegantly posed, young, old, and in between—filled the pages. Maxwell's exquisite exploration of anatomy took Luke on a journey of expression. He didn't look long. Didn't need to, to pick up on the life and emotion in Maxwell's craft.

As Luke turned the pages, the sketches turned into facial designs and one face, in particular, made him pause. Sibyl Marchant.

Maxwell had drawn her glancing over her shoulder, thick dark hair cascading down her back, and staring forward with wide, playful eyes. Deep dimples sat on her cheek and Luke knew she had a second, unseen due to the drawing's angle.

It had been only a couple of years since he'd seen her last. They'd spoken cordially since, but every time they did, Luke's stomach twisted into knots knowing she wasn't his anymore. It was one of the greatest sources of shame and guilt in his life, letting her go the way he did. Perhaps they should've talked about it. Occasionally he considered the idea, but his fear and avoidance tendencies always got the better of him. And Sibyl was so good. She never brought it up, treated him the same way she had when they were just friends. He suspected that she truly was mad but just hiding it, except that didn't track with what he knew of her.

"W…W-Where did you draw her?" Luke asked reverently.

As Luke waited for Maxwell to answer, he internally cringed. He'd never escape the occasional, mild shame that came when he stuttered. At all times he remained hypervigilant of his words, especially the w's, and long a's, using alternative words where possible. Unfortunately, he couldn't get around the damn question words like 'why,' 'what,' and 'where.'

"At La Parfana where I got the flax tow for my paper," Maxwell answered. "When I asked to draw her, she agreed. Her mom is an artist, too."

He knew that. Luke stared at her portrait, a slight smile on his lips. *I remember when her hair would fall around her face like that.*

He looked at her eyes, the light perfectly captured in them, and remembered the almost overwhelming desire to kiss her whenever she peered up at him hovering over her, hair spread across her pillow and a blush dusted across her cheeks. God, he missed that feeling.

Then he noticed Maxwell staring at him, confused.

"Beautiful," Luke said as he sat back. Realizing the word could be read into too much, he cleared his throat. "Your art is beautiful."

"Thank you. When will you have my books finished?"

"They should be ready in about twenty-one days. Stay here and I'll get the swatches."

Without access to traditional printing services, people had adapted, resorting to pre-electric ways of producing books: stitching them together by hand by trained bookbinders. He had spent close to ten years developing his craft and personal style, using handmade leather or linen to create the covers which he then hand-stamped and adorned with gold or silver.

Luke tied his shoulder-length, black hair up and rifled through his workstation at the back of the cabin, passed over the shearing equipment, book cloths, and leathers until he found colored, wax-covered linen thread, ribbons and various sized book boards.

He sat next to Maxwell. "Here's everything I offer," Luke said and walked him through the options. Which thread color? Headband or no headband? What color pattern? Did he want a specific pattern for the sewn spine or the typical saddle stitch?

Once Luke finished laying it all out, he waited on Maxwell, quiet across from him at the table, to voice what he'd chosen.

Maxwell thought for long enough that Luke wondered if he'd overwhelmed the kid. "Need me to go over it again?" Luke asked.

"No, I got it. Just thinking." He went quiet again then said a minute or so later, "Can I exchange the headbands for a ribbon instead?"

"Sure. A headband isn't required but I do suggest it if you expect lots of hands will touch it."

"This is only for me, so, no. And do I choose my cover...stuff later?"

"Yes. Once I bind the pages together, w...w-we'll meet again and you'll give feedback on the product. Once you approve it, w...w-we'll move onto designing the cover. Do you like leather or linen for the cover?"

Maxwell frowned. "Are they much different in cost?"

"They are. Leather is one hundred coins for each book and linen is forty."

Maxwell thought for a moment, looked down at the coin purse he'd set on the table, then back at Luke. "I want linen."

"Alright. I charge half now and half at delivery." Luke accepted the payment. "Thank you. Return in twenty-one days and I'll have the manuscripts ready."

"Thank you." Maxwell stood and grabbed his furs. Before leaving, he said, "I'm grateful you took me on. You were my last hope."

Luke smiled. "Their loss is my gain."

Maxwell chuckled. "That's for sure." He waved over his shoulder. "Thanks again!"

When he closed the door, Luke glanced down at Maxwell's folios still on the table. He ran his fingers across the paper. "It really is beautiful."

Sibyl's picture, her eye showing from underneath some papers, caught Luke's attention and he pulled it free, sitting.

"Sibyl..."

They hadn't spoken for four months, nine days, and five hours. He missed her teasing, their witty banter, and the friendship he'd formed with her, but he couldn't bring himself to face her again after avoiding her for so long. Besides, he'd heard she was dating again.

In thinking of his and Sibyl's relationship, his mind drifted to that night.

The night he'd let her go when she'd begged him not to.

Honestly, some moments in the dark, tiny cabin, Luke wished he hadn't been such a coward. His gloom would only bring her sunshine down, and if he'd told her his true feelings back then, perhaps knowing she'd moved on wouldn't hurt so fucking much.

Sometimes he didn't want to stay isolated in the cabin, but it was safe and familiar, and no one could touch him within the walls. He didn't have to predict how someone would respond or if he said something in the wrong way or any other plethora of issues that may come up in a conversation over a past conflict.

While thinking of his regrets, Luke caught the watchful eye of Boatswain. The dog huffed, shifted his feet, and laid his head on Luke's knee, those big, round eyes telling him how much of an idiot he was being.

"*Just talk to her,*" Boatswain scolded.

Luke stared at him. "I can't do that," he whispered.

"*Coward.*"

"That's not nice."

"*She deserves an explanation. Talk to her. Tell her you're sorry.*"

"She's dating someone else. She's moved on."

"*Coward.*"

"You know w...w-what?" Luke moved Boatswain's head off his leg and stood. "I'm not talking to you anymore."

Levin rapped his tail against the table leg, signaling he wanted food and the racket made Luke jump. He glanced down at the younger dog and smiled.

Leaving the drawings on the table, Luke prepped dinner for both dogs. He used the last bits of rabbit meat from earlier, cracked the final two eggs into the bowls, and sprinkled blueberries and kale on top. He opened a cupboard, looking for apples, but found none.

"Alright boys." He turned, both bowls in hand, and looked at Boatswain and Levin. The only sign Boatswain struggled to be patient were his light paw taps on the wooden cabin floor. Levin, on the other hand...Whining, drooling, and scooting inch by inch closer to Luke's feet with every passing second.

Luke helped to remind him how to wait then gave the dogs their breakfast and watched them for a few moments. "You both eat better than I do most days."

His mind drifted back to the missing apples and his stomach clenched. *Time for some shopping, I guess.*

Grocery shopping wasn't too bad if he went at specific times, preferably at first opening. He had at least an hour before people started filing into Market Town, but with it being past midday and knew the street would be filled with shoppers. Not ideal and highly uncomfortable, but unavoidable. He'd neglected entering town for so long, if he waited any longer the dogs would go hungry.

After they finished eating, Luke clicked on each dog's pack, struggled into his tattered, grey traveling cloak, and set off down the frozen trail to town.

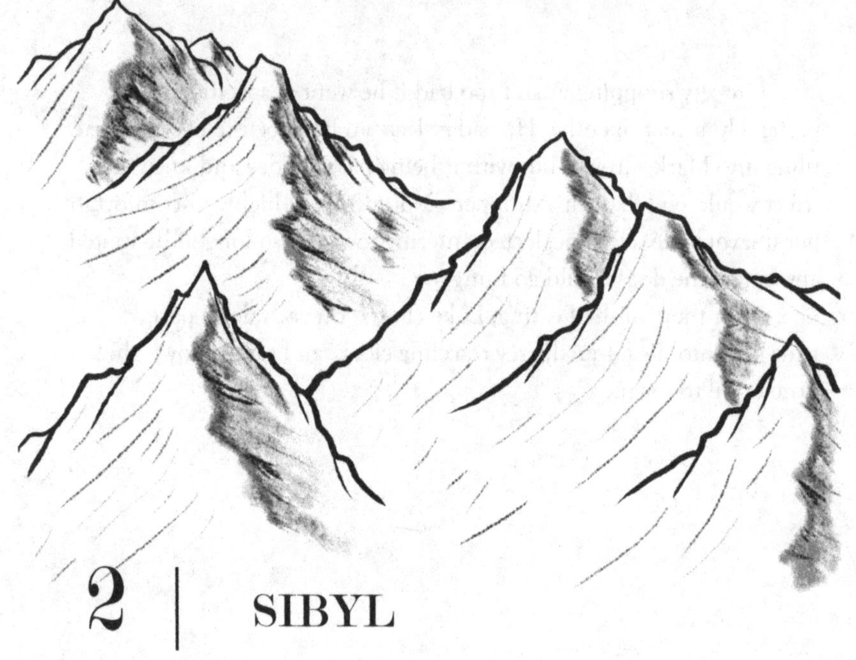

2 | SIBYL

We are the sun and moon, the earth and sky.
Where you are, so too, am I.
We travel together, and never touch,
yet 'tis what I wish for, above all else.
A touch of comfort, of peace, of belonging,
my heart is yours, if only you shall take it.

Her roses were wilting.

Despite covering them at night, sprinkling on eggshell powder, pouring compost tea and fishpond water over the dirt, and mixing in horse manure, they were still drooping, some having lost their petals altogether.

"You're still freezing." Sibyl touched the underside of a bloom. Two orange petals fluttered to the ground and she pulled her hand away. "I'm so sorry, guys."

She shivered. The afternoon should have been a typical early fall day: not too warm and not too cold and with a slight breeze that pricked the skin, but the snow changed all that. It fell in quarter size chunks, turning the ground white and threatening to weigh down the bushes and plants that had no time to acclimate to a cold temperature.

Sibyl draped her shawl around her shoulders and turned to Eloise perched atop the half wall of stone that kept plants like the chocolate mint and oregano from spreading where they weren't wanted.

As always, Eloise perched atop the rock wall pushing the plants trying to escape back into their concrete cage. Sibyl scanned through her log book, wondering what went wrong with her roses in a greenhouse that should keep them warm enough to stay alive.

Eloise's voice broke through her focus. "What do you want?" Eloise asked.

"I want these flowers to stop wilting."

"No," Eloise chuckled. "What do you want?"

Exasperated, Sibyl set down her pencil and picked up her pruning sheers. "Are you getting reflective in your old age?"

"We're practically the same age, Syb." Eloise laughed and folded her arms in mock annoyance, muttering under her breath, "I hardly think twenty-four is old."

"Here," she handed Eloise a bundle of overwintered tulip bulbs she in a crocheted cotton bag and pointed to a group of crates. "Put those with the others."

Eloise hopped down and walked over to the boxes while Sibyl returned to her plants.

Roses, tulips, daffodils, hollyhocks, peonies, and many other flowers lined rock pathways, sat in pots, or huddled in raised beds within the greenhouse walls made of windows harvested from the abandoned homes around Market Town. Pillowy ground cover, some on their last days of flowering, pooled over the thin paving stone's edges. A picnic table sat on the far side, Hunter, her apprentice, occupying it as he bundled herbs for drying.

His toe-head, white blond hair complimented his dark eyes and strong jaw. By the way he moved, Hunter bled confidence. When he had arrived at La Parfana, he was a new amputee and had recently lost his third job due to the struggle of adjusting to the use of one arm. Some shop owners had told her hiring him would hurt her business, but she saw the desire for growth and innate ability to pick up new skills quickly, and after eighteen months of determination and a heaping dose of altering the shop to make Hunter's job easier, Sibyl proudly named him co-owner.

"You never answered me, Syb," Eloise said.

Sibyl didn't glance up as she handed Eloise a couple bundles of herbs. "I have my shop, my family, and Peter. I don't need much else."

She ignored the mild tensing of her stomach at the mention of her boyfriend.

"Blech," Eloise rolled her eyes, but Sibyl knew it was an act. "You're so sappy," Eloise continued. "I'm not talking about that, I want to know what you want. There has to be something beyond," Eloise's voice raised a few octaves to imitate Sibyl's voice, "your boyfriend, your family, and your shop."

Sibyl laughed. "Shut up." She shoved her shoulder into Eloise, which made her stumble a bit and chuckle.

"Seriously," Eloise said, propping up on her elbows. "What do you want from life? What are your goals?"

Honestly, Sibyl hadn't thought of it much. While Elosie preferred to pile life high on her plate, Sibyl chose to take life in smaller portions, and she was happy with that. It worked, even if Eloise didn't understand.

"I want my life to mean something. I want to help others. It's why I have this shop. I can use the clothes, make-up, and perfume I make to give people back a bit of normalcy."

"And what about something more?" Eloise asked, then clarified when Sibyl gave her a tired stare. "What I'm trying to say is that your shop's amazing – I'd never have the patience to grow all of this and keep it alive. I can barely keep myself alive – but this is only a small piece of you. Don't you want to expand things and help people in a different way?"

"Like how?"

"I don't know. You gotta figure that out."

Sibyl tossed a handful of basil at Eloise's chest. "Don't go all deep on me then leave me hanging."

Eloise laughed and wiped at some stray leaves. "I'm not you, but I can't help but think you were meant for more than a humble shop owner who has the occasional romp in the upstairs broom cupboard with her boyfriend."

"You are impossible."

They both laughed, Sibyl leaning against Eloise. They'd been best friends since they were young teens. Back then, Sibyl was shy and quiet, but she'd had a moment of bravery when she decided to take in some nice clothes she'd outgrown and give them to Eloise. It had been terrifying, especially since Eloise intimidated her, but that act began a strong friendship Sibyl wouldn't trade the world for. Their bond was timeless. Sisters.

"Well, lunch is over for me," Sibyl announced as she fixed her braid. "I need to get back to my customers."

Eloise stood and smoothed out her shoulder-length red hair. "Don't fade into the background, okay? That's not where you belong."

Sibyl chuckled and waved Eloise away, who waved back and slipped out the greenhouse door. Sibyl watched her leave, smiling.

She's so happy now.

She remembered how bad her trauma had been and even though Eloise would never truly be rid of it, she was in a really good place. It had taken Eloise years to get to it. Sibyl hoped it never changed.

She gave one last look at her wilting roses, frowned, and picked up her basket of freshly harvested flax, the season's final crop, and walked into the warm interior of La Parfana, heated by burning madrone wood. Sibyl set the basket on the table in the middle of the shop amid the handmade soaps, wooden toys, and perfumes. Everything, aside from the toys, were handmade from the plants in her greenhouse, the trees and plants outside, and what she could purchase at the trader stands out on Market Street. She'd spent three years caring for and cultivating her small empire.

Placing her shawl on the back of a chair, Sibyl removed her gardening gloves. She loved the shop's wooden tones and happy indoor plants covering nearly all empty spaces, a forest within four walls. Dyed linen scarves, dresses, and shirts were folded neatly in one corner, while in another sat her makeup line of rouges, lip stains, and eyeliners. Her perfumes at the storefront were by far the most popular and she sold out often, which reminded her...how could she keep up with the demand of her rose scents if they were falling out of season three months too early?

The ringing of a bell sounded and Sibyl turned to greet a customer with a smile on her face, but her smile faltered.

Peter squeezed her midsection with an attempt at a low, playful growl.

She gasped. "Put me down, Pete!"

"No."

A familiar jolt of fear soured her stomach and Sibyl pushed harder against Peter's arms. Her eyes flicked to Hunter distracted by a customer and she plastered a smile on her face.

"Now." Sibyl's whispering voice lifted an octave when he tightened the embrace and she struggled to breathe past it. "You're hurting me."

Peter's voice had a cruel edge that sliced at her fears and multiplied them. "How can I be hurting you?"

"You just are. Stop."

"Ask nice and I will."

Again, Sibyl eyed the customer and Hunter, now dreading they'd turn around and see she needed help, but they didn't seem to notice. Good.

"...Please," whispered Sibyl finally. "Please put me down."

When he set her on the counter, Peter gave her a peck on the cheek. "That's my girl." He moved between her legs, and smiled again. A chuckle complimented Peter's sparkling green eyes. "I couldn't wait to see you."

She smiled past the nausea in her stomach. To sell her lie, Sibyl laid her arms around his neck to play with his tawny hair. "You couldn't, could you?"

Peter nuzzled at her neck, his hand drifting to her waist. "You're too beautiful to leave for too long. I felt deprived."

Sibyl laughed quietly. "And what did Thea say to you leaving early from your courier job?"

"You smell so good." Peter lifted her wrist to his nose and his lips brushed the tender skin. "Rosemary and..." he took another whiff, "something else. Very nice."

It's bay, Peter. Rosemary, bay, and pine.

She hated that she cared about something as innocuous as a perfume scent, hated that it mattered, but when he cared about nothing except what made him happy, could she blame herself? It was like he'd conditioned her to crave crumbs of attention.

"Peter," Sibyl warned, pulling away and jumping from the counter. She made sure to let her gaze linger, knowing he'd always been a bit insecure of their height similarity. A little way for her to fight him without him knowing. She stuck her hands in her pockets. "You lied again, didn't you?"

Peter made a pouting noise at the back of his throat, then stepped forward to hold Sibyl again. "What's it to her if she thinks today's our anniversary instead of next week? I had to see you."

She squirmed out of his arms and deftly snatched up her basket. "I care. What happens when she finds out? This is the fifth job in a year."

Peter's excitement dwindled. He rubbed his toe on the floor. "I'm not going to mess this job up. Promise. It's one lie, and not even a big one. She knows me, so I'm sure she'll understand."

Now Sibyl felt like a mother scolding her child and her irritation sparked into anger that she struggled to hide. "We agreed when we started our relationship back up that there'd be no more lies—"

"I know—"

"And that you'd try really hard to keep your job—"

"Yes, but—"

"You really gotta stop interrupting me." Sibyl turned away, her face red and insides trembling. "I want us to work because I love you, but I need you to step up."

An arm snagged her wrist and Sibyl whirled around straight into a stinging slap across her cheek. She stumbled away, shocked he'd do such a thing with an audience then realizing no one lingered in the shop.

Where's Hunter and the customer he was helping?

"Don't tell me what to do." Peter's bright eyes blackened. "How dare—"

Hunter, oblivious to the altercation, entered from the back, carrying a bundle of dried herbs and Peter immediately shifted into happiness again.

Sibyl tilted her face away, pretending to be distracted with a box of rouges that needed unpacking. She rubbed her cheek with her shoulder which also wiped away her tears.

"Where do you want these?" Hunter's asked from behind her.

Plastering a smile on her face, Sibyl turned to Hunter still holding the herbs. She pointed towards a café table with two chairs then back to the box in her hands. "Over there. We can get to them on Thursday."

Hunter chuckled. "That's today."

With a start, Sibyl whirled around toward the calendar on the wall. "What?"

"Uh...today's Thursday. What's wrong?" He leaned in slightly. "You hit your cheek?"

"Shit," Sibyl jumped into action and fluttered about the shop, searching for her coin purse. "Shit, shit, shit."

Peter's voice sounded in her head. *"I told you not to swear."*

He didn't need to say anything for her to feel the toxic energy of those words down to her bones.

"What's your hurry, anyway?" Hunter asked.

"I'm meeting with a traveling salesman. This is the first time in two years he's coming back to the market and he carries rare items." She talked as she rummaged through the drawers, nearly emptying them completely in her rush. "Damn it! Where's my—"

Coins jingled and she flicked her head up to look at Peter with the leather pouch in his hand. "Found it under the scarves. I'll give it to you for a kiss."

She paused for a split second, knowing if she said no, he'd make a scene and Hunter would ask questions, so Sibyl snatched the bag from him, gave him a kiss, and rushed out the door.

As soon as it closed behind her, she skidded to a halt, and popped back into the shop. Peter put down a scarf.

"Back so soon?" he asked.

"I need you to watch the shop."

Peter's acknowledgment didn't come fast enough. She'd miss out on the chance to purchase anything, and couldn't believe she was placing the fate of her baby into his hands, but she knew with Hunter there, Peter would be on good behavior.

Putting a sly smile on her face, Sibyl said, "There will be a prize if you help."

Even as her stomach squirmed, she watched Peter consider her offer within seconds. "Fine."

She didn't offer any thanks, just rushed down the road, twirling around people so she wouldn't bump into them. Frozen grass crunched under her feet as a group of kids ran past, several wearing helmets from surrounding countries when they'd fruitlessly offered their help to the Unites States people. The cold wind bit at her face. She pulled her coat tighter.

Briar Lane slowly woke, named as such by the sign discovered half torn and hidden by grass growing untamed from the cracks in the road. As one of three main streets that made up Market Town, Briar Lane's provided trade and provisions for local clan members and Compounders.

The salesman beamed when he saw Sibyl. "Hello, friend!"

Breathless, Sibyl shook his hand. "I hear you have some citrus from down south."

"I do." He grabbed an open crate filled to the brim with various fruits. Oranges, lemons, limes, and grapefruit. "Take your pick."

Sibyl's mouth watered. The light, zesty notes clung to the air around the box, filling her nose with memories of childhood summers spent playing and snacking on cold oranges on the back deck. She wanted all of them.

"What are they going for?"

"Four coins per pound."

Ten minutes later, Sibyl happily snacked on an orange she had taken from the bag filled with grapefruit, lemons, and limes. She pulled back the peel and squirreled it away. The impossibly sweet fruit broke and snapped juice into her mouth as she chewed, tears forming in her eyes.

This was so worth it.

"The orange is just that good, huh?"

His deep voice caught Sibyl off guard and she inhaled the last slice of orange. She coughed, stumbling to her feet.

Luke stood underneath the shade of a large tree, watching her with a blank stare.

"Don't mind me," Sibyl hacked, inhaling around the orange pieces, put her palms to her knees, and hacked again. "I'm...I'm just—" she wheezed, "dying."

He gave her an awkward single pat on the back. "There, there."

Still bent over, Sibyl craned her neck around, and glared at him. "Really?"

From her position, his large, imposing mass was even more so, and her stomach went all fluttery. He was just as gorgeous as she remembered. He kept his dark beard neat, a worn travel cloak and large scarf loosely wrapped around his neck and hanging down by his knees, wore distressed jeans complimented by a green flannel hanging at his waist and thick black boots. She'd always been fascinated by the white scar through his left eyebrow, wondered where he'd gotten it, but had been too afraid – stupidly – to ask about it during their brief, tragic relationship of six months.

"If you're talking, you're breathing. Looks like you have it handled."

Boatswain shoved his great body against her legs, his head tilted back as if it were broken, and gave her an open-mouthed stare. His large tongue flopped out the side of his mouth just as a second, familiar dog latched to her other leg. She coughed through the final stages of choking on her orange, sighed, then crouched and ruffled their fur. "You'd help me if I were choking, wouldn't you, boys?" She noticed the second dog, almost forgetting completely Luke had rescued him. "Is that the dog that bit you during that fight?"

"Levin was *holding* me," Luke clarified. "Not biting me. Took a bit to find him, but now he's mine."

She smiled. Luke always had a soft spot for big dogs and the chestnut brindle mastiff standing at his side was proof of that. The dog's coat gleamed, he'd gained beautiful muscle, and his eyes shone bright. All under Luke's care.

Sibyl knelt before the dog and held the back of her hand out to him, remembering how Luke had taught her. "What's his name?"

"Levin," Luke answered.

Part of her felt awful for indulging, but his voice rolled over her back like a soft, warm blanket and she closed her eyes to savor its effects. "That's from a book, isn't it?" Sibyl asked and couldn't stop the smile from brightening her face when Luke's lips twitched and he glanced down.

"No."

"It is. It so is. Don't deny it!"

A gleam in his eyes appeared and the corner of his mouth twitched. She'd known him long enough to recognize the micro-expressions of amusement.

"Alright."

Caught up in the moment of how they used to talk to each other, Sibyl let her gaze take him in. His height that challenged her own six feet. Wide shoulders. Slender waist.

The cold, fractured sunlight bounced off his unruly, mid-length hair, its waves and flips kissing the top of his shoulders and brushing his cheeks. Sibyl wanted to dislike him. He was too pretty for his own good, especially those dark eyelashes set upon angled eyes that somehow held a duality of piercing feminine and a slice-through-to-your-soul experience.

His stoic, sometimes cynical nature could land him a part in 'Snow White' as Grumpy. But she'd seen him do things, like argue with Boatswain about the log he'd chosen for throwing, or tell a story to frightened children with individualized voices. She'd seen him sneak food to those who needed it and help when no one else did. Then there was his ability to quote just about any classical novel, including the romances.

With as much as she enjoyed seeing him again, hurt lurked within her. He'd still yet to give her an explanation as to why he broke off their relationship so quickly and of course she blamed herself. Maybe she'd done or said something, or didn't? He hesitated talking about the why and so she'd dropped the idea after trying for a whole month. She and Peter got together less than a year afterward and the idea of a conversation or any kind of closure.

As he adjusted the pack on Boatswain's back, Sibyl noticed a light purple piece of fabric tucked into a bag – a scarf from her shop – just as Luke stuffed it further into the pack and grabbed a thicker, woolen one, wrapped it around his neck, and buried his face up to his nose in the accessory.

Dread flashed through her.

She'd forgotten about La Parfana and Peter watching over it.

"Oh no!"

She sprinted back to the shop, hair slipping from the confines of her twin French braids, winding around and between people who mingled about the marketplace. She shoved through the door to Peter stocking inventory.

"Did you get the fruit?" Hunter asked as he poked his head in from the back.

Sibyl tapped her forehead. "I sat down to enjoy an orange and ended up forgetting the others on the ground."

Hunter stepped into the main shop area. "Want me to go grab it?"

"No, no. I forgot it, so I'll get it."

Hunter nodded and disappeared again.

"You look winded," Peter commented.

"Yeah. Well, I sprinted here after realizing I left two hooligans alone and I'm the only adult between us." She handed some empty vials to Peter. "I left them just outside the tradesman's booth. In a couple minutes, I'll head back out and—"

Peter grabbed her hand, sending two vials crashing to the floor. Sibyl gasped, Peter's strength overpowering her own to bring her close to him. His hot, angry breath clawed across her face.

"You never thanked me for looking after your shop."

Every bit of her screamed to get away. She used to be stronger, braver, but now as she stared at his white knuckles, fingers squeezing the blood from her hand, and his bared teeth, she couldn't bring herself to fight back. "Thank you for helping me," she quietly whimpered out and tried a smile, tears threatening to fall.

The shop bell rang. Luke's baritone reached her ears and she turned to greet him, Peter's hand flashing away.

He held up her bag. "Forgot this."

She flipped from terrified to happy in a second, mental exhaustion pricking at her eyes. "Thank you!"

Sibyl ran over and went to grab the bag but Luke wouldn't let go. At that moment she noticed the slight shake of his hand and his eyes weren't on Sibyl but aimed at Peter.

"Your arm?" Luke asked under his breath. "He got rough...Sibyl," his dark eyes flicked to hers, "he's abusing you."

"It's not your business," she whispered back, insides shaking. "Now give me my bag."

Luke held her gaze. His jaw twitched and nostrils flared. She'd never seen him so severely angry and as much as it shocked her, it sent a wave of safety down to her toes. Luke released the bag and took a half step back.

Sibyl handed the bag to Hunter, who immediately inspected each fruit as if it were a priceless jewel.

"Thank you for bringing the bag back," Sibyl said to Luke. "I was just about to head back out and get it."

Without speaking, Luke nodded and watched Peter disappear into the back. He eyed the door until it closed then pulled her aside. "Peter charged me too much for the scarf I purchased earlier."

"He did what?" Sibyl's voice rang a bit too loud and she covered her mouth, glancing around to make sure Peter wasn't close by. Anger rose in her gut. "How much did he charge you?"

"Thirty coins."

Under her breath, Sibyl said, "Damn him," then she waved Luke over to the counter and pulled out her money box. She gave him back five dollars. "Here. And for the record, he's not an official employee. This is my shop and I asked him to watch it while I went out to get the fruit."

Shocked anger spread across Luke's face. His nose crinkled in the way it always did when someone got a rise out of him. "He hurt you. I saw it." Then an unexpected gentleness in his voice rose from the fire of his fury. "Sibyl, you deserve so much better."

Her mouth didn't work. When her brain processed what she wanted to say, Sibyl realized, unexpectedly, to find out that she was angry. "You mean you?"

He blinked at her then his shoulders relaxed. "That's not what I meant. I wish I could take what happened back. We need to stay on topic." He shifted. "It's not my place to judge but...him?"

Fine. She'd focus on what he wanted to focus on, not what they desperately needed to address between them. Sibyl crossed her arms. "What's wrong with him?" Even as she said it, she knew the answer.

"First off, he overcharged me on purpose. I suppose you're going to tell me it was an honest mistake on his part, then you'll give him a little slap on the wrist for his idiotic joke. I also suppose he has an amazing job, is the perfect image of responsibility, takes time to spoil you, and makes you laugh. And never hurts you."

She blinked rapidly, stuck in place, with her arms locked at the elbows. With each word from Luke, she boiled and steamed, her lower jaw slowly jutting out further and further. It hurt to hear from another person what was wrong with her relationship with Peter, but most of all, Luke had picked up on it within minutes and she'd taken years. Inadequacy set in.

"My romantic relationships are neither your business nor your concern. I will deal with my stuff as I see fit. Now..." she took a deep breath through her nose, "can I interest you in anything else to apologize for Peter's carelessness?"

Without taking his eyes off her, he flicked his arm out and pointed to a vial of perfume. "That one."

"You didn't even look at it."

"I want it anyway. How much?"

Simmering, Sibyl looked at the bottle and released a small puff of air at the irony. "Five coins."

Luke handed the money over, took the bottle, and slipped it into his pocket. "Thank you. I'll see you around."

No sooner had Luke left than Hunter and Peter walked in from the back.

"What's the plan for the rest of the day, boss?" Hunter asked, scratching at a mark on the wooden countertop.

Sibyl didn't answer right away, occupying herself with staring at the door Luke had left through. He made her so mad sometimes, thrusting irritation and anger at her without a care for her own emotions, nosing into her business.

He was right, though.

She glanced at Peter. He smiled at her. If she were to spend her life with Peter, she'd be the adult taking care of him, and used as a personal verbal and emotional punching bag whenever Peter saw fit. She hated being stuck with him, but how could she even leave?

"Hello?" Peter waved a hand in front of her face.

She scoffed and batted it away. "Hunter," Sibyl said when her eyes focused. "Go home early."

"Really?"

"Yeah."

He ran off, not needing any more convincing, and Sibyl chuckled as the door closed. She was alone. With Peter.

"So..." he drawled with an eyebrow raised, "about what you said earlier." Peter stepped forward and slid his hand along her waist. "I saw a cot in the back room and it's just calling our names."

A prickling lingered on her skin then settled in her stomach, turned it rock-solid, and she wanted to throw up. Despite all the sensations hitting her at once, Sibyl whirled on him. "You honestly think I'm going to want to have sex with you after what you just pulled?"

"I was trying to help you."

Frustrated anger hovered in Peter's voice like Dracula waiting for his first nightly victim. He wanted a reaction. She wasn't oblivious to the slight sparkle in his eyes whenever he hurt her. She had to calm down or he'd get what he wanted.

Sibyl sighed, evened out her voice, and said, "Overcharging my customers is not helping. It's stealing."

Peter's confusion worsened her stomachache, and she fought to stay calm. Luke's words about Peter earlier echoed in her head. She shooed them away.

"This is my shop," Sibyl said. "I asked you to watch it, not steal from someone."

"Is it really stealing if they don't know?"

Sibyl lost her composure. "Of course, it's still stealing!" She spun around, gathering up his coat and scarf, her heart pounding in her ears and face. "I can't believe I let it get this bad."

"What're you doing?"

She handed his jacket back, hot tears pouring down her cheeks.

"What does it look like? I need you out of here."

"Sybie, I—"

"Don't call me that. You're damned lucky it was Luke and not someone else."

"Please. I'll do better."

Laughing through her tears, Sibyl put her hand against his chest. "We're not over, just...I need a break." She turned around, her hand on her forehead and spoke under her breath. "Luke was right."

"Luke?" Peter snarled. He reached her in a few long strides. "That emo bad boy's the reason you're kicking me out?" He paused, his eyes narrowing. "You two didn't..."

"Get out!" Tremors shook Sibyl's entire body. Anger and fear seared her head. "Just...just leave."

He stepped closer to her, ruse of innocence long gone. "You're not going to kick me out. This behavior isn't good for our relationship, Sybie. We're meant to be strong, a team, and I want us to work." Peter rubbed the end of her braid between his thumb and index fingers. "We're endgame. Remember? But we can't be if you keep pushing me away and working with Hunter and talking to Luke. It's dangerous. I really think we should work on us before you meet with your family. Please don't push me away. I'm nothing without you."

His eyes drew her in. They had a way of doing that, as if she were a magnet and he metal, and she desperately wanted to believe everything he said. He was so gentle and so loving normally, only struggling on the anxious or sleepless days. Couples had bad days, right? Times when one or both would struggle and, in those moments, needed their partner's support. She wanted to see him through those days.

Before she could say, 'You're right,' the door jingled downstairs to signal a customer had walked in. Sibyl had purposefully turned the sign to OPEN, even though it was after hours, holding onto the hope that someone would walk in to keep Peter in check because she didn't know if she could.

Working his jaw, Peter left. The door closed behind him.

Sibyl lowered to the floor, heaving and squeaking as she cried. Hers and Peter's relationship had already crumbled by the time he came to her on his knees several months ago, begging for a restart, and she had agreed because she couldn't stand to see him so distraught.

The abuse? That was new. It crept its way into their lives before she even realized. By the time it had surfaced, she'd forgotten how to be strong or funny. Just a shell.

She crawled to her feet, helped the customer find a shawl for her granddaughter, and closed up shop. Then she stumbled her way into bed upstairs and covered her face. Shame crawled underneath her skin. She had used him as a tool to distract her mind, and she felt like the worst human being. Dirty. Toxic.

Unable to get out of bed to close her curtains, Sibyl took hours to fall asleep until the black night sky turned navy blue.

3 | SIBYL

Red-eyed and sore, Sibyl opened her shop to the public the next morning after only a few hours of sleep. As always, a small line of her most loyal customers meandered inside. Some picked up what they wanted right away – a refill here, a replacement there – and left Sibyl two hundred coins richer, but there were a few indecisive shoppers who remained.

Sibyl approached one such customer, a woman squinting at a collection of rouges.

"How's your grandchild doing, Mrs. Gallagher?" she asked.

Mrs. Gallagher, still squinting, looked up at Sibyl. "Well enough. He – Oh! I need to remember – they ran out of the lip stain, and I can't seem to find the kind they like."

A customer gave them a side-eye as he passed by with his wife.

Sibyl remembered the first time Peri came into her shop, sticking to the back walls and wringing their red-freckled hands. She'd spotted them standing away from the lip stain section, peering over two women's shoulders as they browsed.

"Can I help you?" she had asked and when they had explained they were looking for lip stain but were too shy to approach, she had helped them pick the perfect color for their light skin tone. Their eyes lit up, and they walked to the counter with a slight bounce in their step, four cylindrical containers in their hands.

She guided Mrs. Gallagher five steps to her right, picked out a red color with an orange undertone, and placed it in her hands. "Peri likes Bottled Sunshine, if I'm not mistaken."

"Oh!" Mrs. Galagher held it at arm's length, squinted, and read the side. "That's the one. They go through them so fast; I can't seem to keep up."

"It's my pleasure. And let Peri know," Sibyl walked with Mrs. Gallagher to the counter Hunter waited behind, "that they should come visit. I'd love to show Peri my upcoming new line sometime before it releases this summer."

"I'll relay the message, but I'm not sure they're ready. Being gender-fluid – I think that's the right term – is all very new to them."

"I understand. Well, let them know my door is always open when they're ready."

"Thank you," Mrs. Galagher said and squeezed Sibyl's forearm. "You're a bright spot to my morning. Always have been."

Hunter watched her go. "I want her to be my granny."

Sibyl laughed. "Don't we all?"

When the door closed for the day, Sibyl sunk into a nearby chair and sighed heavily.

Hunter approached. "You okay?"

"Yeah." Sibyl sighed again. "I'm gonna go in the back for a bit."

"Alright," Hunter nodded. "I'll start on lock-up."

Sibyl smiled, thanked him, and escaped behind the closet door by the entrance to the greenhouse, her heart beating through her entire body. She'd had a distraction from the hurt Peter caused while helping her customers, but now that the shop sat in silence once more, a roar of thoughts hit her violently.

She sunk to the floor, watching the tiny tremor in her hands as she rested her arms on top of her knees.

For a long time, Sibyl looked at nothing and allowed herself to only feel the effects of Peter's hurt. It had wedged into her being for so long, she'd forgotten it was even there, poisoning her, making her easy to manipulate.

How could I have forgotten myself so much?

She used to be brave. Not anymore. She didn't know if she had the strength left to break up with him after he'd drained her bone dry. He lived in the area. She would see him places and how could she not worry about who or what he'd go after to force her back with him? Her family? Her shop? Her friends?

After several minutes, the shaking subsided, tears were dried, and she steeled herself as she walked back into the shop.

The front door opened and Sibyl's mom walked in. Every time Sibyl saw her mom, her heart leapt in her chest. For nearly ten years, Sibyl had been separated from her family. They'd sought shelter with many other displaced families and it had collapsed during a nasty earthquake a few weeks later, separating Sibyl from her family when they thought she'd died.

Sibyl spent nearly two weeks with amnesia and would have died had it not been for the couple who took her in and helped her head from the resulting healing from the head injury she'd sustained. By the time she'd fully recovered, she'd been separated from her family for too long to know where to look. That's when she decided to start a new life at the Compound.

By pure chance three years ago, Sibyl had been reunited with her family and she'd held onto them with a vice grip ever since. Best part? She'd gained a sister after finding out her mother had been unknowingly pregnant when the accident happened.

Charlotte Marchant was a tall woman, nearly six feet, and solid. As a farmer's wife, she wore practical clothes, kept her appearance well-groomed, and ran off of a never-ending supply of energy. Her gentle, honey brown eyes scanned the interior of the shop as she entered.

As kind as she was, Sibyl had to get used to her mom's no-nonsense and sometimes forgetful nature, which occasionally affected Charlotte's ability for small talk. In a perfect example of that, Sibyl watched her mom peruse the shelves for a bit, ignoring her daughter and Hunter, and finally settled on a bundle of dried oregano, thyme, and rosemary, then walked over and set her items on the counter.

Charlotte seemed to notice she had company, blinked as she processed the information, and a soft smile bloomed on her face. "Are you coming to dinner tonight?" Charlotte asked and touched Hunter's forearm without looking at him to let him know she'd seen him, too. Hunter moved to grab a bag, which pulled Charlotte's attention. "Thank you. I won't need a bag, no."

"Of course I'm coming, Ma. I just have a few orders to fill after La Parfana closes and I'll be there."

"Good. Alice misses you."

I miss you, is what Sibyl knew her mother wanted to say but struggled with the words. Sibyl had seen her try, every time growing too emotional to get out more than, "I mi—" before she worked her mouth and tears wet her eyes, then settled on complimenting Sibyl.

"I've been gone two days. She can't miss me that bad. Plus," Sibyl put on an easy smile and leaned forward onto her elbows, peering up at her mother with a few exaggerated blinks, "Are you sure it's not you who misses me?"

Charlotte smiled, worked her mouth, and sniffed; eyes alight with every bit of a mother's love that Sibyl had craved for so long.

"Perhaps." Charlotte shrugged then cocked her head slightly. "Are you okay? You look like you've been crying."

Sibyl's face heated and she busied herself with folding already folded scarves sitting in a box. "Not recently."

Her mother put a hand on Sibyl's. "There's no point in hiding it, I'm the same way. After a good, cleansing cry, my eyes stay bloodshot for ages. Seems you got the gene. Did Peter cause this?"

Funny how she went right to blaming Peter, and despite loving her mom fully, she still wanted to scowl at her. "It'll be fine."

"It's not, though, if you're crying."

Tears formed in her eyes as her mom's attempt to get Sibyl to talk finally clicked in. "I thought that he'd changed, Ma. I don't know what to do."

Charlotte gathered her up in her arms. Sibyl didn't care that she looked allergy-ridden, with her puffy eyes and red, stuffy nose; her mom was holding her. Charlotte's comfort hit Sibyl like a wave, the relief crashing into her chest with such force that she stopped simmering over Peter and wept over the sensation of a mother's love.

"Now," Charlotte leaned back, arms still around Sibyl. She smoothed out her daughter's hair. "You're coming to dinner. We won't talk about anything unpleasant and we'll be together. Play a board game. Stuff our faces. Just us. 'Kay?"

Sibyl nodded. "I love you."

"And I...love you, too," she whispered around what Sibyl knew to be a tight throat, paused for a few moments, then clicked her tongue. "Well, I've got my herbs. I have a few more errands to run and I'll see you in a few hours. Don't be late."

"Alright," Sibyl said as she waved.

Hunter, who still stood behind the counter, rubbed his hand on his apron and said, "I want her to be my Ma."

Sibyl swatted playfully at him then walked into the back to check on her wilting roses.

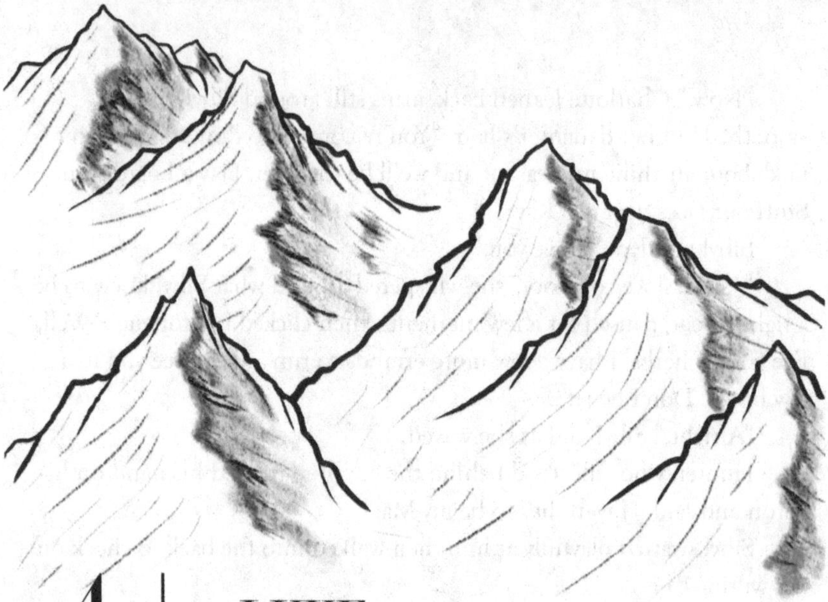

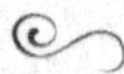

4 | LUKE

She is the sun, and I the storm.
Just as I crash upon the rocks,
she rises.

"Yo, Fade spy!"

Someone pinned his arms behind his back before he could turn around. A punch sent Luke crumbling to the ground, arms still behind him, then a second had him pressed against a brick wall. The coarse bricks scratched his face and arms as he sank to his knees, nose dripping blood. He glared up at the blond boy standing over him shrouded in sinister shadows. Four other kids flanked him.

"Why don't you say something? Huh? Maybe run back to your Fade friends and leave all of us alone."

Luke trembled but said nothing. It wouldn't matter anyway. Peter would just make fun of how he spoke, then hit him again as his cronies held him down.

"Yeah," Peter sneered. "That's what I thought."

Peter drove the tip of his boot into Luke's stomach. Bile forced itself out of his throat.

"Leave me alone. Please."

Laughter. So much laughter.

Peter had grown into his body much quicker than Luke, his broad shoulders and honed, teenage muscles – except for crumbs of adolescence in the slight roundness to his cheeks – leaving little opportunity for Luke to come out on top. It also didn't help that he'd given up defending himself long before Peter landed a punch.

"Look at him," Peter egged his acolytes on, their jeering and laughter mixing with the ringing of his ears and burn of his stomach. "You're pathetic."

That last word, punctuated by a terrifying hate, contorted Peter's face.

By heavenly intervention, the verbal attack stopped. Luke peered through gaps in his arms, half expecting Peter to be waiting for him to uncover his face so he could personally punch him, but he just crouched in front of Luke, glaring. "Why can't you just stop?" Peter asked.

Luke looked at him, confused.

"That idiotic stutter you do to get attention. No real person talks like that."

Luke's heart dropped. He expected something cruel to come out of Peter's mouth, so hearing the words destroyed any confidence Luke still had.

"It doesn't just go away," Luke managed to whisper.

Peter scoffed and rolled his eyes. He lashed out his hand, fisted Luke's shirt, and pulled him up to his face. "You're so delusional, even you believe it. Figures. Why don't you do us all a favor and leave so we don't have to listen to you speak ever again?"

And he tossed Luke in the mud.

L uke snorted awake, his arms flailing as he fell but realized he was safe in his bed. Early morning light shone through his loft window. He spread his fingers over his chest, heart slamming against his ribcage.

I'm okay. I'm safe. It happened in the past and I'm safe.

That's what he told himself every time he relived a memory. Watching Peter try to hurt Sibyl awoke a fear he thought long dead. Anger had nearly overwhelmed him and Luke had to hold the door jamb to avoid punching Peter in the face.

He'd hid in his parent's home to avoid Peter until he turned eighteen, old enough to move out, and found his cabin shortly afterward. A place just his own, away from prying eyes and judgmental whispers. A spot to just be himself. No one to care about the scars between his fingers. No one to care about the stutter. It was just him, the forest, and Boatswain, Levin joining later. He could be free.

No one to care.

The loneliness got to him more often than he wanted to admit it, but how could he keep trying when those around him wanted him face first in the dirt?

That is...until Sibyl, Bannack, and Eloise showed up and adopted him into their group. They immediately accepted him. Every part, even the broken bits. Friends. Allies. They protected him and each other, made sure to include him, stood beside him when he needed it, and pushed him to grow. Called him out on his bullshit then invited him for drinks minutes later.

After all that, he'd still gone back to the comfort of solitude.

Luke stared at the ceiling, trying to understand why he so often restricted himself from true growth, Levin and Boatswain squished against him. One of them snored; a quiet, grumbling noise he couldn't sleep without.

He simmered over the memory of Peter grabbing Sibyl's arm. The fear in her eyes. The malice in his. It had been too much and instead of helping, he stood there, completely useless, his legs frozen and shaking, fist clenched around the scarf. He knew what Peter was capable of, the proof a white slash through his black eyebrow. That day, he'd nearly lost his vision, and seeing Sibyl cornered by him brought all the pain and terror back.

I should have fucking punched his lights out on the spot. Luke let out a quiet, frustrated grunt as he laid his arm over his eyes. *But I let my fear control me. Again!*

Dust sprinkled onto his cheek. He jerked, waking Boatswain who glanced at his human with a sleepy eye, sighed, then settled back down.

Sibyl had looked so different from the last time they saw each other with her dark hair worn down to her waist and a deep purple shawl hanging off one shoulder as she snacked on an orange. He almost didn't recognize her at first, then her love of a simple moment, enough to shed tears, had captured his interest and he'd watched from his place underneath the tree, adoration blooming in his chest.

Her crying had intrigued him so much he just had to talk to her, ultimately making her choke on the fruit by accident. Luke's cheeks warmed. She was beautiful and he a bumbling worshiper.

More dust, mixed with small slivers of wood, landed on his face.

"What the—"

The entire home groaned. Levin snapped awake. He whined, tail between his legs, and jumped from the bed, thumped down the loft stairs, and stood by the door.

A terrible deep moaning filled the cabin, making both Levin and Boatswain whine-bark. A shock of terror slammed into Luke's chest, robbing him of breath. Boatswain lurched to his feet, half-dragging Luke by the sleeve down the stairs.

Luke slammed his shoulder against the crooked door, cursing the cabin's inability to stand straight. It wouldn't budge. He slammed again, vaguely thinking his aunt would kill him if he ripped his stitches, helplessly listening to the creaking and groaning of what sounded like a deranged whale.

Something cracked above the loft, the ceiling too dark to see exactly where the damage came from.

The dogs cowered, Levin screamed, and Luke, desperate to save his dogs, switched from trying to open the door to breaking the glass of his only window. He tore off his shirt, wrapped it around his fist, and punched the glass three times before it shattered.

Levin, driven by terror, immediately jumped out. Luke tried to catch him, but the mastiff sailed over his shoulder and slammed Luke's spine against the sill, knocking the wind out of him. He grunted and eyes bugged when his ribs cracked.

Boatswain, though terrified, had emergency training Levin lacked, allowing him to stay by Luke. He'd been with Luke's dad, Isaac Blackwood, during the bombs. They'd worked together to rescue people from the explosions and wars that emerged after the Day of Ashes.

Luke knelt and held onto the dog's face. "Go. Find. Okay?"

He swallowed down the knot in his throat not knowing, truly, if Boatswain understood. It had been years since Boatswain had seen action. He knew to find the scent of birch, but had Soora, Sibyl, Eloise, Bannack, or his mom kept their bark pieces? Luke had no choice but to put faith in Boatswain that he would find someone and bring them back, so he cleared the window frame of glass and gave a command.

"Seek!"

Boatswain didn't need to be asked twice. The large black and white dog leapt through the window as if on wings.

Luke immediately covered his head with his arms as the roof caved in.

5 | SIBYL

I can give you more, should you only ask.
I can give you my kiss, my smile, or my love.
Alas, there is but one, I cannot give.
For 'tis my soul.
Of which you already possess.

Alice hugged Sibyl when she opened the door and smiled as she pulled her into the warm house.

Her little sister was curly-haired and round-eyed with a sprinkling of dark freckles along the bridge of her nose and a single dimple above her lip.

"Did you miss me?"

"Not even a little bit," Sibyl said and let her smile spread across her face when she couldn't hide it anymore.

Alice blinked up at her. "Liar."

"Girls!" Charlotte called from the kitchen.

"What, Ma?" they asked at the same time.

"Close the door. It's freezing. And help me bring the food to the table."

They took turns carrying dinner – trout with herbed carrots, mashed potatoes, and buttermilk rolls – to the table.

"How is La Parfana running?" her dad, Henry, asked. He stared at an empty place over her shoulder, blind from glaucoma he'd contracted after they'd been separated. At first, communicating with him was strange and she took some time to grieve the loss of his eyesight after each visit. It took her about a year, but she grew used to the condition.

"It's good. Hunter's learning a lot. He can run the shop alone now and I think it's almost time to teach him about making perfumes. They're very delicate – some – and you have to know what scents blend together and which ones are meant to be top notes or middle notes or low notes."

"Have you made any poisons?" Alice asked, eyes round and excited. "Like that lady in the 1800's, or something. You know, where she made poison for women who had abusive husbands."

Sibyl laughed but realized quickly that both parents were silent. She gave them each a quick glance then answered. "...Madame Giulia Tofana?"

Alice nodded vigorously.

"How do you know about her?"

"I found an old book in Mr. Akido's bookstore. Millie showed me." Alice smiled shyly and pushed her fork around in her potatoes. "She loves spooky stuff."

Sibyl eyed Alice, hiding a smile at her reaction. "Spooky stuff, huh?"

Alice nodded. "Yeah."

"Well," Sibyl replied after chewing a piece of her roll, "you know I named my shop after her. It's a combination of, 'perfume' and her last name. So yeah, I know about Madame Tofana."

Alice leaned forward. "Do you know how many people she killed?"

"Alice!" Charlotte exclaimed and the conversation cut off. When their mom wasn't looking though, Sibyl held up her fingers on a single hand. Five, one, zero, zero. Six-hundred victims. Sibyl smiled over her cup at Alice's joy.

After a good meal with her family, Sibyl and Alice opened the wooden storage chest by the fireplace. Sibyl handed Alice a few rolled up blankets, went to close the chest, but paused when she noticed the maker's initials on the wood.

L.N.B.

She knew who'd carved them and she couldn't stop the softening of her gaze and tiny flutter of her heart.

Luke Noah Blackwood.

Sibyl ran her fingertip over Luke's flowy initials, admiring the calligraphy-like penmanship, imagining the movement of his hands during the moment he stamped his mark. It made her stomach go all funny.

Even though he'd dropped their relationship when she thought it was going so well, Sibyl couldn't stay mad. She'd tried, and still wanted to understand why, but her crush on him and curse of forgiveness wouldn't let her be upset for long. A toxic trait? Maybe. For Luke, though, she'd wait for as long as it took him to realize he was braver than he thought.

"Hey." Alice bumped her. "I need another blanket."

"Oh. Yeah. Here."

She couldn't be thinking about another man while in a committed relationship with someone else. Too close to cheating for her comfort.

As Sibyl turned around and stood, she caught sight of her mom and dad sharing a tender moment, Charlotte tucking Henry's blanket over his lap and Henry responding with a kiss on her forehead. In the moment of seeing their love, Sibyl's stomach hit her with a ping of bitterness. Why couldn't Peter do that for her?

"Ew! Yuck!" Alice teased, flopping backward on the couch and right into Sibyl's lap seconds after she'd sat.

"Your head is so heavy," she said while pushing on her sister's shoulders. "What do you keep in there? Rocks?"

Alice sat bolt upright and looked at Sibyl, fake shock comical. "You take that back!"

"No."

"Right now! Or I'm gonna take the rocks inside my head and throw them at you!"

They were standing now, the couch between them.

"If you do that," Sibyl rotated around the piece of furniture as Alice tried to catch her, "you'll have less in your head."

The sisters shot quips at each other for another few seconds then fell into a heap on the thick cushions, tumbling over and onto the floor. Charlotte laughed and Henry smiled. Sibyl laid on the ground and let Alice sit on her chest.

"Get off!" Sibyl squirmed. "You're so heavy!"

"Am not."

"Are too. Get...off!"

With a giant thump, Alice landed on the ground, taking the coffee table contents with her. Shocked, both Sibyl and Alice cackled and snorted.

Moments later, laughter died down and they settled in for a quick board game. It took longer than Sibyl expected, but she was glad to stay with her family. Alice followed her to the front door, her presence reminding Sibyl to pick her up for another sister date soon.

"Thanks for the dinner." Sibyl hugged her parents then turned to Alice, and in a hushed tone said, "Listen to Mom and Dad, okay?" When Alice said nothing, Sibyl repeated, "Okay?"

"Yeah. Okay."

Once on the porch, Sibyl looked to the waning sun, still bright enough to collect herbs before nightfall.

"Goodnight," she said to her parents. "Thank you for dinner."

She waved to them and wrapped her scarf around her neck to shield her face from the cold.

Sibyl wandered through the forest, fingers stiff with a fanny pack on her waist where she nestled the herbs and plants she gathered in the twilight. Mint, birch, wild hazelnut, huckleberries, salal.

The lilac was especially exciting and collected some twigs to propagate. Glee sprung through her, dancing and bounding, as she thought of all the glorious scents she could mix with lilac once she broke down the blooms. Pine, rose, and orange were at the top of her list.

A familiar bark sounded in the distance. She straightened, and spun to find the source. Luke never let his dogs out of his sight. She clenched her teeth and listened. Seconds ticked by then came the booming bark of—

"Boatswain?" Sibyl called.

He appeared on the ridge, tail wagging to the left and tongue dripping with saliva.

A few years ago, Luke had asked her to keep a small pouch of birch bark on hand for emergencies. She'd agreed. Even though she thought the request strange, she still kept it tied to her belt loop or in her pocket at all times. Seeing Boatswain in the distance, barking in a way that sent chills over her skin, reassured Sibyl she'd made the right choice.

She rushed to the dog, noticing signs of distress the closer she got to him. Whale eyes. Shaking legs. Whining pants. Mud up to his knees and sticks in his coat.

"Hey, boy," Sibyl crooned as she knelt and quickly ran her hands through his fur to pick out the forest litter.

Sibyl fought through her worry. "Where's Luke?" She glanced around. "Where's Levin?"

Boatswain took off, pausing several yards away to spin in a circle and glance at Sibyl. She followed. The dog led her to a trail and they ran along it until they reached Luke's cabin.

What Sibyl witnessed froze her to the spot and Boatswain's whining faded away into silence.

The cabin, on its last legs years ago, the front door unable to open properly, had imploded. No...collapsed.

Her heart twisted. She knew what it was like to be buried alive. Trapped. Suffocating. No way to know if help would ever come. Broken bones and bleeding into the darkness. Painful breaths as dust filled the lungs.

Sibyl stumbled backward a step. A wet tongue made her jump and she looked down at Boatswain who plunged forward, sniffing and zig-zagging. He didn't climb into the wreckage and instead returned to darting back and forth with his nose pressed to the earth, and sat by the door, staring at Sibyl.

Finding her strength, Sibyl rushed forward and fell to her knees in front of Boatswain. He gave her a lick then turned to scratch at the threshold. She didn't dare touch the rubble, knowing first-hand how fragile a collapse could be, but didn't know the first thing about search and rescue in order to get Luke and possibly Levin out. Boatswain clearly had been trained in it, so she turned to the dog.

"Where are they?" was all she could ask. The dog ignored her. She didn't even know what commands he'd been trained to recognize. Switching tactics, Sibyl called out. "Luke! Let me know you're alive!"

Where's Levin?

She had to focus on Luke. Levin, regretfully, needed to wait. One emergency at a time.

Waiting lasted eons, her heartbeat pounding in her head until she only heard the blood coursing through her. Maybe she was panting? She didn't know. At some point, she joined Boatswain in his digging, together forming a deep gouge in the earth in front of the door.

Then she heard it. Some kind of moan or words seeping out from under the roof. But from where exactly?

Desperate, Sibyl grabbed the doorjamb and screamed, "Luke?"

Proof of life didn't come again for several moments. She heard a faint scratching. Proof of life! Fear drove her mind to think of terrible, horrible things.

On the verge of hyperventilation, Sibyl turned to Boatswain. "Find Luke. Show me how to help. Oh God, I hope you can understand me."

The dog inspected her face, let out a quiet whine, and leapt into action. He padded up a pile of logs covered in a tarp leaning against the cabin and tested the collapsed roof with his paws. Sibyl followed, unable to calm her beating heart and hot tears.

The devastation of the cabin was gut-wrenching. The load-bearing beam had shattered, possibly hitting the ground before crumbling. Luke's bookshelves of carefully curated novels covered the floor, roofing on top. She knew how important the cabin was to Luke and to see it mutilated, hurt.

She and Boatswain continued to hike over the fallen walls and roof rubble. Sibyl ducked underneath the shattered beam, and pushed aside a few chunks of shingled roof and when wood cracked underfoot she froze for just a second until Boatswain sat at the center of the cabin and barked once.

"Here?" Sibyl asked when she approached.

The rubble moved just a bit. She hauled metal, shingles, and splintered wood away, most of it basically disintegrating the minute she touched it.

How in God's name has it stayed intact for so long? Why did Luke never leave if it was this bad?

The way the beam leaned – the front against the only wall currently standing – and created a small lean-to that could have protected a small child, not a six-foot-tall grown man. Except his hand peaked out from underneath the rubble, scratching at the floor. Hope leapt in her stomach.

Sibyl slowly cleared the wood and metal away, the hand became an arm, then an elbow, then a shoulder, and finally a head. At first, she noticed no injuries, but as she looked closer, she noticed blood coating the back of his scalp, black hair hiding it so well only the moonlight shift revealed its glossy shine. His other wrist, once she cleared a heavy board off it, was covered in purple black bruising.

Sibyl's heart dropped from her chest. "Luke?"

He coughed. "Levin?"

"I don't know. I haven't seen him."

"Damn it." Luke's voice was more gravely than usual and he smiled weakly when Boatswain licked his cheek. "Good boy."

Sibyl reached out to help him up but thought better of it and pulled away. She zipped through questions about his condition. "Where are you hurt? Do you have any tingling in your hands and feet or pain in your neck? Are you disoriented in any way? Can't breathe? Where does it hurt the most? Can you wiggle your fingers for me?"

Luke winced. "My wrist is broken."

She waited for more, but he just laid on the ground. "That's it? You had an entire house fall on you and all you can tell me is your wrist is broken? I need to know if I can move you."

"Sibyl," Luke groaned. "Help first. Freak out later. Yeah?"

She stopped and exhaled. "Okay. Yeah. Yeah, you're right."

Sibyl and Boatswain worked for nearly half an hour, pushing against wood and metal to uncover Luke to fully see the devastation. His side and back had been cut by something, and blood covered his bare torso. Sibyl sucked in a breath and blinked away tears as she scanned him. A dark purple bruise ran horizontally over his spine, and when Sibyl leaned over to inspect the injury at his side, noticed someone had already stitched him up. He must've been hurt there only days earlier.

Why didn't he say anything?

When he'd visited her shop, he hadn't moved differently or winced at any point.

Before she could uncover his right leg, Luke shoved a log away with a kick. Sibyl gasped as he sat up, grumbling, hissing, growling, and swearing.

"What are you doing?" she yelped, instantly trying to keep him still. She pressed against his shoulders, her fingers remembering his warmth.

He gave her a blank look. "Getting up."

"You could have a neck injury, or a concussion, or—or an impalement." The fussing did no good, so she squawked at him again when he shoved her hands away. "Stop moving! I still don't know if you have any spinal injuries."

"I'm okay enough. I've been stuck underneath that rubble for almost two hours. My body's sore. I need to move."

"Of course your body's sore. A house dropped on you. No matter how much you want to, you can't just move after that!"

"I'm aware," Luke said as he unwrapped his bloody shirt from his broken wrist, his mouth open in a silent scream and face twisted.

Sibyl's stomach lurched. "Stop that! Let me."

Luke relented, his brow sweating, and gulped as he let her create a makeshift splint to secure his broken extremity. She glanced at him. "You know," she said, ripping another strip of fabric then tying it around his wrist smashed between two boards from his bookshelf, "you can scream."

He kept his eyes closed. "I don't feel like it."

"Suit yourself. We need to get you checked out, though. The Compound's closest."

"Sure. Then we find Levin."

"Of course." Sibyl ducked underneath his arm and with a heave – and a pained grunt from Luke – helped him stand and navigate the rubble. She glanced sideways at him, to gauge his facial expression.

He looked at her, then, and she jerked her head away, embarrassed.

"Like what you see?"

"I wanted to make sure there wasn't anything on your face."

"W...W-What? Like chocolate cake?"

Sibyl sniggered, despite her utter embarrassment, and her face heated. Then his eyes sparkled in the way they did whenever he tried to stifle a laugh or smile and her stomach tumbled and fluttered. The reaction caught her so off guard that she laughed, a single guffaw that burst from her mouth like a deranged horse shriek. She clamped her hand over her mouth a bit too hard and ended up slapping herself.

Luke, in an amazing display of self-restraint, smiled briefly and turned away, focusing on stepping over the last bit of rubble before they finally reached the grass. He slowly sat and covered his face with his hand.

She left him there and trudged through the rubble again, searching for his personal chest, remembering its location from the last time she visited the cabin years ago. Hopefully he hadn't moved it.

Sibyl found the corner of it – or at least she hoped – not too far from where it had been and her carefully maintained heartbeat and breathing sped up.

Please be in here.

In her rush, Sibyl didn't pay attention to a shattered shard of wood on top of a board and as she stepped forward, the fragment lanced through her winter leggings. She gasped and fought the urge to scream, then reached down to assess the damage. It didn't feel too bad. Nothing stuck out of her leg. She could still put weight on it, albeit a bit uncomfortable, so Sibyl left it alone to focus on Luke.

Heaving a broken roof piece off the chest, Sibyl found an extra coat, two warm pelts, some basic first aid supplies, leaves for grinding into a poultice to fight infection, and some cut strips of fabric. Shoving the items that would fit into a drawstring bag and carrying the others, Sibyl brought the items back to Luke, crushed the leaves in her mouth, and wrapped the fabric strips around his torso.

"Your saliva is inside me."

"Oh shut up." Then she smiled and teased, "Call it revenge for not letting me peg you."

The deep flush of Luke's face was barely noticeable in the moonlight and she smiled wider.

"Tell me what cut you," Sibyl said after the moment left and moved around him to get the fabric around his back.

"Glass." Luke lowered his arms with a groan. "Levin jumped through the broken window before I could clear it and slammed me into the sill. I'm concerned he's hurt."

Her heart dropped. "We'll find him. Maybe see him on our way to the Compound?"

"Maybe."

Sibyl watched him closely. He was broken, bleeding, and bruised, but he only cared about his dogs. Admirable and endearing, except he needed to be cared for too and if he wouldn't do it, she would. She cared for his wounds, working from major to minor, even going as far as to wrap a small cut on the palm of his hand that wouldn't stop bleeding.

As she draped a coat around his wide shoulders, Luke's head snapped up and she paused, fingers clenched around the collar of the coat. They stayed there for several heartbeats, sharing cold air. A few stray snowflakes landed and melted on her cheek, and her breath halted as Luke reached up with his bandaged hand and brushed the water droplet away, lingering on her skin. The back of his index fingers twitched, as if he restrained himself from touching more. Luke's eye softened, his mask of boredom falling away, and he looked at her again like he used to: completely, utterly, and irrevocably in awe.

"Luke…"

"Sorry," he mumbled and dropped his hand. His expression changed back to the jaded, halfway to boredom Luke.

That's not what I meant.

Talking would do no good, so she pushed the moment aside and attempted to alleviate some of Luke's worries by asking, "Do you need any help getting your other things? I could get a group together and—"

"No," he snapped. Then he sighed. "Sorry. I'm on edge. Let's head to the Compound and I'll figure something out…I'm glad you came to help me."

"You're welcome." Then she remembered the birch bark in her pocket and fished it out. "Do you want me to still keep this?"

Luke nodded. "In case another house falls on me."

Sibyl chuckled. "Ready to go?"

Luke nodded. "Soora's gonna kill me."

"Soora? No."

He gave her a slightly amused glance. "She already patched me up a few days ago. I promised I'd keep out of trouble but," he motioned to his bandaged side, "that didn't happen. I'm also probably going to miss my mom's birthday."

She tried to slip underneath his arm, to steady him, but his cry of pain made her jerk away.

Luke groaned with his hand on his torso. "Broken ribs, I think."

"Sounds like it." She eyed him for a few moments, trying to figure out what to do. "Think you can walk okay?" To Luke's nod, she replied, "Alright. Walk next to me, then. That way I can be there in case you need to lean on me."

"I'll be fine."

Slowly, they made their way through the forest, each step calculated to avoid tripping over branches or holes in the ground.

Luke used Sibyl as support and after many long minutes, nighttime fell completely, darkening the world around them to the point where they could only see a few feet ahead. The air froze, too, driving Luke to shiver and his teeth clatter. She'd almost reached her tipping point as well and suspected with his fewer layers and injuries he'd succumbed quicker than her. Frozen misting rain slashed against her cheeks and forehead like glass.

"We gotta get out of this cold," Sibyl placed her hand on a pine tree while frozen needles crunched underneath her feet, "or you're going to freeze.

"I-I-I'm fi-fine."

"No, you're not. You're shivering."

Luke chuckled; an airy sound that gave the effect of his breath being pulled from his body. "P-P-Perhaps I'm regress...ing. F-F-Fucking c...cold."

"Come on." Sibyl pulled on him and he hissed in pain as he went with her.

Her leg stung and twinged and Sibyl closed her eyes for a few seconds, hoping the pain wouldn't get worse.

Sibyl sucked in a breath when a stray branch hit her in the face. "I don't know what else to do."

She turned around to look for Luke. He stood behind her, a hand on Boatswain. He'd stopped talking and now swayed and shivered, eyes half closed.

"Luke?"

All six-two of him hit the ground face first with a hard thud. Boatswain yelped, licked his face, and shoved him frantically.

"Luke!"

Sibyl reached him in seconds, fear shooting to the stars, dropped the bag to the ground then fell to her knees beside him, took large handfuls of his soaked shirt, and heaved him onto his back, shoving away the animal hide.

She paused, hands stilled on his chest, and tears welled in her eyes. What would happen if she couldn't help him? They were stuck in a forest, in the dark, with no way to find shelter any time soon. Her leg was injured and Luke was worse off. Would she even be able to drag him?

I'd be able to track us out of here if I could just see.

She looked down at Luke's dark form with Boatswain panting beside him. Warm tears formed as she tried to keep a level head. She folded in on herself and a single sob escaped her.

I don't know which way the Compound is.

Boatswain laid on top of Luke, and she gave him an appreciative scratch on the ear. "Good dog," she whispered.

What am I going to do?

Despair set in and she temporarily gave into it. Her shoulders drooped and she cried. She had to figure out a way to get them out of the weather and dragging Luke through it would worsen his injuries.

Unwilling to give up so easily, Sibyl wiped at her tears, stumbled to her feet, and began screaming, "Help! Help us!"

Shrouded by dark clouds and trees, the moon sat in the black sky. Cold seeped into her veins, freezing her fingers and toes inside her boots, and she returned to Luke, still unconscious, and surrendered her own pelt. It was a bit wet but the underside was still dry.

Please let this keep him warm long enough.

Sibyl waited for as long as her anxiety would allow her, alternating between screaming until she was hoarse and warming Luke up with her body heat.

She couldn't feel her fingers anymore. They resisted movement. Luke's breathing had gone ragged and he still shivered.

Someone. Sibyl pressed her face against Luke's chest. *Please...*

6 | SIBYL

oving was painful. Stiff. But she sat up anyway and checked Luke.

Warm air puffed onto her frigid hand. She pressed her shaking hand to her mouth, nose stinging as tears warmed her eyes.

"He's alive," she whispered, unable to speak louder than a whisper and turned to Boatswain. "You're a *good* boy." She scratched his chin. He refused to move from Luke's chest. "Now," she stood, stumbled a bit, and looked for a rising sun, or campfire from possible travelers, or the moon reflecting off the ocean. Something to point her in a direction. "Time to be less helpless."

Sibyl worried about Luke's bleeding. She could care for the external, but didn't know what went on inside him. They needed a campfire and a roof over their head and still she expected to miss something vital.

"First order of business: shelter."

Everything that could be used for fire was soaked and unusable.

As she squinted through the black, a flicker of silver caught her eye and she gasped. Sibyl ran, half-frozen, straight for the light that grew bigger as the trees thinned.

There. Moonlight on the water.

As she scanned the horizon, searching for the Compound's light, she noticed a white lighthouse standing at the entrance to the harbor not far from where she stood.

Did we really end up this far out?

The disorientation from the freezing rain and darkness, aggravated by her worry over Luke's injuries, had completely screwed up her internal navigation. They were now several miles from Luke's cabin and even farther from the Compound. With Luke's injuries – Sibyl turned to look in his direction – who knew how long it'd take them to get to where they needed to be?

Ghostly white and falling apart, the antique lighthouse was their only hope. It had stood as a beacon for generations, welcoming travelers in the town's early days of muddy dirt roads and horse drawn buggies, and still stood for bigger ships a hundred years later. Now, in her most desperate time of need, it stood as a beacon once more, igniting its purpose and reliving its glory days.

Sibyl rushed back to Luke, guided by the stark white of Boatswain's spots, and shook him. The bag slammed against her back as she did so. Luke moaned at first, and as consciousness took hold, loudly and aggressively swore.

"Go away!"

"You can be mad later." She shoved him. "You're going to die if you stay out here."

By now, she struggled to move her frozen limbs. Sibyl shivered, her teeth clattering as she fought to activate her muscles.

"W…W-What did you do to me? I hurt. Everywhere."

"A cabin fell on you. Now move!"

With a giant heave, she got Luke to his feet. He swayed, stumbled, then caught his midsection with his arms, groaning.

Boatswain trotted beside them as they walked. Luke mumbled curse words under his breath.

"You know," Sibyl said as she helped him over a small wall of rocks, "we haven't seen each other for nearly three years, and in one day we both almost die."

He sniffed. "Karma's a meddlesome shit goblin."

"Karma?"

"Yes. The thing w…w-where past actions come to bite you in the ass."

"I know what it is, but what are you talking about?"

"You choking on an orange that day in Market Town is the thing that started all of this."

"Seriously?" Sibyl paused and exhaled, the trek to the lighthouse taking longer than she wanted, but she could see it now, a white pillar of hope, off in the distance. "I don't think the two are connected."

"And I refuse to believe coincidence put us together."

"Luke," Sibyl smiled and shook her head, "Market Town, where I work and live, is literally across the bridge from your parents. The Compound is a half-day's walk, easily, and all other clans can be reached within a day. You're saying running across me yesterday was just chance?"

"Karma. Not chance. It's meddling with our lives, forcing us together, and I don't like it."

Ouch. He didn't like that they were spending more time with each other? Did he hate her being around him that much?

I'm so dumb. He's not happy with me here. Once I get him settled at the Compound, I'll leave like he wants.

Luke's shoulder whacked the back of her head as he threw up. She stumbled forward, using a tree trunk to stop her fall.

Sibyl wasted no time helping Luke to his feet as she nearly tripped over Boatswain fussing over him. "I think you have a concussion."

"You think?"

The retort hit her in the stomach, mixed with the stench of vomit, and she clutched at her shirt, trying to hold back tears. Why did she have to cry in any moment of stress? It was so embarrassing.

Luke's in pain. That's all this is. I need to fix him, get him back to the Compound, and he'll feel better.

Satisfied with the reassurance she gave herself, Sibyl pulled Luke to his feet and walked with him to the lighthouse.

The musky scent inside mixed with years of birds roosting in the rafters high above did nothing to encourage visitors, but Sibyl was desperate. It had to do.

Against the walls were dust covered boxes, bed frames, tires, and an assortment of discarded bikes. The floorboards creaked with every step. Sibyl glanced up. A section of the spiral staircase had broken and laid on the ground. No hope to reach higher. Birds, specifically doves judging by their noises, roosted in the dark rafters, but she couldn't see them.

Luke settled on the ground with a grunt, and he shuddered audibly with his eyes closed and head resting against a wall. Boatswain immediately climbed onto his lap.

Sibyl rushed to the door – a flimsy thing with a gaping, rotten hole in the bottom of it. Before closing it, she noticed a metal barrel drum outside sliced in half long ways, and dragged it into the lighthouse. She rifled through the pile of rubble, and found a piece of sheet metal that she combined with the drum and used to block the wind from coming through the hole.

"W…W-What's the plan now?" Luke asked.

Back to rifling through the piles, looking for anything that she could fuel a fire with, Sibyl didn't answer until Luke repeated his question.

"We," she said, inspecting a third piece of wood with paint on it, "are going to get warm, spend the night, and get up tomorrow morning to walk to the Compound."

"Food?"

"I don't know yet." The drum clanged as Sibyl tossed an item into it and her leg twinged again. She froze and her hand went directly to it.

It has to wait.

Thankfully, in his delirium, Luke hadn't noticed, and Sibyl was too pumped full of adrenaline to care too much about what germs her leg had been exposed to, so once the pain faded in a few moments, she went right back to work.

Sibyl gingerly sat down by where she intended to start a fire and busied herself with the grueling task of making enough friction for a spark. Back and forth she sawed the bow she'd made of a string and a stick, her arms burning and shoulders aching from the exertion, always turning to glance at Luke. She couldn't see much, but she could tell if he'd shifted positions.

"Once I get this fire going," Sibyl said, wiping her forehead, "we'll start to feel better."

She talked to Luke for a while because he seemed unable to stop himself from replying to her, but after a few minutes, he went silent.

Undeterred, Sibyl said, "Food's coming. We just need to get this fire started."

Nothing. Just the sleepy dove coos above and when Boatswain rushed over to her, pawing at Sibyl's thigh then rushed back, Sibyl knew he was in danger.

"Hey! You need to wake up!"

Nothing again. She couldn't stop her sawing, so helplessness took hold. A nauseating tingling shot through her. The only thing that kept her from dropping her tools to take care of Luke was seeing Boatswain lick, nudge, and bark at Luke.

"You can't fall asleep on a concussion right now. Wake up. Luke!"

"Huh?" came his irritated, complaining voice.

Sibyl sighed, tension relaxing a bit.

An ember ignited the kindling and she tossed her tools aside, nursing the newborn fire to life. Soon, a hot fire crackled in the metal barrel. Sibyl sighed as her body tingled in the heat and it spread over her body as she relaxed into the floor.

With a jolt, she remembered Luke and rushed over to his side. Luke barely opened his eyes to look at her. "Hi," he mumbled and barely got his hand in the air to rest it on Boatswain's head.

"I need to check you."

He smirked and titled his chin down. "You wanna check me out?"

"No. *Check you.* As in you fell and you're probably bleeding again. I need to make sure your bandages are still clean."

Luke tried to adjust but he didn't move much before his eyes widened, and he jerked and froze. She heard the slightest hint of a whimper slide out from between his tight lips and she furrowed her brow when the glance he gave her screamed at her to save him.

"I'm so sorry to ask, but can you make it to the fire? I'll be able to see better."

"I..." he paused then reached out to her thigh where she'd cut herself and delicately put his fingertips a few inches lower and came away with blood on his skin. "When did you do that?"

Sibyl tented the injury with her hand so she didn't aggravate it or inflict a higher chance it'd get infected. "When I was looking through the wreckage. It's fine. I'll take care of it later."

He leveled her with a calm yet stern look and used the wall for leverage as he groaned and stood.

"Luke—"

Luke pressed his finger to her lips, kept his neutral expression, and walked over to the bag Sibyl had left by the fire. She watched as he returned with it and barely made it to his knees in front of her.

"You don't have to—"

"Sibyl." He struck her silent with a single look. Flickering orange and yellow framed his large shoulders and solid torso, her pelt hanging from his forearms and long waves brushing the collar of his coat. Only one eye caught the light, the other shadowed, a contrast of pitch black and golden brown in his irises. Without breaking the eye contact he'd captured her with, Luke hooked his hand at the back of her knee and pulled her hips forward in one motion. She bit back a gasp.

He was injured. His brow had a slight sheen of sweat on it, and he could barely move his hands, yet he took care of her.

"I told you no, Luke. I can fix it myself."

"I know."

"Then why won't you stop?"

He looked at her. "Because you don't actually want to tell me no." Luke glanced down at his hands, cut off a groan of pain before it could fully mature, and said softly, "because I'm fucking tired of you taking care of everyone else before yourself."

Oh.

She had a boyfriend. Sure, he was abusive as hell and she would definitely be breaking up with him once she got Luke to the Compound, but he was still her boyfriend. The thoughts she teetered on the edge of indulging would stay put if they knew what was good for them. They remembered, whispering sweet nothings of her and Luke's short and ill-fated time as a couple. Ignoring them only made them scream louder, "he made you feel fulfilled and cherished."

And when he said things like that, her heart broke all over again that they hadn't lasted.

In awe of the line of his stubbled jaw as Luke gently rolled up her pant leg and inspected it.

"You'll need stitches."

"That bad?"

He nodded. "We don't have anything like that in our magic bag, do we?"

"No."

"Hmm. That's fine." Then he set about cleaning her injury, applying a poultice, wrapped her thigh, and rolled her pant leg back down. Sibyl couldn't move. She was a doll and he the carpenter manipulating her limbs to craft them to perfection, and she couldn't look away. The way his hands slid over her leg...

"Thank you," she said quickly and twisted from his light grip. "I can finish up."

Every piece of her hated rejecting Luke, but she couldn't let him touch her. Not when they were both vulnerable and easily could succumb to their desires. Or was that just her? He seemed unbothered.

Sibyl quickly tied off her bandage and shifted to caretaking mode. "Your turn."

He watched her for a few seconds, his shoulders dropped just a hair, and he nodded. "Might as well take off the rest while we're at it."

Sibyl snapped her attention to him. "What? No one is taking off anything."

He smiled just a smidge and she wanted to erase it from his face. Luke said, "because our clothes are wet from the snow and rain? You might be fine with freezing, but I'm not."

"Oh. Yeah. Yeah, that makes sense."

Sibyl caught glimpses of Luke struggling out of his wet things as she easily shed hers. The fabric and fur clung to him like a second skin, and as soon as Sibyl heard him cry out when he'd expertly kept his reactions to pain just underneath the surface, she limped over as fast as she could.

When she reached for him, he turned, panting and silently begging for help.

"Sit down," she urged, barely keeping her worry over him to herself. "I'll help you."

"Damn I hate this feeling," he mumbled.

Sibyl peeled the second leg of his pants off. "What feeling?"

"Helpless. Being coddled."

She smiled a bit. "What happened to being tired of me taking care of myself last?"

"That's different."

"How so?"

Luke looked up at her, eyes misty. "Only one of us is allowed to care for the other person and it sure as hell ain't you."

"So you can dish it, but you can't take it?"

Luke grunted. "Shut up."

Sibyl chuckled and hung his pants on a nail.

"Now for step two." Sibyl grabbed the first aid supplies she'd brought from Luke's cabin and sat down in front of him. "I can't really see with this limited light, so I'll need to patch up the immediately dangerous injuries and save the rest for Soora."

Luke swayed a bit, breathing labored. "Do your worst, Doc."

She made a face at him. "Lift your arms."

He did so.

She didn't comment about the peppering of scars and wished she'd been curious enough to ask about them before. They painted his shoulders, sides, hands, between his middle and ring fingers, on the underside of his arms. What were they all from? Some looked like stab wounds, others from...hunting, maybe? Although, she couldn't imagine Luke willingly in a fight.

Luke sat still for her while she worked, but she could feel his breath and gaze on her as she did so. It unnerved her, yet she didn't want to move away. His breathing was...calming, somehow, and her nerves were triple fried, awareness of their state more potent now that adrenaline had worn off.

As far as she could tell, no large areas of bruising was present, a positive considering the damage he could have sustained. Tears welled in her eyes at the thought of losing Luke. His hand lifted, fingers in position to touch, but partway there Luke stopped, closed his fingers into a fist, and dropped his hand. Sibyl pretended not to notice.

Once she finished wrapping fresh bandages, Luke thanked her and scooted closer to the fire with Boatswain attached to him as if they were one. Sibyl watched Luke for a bit, the firelight settling on his face and brightening the bandages covering his torso, arms, and splint on his wrist. The bridge of his nose was long with a slight convex curve, and his cheekbones high. Stubble framed his face well, even though it needed a bit of refining, and his shoulder length, soft wavy dark hair kissed his skin.

"You're staring again," Luke said in a deep tone that made her want to shudder happily, watched the fire for a moment, then flicked his black eyes in her direction. He had a quiet command about him and Sibyl suspected she couldn't avoid its allure for long.

"Am I a fascination?" he asked.

Realization snapped her out of staring at his finger scars. "No. God no. I'd never—" She paused, wanting to be sure she chose the right words. "I'd never see you as that. Ever. It's just...I'm just now realizing I never asked you about the scars on your fingers."

Luke shrugged in a way that made Sibyl wonder if he wanted to move away from the conversation, and she was prepared to discontinue the line of conversation, except Luke spoke up, so low he almost whispered. "They're from a surgery I had when I was a toddler to separate my fingers. A small portion of the bones were fused as well, which is why I prefer the bow. Keeps my fingers strong." He inspected them. "It's only been recently that I wasn't ashamed of them."

"Why?"

"Bullies," he answered plainly.

"Oh. I'm sorry."

He grunted. "It happened a long time ago."

"But it clearly still bothers you."

Luke looked at her then turned away without another word.

Sibyl tossed another piece of wood on the fire, then tested their clothes. Dry. So, she tossed Luke's to him and wiggled into her own. When she finished, Luke still hadn't put on his shirt and instead shifted his eyes from her to his clothes.

"Did you..." she narrowed her eyes, "wait until I got dressed so I wouldn't feel obligated to help you?"

"The world may never know," Luke muttered back and worked on getting dressed. He stopped halfway through, arms in, but struggling with getting it over his head. He furrowed his brow apologetically. "I need help."

Sibyl helped Luke into his shirt, basking in the effect his thoughtfulness brought, and helped him to the ground. He grunted as he settled into position and sighed.

Sibyl thought back to her thigh and glanced down, realizing she'd bled through the bandages. She glanced over at Luke in case he wanted to yet again not allow her to take care of herself to see him dozing against Boatswain. She sat to look at it.

Yup. Luke was right; it needed stitches.

Shoot.

She quickly escaped into the snow outside and rubbed it on her cut, biting the inside of her cheek when the freezing cold shocked through her wound, and snuck back into the lighthouse to grab the shortest strip of fabric she could find. She couldn't take too much. Luke needed it worse than her and if she needed to go without, she would.

"Don't you dare," Luke mumbled, draped over Boatswain. "You need the bandages as much as me. Take what you need." He sighed sleepily. "As your doctor, I command it."

She smiled and chuckled lightly and took what she needed.

7 | SIBYL

For a time, silence fueled me.
Then it stole joy and sucked my life dry.
You shared in my loneliness.
Welcomed it like an old friend.
Now, you are my life and my joy.
We share silence together.
And I have peace.

Now that warmth and her leg had been taken off the to-do list, Sibyl set about figuring out the next issue: food. The doves cooed above and she tilted her head slowly like a predator stalking its next meal.

As if knowing what she was thinking, Luke handed her a small stone. "If we can find something to build a sling shot, we can eat them."

"Those poor birds." Sibyl glanced up again, rolling the rock in her fingers.

"Anyone w...w-who shits on me deserves to be eaten." He lifted his arm and pointed at a white spot. "See."

I don't even know if I can hit one." Sibyl smirked as she got up to look for some leather string and fabric. "I make perfume. I don't hunt birds." She turned around, pointed at him, and bounced backward on the balls of her feet. "That's your department."

"What about that spear you had three years back?"

Without hesitation, Sibyl lied, "I got rid of it." Luke didn't need to know she'd fibbed to avoid the hard truth: Peter had sold it right from under her nose when they started dating the first time and he'd kept it a secret until she'd asked him to stop slapping her butt in front of customers a few months back. He'd stopped, but later that night revealed the truth in a fit of anger.

Originally, Peter had said it was stolen. Even took time to look for it with her, expertly showing true concern at its loss and comforting her. At the time, he was perfect. Sweet and gentle and caring.

Oh how stupid she'd been.

"Pity," said Luke and he rubbed Boatswain's back, then he smiled. "You w…w-were a force of nature."

"Is that," Sibyl leaned back, "a compliment?"

Luke turned away and mumbled, "No."

"You're impossible, you know that, right? Have you been a hermit for so long that you can't compliment someone without trying to hide it?"

Why is he hiding in the first place? What's he running from?

Instead of pressuring him, Sibyl stood and rifled through the pile of rubble again. The whole thing was beginning to feel like their personal treasure trove. She found a small fabric mask with the elastic ear loops still intact, tested it out, and both snapped the second she applied tension.

Well, I guess the mask can be a pouch.

All the elastic items she found were either too disintegrated to be used or snapped under any amount of pressure. Her body cast a dark shadow over the items, hindering the efficiency of her search.

"There's a boot by your foot," Luke piped up, scaring her.

"It's not what I'm looking for." Sibyl removed her hand from her pounding chest and picked up a rotted branch she could've used to make a bow, but that thought fell away after she realized she didn't have a way to make arrows.

Luke called out again, "You've got a pouch. You could make an old school sling?"

She glanced down at the boot, realizing he was right, and walked back to the fire with her items.

Luke scratched the back of his neck. "Hey. So, I realize I haven't been much help. You've done much and w...w-without you, I w...w-would've been a goner. So...thanks."

Sibyl blinked, wondering if the real Luke was somewhere else instead of standing in front of her. An apology? She'd never known him to be the first to apologize. Most of the time, he went about his day doing and saying what he damn well pleased. He wasn't mean, but he also didn't care if someone either got offended by honesty or if they completely misinterpreted his words, So his apology, even if it was awkward and delayed came as a surprise.

"You were—are—injured and pushed through that to wrap my leg. You don't need to apologize."

"I'm just...not used to being so useless."

There was that word again. Useless. What's going on with him?

She watched Luke rub his face in the dog's neck fur, muttering in a low tone. Boatswain's tongue flopped out of his mouth and he scooted against his human, rolling onto his back for belly scratches. Luke obliged.

"Look at you and your soft belly," he muttered.

A tiny flutter settled in her stomach and she smiled.

Luke flicked his eyes to her, a sparkle in them from the firelight which made him look devious and delicious—

Delicious?

Sibyl jerked her head away and crossed her legs, busying herself with pulling the boot laces out to distract her mind from images of his face peering at her from behind dark eyelashes.

He was the grumpy one, the one who crossed lines of social etiquette as if they weren't there. No one was supposed to like being around him, yet, that's exactly where she found herself, intrigued by his prickly exterior that held a deep chasm of mystery, intrigue, and kindness.

Even though he'd dumped her without warning years ago and she'd been furious that he hadn't spoken to her about why, Sibyl could see a change in him that drew her closer. Maybe, just maybe, things had changed?

She willed her mind to shift to the task on hand, used a rusted nail to rip holes in the mask, then tied the shoe strings into each hole. At the end of one she tied a loop and the other a knot, and stood, ready to throw.

Luke's outstretched hand stopped her. "Can I try?"

"Seriously?" Sibyl asked. When he didn't break his gaze, Sibyl sighed. "You're hurt."

"I'd still like to try."

She looked at him for a moment, taking in the beaten up condition of his body. Who was she to stop him?

"Here," Sibyl said after a moment and handed the makeshift sling to Luke. "I need a laugh today."

"Ha ha." He groaned as he stood slowly, holding his ribs, and slipped his finger through the loop at the end of the lace, lifted his arm, and lowered it immediately. He glanced at Sibyl, quickly hiding a pained expression, and tried again with no success.

Sibyl watched him; her stomach growled. She couldn't stand seeing him push past pain to avoid his feelings, so she got to her feet. "Okay. Your personal doctor says it's time to stop." Sibyl touched Luke's forearm. "Go sit by the fire, broken man."

It took him a few moments to give the sling back and did so with a quiet, disappointed groan. Sibyl helped him to the floor.

She aimed, held the string at arm's length, and swung as if she were throwing a ball. No one had ever told her how to use a sling, so she entered the activity blind, a small section of her mind worried about how she might look trying to figure out the technique.

After several minutes, the rock hit a beam, the sound bouncing off the structure's interior, and the birds awoke. They fluttered, frantic to escape, but couldn't with the only door blocked. Sibyl ducked and put her hands over her head. Boatswain barked. She could hear him bound around the lighthouse.

Once the birds calmed, Sibyl tried again.

And again.

Each time she shot the rock from the sling, it hit a beam or poked a hole in the roof.

"You're doing great!" Luke called from the spot Sibyl had banished him to.

Sibyl glared at him and his stupid, perfect grin. "You're so lucky your ribs are broken, asshole."

"You really are doing great. Those holes in the roof are the perfect distance apart."

"I've hit exactly zero birds."

"And the pigeons thank you."

She scrunched her nose up at him, huffed, and turned around. "Well," she aimed, "my stomach doesn't!"

By some miracle, the rock hit a pigeon and it fell from the rafters with a soft whump.

"I did it." Shock fell away and Sibyl jumped in the air, dancing and spinning. She grabbed the bird from the ground. "I did it! Do you know how long that took me?"

Her toe hit a beam lying on the ground and she pitched forward...straight onto Luke on the ground. He cried out as she collided with him and Sibyl ended up anchored, for a moment, against him. Luke's barrel chest heaved against her shoulder. She could hear the heavy breaths he took.

"I have some idea, yes."

His voice was in her ear, quiet, pained, and rough. Then she looked at him.

Their faces were close. Too close. Luke's eyes shone golden brown. His hand shifted against her back. Fingers splayed out. Slowly he reached up to wrap a finger around one of her braids hanging down her back and gave it a tiny tug. Sibyl's lungs squeezed together and her heart leapt and she scrambled away.

Sibyl's throat was almost too tight and dry to form words properly, but she managed a, "Wanna pluck the bird—"

"Yes, I do."

Luke grabbed the bird and she closed her eyes.

8 | LUKE

Almost there.
Almost a sign.
Almost a possibility.
Almost thine.
"Almost," I thought. "We've almost arrived."
"Almost," I thought.
And then you were mine.

Sibyl wouldn't stay out of his head and he had half a mind to let her stay, and as he sat with the bird between his knees, plucking it awkwardly – damn his broken wrist – he struggled to keep his gaze to himself.

She sat by the fire, bundled in a brown fur pelt, knees to her chest, and there were several times Boatswain had to remind Luke with a gentle nudge that he had a job to do and couldn't skip off to Daydream Land. Sibyl's earthen scent of rosemary and pine caressed the shadows of his mind, pushing, shoving, and spreading with a voracity that startled him. She was so warm, so feminine. The glimpses she'd given him of her grit throughout the years, and especially in the past couple hours, sucked his throat dry.

She'd been an angel in the darkness the moment she pulled a piece of his roof off him.

What am I doing?

She's off limits, idiot.

Luke glanced her way again.

I should say something.

He yanked hard on a bundle of feathers and bit down a pained groan.

Should I?

No. No. Bad idea.

Sibyl stood, mumbling something about water to clean his hands, and left with a cloth. She didn't come back for several minutes and Luke's insides tumbled with worry. Would she come back? Was she safe out there? Was he being too forward? Did she forgive him for breaking up with her enough to have a conversation about it? Did she even care anymore? Why wasn't she coming back? Had she left him after realizing he couldn't pull his own weight?

By the time he'd pulled all the feathers off, he was sweating and his body damn near cramped up with his legs slightly bent and back hunched over the bird carcass. He straightened as much as he could, but he remained in the awkward position until Sibyl returned with a bucket of snow she set by the fire and knelt down beside him.

"Alms for a poor, broken old man?" Luke asked, trying to make light of his situation.

A bright, warm wave of joy ran through him as she smiled with her nose scrunched. Three little wrinkles right on the bridge. How shameless of him to hope he could bend forward and kiss them, but shameless he was. He almost smiled back when he shifted and his muscles spasmed and he was holding his mid-section, Sibyl fussing over him.

"I knew I shouldn't have let you pluck that bird," she chastised herself.

Luke tried to grab her, to stop her, but she stood too fast and he was too slow due to his injuries, and could only watch as she hurried over to the bucket, dipped a rag inside, wrung it out, and returned to him. She blotted at his forehead and cheeks, lifted his shirt without so much as a warning, muttered to herself, and gave him a hard glance.

"You are not going to be helping anymore. Understand?"

He blinked. "Yes."

"Good."

Sibyl spent the next few minutes refreshing his bandages, all the while sighing and mumbling to herself for thinking it was a good idea letting Luke help. Part of him blamed himself for ignoring his health to avoid facing reality and the other part, the immature, toxic side he'd spent too long fighting, absorbed the attention she gave.

God, fucking damn it. He was touch starved. So much time away in his cabin with only his dogs for comfort had driven him to stoop lower than he cared to admit. He wanted her, but he'd never allow himself to have her unless she, too, wanted it. Wrapping his wounds for a third time in silence gave Luke time to fight his demons. Peter became an obstacle to overcome, a warlord coming for his girl after she escaped his domain and ran straight into Luke's.

In the silence of that moment, Luke knew one thing, irrevocably and unequivocally: he would fight for her. His chances were slim, mountainous walls stacked against him, but he would do it. If he lost, so be it, but he would know he gave it everything he had, starting with...

"Letting you go was the foulest mistake I ever made, and I'm so, so sorry I hurt you."

Sibyl, her arms reaching around him to tuck in the end of the bandage, froze. The fire crackled in the background. Luke waited, practically on Death's door, for her to say something, anything.

"Sibyl?"

"Uh...Yeah?" She didn't move.

"You good?"

She let out a light chuckle, somewhere in the region of disbelief and shock, slowly tucked in the cloth strip, and silently went to tending the bird.

Luke gingerly slid his coat back down and pulled the fur pelt against his lower spine. He watched her carefully, eyed the slight shake of her hands and avoidant gaze of her eyes.

"I shouldn't have brought it up."

"No," she replied wistfully. "No, it's okay."

"Is it?"

She flicked her attention to him, down to the bird in her hands, and closed her eyes. "I just have one question."

"Yeah?"

When she opened her eyes, Luke saw the misting of tears glistening in the fire's glow. "Why—" she swallowed, set the bird down on a clean sheet of metal, and hugged herself, "why didn't you talk to me? You left me high and dry. I thought—I thought I'd done something irreparable. Been thoughtless and hurt you."

"You didn't—"

"I've been over and over it in my mind for years, wondering what I did, how could I have hurt what we had so deeply that it warranted complete silence, and—" She pressed on her eyes with the heels of her hands then pulled them away just as Luke tried to stand to go to her, unsure what to even do. "Why did you abandon me?"

That gut punch hurt more than he expected. They stared at each other, Sibyl with tears trickling down her face, and Luke with his hands limp in his lap, unable to feel any extremities. She was right. He'd abandoned her.

"I don't understand. I just don't. We had it *so good*, Luke. So good. You were—" her breath hitched, "you were everything to me. I loved us together then you just, what, woke up one day and decided to drop me?"

What could he say? Yes? Not exactly? Even after three years, he still didn't know why he'd dumped her. Luke opened his mouth to speak, but Sibyl was crying now, trying to speak through her emotions, and all he could do was watch her unfold everything she'd kept hidden behind her smile and kind personality.

"Do you even know how long I waited at your cabin, banging on your door, and pathetically begging you to just come out and talk to me and then feeling like an absolute idiot because you showed up after a three day long hunt when I thought you were inside ignoring me? And then you told me, when I asked if we could talk, that you didn't have time.

"And then you never replied to my letters, except one where you showed up with it in your hand, face blank, and told me you needed time and you'd come to me when you were ready, and you never came!" Sibyl stood and paced. "You *never* came to find me, *never* apologized, *never* explained just what had happened."

She spun on her heels. "All I wanted was an explanation. Instead, I got static. Silence. And I have still...been there...when you needed me!" Before Luke could reply, Sibyl contorted her face, ran her hands through her hair, and practically yelled, "you are a coward. You're a coward for running and a coward for ignoring me."

Words spilled out of her and he sat there, helpless against the onslaught of seeing what he'd done to her, and he had to wonder if he could ever make it up to her. So, Luke softened his shoulders, opened his hands, rotated them to the ceiling, and peered up at her.

"You didn't deserve that. I was running from everything back then, but I should never have turned away from you." He knitted his eyebrows together. "You have every right to be angry. I understand if you would rather leave and never look back."

Sibyl blinked through her tears, frowned, and put her finger in the air. "I am not going to do what you did to me. I know how awful it felt, how it still feels, and no matter how angry I am at you, you will never get the same treatment. I won't—I can't do it."

She was a much better person than him, and he would do everything in his power to make up for what he destroyed.

"Fair enough," he said.

She inhaled as if releasing a built-up pressure and blinked. "I'm going to bed," Sibyl said quietly and walked away.

Morning came, unwelcome and vibrant. A hole Sibyl had shot into the roof beamed light into his eyes and he groaned, his body angry he'd slept on the ground. Right as he moved, pain from his temporarily forgotten injuries stole his breath and forced him to remain immobile until further notice.

"Sibyl," Luke croaked and looked at her form curled up on an almost flat pad, the fire smoldering next to her. "Sibyl, wake up."

She moaned and moved. "What time is it?"

"Morning."

The smile that bloomed across her face did fuzzy things to his insides.

"Good morning," she said through that smile.

"Morning," Luke grumbled and moved. Pain pushed a grunt from him. Sibyl jerked forward to help, but he didn't want her anywhere near him or he'd explode at her touch, so he shook his head as politely as he could. God, even that took too much out of him. "I can do this."

She backed off, nodded, and waited by the door for him. He was the old grandpa hardened by a life of survival who struggled to walk without his cane. It infuriated him. He was supposed to be strong, agile, but he was now struggling to even stand.

"I need to double check your bandages."

"Again?"

She gave him a look. "Yes. Again. We have one more roll, so if you need a change, we can do that."

Luke's attention caught on the limp and grimace Sibyl tried to hide. "Use it for yourself," he said.

"What?"

"I'm fine. I can suck it up until you, me, and Boatswain get to the Compound." When she didn't move, he clarified, "Your leg needs it more than I do." He patted his leg. "Come on boy. Let's give her some privacy."

Luke and Boatswain waited out in the cold sunlight for a few minutes with the leftover supplies Sibyl had brought from his cabin. He leaned against the lighthouse's white exterior, lost in thought.

I really messed things up.

He glanced down at Boatswain for a moment as if the dog knew anything about the complexities of human relationships. "I'm jealous of you, you know. All you have to do is tick your head to the side, flop out your tongue, and people love you."

Boatswain did exactly as Luke described, pressing his massive black and white body against Luke's thigh and nearly toppling him over with his weight. Luke chuckled, and scratched his jowls.

"Yeah. Exactly like that."

Movement caught both of their attention and Luke glanced up to see Sibyl standing at the mouth of the lighthouse, her cheeks slightly pink and body bundled in thick furs. They watched each other for a few moments until Boatswain loped over and got attention from Sibyl. She smiled down at the dog, knelt, and said something to him before she glanced back up at Luke.

His heart leapt seeing her. The night before had been rough, to say the least, and he wondered if it still affected her. He hoped it didn't, hoped that Boatswain's antics would help soothe the sting if it did.

Sibyl's breath puffed away from her face. "Ready?"

Luke nodded and they walked toward the Compound together, boots crunching in the half inch layer of snow. Boatswain, able to read emotions better than Luke, stuck to Sibyl's side.

He could walk mostly on his own without much pain, a relief, but still tired easily. They rested a lot, which turned the journey into a longer trip than expected.

"This feels like old times, doesn't it?" Sibyl reminisced when they were about a mile from the Compound.

The bounce in her step and cheery smile gave him goosebumps and he rubbed his arm. The more they walked, the more she fidgeted.

He sensed she needed to chat, even if the topic was mundane. "It's been a while, hasn't it?"

"Yeah...it has." She took in a quick breath and said, "I'm sorry. I don't mean to make you uncomfortable. I know how much you dislike small talk and," she grimaced, "I'm probably making things awkward."

"You're not."

"Okay. Good. I just...I need to babble," Sibyl wiped at the outside corner of her eye, "to release leftover tension from last night. It was a lot."

Luke nodded. "Makes sense...You can talk. I don't mind."

A slow, shy smile brightened her eyes, and she paused for a bit to look out over the Spit, a narrow land formation connecting the peninsula beyond them to the mainland they walked upon. They were minutes from the Compound - it stood strong upon one of the tallest hills in the area - and all he wanted was to lay in an actual bed.

Wind blew past them, salty with a slight scent of decay. There was a tranquility to the ocean but it held a quiet power, one that went unnoticed until it roared to life and battered those who entered it upon the rocks.

Like her.

Sibyl smiled, leaned into the crisp wind, and closed her eyes. When she tilted her chin to the sky like a sunflower desperate for light, Luke couldn't tear his gaze from her until she opened her eyes again.

"I've always loved ocean smell. It reminds me of life." She turned to him and he quickly wiped away his disagreeing scowl. "Have you ever had seaweed salad? It's so good and the ocean's just full of it."

"Full of seaweed salad? Gosh."

"No," Sibyl giggled a bit. "Seaweed. To make seaweed salad."

"Now I'm confused."

Of course she didn't explain, just launched into a monologue, words fluttering about like a hummingbird looking for a flower. He listened. By the time they were halfway up the hill, she'd turned his brain to mush, yet he enjoyed listening, even though following her train of thought was a maze. Her voice held a musicality, a lightness, that brought Luke warmth and peace.

Luke and Sibyl walked slowly up the hill, Luke leaning against her for support. He'd felt fine – considering – that morning, but whether it was the journey or his injuries worsening, Luke could barely hold his head up. Several times he had to remember to lift his feet and almost pitched forward several times if it weren't for Sibyl's support.

A single Sentinel met them when they reached the hill's summit.

"Ho!" He held his hand in the air, paused, squinted, then clapped his hands. "Well, if it ain't Sibyl Marchant! I was wondering when you'd crop up. Been too long, hasn't it?"

"Hello, Ben."

Luke didn't like the way she'd said his name all gentle-like. It made him cranky and he wanted to punch the guy.

Sibyl laughed as Ben pulled her into a tight hug. More irritation pushed on Luke's stomach. Boatswain's wet nose nudged into Sibyl's hip and she nearly toppled into Ben. Luke called his dog to his side.

"Not unless you count the time I helped you off that roof," Sibyl said with a chuckle.

"I was pretty drunk, wasn't I?"

She gave him a sideways look. "You were crying."

Ben rubbed the back of his neck sheepishly then seemed to notice Luke for the first time. "Awe, man. Between you and Eloise bringing home strays, we're losing space."

Luke raised one eyebrow and found his voice, irritation driving him to speak. "I'm Mason and Soora's nephew. I'm not a stray."

Ben smiled. "So, you're the mysterious nephew he talks about. Well, welcome to the Compound." He paused then pointed. "They're still in the same place. Good luck!"

The Compound was a red brick building built in the mid-century modern style popular during the 1950's and 60's. A double glass door sat underneath a bowfront awning with three stories of identical windows to the right. They used to be classrooms, but had long been converted to small apartments for the resident Compounders. A long beige wall stretched out to the left of the door, covered in ivy, and leading to the main building and Soora's medical wing.

"W...W-What did Ben mean about Eloise?" Luke asked after leaving Ben to his job. Good riddance.

Sibyl sidestepped a small group of children who shot past them. "He

was talking about Eloise bringing Bannack home when they first met."
She released a tiny chuckle. "And the girlfriend I found nearly drowned
after she fell off the Spit Bridge."

"Girlfriend or *girlfriend?*"

A smile tugged at her round lips. "The latter."

Interesting. He hadn't expected that answer. "How do I not know
this?"

She chuckled. "Well, we rarely see each other."

"I meant before."

"You seem so confident I knew back then."

"Did you not?"

She shook her head. "I didn't realize I was bi until a little after we
broke up."

"So that girlfriend you mentioned..."

"Was short lived but happened about a year ago. Before Peter and I."

Peter. The universe was so keen on reminding him of his childhood
bully any moment it got.

When they entered the bustling Compound, Luke was met with
loud conversation, foot traffic, and various sounds of goats or chickens
currently transported inside or outside. People noticed them and parted.

Between the three-hour trek to get to the Compound and the
climbing of its hill, Luke's body finally forced him to stop. It was a
miracle he'd made it as far as he did.

The color drained from his face, his skin clammy and cold. He
struggled to see and kept alternating between looking through his right
and left eyes to clear out the haze that settled in them.

"Cici!" a child called. Luke squinted through unfocused eyes and
watched as a group of five kids between the ages of eight and ten
surrounded her. "Cici, you're back!"

He vaguely heard Sibyl chuckle. "Just...moment." The words blurred
in his mind. "Need...help...friend."

Luke stumbled a bit.

"Hey." Sibyl gave him a shake.

It hurt, vaguely aware someone moved him, so he groaned loudly
and looked at her, eyes drooping.

"You gotta...wake," Sibyl mumbled again. Was she mumbling?

Luke moaned.

"...close," she said, grabbed his waist, and heaved.

Luke cried out, waking up fully to agonizing pain smashing through his bones. "Ach! Damn it! Do ya have ta hurt me?"

"If it prevents you from falling asleep on me, yes."

His head rolled forward. "Jerk."

"Asshole."

Luke's eyes twinkled.

Soora rushed up from the end of the hallway, two assistants following with purple arm bands signaling their status as nurses and medical assistants. Someone had probably alerted her to their arrival.

"Luke," she breathed out and immediately inspected him. "What happened to you?"

"Curious, that," Luke said through a lazy, sideways grin. "Old cabin roofs are quite heavy."

His aunt rolled her eyes. "Glad to hear your humor is still intact." Soora looked to Sibyl for clarity.

"His cabin collapsed with him and his dogs inside," Sibyl explained. "Levin's missing, but Boatswain found me. I pulled Luke out of the rubble. We tried coming here last night but got caught in the rain and snow and stayed in the old harbor lighthouse until morning."Soora nodded a thanks then looked to her assistants. "Help Sibyl. Let's get him to the med bay and see what the damage is."

"Come on," one of the medics, a woman with dark brown locs and many golden piercings, urged. "Let's get you checked out, too."

Luke glanced over his shoulder, arm draped over the pierced woman's shoulders, and watched Sibyl stand awkwardly in the center of the lobby. He wished he could wave to her or smile, but he was too heavy everywhere to even lift a finger.

"Her leg," he managed to his aunt when she stepped up to assist with bringing Luke to the exam room, "...stitches."

Soora nodded her understanding – or at least he hoped she did – and whispered something to a nurse before the med bay double doors closed on Sibyl, still watching them take Luke to the back.

9 | SIBYL

Careful.
For was it not the fisherman
who mistook the sea's calm for safety?
So, too, have you done.
With her.

Soora returned from settling Luke in his room and tended to Sibyl's leg. She ended up pulling a few micro-slivers out of Sibyl's thigh, gave her four stitches, an anti-bacterial for her leg to stave off infection, and ordered her to stay in town for the next two days to make sure no infection hit.

After her release from the quick doctor visit, Sibyl limped back and forth in the gathering area directly outside the medical bay, rubbing her palm aggressively with her thumb.

"Syb!"

Eloise crashed into her. Sibyl grunted in surprise then reciprocated the hug. Boatswain's excited bark boomed through the building, and he received a highly anticipated scratch of his jowls that left a string of drool on Eloise's hand. Bannack appeared shortly after and gave Sibyl a gentle hug.

Sibyl had always admired them as a couple. Bannack was an imposing Black man with a heart of gold that had remained intact even after all he'd experienced as a mercenary and Second Hand to the woman who'd used him to terrorize people for years. He never left his and Eloise's apartment without his sword at his hip, and today was no exception. Eloise was short, lithe, as fiery as her red hair, and liked no one except Bannack. They were strong together and a terrifying force when protecting those they loved, him with his exceptional skill as a sword fighter and her with her seven knives. To see them fight? Pure poetry.

Her best friend smiled, bright golden eyes crinkling at the edges and intense scar down the right side of her face struggling to follow suit. "I heard from Ben that you showed up." Eloise pulled her onto a bench. "He filled me in on what happened. Are you okay?"

"Considering why I'm here," Sibyl sat, "I could be better."

There was a short silence then Eloise chuckled. "I'm glad you're safe. How's your leg? And Luke?"

She glanced down at her thigh, a change of sweats covering the bandage wrappings. "It'll heal. Luke's a bit banged up. Broken wrist and probably a broken rib or two. Has some deep cuts that need looking at and some bruising, but otherwise okay." Sibyl looked at Bannack. "How did your work trip go?"

Every month or so, Bannack traveled south with some provisions to help a struggling community. He shrugged and sighed. "With the weather like it is and the Compound struggling, I couldn't get away. I look forward to going, but it's safer if I stay here."

Eloise leaned forward in her seat to stare down the hallway, bracing herself with her hands on the bench seat, and her face reddened.

Sibyl turned to see Peter with his back against a wall by the back door, too far away to get his attention, but she recognized him all the same.

"What's he doing here?" Sibyl started to ask, then as she continued to say, "he doesn't live...here," her words fell away as a woman approached him and kissed his neck.

Sibyl's heart crashed through the floor and her vision tightened, focused on the way the woman held him, and the way a smile bloomed across his face. A smile he never gave her, not even before he turned horrid.

Eloise huffed angrily. "Here," she said to Bannack as she handed him the kukri she always kept strapped to her thigh. "Hold my knife."

"Leese, don't —"

Eloise put her hand in the air to cut off whatever Sibyl started to say and she watched Eloise stomp over to Peter. He noticed her seconds before receiving Eloise's fist to his face.

"What the hell?" Peter yelled as he stumbled back and put his hand on his eye. His woman scurried away when Eloise looked at her.

Bannack's single chuckle caught Sibyl's attention and she turned to him smiling beside her, arms crossed, kukri dangling lazily from his hand. "She's been wanting to do that for ages."

"Oh. Cool...I guess."

She was too afraid to punch Peter herself, so she was glad Eloise was so willing to do it for her.

Without so much as another word, Eloise stalked off back to Sibyl and Bannack.

"You're braver than me," Sibyl said through tears when Eloise returned.

"Now you don't have Peter hanging over your head preventing you from relearning how to get your bravery back."

"But — Oh God, he's coming over." Worry pounded on Sibyl's chest and she took a step back.

He shoved through the crowd. "Do you have a problem with me?" Peter demanded, eye swollen, and loomed over Eloise.

She stood her ground, hands balled into fists, and glared up at Peter.

"Stop it." Sibyl pulled Peter away and sniffed. "I'm sorry she hit you—actually," she shook her head, "no, I'm not because I won't apologize for her giving you what you deserve. You know we both saw you with another woman. Why? You said you wanted to work on us."

Peter shrugged. "I figured revealing who we're cheating with was our thing, now," he said.

A shock of terror lanced through her and Sibyl barely spoke. "What's that supposed to mean?"

Peter sneered. "*You* went behind *my* back and slept with *Luke*."

"What?" She squeaked out the word.

"You know *what*. Traipsing around with him, coming in through the front fucking door with him around your shoulder."

"That's *not* what happened."

"Deny it all you want." He took a step and leaned forward, inches from her face. Liquor hung on his breath. "He's got his cock in you any chance he gets." Peter scoffed, eyes roving over her possessively. "With those big curves, I don't blame him."

Peter's words twisted maliciously until she stopped breathing. Her throat burned with each intake of air. She found her voice, then, shifting her gaze from his chest to his face. "I am not...in his pants and how dare you talk about Luke that way." A rush of anger drove her to shove him. "I have always been kind to you. I welcomed you back even though you did nothing to deserve it. 'I'll do better,' you said. 'We're endgame.' Those were your words. And I —"

"I'm not listening to this." Peter turned to walk away, waving his hand through the air in dismissal. He stopped dead in front of Bannack, who stood with his arms crossed, reserved fury on his dark face.

Sibyl knew that look and Peter didn't. It meant danger. It meant run.

"You're going to listen," Sibyl snarled, "because I'm sick and tired of you interrupting me or thinking you're allowed to walk away like a child."

Peter tried to walk around Bannack, but his hand shot out, startling a few eavesdroppers, took a fistful of Peter's shirt, and spoke in a low, snarling tone. "I have squashed bugs with more emotional maturity than you, white boy. You stay and listen, or you will have me to answer to."

Peter scoffed but he didn't leave when Bannack released him and stepped away. Sibyl walked around to look Peter dead in the eye.

"I've done everything to keep this relationship afloat because I believed you were capable of changing, but now I realize how much of an idiot I was. You did nothing to fix things, nor did you care to change who you are."

"We're done."

Sibyl gathered her wits. "It's cute how you think you're ending the relationship." She almost laughed when Peter darkened. "You paint yourself as this White Knight, this perfect little man who does nothing wrong, when you're the cheating scum."

Shaking from anger, Peter worked his jaw. When he finally spoke, it came out in a slow drawl. "Are you finished?"

"Yes." Then loud enough for everyone to hear. "We're over, Peter. I'm glad to toss you out with the pig slop."

Dismissed and humiliated, he scuttled off and disappeared. Only then did Sibyl's knees buckle and she crashed into Bannack, who grunted and helped her to her feet again. Her entire body trembled.

"Thank you," Sibyl said as she sniffed.

Eloise wrapped her arms around Sibyl. Tears fell and she cried into Eloise's shoulder for a good while. Peter didn't deserve her tears, but she'd just done the hardest thing she'd been asked to do for a long while. When she finished, Eloise gave her hand a squeeze.

"Punching him was worth it," Eloise whispered.

Sibyl let out a wet, disbelieving chuckle. "Anyway. *That* happened." She looked at them both. "What's the plan for the rest of the day for you guys?"

"I thought you guys would be gone by now."

Bannack's arm draped over her shoulder and Eloise said, "We can't leave until Soora lets us know how Luke's doing."

Sibyl smiled, happy to know Luke had friends who cared so much about him. He wasn't the easiest to get along with and she knew his track record wasn't the greatest, but here were two of the best people she knew eager to check up on him.

Soora appeared. "Hey guys."

Bannack was the first to bring the conversation to the part they were all waiting for. "How's Luke?"

"He has two broken ribs, a wrist that I had to reset, and I re-stitched the laceration on his side," Soora informed them. "He's very lucky that his head wound wasn't more serious because I don't have the equipment to care for a brain injury." She looked at Sibyl. "He's asking for you."

Boatswain, who'd been lying spread-eagle on the floor, forcing people to walk around him, jumped to his feet at Sibyl's call and immediately slipped. He didn't seem to mind but Sibyl couldn't stop her cackle of surprised laughter. The large dog padded to her side and his tongue flopped out of his mouth as he smiled up at her.

"Ready to go see your daddy?"

In response, the dog's entire lower half of his body wiggled.

Sibyl laughed, still feeling the residual effects of crying, and ran her fingers over his ear. "Wiggle butt."

10 | LUKE

You are the glass, shattered and in my skin.
Heed my warning, you said, listen to the pain of my soul,
yet I did not.
So, I shall gather the pieces,
and build you a new window,
one that cannot shatter.

Damn, he hurt.
Leave it to the apocalypse to wipe out all the good drugs.
He was reduced to snacking on bitter leaves and herbs to
stop his wrist from throbbing. Angrily chomping on one, Luke glanced up
as the door opened.

"Boatswain!" Sibyl yelled in surprise.

Luke only saw a black and white blur of fur followed by an
enthusiastic smearing of something wet and slimy across his face. A nasty
jab to his stomach made him cry out and grab his broken ribs. If he
hadn't hurt enough before, the fire over his entire chest made sure of it.

Sibyl pulled the dog off Luke.

He leaned his head back, blinking back tears, and groaned heavily.
Any other time he would have gladly accepted Boatswain's smothering

affection. He didn't blame the dog. Boatswain never fully got over the separation anxiety he suffered from as a young pup.

"Thank you," Luke said through a cough, weaving fingers through Boatswain's thick double coat as the dog laid beside him. "I missed him."

Sibyl only stood with her back against the wall and arms crossed. Luke drew his eyebrows together and she raised hers.

"W...W-What?"

"You know what."

"No. I don't."

"Do I really have to spell it out for you?"

Luke laughed once. "Apparently. I have absolutely no idea w...w-what you're going on about."

She sat on the bed. Luke's hand tightened in Boatswain's fur. "You're welcome, ya know, for saving your life," Sibyl coaxed.

"Oh. I see." A mixture of amusement and irritation at himself muddled around in his stomach. "Thank you."

"With everything that's happened, I'm glad you're okay. For a moment, you really scared me."

"Scared you?" Luke slowly nodded. "Do you have x-ray vision? Can you smell blunt-force trauma?"

"No," Sibyl blinked at him several times then glared. "There's no reason to be a jerk to the person who saved your life."

She was right, as always, and he tilted his head to one side, closed his eyes, and sighed. "I'm sorry. I should have been more thankful. You did a great job."

"Hell, yeah, I did." As if realizing a mistake, Sibyl covered her mouth. "I mean, I was pretty amazing."

Luke straightened. "...Do you feel guilty about something you just said?"

"No. I..."

She didn't speak for a moment and while he waited, Luke ate another leaf. The pain wasn't subsiding as fast as he wanted, and he really, really wanted to snuggle up with Boatswain and sleep it off, but Sibyl's reaction to a small swear word concerned him.

Sibyl pulled her knees to her chest and placed her mouth against her knees, focusing on her toes. "It's embarrassing."

"And?"

She turned away. "Peter...he never liked it when I swore. He never did anything more than just a whisper under his breath, or a disapproving glance, but I knew. I always did. So, now my first reaction is to cover it up. I'm not a big swearer anyway but it comes out when I get excited or forget to think before I talk."

A jolt of fury and hate soured his stomach, and he placed his hand on his mouth to mask a frown. Letting her see how he felt wouldn't be productive, and it made him want a long, angry walk.

He looked at Sibyl. "So, 'cause of Peter, you don't swear as much as you would?"

"Among other things..."

Luke's blood boiled. *Among other things?*

He nearly jumped out of bed, grabbed Sibyl by the shoulders, and shook sense back into her. Peter did this to her. He'd clouded Sibyl's sunshine.

"Other things? Sibyl..." Luke put his hand on Boatswain's back to avoid holding her hand. "Did he hurt you worse than I saw the other day?"

Her eyes widened then she furrowed her brow. "No. No, nothing that extreme."

Something was being omitted, some revelation she kept secret. He detected it in the redness of her eyes, the flush of her cheeks, and the tone of her voice, as if she'd just finished crying.

"He hurt you. He's immature and dangerous."

Sibyl glared at him. "You interacted with him once and now you're an expert?"

"No, but he did something to you that you're not telling me."

"Which is none of your business!" She stood suddenly. The bed returning to its normal position hurt his ribs, and she stomped to the door.

Luke called out to her before she opened it. "And you're still with him?"

Her shoulders raised to her ears, then she shuddered slightly and spun on her heels. Anger flashed in her eyes. "And you know what else? You're lucky I came. You're lucky I care because right now, you'd still be trapped underneath your house if I hadn't followed Boatswain. You don't get to lecture me on who I date, and you certainly don't get to lecture me on how to feel about how my ex treated me. You're assuming everything."

"Sibyl, I—" Guilt settled in his stomach.

She pursed her lips. "I'm not ready to talk about it. Okay? Not with you, not with anyone. It's absolutely none of your business and if you keep pushing me, the last you'll ever see of me is my back when I walk out of that door. Alright?"

"Yeah."

"I should go," Sibyl turned around. "And because I'm such a suck-up and can't help but try to fix everything..." She paused and turned back, rolled her eyes to the ceiling as if her words were mostly to herself, then looked at Luke. "I'll find Levin for you."

"Sibyl—"

"It's fine, really. I'm glad you're safe."

He knew it wasn't fine. Fine was a dangerous word. Once again, he'd bumbled into something he shouldn't have, hurting her. He should have let the topic of Peter go. He had no right poking around.

"I shouldn't have pressed you."

She smiled flatly. "I can figure things out on my own."

"I know you can."

"I'll keep you posted about Levin."

Now his worry grew from his chest to his stomach, and he glanced down.

"Thank you."

He hated seeing her leave in her current mental state, and, in that moment, he hated himself. How much of her shutting down could be blamed on him?

As soon as she took a step to open the door, she stumbled and grunted. Her hand jerked to her thigh.

Without thinking of his actions or caring whether he'd aggravate his own injuries, Luke moved from the bed and reached Sibyl in a few long strides. She made a small noise of surprise as he closed in on her space.

"You're hurting."

Her eyes darted back and forth as she stared at him, tall enough to look him straight in the eye. "Am not."

"Don't lie to me Sibyl. Please." His voice came out deeper than he intended, and he watched her brown eyes dilate in response.

Interesting.

"It's just a few stitches Soora put in. I'm fine."

"Come sit down. Rest a bit."

Her eyes darted to the bed, and he watched a small crease between her eyebrows form. "Luke...I couldn't."

Luke had known Sibyl long enough that he recognized the look of her wanting to do something but resisting. For whatever reason – whether through Peter's doing or her natural tendency to overlook her own needs and wants – he refused to let her leave without resting her leg.

"Sit."

Sibyl watched him as she lightly chewed on her lips. Thinking. Deciding. She reached up to her shirt collar tucked underneath her jacket and he saw the shake of her hand.

He only wanted to stop it from shaking. That's all. As soon as he grabbed her hand, her mouth opened slightly, enough that he could see the pink of her tongue, and he lost control of his senses.

Luke reached up and brushed a stray hair that had fallen from her Dutch braids. His hand fluttered down the side of her face and locked behind her neck. Everything within him trembled. He wanted her.

He wanted to say a lot of things. Do countless more.

"Sibyl..." he started but couldn't finish, instead leaning forward to press his forehead against hers.

"We aren't together anymore," she whispered, and when Luke pulled back, she clarified. "Peter and I. We broke up a few minutes ago."

Shit, I'm being insensitive.

She'd just broken up with her long-term boyfriend and as much as he hated him, he couldn't bring himself to do anything that would tarnish Sibyl's reputation.

"Come sit beside me?" he asked.

"Okay..."

Sibyl took one side and Luke the other, Boatswain happily occupying the entire foot of the bed plus more as his giant body splayed off both sides.

Sibyl chuckled. "He's such a goofball."

Luke smiled a little. "He is."

After a few beats, Sibyl said, "Luke?"

He turned.

She actively avoided his gaze, and said, "Can you hold me? I don't want anything to happen but...I need someone to hold me."

Luke obliged. He wrapped his good arm around her, anchoring her trembling body to his side. Slight pinpricks of pain zapped his body, a small price to pay to comfort her.

Whatever she needed, he wanted to provide, even if it meant this moment would be all they got.

"Can you put your hand on my head?"

Luke did so, enjoying the feel of her soft hair beneath his palm. As soon as he lightly stroked her hair, careful not to catch the strands and pull them from the braid – who knew how long it had taken her to do – excitement bloomed in his chest when she melted against him.

"Mmm," she mumbled. "That feels good."

He continued, slowly testing the waters by putting his cheek against the top of her head.

God, he could die like this.

Sibyl relaxed against him. "I shouldn't have said the things I did," Luke whispered as he continued brushing her hair with his hand. "I shouldn't have pushed you. Our friendship is important to me and my asshole actions w...w-weren't right or kind."

He hoped she would accept his apology, that she'd be able to sense the regret in his voice.

This is harder than I thought.

Was he sweating? Probably from the burning ribs with every breath. Yeah. Good explanation.

Why won't she say something?

To his amazement, Sibyl's tense shoulders relaxed. "I will admit, snapping at you was a bit of an overreaction, but could you blame me?"

"Not at all."

"You're a bit of an asshole."

Luke chuckled, his eyes crinkling as he smiled wide. "Took you this long to realize?"

Sibyl chuckled with him and sighed.

"Don't leave," Luke said into her hair, then clarified. "Yet—Don't leave yet. Give me time – a day or so – to apologize properly."

"Why?"

"Does it matter?"

"Nevermind." She turned toward him, almost nestling her face into the crook of his shoulder. "Forget I said anything."

"Give me until tomorrow evening, okay? I'm staying at my parent's on the Island. Meet me there?"

Sibyl inhaled and exhaled, the sound shaking as it left her and Luke had to close his eyes and focus on the way her hair smelled faintly of sweet rum so he didn't say something he regretted.

She nodded. "I'll leave in the early morning in two days. I have to stay in town anyway to let my leg heal a bit."

Luke thought for a moment. "I can juggle that. You know their home's location, right?"

Sibyl nodded and the conversation lulled.

After a long while, Luke noticed the slow breathing of sleep coming from Sibyl, so he carefully shifted, made sure the pillow sat just right under her head, and braved through pain to get an extra blanket from the bedside storage chest to put on her. Luke grabbed a worn copy of "The Last Unicorn," not a typical choice but a story was a story, and settled beside her to read.

She slept for hours. Luke had finished the book by then and had started on another when she shifted and sat bolt upright.

"Why didn't you wake me up?"

He looked up from a gunslinger standoff scene to blink at her. "Did you have somewhere to be?"

"Yes!" She jumped to her feet, cringed, and mumbled, "I can't believe I forgot about the shop." Sibyl turned, took a step, then seemed to rethink, and turned back around to him. "Thank you."

Then she was gone, just as much of a whirlwind leaving as she'd been entering.

Boredom crept up an hour later, driving Luke to plot an escape plan. Priority number one? Avoid Soora. She'd send him right back to his cell if she caught him out and about. He needed to do something, and willingly risked detection for freedom.

Unfortunately, almost fifteen minutes into his journey Luke sunk into a nearby chair, breathing hard and hurting everywhere. He wiped at his forehead with his shirt sleeve and when he lowered his hand, Soora stood there, lips in a straight line, silently scolding him as if he were a small child as she rubbed Boatswain's ears. Soft groans of satisfaction rose from his dog's throat.

"Yeah?" Luke asked, stupid enough to hope she was clueless.

"I told you to stay in bed." A small smile played at the corner of her mouth. "Were you chasing after her?"

"Ugh." Luke tilted his head back against the wall. "She left a bit ago, so, no."

Soora's eyes changed, a warning hardening her gaze, making Luke fight the urge to stand at attention. "Be careful," Soora hinted. "She needs a gentle hand."

"She and I aren't a thing."

Soora smiled as if to say, *'gotcha.'* "Who said anything about you guys being a thing?"

Luke glared at her. "I hate you."

"Love you, too." Then she left without waiting for him to say anything more.

"You're not going to force me back?" he called.

Over her shoulder, Soora called back, "I figure you have less than an hour left of strength and by then, I'll be passing back this way anyway."

Luke smiled at that. So, he stayed on the bench a bit longer, watching people bustle through the Compound's hallways. They wore fur coats, blankets, and woolen hats. Some stoked open fire bins set up at varying points in the common areas as others huddled together, rubbing their arms, warming their hands, and conversing in low mutters with their neighbors.

Luke listened as a group of people standing around the closest brazier mere feet from him talked in hushed tones.

"I had to break the ice off the horse troughs again this morning and it's barely August." The taller man shrugged his blanket higher on his shoulders.

"Did you hear about the Talmhai clan?" asked an older man with grey hair. "They blocked all trade coming in or out."

"Why?"

"Rumor is, they're all sick."

"Yeah," said a younger woman. "It's in the Portugai and Nongshi clans too, but they haven't blocked trade yet. It must be really bad there."

"Well, what about the Rhondians?" asked the tall man. "Any sign of sickness with them?"

Intrigued, he sat up straighter.

"As far as I know, no," the older man said. "Healthy as horses, they are."

"Well," said the woman. "It better not get in here. We're already short rationed as it is with this early winter."

"It's only going to get worse." The older man. "We aren't prepared for something like this."

Luke stood, his ribs angry that he bent at the waist, and walked over to the group he'd been listening to. Boatswain velcroed his body to Luke as if attempting to keep him upright. The fire in the short metal cage made his skin tingle. All three turned to him.

"I'm looking for Eloise."

They blinked at him, as if waiting for something more, and for a few moments, he almost told them to piss off and he'd find her on his own, but they'd done nothing wrong except look at him.

He clarified, irritated that he felt the need to do so. "Eloise Oliver? Married to Bannack Owusu?"

"We know who she is. Why do you need her?"

Luke forced his jaw to relax, aggravated he had to pry the information free of their lips. Who were they to gatekeep Eloise? What was their goal, other than to dig in the fact that he didn't belong? "I need to talk to her. W...W-Where is she?"

"Oh," the woman piped up. "She should be in her office. It's halfway down the hall." She stepped out into the hallway, waiting for a group of people to pass by before she pointed. "Take a right at the brick column there and go up the stairs to the right of the library. She'll be at the top."

"Thanks."

As Luke turned the corner, he heard the woman hiss to the men, "What's your problem?"

Luke allowed a group of people to pass him so he could listen in on the answer. Despite his distance from them, he'd spent years strengthening his hearing as a hunter and had no issues listening in when the typical person wouldn't be able to distinguish words. He made sure Boatswain stayed close.

"You don't know who that is?" one man asked, shock in his voice.

The other man filled in the question. "He gave Peter a black eye years ago."

Fucking idiots.

Luke ground his teeth as heat rose into his ears. He ducked around the corner at the top landing, straining to hear.

"Why does that matter?" the woman asked. She seemed to be the only sane one. "They were kids."

"And he's never taken accountability for his part in what happened to Peter then disappears almost completely afterward? I wonder why, is all."

The woman scoffed. "Or you're tossing judgment at some rando because your childhood gang leader told you a story. You're both grown, haven't seen him in several years, and you're *still* letting him call the shots." A short pause. "You know what? Whatever."

Why was he even listening in? He'd already moved on from what happened with Peter.

He gave up on the conversation and followed the woman's directions, stopping by each fire to warm up so he wouldn't shiver his stitches off. Boatswain leaned against Luke's leg every time they paused.

Luke looked down at his dog smiling up at him.

"Enjoying that toasty double coat?" Luke gave Boatswain a scratch and walked the last leg to Eloise's office and finally managed to shake off the intrusive auditory reminder of the conversation between the two men and the woman.

Eloise sat in her office, door ajar and, warmth from a brick fireplace that didn't seem to fit with the rest of the office, almost as if an addition after the school's construction. Her dark red hair cascaded down one side of her body, adjacent to a healed yet brutal scar down the right side of her face. While she'd never shared how she'd received it, the bits and pieces of information Luke had picked up over the years led him to safely assume her sister's death had occurred at the same time she'd received the injury.

She leaned over some papers, lifted her eyebrows, blinked hard, then rubbed them. She was short – maybe five and a half feet with boots on – the imposing desk shrinking her even more and she made up for her height with intimidation. She was mostly harmless...except when it came to protecting her loved ones. Luke would be her next meal if he didn't choose his words carefully about how he and Sibyl had been communicating lately.

"Think a quick prayer to whatever gods are out there is a good idea, B?" Luke asked in a hushed whisper.

The dog gave no hint of ever answering.

"Worth a try," Luke muttered.

He nearly fell over when Boatswain suddenly slipped inside the cabin as if he were an octopus and cried loudly. Curious what had the calm, older dog so excited, Luke curiously stepped over the threshold. His heart jumped at the sight of Levin. Somehow, he'd found his way back. He danced around Boatswain, falling and rolling around the room with him. Luke watched them, struck completely still.

When Levin noticed Luke, his body folded like an accordion before he leapt through the air and tackled Luke. He fell against the couch, laughing, crying, and using his uninjured forearm to shield his face from the dog's tongue. Levin danced around him, licking and whining, and Luke didn't have the physical strength or desire to push the dog away.

"Alright, boys," Eloise said seconds later and pulled Levin away.

Luke layed on the couch for a few moments, eyes watering and wondering how the hell he'd manage to move. Hopefully he hadn't torn any stitches.

"How?" Luke asked through deep breaths.

"You've got a smart dog here," Eloise replied. She stood next to Levin, rubbing his snout. "Showed up about an hour ago."

Luke smiled and knelt slowly in front of Levin, grabbed the skin of his neck, and peered into his golden-brown eyes. "You're a good dog."

Levin panted, whined, and shifted. Luke noticed the stitches on his flank. He turned to Eloise. "Someone helped him?"

She nodded. "I'm not sure who. Came in like that."

Whoever had fixed his dog, he owed them a debt of gratitude. Luke sighed and pressed his forehead to Levin's and exhaled his worry.

I need to tell Sibyl.

With the commotion calmed and both his dogs at his side, Luke sighed into the couch and tilted his head back. Relief rippled over his skin. He just needed to make sure he didn't move and aggravate his injuries.

Eloise's voice rang through the air. "Feeling better?"

"Not really," Luke groaned as he lifted his head to look at her. She'd sat back behind the desk. "I feel like shit, all I want to do is nap, and I'm sweating profusely."

Eloise grabbed a stack of papers, tapped them on the desk, and placed them in a pile to her right. "Good to know you're still grumpy."

"I'm always grumpy." Luke carefully folded his arms.

She ignored him. "You can take a nap."

Luke watched Boatswain grunt and spin beside Levin then lay down next to him at Luke's feet.

"I'm good," he said.

"Luke...you're turning pale."

His eyes drooped and his head tilted sideways. Being with people had always been draining, but he found comfort in Eloise's presence for nearly the entire time he'd known her and her office seemed to have the same effect.

"No thanks."

"Suit yourself. So, why'd you visit?"

Luke sighed and rubbed his thigh. Nerves took over. He tried to say, "I need your help," and at the same time, thought, "Sibyl's mad at me," so what came out was, "I need Sibyl."

Eloise stared, her shock slowly, painfully, turning into a smirk that twitched at the corner of her lips. She snorted, and covered her mouth. A furnace of heat blossomed on Luke's face so hot his skin would surely melt until he morphed into an awkward mess of bones on the couch.

"You...need Sibyl?"

"No." Luke cleared his throat. "I don't need Sibyl."

Yes, I do.

Shut up.

Eloise nodded slowly. "But you'd like Sibyl?" Luke gave her an embarrassed stare and she lifted her hand in surrender. "Okay, okay. What did you actually want to ask?"

Luke sighed. "I need help."

"With Sibyl, I'm assuming."

Luke shot her a death glare. "Yes." The next words out of his mouth, Luke knew, would turn Eloise into Mama Bear and he cringed thinking about his possible fate. "I...hurt her."

There it was. That gleam in her eye he'd seen so many times. A gleam that told him he better run and hide. Not many people frightened Luke. He was big, burly, and people generally avoided bothering him because of it, but Eloise was like a miniature Doberman with a death wish and barely concealed anger issues.

"What did you do?"

Luke swallowed.

This so hard.

Alongside willingly accepting the consequences of his admission, the act of asking for help nearly paralyzed him. His idiot brain and mouth had eloped together, leaving him a bumbling, muttering, brainless lump on the couch.

"I sorta...pressured her into talking about how Peter treated her."

"You shouldn't have done that."

"I know."

"It wasn't your place."

"I know." He gave her an apologetic look. "I'm out of practice." Then he lifted his hands. "Not an excuse for my actions, though."

"So, why are you asking me for help? Go talk to her."

"I did." Luke paused, staring at his hands fiddling with each other against his will, so he jammed them into fists. He looked at Eloise, her stare searing, and took a hesitant breath. "I need to show her how sorry I am."

"Why?"

Luke glanced up at her. Her unexpected question confused him and heat blasted up his neck. "I...huh?"

"Why do you need my permission?" Eloise leaned forward and Luke's heartbeat echoed in his head. Despite his discomfort, he silently thanked Eloise didn't making it easy for him. He needed a good kick in the ass so he didn't risk hurting her ever again. Eloise said, "figure it out, pretty boy."

He worked his jaw. "You're not going to give me anything, are you?"

"No."

Luke's hope crashed and burned.

Eloise smiled. "I like watching you squirm for this."

He sat back, annoyed, and crossed his arms. "Oh joy."

Smiling, Eloise leaned back. "Go talk to her, but if you make things worse..."

The threat, even though he knew Eloise wouldn't do much other than tell him off, hit home. He knew she meant business.

"Don't w...w-worry," Luke stood and called his dog. "I'll behave myself." Right before he left Eloise's office, he turned in the doorway and asked, "Oh. Can you get a message to Sibyl about Levin being back? It's just...I could, yet Soora is most likely hunting me down right now and is probably going to post guards outside my room until I'm healed up enough to leave. Not sure I'll be able to let Sibyl know in time."

Eloise smirked. "Sure. I'll let her know."

He patted the door frame. "Thanks."

Luke made it back down the steps just as Soora rounded the corner with two large Sentinels behind her.

"Hi," Luke said as she stopped him.

"I told you to stay in bed."

"I had to take care of something."

Mock surprise widened her eyes and opened her mouth. "Oh! Is that what you were doing?" When Luke tried to walk past her, her hand connected with his torso and he stopped cold, not wanting to push past. "Aren't you the least bit curious why I have these guys with me?"

He hoped she wouldn't bring it up. "No."

"If you don't get in bed, right now, they're going to force you there. You need to heal and walking around makes your injuries worse."

Luke assessed the situation with a few flicks of his eyes. He knew Soora would follow him wherever he went, nagging to rest until he dropped dead of annoyance. "Fine. I'll go."

She kept her hand on his chest, eyes squinting at him, then gave a satisfied nod. "And leave again."

With a tiny smile, Luke said as he left, "Yes, *Mom*."

Soora kicked at his behind, smiling.

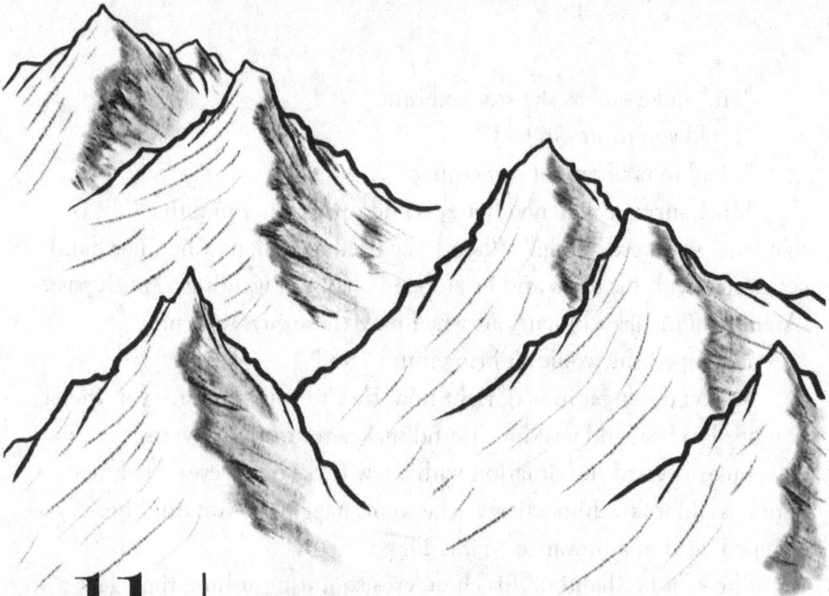

11 | LUKE

Forgive me of my blunder.
Forgive my stumble.
I am learning how to love.
And to love you, despite my clumsy heart,
shall be the greatest accomplishment of all.

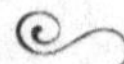

As Luke walked with Boatswain and Levin through the town square a couple weeks later, early morning snow crunching underfoot. An eerie silence hung on the frozen wind that slipped underneath his cloak's hood and aggravated the healing bones in his still splinted wrist.

A tiny snowflake melted on contact when it landed on his nose and Luke paused to stare up at the monochrome grey sky, the white of his breath spreading from his mouth after each breath.

Silence.

Before, the lack of noise meant contentment among the islanders. Now, grief and death caused it, Rhondians only leaving the warmth of their homes to find food to fill their shrinking bellies or bury their dead.

He'd seen so many live for months off scraps. People weren't meant to live like that. Animals had escaped to warmer territories and ones that hadn't, gave their lives to help starving humans survive.

Luke shivered then groaned when his ribs pinged, healed enough to give Soora the confidence he could return to normal life, but still causing issues if he slept wrong. Plans with Sibyl had changed as well. After the revelation of Levin showing up on his own, Sibyl had opted to visit his parents once he'd healed, and Luke was fucking nervous. For two weeks, he'd waited in anticipation, planning and preparing what he would say and do to start making amends, and even though he trusted her to be honest with him, Luke couldn't help worrying she'd changed plans because she didn't want to talk to him. That worry worsened when, at the end of two weeks, he and Sibyl had had exactly one other conversation, when he'd run into her and Soora on one of his agonizing slow morning walks.

A small group of five people appeared on the hill's rise ahead, braving the ankle-deep snow to carry two of their dead to the canoes then to the ocean. The Rhondians were lucky in that way. They could admit their dead to the sea rather than pound shovels into the rock-hard ground like the other clans.

Luke's heart clenched and he stood silently as the funeral attendees passed by, pressing his fingers to his lips then his chest to share condolences. The oldest woman in the group, grey-haired, eyes filled with tears, approached and gave his arm a quiet squeeze.

He left the mourners to attend to the funeral and continued ambling gingerly, eventually stopping to rest on a rock. His breath puffed out from his mouth as he struggled with the zipper. Even with gloves and a brace, Luke's fingers wouldn't cooperate. His fingers barely moved and his wrist would twinge randomly, making Luke hiss as he sucked in a breath through his teeth. When Levin nudged Luke's elbow, he gave up on the zipper.

"Having issues?"

Luke glanced up from his sulking to see Sibyl wrapped in a thick fur coat, black braid hanging off one shoulder, and holding a wicker basket of vegetation. She poorly hid her amused smile. Luke's heart jumped, the traitorous bastard. He waited in anticipation for her to speak again.

"That depends. Do you often help a man at the mercy of his injuries?"

Her mouth shifted. "Depends."

"On what?"

Sibyl stepped closer and rubbed Levin's head after he came over. "On if you're going to make this saving you from your injury-related problems a habit."

He huffed quietly. "It's not my fault the cabin fell apart."

"No." She set the basket down beside Luke and while Levin and Boatswain entertained themselves by sniffing the contents, said, "But there's an easier way to ask me, you know." Sibyl knelt beside Boatswain, unzipped his pack, and handed Luke partially frozen bread, a ceramic jug of goat's milk, some jerky, and cheese. She peered up at him through dark eyelashes and he was done for. "Whatever happened to, 'Hey. Wanna hang out?'"

"What?"

"What?" Sibyl parroted.

Holding onto his food items, Luke leaned down and narrowed his eyes. "You want me to ask you out?"

For a few moments, he thought she might stay silent and blush until he lost interest, but he knew exactly what she'd said and he wouldn't let her get away without explaining. Then Sibyl snatched the bread out of his hand, ripped it in half, and stuffed the whole thing in her mouth.

Only then did she speak with the bread crowding her mouth. "Diff brehb iff fo goo. Mmm. Dewiffuff."

"I'll just wait until you're done." Luke enjoyed his quick meal and shared his jerky with the dogs until Sibyl finally finished. The nerve of her. Stealing his food without asking. Knowing exactly what he wanted from Boatswain's pack. Bribing his dogs to like her because she gave good scratches. Honestly, she was the most annoying woman and often did it for one thing...

"You did this on purpose to get back at me." God, he sounded so paranoid, but he knew Sibyl well enough to know she'd pull something like this.

She made a little noise at the back of her throat. "Did what? Please be specific."

He couldn't tell if she was serious or not. Luke narrowed his eyes. "You're taking my food. Stealing my dogs. And I know why." To her raised eyebrows, he said, "you're upset."

A soft smile spread over her face. "Whatever makes you feel better." She grabbed her basket and stood. "For the record, I'm not. I just feel like messing with you like old times."

Luke very much wanted to act like a child and tell her to, "prove it," but she was already leaving and he found himself reaching out to grab her, but his fingers came away with only air.

"Well, it was fun running into you," she said over her shoulder. "Enjoy your afternoon."

Suddenly and inexplicably desperate to keep her close and afraid she'd disappear completely from his life once she left, Luke gathered his strength, nearly ran to catch up, and caught hold of her wrist. She stopped immediately with a tiny gasp. He took a few moments to pause, then glanced up at her pink cheeks and wide brown eyes, the soft wind blowing stray strands of brown hair across her cheeks. Oh no. He'd messed up again. Acted before thinking.

This is what had gotten them in trouble last time. They'd moved too fast, gotten in too deep, and he'd frightened himself.

His attraction to her wriggled in the deep recesses of his mind, a being he never fully banished. When Luke opened his hand, the creature faded back into the darkness, but Sibyl, with her wet eyes and expanding chest, stayed.

A silent begging passed between them, weighing on his chest, whispering to finally make good on all his forgotten promises from years ago, but he couldn't. He could offer nothing, so he let her go. And damn it, her eyes were still doing that thing. That thing where they pleaded with him not to.

"I'm sorry," Luke mumbled and stepped back.

"Luke…" she whispered. She took a half step forward, seemed to think better of it, then cleared her throat. "I'm glad we ran into each other."

She smiled a little, those weeping eyes skewering him with guilt. "You don't know what I'm talking about, do you?"

He shook his head.

Sibyl released a breathy chuckle, wiped at an eye, and blinked skyward. "It doesn't matter anymore anyway. I'll see you tomorrow."

As he watched her leave, he couldn't help but worry she'd tried to tell him something and it soared completely over his head.

The well-kept driveway led down to a brown house with dark green trim. The last time he'd spent any significant amount of time in the home, he'd vowed never to return, convinced he didn't belong in the world his parents lived in. Now, as he waited for one of them to open the door, he wished he'd stayed. He still had a laundry list of things to learn and by isolating, especially in his late teens through early twenties, he'd lost growth he would have had otherwise. That needed to end.

Luke's dad opened the door and smiled. The dogs entered and Isaac let his fingertips graze the top of their back as they passed.

Isaac stood tall with a thick mass of wild bronze hair caused by the five cowlicks wreaking havoc on his scalp, his build stocky, and skin so pale he could almost blend in with snow. Luke enjoyed teasing him about it. The man burned to a crisp in the shade.

"Hey, Dad," Luke said and patted him on the shoulder as he walked past.

Isaac closed the door. "Enjoy your walk?"

Luke knew his dad well enough to detect the, "*I hope you learned your lesson and will slow down now,*" words tucked between the lines.

He chose to ignore what his dad didn't say as he sat on the couch, sweet relief flowing through his body. "Quite refreshing. Thanks for asking."

His dad stared then a few moments later, guffawed. "You're lying through your teeth." As Luke glared, Isaac sat with him. "By the way, your things are all moved in downstairs."

"Thanks for that." He perked up, realizing he hadn't seen his mom yet. "Mom's location?"

"A meeting. Should come out soon."

"About?"

"The winter freeze mostly, but she has a guest today that's talking about gathering a team together to go investigate something upriver." Isaac stood and walked to the kitchen. "Hungry?"

"Starved." Luke followed him. "Something's upriver?"

Shrugging, Isaac handed him a small meat pie. "Didn't hear what." Then he smiled. "Unlike you, I'm not nosy."

Through a mouthful of food, Luke said, "I resent that." He swallowed. "I'm invested."

"I sense your hesitation to take over for Clara has something to do with your stutter. Am I correct?" When Luke didn't give a clear answer, Isaac shrugged. "If the Talmhai clan can accept a trans Leader, the Rhondian clan can accept you. They just need a chance."

"I'm not sure I believe you."

"Well, believe me or not, if ya still want the Leadership, now is the best time to tell yer mother."

Luke shook his head. "I'll think about it."

They spoke for a while longer congregated around the kitchen adapted to off-the-grid living. The appliances from before Day of Ashes were for storage just the same as the kitchen cupboards. Drying herbs hung from hooks under the cabinet, meat salted in the kitchen sink, water glassed eggs sat on the counter. If Luke had visited during the summer, jerky would be smoking outside, hides would be tanning, and his mom would be out in the back yard she and Luke's dad had converted to a community garden. Now, the whimsical mismatch of raised beds grew weeds until the season changed.

The split-level home's lower half had been remodeled by a previous owner to resemble an apartment with a back room that Luke's mom had quickly claimed as her office space. Luke often found her there on his visits watering her garden as she worked out how to deal with a trade agreement not going her way, a prickly adviser, or a quarrel between two clans.

After half an hour of Luke's arrival, a door opened and muffled voices followed.

Luke stood, hoping to catch his mom's eye as she followed four advisers representing their respective clans. His mother, Clara, was short with hair just as dark and vibrant as the day she was born and dressed as if stepping out of an archaeology dig under the scorching sun. Clara ran hotter than most, comfortable in the warm white linen shirt and tan linen pants that billowed around her bare feet as she walked.

Nongshi clan's Leader, Chizu Doi, the group's bright-eyed darling appeared first; young, spry, and full of blazing spirit, who carried a pair of katanas against her back.

Then came the twins, Quinn - Portagai's leader - and Thea - Equida's - the quiet ones. What they lacked in height, they made up for in pure, brute strength. Rumor had it, both Thea and Quinn together pulled a truck from a pond with only a rope, and even though Luke had never witnessed a feat similar first hand, he had no intention of testing it.

Talmhai's clan Leader was a slight, hand-wringing woman known only as Rome and even though she appeared nervous and vulnerable, she possessed a sharp wit that always put her two steps ahead of anyone in the room. The true reason for the hand-wringing was a well-kept secret, one only Luke and his family were privy to, and if people knew the action was simply a nervous tick, Rome's entire cover would be blown. She wanted to appear like a mouse so no one realized a lion sat before them.

Each leader inclined their head toward Luke and Isaac as they left until one visitor remained. They stood with their hand on the door, locked in conversation with Clara, nodding every so often. Luke didn't recognize them, so he wondered if they were the person invited to talk about traveling upriver.

The visitor spoke in hushed tones, and kept shaking their head, frowning, and pulling at the short hair at the nape of their neck.

"I don't know what to tell you, Diana. Without proof..." Clara's voice trailed off, as if alluding to something.

Diana released a quiet, disappointed groan. "That's just it. Proof means it's too late."

"I'm sorry. Sending a party two weeks away up in the mountains would pull people who are needed here and as much as I hate to admit it, I can't give the command when you only have a hunch. It would put them in danger, too. You know as well as I do that the wild animals are starving and helpless humans wandering around would put them in harm's way."

"I'm telling you, there are people in the Pass who shouldn't be there." Diana sighed. "Isn't there anything you can do?"

Clara leaned against the railing that led downstairs, her arms folded. "I..."

"Please, Clara, I'm begging you. Something's wrong. Danger is coming this way. I've been as close as I can get and I've heard their whispers to seek revenge."

His mother released a drawn out, heavy sigh, keeping her eyes on the floor, and shook her head. "Okay. I'll see what I can do." When Diana jumped out to grasp Clara by the shoulders out of sheer excitement, Clara stopped them with a hand in the air. "Only a small group. Two people and no more."

"Thank you!"

"Don't thank me yet. You'll need a guide who knows the landscape. Find one and then we can talk. Okay?"

Diana nodded fast, a smile brightening their face. "I will."

The minute Clara closed the front door, she approached Luke to wrap her arms around him. "I'm so glad you're safe," she whispered.

Luke crouched and her hand touched his cheek, warm and soft. He smiled for her. She loved when he did.

"I'm okay, Mama." He pulled the scarf out from Boatswain's pack. "Happy birthday."

She smiled. "Thank you. And don't worry about the party. Soora makes a big deal about it but I don't mind that you don't come. I know it's hard for you."

He tried to smile but he sighed heavily instead.

Clara took his free hand and pulled him toward the couch in the living room. "You're exhausted. Come sit."

He followed her, laid down, and placed his head in her lap. Her smell hung in the air, a scent of comfort, love, and peace. When her fingers slid into his hair, he melted.

"Go ahead and get settled." Luke's dad called from the kitchen. "In a few days, we'll chat about finding you another home."

"Sure, Dad," Luke tried to say but his mouth was heavy and his mind uncooperative, so the words came out in a garbled mess.

His mom kept running her fingers through his hair, turning every bit of his body into mush. For as long as he could remember, she soothed him that way, and just like then, he melted in her lap.

"You can sleep on the couch, if you need."

Luke mumbled with his eyes closed. "I can sleep here."

Vaguely, he felt her chuckle but he was too far gone to register much more than movement of his head, footsteps leaving, and a warm blanket over his shoulders. Someone touched his feet. He wanted to move and be productive but his body vetoed every effort.

Luke awoke on a cloud. He snuggled further into it, rubbing his itchy morning stubble on the soft surface then opened his eyes. A great, black beast loomed in front of him.

"The hell!"

It licked him and Luke realized the creature was Boatswain. The dog sneezed.

"You gotta stop doing that."

Boatswain accepted a scratch on his shoulder then padded away and disappeared around the corner.

With a groan, Luke sat up from his position on the couch, keeping his torso as straight as he could.

"Hello."

Once again, Luke jumped out of his skin. He gasped, his ribs burning, and glared at Sibyl who sat in a chair by the fireplace.

"Is everyone here trying to get me killed?"

Sibyl smiled at him and held her thumb and index finger parallel to each other as if she were pinching a thick piece of air.

He grunted. "You're early."

"No, I'm not," Sibyl said through a small giggle.

"What? How long did I sleep?"

Just then, Clara walked into the room in sweatpants and a large tee, and smiled at Luke. "Oh good! You're awake. You slept for a whole day." She smirked. "I almost called for the doctor."

Luke's stomach dropped. "And Dad?"

"He left a while ago," Sibyl said.

"The Walsh family is sick," Clara explained. "So, he brought them food." She bit the inside of her bottom lip and turned away.

"Mom? Something's the matter. Tell me?"

"It's just..." Clara sat in a round chair, leaned back, and pulled curled into a ball. "Food is scarce. The hunters are bringing less and less food every day. I worry about the clan's future."

Luke scooted to the couch's edge. "And?"

"You haven't been here. You haven't seen."

The words weren't a reprimand, but they sure felt like it, and Luke's shoulders drooped. He'd spent too long cooped up in his cabin, hiding from the world, his clan, and the responsibilities that came with being the Leader's son. It was a huge weight, but his mother needed him now more than ever. Sibyl sat beside him and smiled gently.

"Mom," Luke crooned, "it's true, I haven't been a support like I should have. I'm here now and if you need me to, I am going to stay and help."

She nodded, glancing away and biting the inside of her bottom lip again. It quivered.

Luke walked over and knelt in front of her, his hand on her knee. "Tell me more."

She looked back at Luke. "Predatory animals have started attacking clan outposts. Everyone's still safe, but only thanks to our reinforcements. Three of our Ambassadors went out to fix the holes a pack of wolves put in the fence and..." she looked at her hands, "they're dead."

Sibyl put her hand to her mouth. "Oh no."

The Ambassadors operated similar to a board for a company, making decisions behind the scenes with the Leader to enact changes for the member's benefit. Six typically held the position, and if three were dead, that left three empty seats to be filled in the middle of a winter that came too early when most people didn't have enough energy to maintain their homes and families, let alone take on a physically and mentally draining job.

Keeping his cool was more difficult than he imagined and he had to take in a deep breath before speaking. "Need me to do anything?"

Clara looked at him, her eyes twinkling, and put her hand on his. "Stay here. Nothing's changed for you. This isn't the first time I've dealt with an emergency."

Luke lowered his head. *I should have never hid away.*

The back of his throat burned as he swallowed. Leaving for the cabin began as a getaway from hurt and turned into a full-blown escape from reality. It wasn't until Sibyl showed up with a freshly lightning struck Eloise and terrified Bannack three years ago that he'd slowly tried – and failed – to re-enter into society.

"Well," Luke's mom put her hand on his shoulder and smiled, "I'll leave you to your date."

Luke blanched and ducked his head, Sibyl's suppressed snort coming from beside him. "Mom," Luke said, embarrassed, "she's just a friend."

Clara smiled in the way that she did when she didn't believe him and accepted Luke's kiss on her cheek. He waved at her as she left wrapped in a large fur coat and hat.

When Luke turned around, Sibyl stood several paces away, hands behind her back, teetering on her heels, with a shit-eating grin on her face.

"Yes?" He walked past her into the kitchen and started pulling glass jars of ingredients from the cupboards, smiling when she couldn't see.

"Oh, nothing."

"That sing-song voice is annoying."

Sibyl chuckled. "Your point?"

Luke narrowed his eyes at her as he walked past and outside. He pulled some berries and water-glassed eggs from the underground refrigeration system and returned to hand them to Sibyl.

"Ooh. What are these for?" She grabbed a blueberry and tossed it in her mouth before he could snatch the basket away from her.

"Breakfast."

Munching on more berries she'd snuck – he'd moved the basket full of them twice already – Sibyl stepped forward and peered into the bowl, Luke taking a half-step sideways without breaking stride in his creation of food.

"What are you making?" she asked.

"It's a secret."

She was so close, so fragrant with that subtle and alluring scent of rosemary and pine and it made his head spin in happy circles. If she lingered much longer, he'd forget everything, from what ingredients he already added, to his goddamn name, to the fact that a hard-on pressed against his sweatpants and he couldn't turn or she'd see.

Luke sighed and the spoon clacked against the metal bowl when he released it. "I need you to go into the sitting room down the hall and wait. I'll let you know when I'm done."

"You wanna be rid of me that quick, huh?"

Luke squinted at Sibyl. She was being strange, too happy and pleasant for someone he had hurt the day before, and he wasn't buying her ruse or playfulness or whatever she was doing.

Deadpan, Luke said, "Yes. You're breathing in the food."

She barked out a laugh. "Fine," she stalked away, adding a little playful bounce to her step. "I'll just be over here. In a room. Alone. While you make delicious food."

She disappeared into the room he'd told her to go into.

"That woman…" Luke grumbled, hand resting on the unmoving spoon, head bent, and eyes closed. He could still smell her as if she never left. He looked down at Boatswain staring at the floor, tongue making a puddle of drool on the hardwood. "You idiot," Luke said with a smile and dropped a towel on the ground to put under his dog.

12 | SIBYL

Sibyl peeked in each room in the hallway. A clean but unused small bedroom. A guest bedroom with its door open sat parallel to the bathroom and a third room, the sitting room with a couch, bookshelves, cold fireplace, and coffee table with a few trinkets on top. Blinds on the three windows blacked out the sun. Sibyl pulled them open, smiling as sunshine flooded the room, then turned to take a better look at the space.

There wasn't much else. Some boxes of things stacked in a corner, a round, overstuffed chair sitting diagonally in front of them, a dark wood dresser, a rug of every color imaginable made from – she ran her fingers over the surface – t-shirts. One photo hung on the wall and she walked closer to it.

Young Luke posed with a puppy with white and black spots, his eyes squinted almost shut as he smiled, and cheek buried into the dog's fluff. Luke and Boatswain. Sibyl smiled, a puff of air exiting her nose.

Is that what a true smile looks like on him?

She wouldn't know. She'd never seen him like that, even while they dated. Most of the time, she noticed tiny twinkles of his eyes or reserved smiles, and he rarely laughed. Sure, he chuckled, but true, unbridled laughter? She rarely saw it.

What happened? Why aren't you like that anymore?

Turning away from the photo, Sibyl sat on the bed and smiled. Had he really used the word 'annoying' as if she were his sister hovering her finger inches from him and claiming she wasn't touching him? Such strange flirting, but endearing.

The smile faded when embarrassment set in. She'd been weird, too, with her bouncing and animation and Luke had caught onto it.

"Oh, God," Sibyl groaned, placed her head in her hands, and folded into a ball of anxiety.

Why can't I ever stay mad?

As a child, when she got in trouble, she'd be banished to her room, sit on her bed, and desperately grapple with her receding anger. It wasn't like she didn't want to stay angry. Being mad felt good but it always left long before Sibyl wanted it to, especially if she slept on it.

Yesterday, she'd been furious and hurt by Luke's comments and yet, the same day she slept next to him as if he were already forgiven. God damn it, he put her at ease. She never had to morph into someone else to please him, or bend her needs just so he'd treat her with respect. Maybe that was why it took so little effort from him to convince her to lay down with him in his hospital room? Was she that easy of a mark? Was she a mark to him?

By that morning, their disagreement had been so far from her mind that she entirely forgot the reason for visiting his parent's house until she'd walked in on him drooling on the couch. And when he'd woken up, all delirious and grumpy and his hair mussed...well...her thoughts were as irreverent as his hair.

When padding footsteps preceded Luke's hand holding a plate of food, which he left on the floor, Sibyl was snuggled on the bed reading the third chapter of a novel she found on the dresser.

Sibyl set the book down, walked over, and looked at the offering. Two pancakes with syrup made of some kind of berry, orange slices, and an egg. She stared at it, shocked. How had he known?

Sibyl grabbed the plate like a greedy child, her nose prickling. Absolutely ridiculous. It was just food.

And yet, the breakfast held more weight than that. Somehow, Luke had stumbled upon the last breakfast she remembered as a child, right before the building collapsed hosting her dance recital. She still had nightmares of her little feet running toward them, arms outstretched, desperate to get to them as the building collapsed around her. She'd wake up and realize it had been a dream, but she'd cry anyway as her arm throbbed as if it were still trapped under rubble.

Ten years she would be separated from her family.

So, yes, it may have been just food, something he'd innocently whipped up, but with it came the memory of what happened and what could have been.

Sibyl cried as she ate it, internally reprimanding herself but allowing the tears to come. She shouldn't be crying over food, yet at the same time, she couldn't help it. She needed to cry.

When she carried her empty plate from the room, something rustled underneath her fingertips. A piece of paper? Sibyl wiped her tears, blinked hard, and read it.

I'm so, so sorry for abandoning you.

She stared, shocked, then looked at the half-eaten plate. He was trying to apologize. He'd figured out her favorite meal, and taken extra care to make it look amazing.

Worry entered her mind as Sibyl closed the door to think. Did he want something from her? Was he just being nice? Did he expect something in return for the breakfast? Why was she alone with Luke, anyway? Peter could find out then the cheating accusations would really come flying. Could she protect herself against that? Was she prepared for it? Was Luke? Did it even matter?

Sibyl paced, wringing her shirt into wrinkles. She sat, shifted her right leg over her left leg, and switched. Stood again. Paced.

I have to go out there at some point.

The door, closed and keeping her protected from an inevitable meeting with Luke, seemed to swell larger than its original size. Sibyl huffed.

Get it together. This is Luke we're talking about here.

Revving herself up for what would come, Sibyl paced again.

You're going to be okay. Everything will be okay.

"It's all good," she said to her feet. "Why wouldn't it be? Everything's fine. It's fine." With a whine, Sibyl flopped back onto the bed. "Who am I kidding? None of this is going to go well."

She buried her face in a nearby pillow and sat there for several minutes, only moving to get some fresh air.

"Okay." Sibyl sat up and scrunched up her face. "Let's do this."

Nerves hounded her the entire walk into the house's center and her heart pounded harder as she slunk around the corner, craning her neck to peek into the room for Luke. She didn't see him, even when she wandered into the kitchen and stood in the center of it, confused that he was just...gone.

She checked the backyard. No Luke. He wasn't in the front either, so she made her way downstairs.

She pulled open the door at the bottom landing and paused at the end of another hallway, an old, second kitchen to her left. Something clinked on a desk and she walked around the corner into a small living room framed on two sides by floor to ceiling windows.

Luke's parent's home was a maze.

Luke stood before a tall desk with his back to her. He hadn't noticed her, so she leaned against the side of the red brick fireplace to watch him.

His lack of a shirt, as if he'd been interrupted by a sudden need to create halfway through dressing, drew her eye and Sibyl pinched her bottom lip between her teeth as Luke's back expanded, he leaned over, and blew sharply on whatever he worked on. His feet were bare. Luke stepped to the right and plucked a wooden handled tool from a cylinder with veined arms and leaned over his work again. He scratched the side of his ankle with his foot.

He was simply gorgeous. His black, thick, wavy hair fell slightly past his shoulders, half of it drawn up into a ponytail by a red ribbon, and she pressed the side of her forehead against the brick wall, needing to see it in wet tendrils. His broad shoulders were solid, muscles underneath olive-toned skin tightening and softening with every calculated movement.

That was the thing with Luke. He moved through the world with intention and to others, his existence appeared cold and distant, but she'd found something he didn't show others. A warmth. He wasn't just a pretty face with a body to match; his mind worked in ways she wanted to understand and cherish. A calm to the storm within her. She struggled to sit still, to halt her brain from fluttering off into the forest. Luke acted as a tether so she didn't fly too high.

Luke dragged his large hands through his hair then went back to work and a confusing mixture of desire, eagerness, and forty other emotions soared through her, thrummed in her lungs, stomach, and heart.

Sibyl tapped her nail on the glass of a framed picture hanging against the bricks. Luke paused for a moment, turned his head, and said, "good morning," as he returned to work.

"Where's the dogs?" she asked, grateful they didn't alert Luke to her presence so she could experience the gift of watching him. "I don't see them in here."

"Outside." Luke lifted a book with a dark blue cover, inspected it, and returned it to his desk.

"Oh. Thanks for breakfast."

This entire exchange was going horribly. She might just explode. Her words came out awkward and he was...well, god-level hot but other than that, she didn't know what to think of him. She couldn't gauge him when he wouldn't turn around, so she sighed and took one step into the room. "Do you want something from me?"

Luke turned around then and blinked at her, his hair tousled and hanging in front of his eyes. "What? No. That...I wasn't expecting anything—" he sighed and placed his tools down. "I thought you might be hungry, hence breakfast."

She watched him carefully to gauge his level of sincerity and after a few moments, her worry faded and she hesitantly allowed her heart to warm. "So, you kicked me out of the kitchen only because I got in your way?"

"Yes."

"Not because you wanted to apologize?" Sibyl held up the note so he could read it.

"Oh, that. I'd actually like to talk to you about it." He stepped forward, using the back of a blue fabric couch to steady himself. "Sibyl," he watched her with his soft, dark eyes, "I haven't been the easiest person to be around and I'm really very sorry for how I've acted, both in the past couple of weeks and years ago. I hurt you, I know that—And, you're crying." Luke turned around, his fingers woven through his hair, and mumbled, "Damn. I'm horrid at this."

She released a wet laugh and wiped at her eyes. "It's not you. I just tend to cry. It's rather inconvenient."

Luke's face softened and he moved toward her. She watched him, breath paused in anticipation, and relaxed once he lifted his good hand and gently wiped the tears from her cheeks.

"You keep doing that," she almost whispered.

"I can't seem to stop myself," he whispered back in a deep, smooth tone. "Tears aren't allowed on your face. I won't stand for it."

They shared the same space for the next few moments. He smelled of clean and masculine, and she was aware of a tender touch at her hip. When she didn't push him away, Luke settled the entirety of his hand there, tilted his head to the side, and whispered his fingertips over her cheekbone, tucked hair behind her ear, and slid it down to the tip of her chin. He lifted. Sibyl eyed his mouth, cupid's bow waiting for a kiss, and her breath hitched when his lips parted slightly.

A flash of returning to the present flickered in Luke's eyes and he took a step back but didn't completely leave her, only returned to a platonic distance. He scratched his stubble, then said, "I went to Eloise to ask for help but she basically told me I'm on my own, so now..." He paused, fidgeting with his hair and hands before flexing out his fingers and shoved them in his pocket. "How can I make it right?"

Sibyl stared at him for a moment, Luke's apology note tucked in her hand, and struggled to think of a single thing. "I don't want a grand gesture...I just want you to promise me something."

"Yeah?"

"That you'll make an effort to soften your prickly parts. I don't want them to go away because they're a...a part of you." She almost said, "adorable," and mentally patted herself on the back at her quick recovery. "Right now, they're sharp and barbed and get stuck under people's skin. They hurt. All I'm asking is for you to think before you speak."

Luke looked at his feet. "Think I can do that."

"Good," Sibyl said.

"You're welcome."

"Where did you get the oranges?"

"Huh? Oh. From earlier. Yeah, I still had some left over from trading with that merchant. You were crying over them, so I figured they had to be good, and got some."

Luke turned back around and returned to his table. She watched him for several moments, a smile building on her lips.

He went to Eloise for help. He's trying, even though he's stumbling through the motions.

"What are you working on?" she asked as she came up beside him.

"It's a book for a local kid. He gave me his folio and asked me to put it together." Luke slid the dark blue book her way. "It's not finished, so don't open it yet, but you can look at it."

Before she did, Sibyl asked, "How did it get here then? With your house all crumbled?"

He thought for a moment, then chuckled awkwardly. "You know, I never questioned. Everything happening made it slip my mind, I guess. I did find it in my chest," he gestured a wooden chest similar to the one Sibyl had dug through that night she pulled him from the rubble, "so I assumed someone brought it over."

She nodded. "Makes sense," then leaned forward to look at his work in progress.

The craftsmanship was divine. Scroll work of glistening silver etched into the leather danced around the book edges in crisp and curving lines, the leather a deep and warm brown. On the back cover, all the way at the bottom were fancy, calligraphy letters. She touched them. Couldn't help it.

"Your name, right?"

"Yeah."

She smiled. "It's beautiful.

"Thank you. I sign all my products this way."

Sibyl broke away from his side and walked over to the bookshelf. As far as she could tell, his novels all survived the collapse. "Do you have a lot of customers?"

"I have enough," Luke said from his spot at the desk. She heard some rustling and turned around to see Luke working again on the book, brushing some kind of paste onto the front page. He pulled two clamps from a basket at his feet, lined them up, and spun them until they secured the book to the table. He then turned around, leaned his hips against the desk - hands on the surface - and crossed his ankles. The stance gave him a relaxed appearance. "Keeps me and the dogs fed."

"That's good." She turned back around and ran her fingers down a few spines, wondering how many Luke had rebound himself. "The cabin's toast, I'm assuming."

"Flatter than the pancakes you devoured."

Sibyl giggled and Luke ducked his head. He peered up at her through his eyelashes and she froze, enjoying the way his eyelashes were so dark, they gave him eyeliner and accentuated the brown of his irises. Once again, he flustered her, made her go all funny and thoughtless.

It had been two years. Two long years since she'd begun her relationship with Peter and in that time, she'd lost herself. Allowed Peter to tear her down until she huddled in a naked, bleeding mess before him. But having Luke at her side, she had hope she could heal from it. She would no longer be ashamed of herself, no longer apologize for who she was.

They fell into silence, Luke letting Boatswain and Levin back in when they waited at the door, and Sibyl getting half mauled by them and their wet fur. From her spot on the ground, she watched Luke work and hum, but didn't recognize the tune. It made her smile.

"Looks like you'll be living with your parents for a while," Sibyl teased. "How very fourteen of you."

Without missing a beat, Luke said, "Yes. It's very emasculating."

Sibyl looked at him, heart pounding in her ears. He had to be embarrassed by living with his parents, right? It made perfect sense. Probably her saving him added insult to injury.

Luke turned around, confused, then he put his fingers to his brow. "Ah, hell, Sibyl," he groaned apologetically. "I'm not below needing my parents for help, is all I meant. I didn't mean—"

"Yeah." Sibyl shrugged her shoulders, nodding. "Of course." Boatswain licked her fingers and she was grateful for a distraction from the awkward weight in her stomach. "Hey, I should get going," Sibyl stood then cracked a warm smile. "Thank you for everything."

Luke turned around and nodded. "Alright. I'll be here." Before Sibyl rounded the corner, Luke called out to her and she turned. "I'm truly very sorry for what I said at the Compound."

"Thank you." Sibyl smiled and some weight on her shoulders lifted.

"Hey, uh." Luke massaged his palm. "My mom's party is in a few hours and, uh, it'd be great if you came."

She looked at him, her head tilted just a bit to the side, and considered for a moment. "Isn't that a private thing?"

"Just the opposite. Everyone's going to be there."

Luke said, 'everyone' as if he were expecting to be tortured.

He'd just gone through the extra effort of apologizing. The least she could do was go to a party he dreaded.

"Yeah. I'll come."

People slowly trickled in. Clan leaders, friends, and a few Rhondians who worked under Clara piled their gifts on the table. A humble spread of food sat on the dining table – common foods like smoked meats, breads, winter vegetable chips, and an assortment of cheeses with crackers. And one, single, rather impressively golden chess pie, a dish Clara had settled for after an animated, half-serious tirade around the kitchen when she, once again, couldn't get the ingredients for her favorite: banana crème pie.

Sibyl smiled as she remembered Luke and his mother cooking together for the party while she grumbled about the lack of bananas and "proper sugar."

"Why?" Clara had slammed the cupboard and handed Luke the flour. "I just want my favorite dessert. Is that too much to ask?" She turned, exasperated, toward her husband smiling into the cup of water pressed to his lips. "On my birthday, of all days," she whined, "I want a banana crème pie."

"Mom..."

"And another thing! Whose idea was it to never breed sugar cane to adapt to colder climates?" She'd spun on her son, her finger inches from his face, and whispered, "Psychopaths, that's who. We can't have nice things, apparently!"

Luke turned very scarlet and looked to Sibyl for help. She couldn't. She was laughing too hard with Isaac shaking in the seat next to her. They'd been banished from the kitchen as if they'd offended the Queen, and were relegated to the dining table to watch the wide gestures and rampaging rant that exploded from Clara.

Sibyl smiled at the memory as she walked around the living room, sliding between the backs to two people having separate conversations. One shifted for her to pass and she thanked them before continuing her search for Luke.

She found him standing in a corner, his mom talking with him. The minute Luke smiled at his mom, Sibyl hid behind the wall separating the living room from the house's foyer, and spied on them.

Once again spying. Why can't I just talk to him?

They were just chatting, nothing more, but Sibyl watched Luke hang on every word. He whispered a joke. She laughed. He produced a small box and Clara opened it to reveal a silver chain that she immediately put on and kissed Luke on the cheek in thanks.

Sibyl enjoyed the entire exchange far too much and when someone unknowingly blocked Sibyl's view, she had a very brief thought of drop-kicking them out of the way so she could keep spying. Thankfully, they moved. Luke's gentle affection for his mom turned her stomach into one giant butterfly, fluttering rather ungracefully in her belly.

"You, sir," Sibyl whispered to herself, "are an utter enigma and I am here for it."

The festivities continued with Luke glued to Sibyl's side. She didn't mind. She knew how hard just being in the same house as an event like a birthday party was for him and didn't mind being his support.

Birthday songs were sung, food enjoyed, and Luke disappeared again. Sibyl found him alone with Boatswain and Levin in the home's most secluded area: a tiny nook office.

"You look comfy." Sibyl pulled her hands out of her pockets and sat on the leather ottoman behind the swiveling chair Luke sat in.

"Your opinion is subjective."

"I see your mom enjoyed your gift."

He grunted and rubbed Boatswain's ears. "I never thanked you for saving me. So...thank you. If you hadn't helped, I'd be a lot w...w-worse off."

Sibyl smiled. "You're welcome."

He sat there, flanked by his large, powerful dogs, clad in black jeans and shirt, with his hand hanging lazily off an arm rest. His dark features, especially his untamed hair touching his shoulders, completed the look of a bad boy without the bad.

"You doing okay?"

Luke stared at her, exhaustion in his eyes. "I'd like to hide."

"Aren't you doing that already?"

"No." He scrubbed his face. "I'd like to hide. And if I go in my room, I'll still be able to hear them all."

"Well," Sibyl leaned forward in her seat to stare out the window. The sun splashed brilliant oranges and purples across the clouded sky. She almost suggested a walk with the sky's beautiful colors, but a bout of bravery and, honestly, idiocy came over her and she spoke before she could talk herself out of it.

"I have an idea," she started slowly, then finding traction, continued. "You might find it silly, and if you want to consider it just between friends, that's fine, too, but—"

"Sibyl—"

"—if it's a distraction you'd like...I mean, it's probably not a respectful thing to ask a friend, because what if our relationship as friends gets awkward and weird, and—"

"Sibyl, I—"

"—then it'll be my fault. I don't want it to be my fault. You know what, forget I asked. We should—"

"Sibyl, stop talking for just a sec—"

"—just go on a walk." She gestured frantically to the dogs sleeping at Luke's feet, and stood. "Look. Even they agree asking if you want to kiss is a dumb idea and we should really just go on a walk."

Luke snagged her shirt sleeve, pulled, and she landed in his lap, Luke's mouth meeting her own before she could register anything.

His facial hair scratched at her lips and nose, something she thought she'd hate but it was Luke and he was kissing her and she didn't hate it. She loved the ruggedness of it, the way it made an invisible mark upon her skin. His kiss deepened, punctuated by the gathering of her shirt into his fist, and Luke held onto her as if trying to absorb her into his own body.

Sibyl melted against him as soon as his hand slid up her back to tighten against the back of her neck. She shifted, legs straddling Luke's hips, and titled her hips forward so she could press as much of her body against him as she could. Luke groaned softly.

Tentatively, Luke pressed the warmth of his tongue to Sibyl's lips and in a dizzying loss of her mind, she opened to let him in. Desire cracked down her spine. She inhaled sharply.

Kissing Luke reminded her of fresh fallen snow. Whisper soft, deafening all sound, and breathlessly beautiful, but too much of it would create an avalanche or keep a person trapped inside their cabin for so long, they'd forget their own name. She wanted so much more of him, her hand slowly making its way down his heavy breathing torso proof of that.

With a tiny gasp, she pulled away a bit, but lacked the ability to move further and remained pressed against Luke, taking a moment to process what just happened. He stayed still as well, panting quietly. Her heartbeat thrummed in her head, chest, and between her legs, driving her wild with all possibilities of what they could do with a bit more privacy.

"You've had some great ideas in the past," Luke breathed, "but this one? Genius level."

"Yeah?"

"Yeah."

She giggled at his honesty and tilted her head to look up at him. Beneath the stubble of his facial hair, Luke's cheeks were red. His eyes watched her with a tenderness hadn't seen in too long and Sibyl welcomed a gentle peck on her lips before he released her shirt.

She didn't know what to do with herself, so she went to slide off Luke's lap, but he caught her with a light touch on her elbow, yet she froze just the same.

Luke stared at her mouth, allowed a thumb to linger on her lower lip, flicked his eyes up to hers, and leaned forward to whisper, "Your distraction worked so well, I forgot my own name."

At that, Sibyl shuddered and he let her go. She stood, staring down at him looking up at her, and she reached out to touch his cheek. Whatever came over her, whether a sudden acceptance of her attraction to him or a rare moment of bravery encouraged by their history, Sibyl knew one thing: by all accounts, she shouldn't be kissing Luke Blackwood, yet she did, and he kissed her back harder.

13 | LUKE

Sibyl had been gone for five days, three hours, and twenty minutes.

And he was counting.

Diana had come knocking, looking for a skilled tracker to find proof danger lurked in the mountains, and claimed they'd only need her for one to two weeks. Just a day later, Sibyl left.

Something had changed in the time since she'd kissed him. He couldn't quite identify what, though, and it drove him stir crazy. Every time he thought of her body pressed against him, the warmth of her and the heavy thrill of her on his lap, he stopped breathing. His chest tightened, heart quickened, and his damn mouth smiled of its own accord.

He wasn't one for relationships anymore, especially not with how he lived, and flings bored him to death, with their lack of a challenge and too little attachment.

Sibyl wasn't a fling, nor did she deserve detachment. She was too special, too important, and Luke hated himself for not seeing that before.

After spending the morning in bed with aches ricocheting between and over his bones, he stumbled from the mattress, and padded to his work station brought over by his dad and a few Rhondians.

His parents were out visiting the sick, remnants of a hurried breakfast – a half-eaten piece of toast on a plate and a cup of barley water still warm – sitting on the kitchen table.

Luke worried about his mom's mental state as she returned every day with progressively darker bags under her eyes and would moan in relief as she sat on the couch, his dad flocking toward her to rub her feet as she laid against the cushions, one arm flopped over her eyes. They'd fall into their typical ritual of talking about their day and Luke would disappear downstairs to finish Maxwell's book or reluctantly take a nap, curled against Levin and Boatswain.

Stricken with an unexpected smack of pain, Luke gripped the back of a nearby recliner and waited for it to pass. It didn't – not completely – but he straightened anyway, and stumbled forward to get back to work. The cave-in had pushed his deadline back significantly. He couldn't afford to waste any more time.

Why am I hurting again? Luke put his hand to his forehead and groaned. *Maybe I slept wrong and aggravated something?*

Luke worked slowly, fitting in frequent breaks and lots of naps. Ugh. He hated naps. But one never forgot the agony of waking up after a late work night, hunched over a desk, with broken ribs.

He removed a wide-eyed, curved, heavy-duty needle and threaded it with dark blue wool thread. Then, he cut a thick piece of linen ribbon, stacked the papers together, marked them, and began sewing the spine together.

For the next hour he worked and refused to stop even when his almost depleted mind screamed for reprieve.

Just this last stitch. Luke blinked hard and wiped his brow, his vision blurred, and a cramp shocked him. Luke gasped, hand jerking to the sudden pain.

"Shit."

Boatswain whined and nudged the side of Luke's knee.

"I'm good, B. I'm good."

The event, while small, took its toll, and he barely recovered before a knock came from his door.

"Go away."

He didn't mean to be rude, his brain in a fog.

Luke wanted nothing to do with humans. He wanted a nap.

The knock came again.

Luke growled, scowling at the door. "Huh?" he barked.

His voice came out small, hesitant. "It's me. Max. I'm here for an update on the book."

Luke sighed, embarrassed. "Coming." Then he mumbled, "in fifty years."

Luke opened the small, downstairs apartment suite door to reveal Maxwell standing there with his hands in his pockets. He glanced once at Luke before his expression changed from curiosity to worry.

"I got your message that you're staying on the Island with your family." He entered the room at Luke's gesture and settled in a small chair in the corner, scanning the room as he spoke. "Are you sick?"

"Not sick," Luke said as he lifted his shirt to reveal the scars on his middle then dropped it. "The cabin you visited earlier fell on me."

Shock passed over Maxwell's face. "Holy cow! And you survived?"

"Needed some stitches. Got some broken ribs and wrist." Luke groaned at the end of his words and winced when he bent to bring out the freshly sewn papers. Even with his injuries, the stitching was the best he'd done in a long time.

Maxwell tentatively reached for it, and his eyes flicked to Luke then back to the book, fingers flexing. "This is it?" he asked in almost a whisper.

Luke nodded. It took several more seconds before Maxwell took the item and flipped through the wide pages, fingers grazing over the art as if he were seeing it for the first time.

"Thank you." Maxwell hugged the book to his chest. "This means a lot."

"Of course. Now," Luke reached for his swatches, "time to pick an interior cover color."

They conversed about the art book for a while, Luke guiding Maxwell through the options of a linen interior or paper, solid or painted, and if he wanted copper, gold, or silver leaf edges. In the end, Maxwell left with a bounce in his step and had placed an order for a linen cover, blue-gray interior, and silver edges.

Luke sighed and leaned back in his chair. "Exhausting." Meaning "that was exhausting," but he didn't want to stutter through it. Luke turned to Boatswain. "I'm going to nap."

The dog's ears pricked up. Levin lifted his head.

Shuffling past the stairs, Luke heard a door open followed by hushed conversation.

"There's no way." His mother.

"Clara," came Isaac's voice, almost begging her, "you and I both heard the news. They've been sighted."

"But here? Now? What about Diana and her crew? They could still—" Silence.

Then from his dad, "Are you really surprised?"

"Yes, actually. We were told they were eradicated twelve years ago. Even sent scouts to confirm."

What the hell? Luke, listening with one foot on the bottom stair and a hand on the railing, gripped it tighter. The tone coming from his parents scared the shit out of him.

"I think it may be time to consider someone lied to us," Isaac urged. "You need to lay low until we can figure out what's going on."

"I will not. The last thing my Rhondians needs right now is an absent Leader."

"Please, Clara. If they find you or him..."

Luke heard the padding of feet upstairs as someone walked down the steps toward him. His mother appeared, her cheeks bright red from the cold, and she glanced at him with a blank face.

"Mom?"

Clara shook her head and slipped past him, so Luke went to find his dad.

"Dad?" Luke called after Isaac as he walked into his bedroom.

Isaac turned and sighed. "Your mother's past is catching up to her. I wish I could tell you more, but right now, we have no solid information. When we do, we'll let you know."

"Uh. Dad—"

Isaac paused, about to close the door, expectant Luke would say something.

"Mom mentioned Diana and the people she took with her. Do you know—I mean, have you heard—"

"You want to know if Sibyl is okay?"

Luke nodded.

"We don't know. I wish I could give you more." Isaac blinked slowly, tiredness making his shoulders droop. "I've had a long day. Do you need anything else?"

"No. I..." He debated telling his dad he'd be leaving with the dogs first thing to go find Sibyl to check in on her, but without a trail to follow, he'd be useless. "No. Have a good night."

Again with that fucking feeling of uselessness. Again, he couldn't do anything except wait.

Isaac closed the door.

Luke glanced down at Boatswain, very much not up to napping anymore.

Mom's past?

Luke spent his life unaware she even had a past that could catch up to her and the dire tone of both Isaac and what his mother didn't say worried him. He walked to his room, locked the door, pulled the top blanket off his bed, and wrapped it around his body so only his head and hands were visible. Collecting a book to escape, Luke settled down on a chair, and began reading.

"Your mother's past is catching up to her."

After about an hour, his eyes were heavy and he had to blink hard to get them to refocus, so he hugged the blanket tighter and painfully managed to lay sideways on the bed, quickly falling asleep.

Nearly three weeks later and still with no word Sibyl had returned, Luke dressed for the day and attempted to keep his anxiety in check. The dogs were entertained elsewhere – Levin rooting around the backyard in search of rabbit pellets and Boatswain returning anytime from his run with Bannack since Luke still couldn't exercise for long enough.

As he slid his brace onto his wrist and secured it in place, a knock came from his bedroom door. Luke opened it to see Bannack.

Bannack smiled in greeting. It had been a long time since Bannack's tragic service as a mercenary, but he still kept the same bodyguard-like aura about him, his lean build hiding an awesome amount of physical strength.

"Sibyl not back yet?" Bannack asked as he handed Boatswain's lead to Luke.

"Yeah. Thank you for running with him."

"He's a great workout buddy."

Luke looked down at Boatswain, realizing too late he was soaked. Before Luke could ask why, Boatswain nudged the door open a bit more with his nose, trotted to the center of the room, bent and dragged his head on the floor.

Luke couldn't stop what he knew Boatswain would do next, but tried to anyway.

"No!" Luke yelled.

Boatswain shook his entire body. Violently. Luke scrambled out of the way right before Boatswain's flailing leash whipped his backside, and he crashed into Bannack, both men landing in the hallway with a loud thud, a jumble of limbs. Their heads banged together. Several seconds later, Luke sporting a bruise on his forehead and his barely healed wrist and ribs smarting, they managed to untangle. Bannack stood, swayed, and Luke grabbed him before he took down a painting on the wall.

Bannack laughed long and loud. Luke went hot and red.

Isaac coughed to cover a laugh and Luke turned in horror to see both his parents standing several feet away, smiling, his mother's hand over her mouth as her eyes sparkled.

Luke's neck heated to blistering levels and he slipped into his room, expecting Bannack to follow. Instead, Bannack stood there, awkwardly, and gave a tiny wave. "Hey, guys."

"Get in here," Luke hissed. When Bannack didn't move, Luke stepped forward and yanked on Bannack's arm, bringing out a surprised grunt from Bannack, and shut the door as fast as he could.

"That was embarrassing."

"I thought it was riveting. Awe look," Bannack wiggled his finger at Luke's still hot neck, "it's done wonders for your complexion."

Luke waved his hand away as if it were an annoying bee during summer. "If you didn't have such fast reflexes, I'd introduce you to my fist."

"Which one? Your left hook is phenomenal but your right one...eh...it could do with a bit of work."

"Shut the fuck up." Luke good-naturedly shoved Bannack. "I've beaten your ass more than once and I'll do it again."

Luke rubbed the aching spot where Boatswain's leash had whipped him and grabbed it from Bannack when he removed it from Boatswain's neck.

Bannack seemed to recognize the longing in Luke's face because he said, "You miss her."

"Is it that obvious?"

Bannack smiled in a knowing way that made Luke want to smack it off his face. "I'm a married man," Bannack explained. "I know a crush when I see one."

"Yeah? Says the big, scary mercenary who nearly fainted every time he even thought about proposing."

"Don't change the subject. You need to tell her what's on your mind. Take it from a guy who nearly lost his girl because I wasn't honest with her or myself."

"Except I did lose her."

Bannack's eyebrows came together and he frowned slightly. "If you do nothing, you'll lose her no matter what."

"Shit."

Bannack bumped Luke's upper arm with the side of his elbow. "You got this. She's one of the kindest people and we all love her. She'll see your efforts."

Luke ran his hand through his thick hair. "Yeah?"

"Yeah. Now, I gotta get home to the missus." He bent and scratched Boatswain's ear. "Thanks for the run, friend."

PART TWO

FALLING

14 | LUKE

I have lived in darkness for so long,
I forgot the light.
And you are the sun.

Days later, Luke couldn't stay still. His parents watched as he paced grooves in the floor, and while his dad put all his attention on eating breakfast, his mom was frowning.

Her utensils clattered on the plate. "Will you sit down?"

Luke stopped abruptly and gave her a small glare. "I can't."

"I *will* tie you to the chair." Clara widened her eyes at him, her mouth in a small frown, and pointed at the seat. "Sit. Now."

He sat, his knee bouncing. His mom returned to her meal, and ignored Luke when he all but inhaled his food. Either she didn't care or she actively made the decision to ignore him. He knew she was all talk when she gave him a kiss on the forehead when he finally left.

Luke took a quick detour to Maxwell's house. Maxwell couldn't contain his excitement as Luke laid the book in his hands. He spent only a few minutes there, accepted payment, and set off toward Eloise and Bannack's to tell them of Sibyl's plan to return to town later that afternoon.

Snow whispered to the ground, a fine layer just beginning to thicken. The flakes froze pinpricks onto Luke's exposed cheeks and contrasted against the black splotches on his dog's coats.

Luke looked down at the two. "Race ya."

It felt good to run, to feel his body move and push it to the limit. He adored the cold, crisp wind through his sweaty scalp, the crunching of snow underfoot, the movement of his legs, arms, and torso as he ran.

They made it three miles, running off and on with long walks in between to give his still healing body a chance to recover. Stops occurred at the bridge to Raft Island – where his parents lived – then again in the heart of Gig Harbor amid the matching whitewashed brick of Downtown – now covered in dark greens and blacks from years of neglect, skeletons of what they once were.

As they ran toward Eloise and Bannack's small farmhouse almost a mile from the Compound, snowflakes increased in size and thickness. Giant globs fell from the sky, veiling Luke's vision. Aside from the huffing of a nearby elk herd, the world had gone silent and still and Luke stopped to enjoy a quick lunch with his dogs underneath an overpass as he listened to the quiet.

Perhaps it was the silence, but out in the wilderness, surrounded by the vast world that seemed so small, Luke fully relaxed. He could breathe. No barriers existed. No expectations. For a time, that was enough, but lately, he found himself wondering who he would have been if he hadn't escaped into the quiet. It felt safe and comfortable, but where had that got him?

I'm so lonely.

Time spent with Sibyl were the brightest spot he'd had in a long time and he didn't want to let that go. He knew the cost, though.

If he wanted her, he couldn't escape anymore; he had to abandon loneliness and silence that had been his companion for years.

Luke watched the elk run by, smiled a little when Boatswain's ears twitched from his place beside Luke's thigh and Levin barely managed to keep his bark a whisper.

As always, Boatswain beat them, Levin a close second, and Luke dismally last.

Together, the trio turned down a side road, and walked up the hill, avoiding roots and potholes along the way. No one used cars anymore, not with the loss of gasoline manufacturing, but he did spy tracks from horse hooves. Recent? He wasn't sure.

The road opened up, revealing a black and white farmhouse with a green tin roof and a column of smoke rising from the chimney. Frozen plant carcasses filled five garden beds situated just off the porch. A dark horse, stalled in a converted shed close to the house, lifted its head from behind a wall and hay tumbled from its mouth.

Bannack walked off the front porch just then, a full laundry basket tucked under his arm, shivered audibly then caught sight of Luke. He quickly smiled.

"Look what the dog dragged in," he called and set the basket down and walked over to embrace Luke.

"Don't get so excited," Luke grunted, partly due to Bannack's tendency to hug just a bit too tight when excitement got the better of him.

"Your point?" Bannack asked as he released Luke and returned to the basket. "Wanna help hang this?"

No. He did not. "Sure."

Bannack walked to a shed attached to the house. He opened the door, revealing four taut lines strung the structure's entire width, then handed Luke a cold piece of clothing. While hanging them up, he asked, "How is your bookbinding going?" Bannack smiled. "Still stealing customers?"

Luke scoffed. "Only because the others are insufferable old fools who think thick paper is beneath them."

The unmistakable feel of an arm collided with Luke's shoulder blade and he jerked his head up at Bannack smiling again and laid a shirt over a clothesline. "Which, in turn, makes good business for you."

"Exactly," Luke said and nodded. He picked up a pair of sweat pants, paused, and narrowed his eyes at Bannack. "Did you mean to smack me?"

"Eh." Bannack shrugged. "Sometimes I'm clumsy."

Luke chucked the cold pants at Bannack and they hit his face with a wet flop. He gasped, shuddered, and peeled them off.

"Oops," Luke said. "I'm just clumsy."

Bannack smirked and immediately swirled the pants into a thick rope. Excited fear jolted Luke into action and he jumped at the laundry basket between them, receiving a quick whip to his hand.

Luke yelped and shook his hand out. He pulled the basket with him, jumping away from another flick aimed at his chest.

"Put the pants down and let's talk about this." Luke let out a quick yelp as the clothing made contact with his thigh. "Dude. This is..." he dodged another flick, "so childish!" Luke danced away when the pants connected with the sore spot on his hand from Bannack's first attack. "How the hell can you aim so well? It's unnatural."

"Practice." Bannack narrowed his eyes and smiled. "Years and *years* of it."

Now hiding behind a line of clothing and crammed into the shed's back end, Luke abandoned the laundry basket as a shield and tore down a piece of thin, black clothing, ready to whip Bannack when he came near. He smiled, trying to suppress a laugh, as his target came around the corner, wielding his pants weapon.

"At this point," Luke motioned to the stiff article of clothing, "it's probably frozen over."

"Oh, I am counting on it."

They rotated around each other, locked in a ridiculous stand-off. Luke held his free hand out and slowly shook his head. "Don't do it. Don—"

Bannack lunged. Luke dodged, but Bannack excelled at hand-to-hand combat, which consequently made him more agile. He caught Luke upside the head, twisted, and pulled Luke in a headlock.

"Seriously," Luke groaned, stuck. "You think you're so funny, don't you?"

"Hilarious." Bannack said and refused to let go.

"What are you doing?" Eloise barked.

Bannack released Luke and both men straightened. She stood in the doorway, one hand on her hip, and glared at them. Her eyes drifted to Luke's hand. "Did you come here just to raid my lingerie?"

Luke lifted the piece of clothing he'd snagged from the clothesline. Heat rushed into his ears as he noticed the lace and severe lack of content. Shit, he'd grabbed lingerie. Luke shoved the item against Bannack's chest, who laughed so hard he fumbled with it for several agonizing seconds before taking it from Luke.

"What's going on in here?" came Sibyl's voice.

Luke's heart when he heard the sing-song tone soared. His senses heightened, and he waited in anticipation for her to appear.

She did, her hair pulled back in a four-strand Dutch braid. The sun bounced off the back of her head, giving her a halo. He stood there, his mouth cracked open, and everything exploded all at once.

She's an angel.

Her eyes, her smile, the little laugh she made before covering her mouth. Her nails were painted.

It felt like it had been a millennia since he'd last seen her. He couldn't stop looking.

"Oh, *man*," she chuckled again and their eyes met.

Luke released a shaking breath as she held his gaze. Her dark eyes softened. Did she...did she feel the crackling in the air? Its heaviness? Because he was a complete mess as soon as she opened her mouth. Heart-shaped. A thin upper lip. Thicker lower lip.

He swallowed hard.

"Well?" Eloise asked

Luke shook himself and took a moment to return earthside.

"Uh-oh," Bannack whispered. "You got the eyebrow raise. If the next one goes up, you better talk fast or she'll string you up by your toes."

The second eyebrow rose.

"Yup," Bannack confirmed.

"Shut up!" Luke hiss-whispered and shoved Bannack, who laughed again.

Eloise sighed and jerked her head toward the house. "Come on. The house is warm."

As Luke ran his hands ran over Levin's trunk to check on the stitches, Sibyl knelt beside him. He froze as her shoulder grazed his arm and closed his eyes. She felt so good, he didn't want it to end.

"Is he okay?" she asked in a low voice and placed her hand beside Levin's injury at his ribs, the hair barely starting to grow back.

Did she know how alluring it was? Shit. He was a mess and loving every agonizing second.

"Uh...yeah. He is. Someone stitched him up for me."

Luke watched her lips curl into a smile. "That's kind of them," she said.

"Yeah..." He couldn't stop staring. Mouth dry. Fingers bumbling. "It is—was."

"Took you a long time." An observation Luke hoped she wouldn't read into.

Levin flopped his tongue out in the way Boatswain always did, and let out a bone-rattling bark. Luke released his collar and Levin sniffed around the living room before settling down beside Boatswain enjoying the fire.

"Thank you for offering to find him," Luke said and looked at Sibyl.

She smiled back, eyes squinting a little, and nodded.

With Boatswain and Levin piled by the fireplace, Luke shrugged off his coat to hang it on the hook by the door. He turned around and took in the house that he hadn't visited in close to a year. Everyone gathered in the small living room equipped with the typical items: a three-seater couch, two chairs, some blankets folded in a corner, and macrame wall décor. The home was warm and the decorated soft tones accented well the splashes of dark.

A kitchen lay beyond a wide archway and a sliding door beyond that. As Luke settled into the couch, he slouched and watched the fire crackle and dance. His dog's coats gleamed in the light, their breath slow and deep, ribs rising and falling.

Luke visited for a while, snacking on apple chips brought out from the pantry, falling into conversation with Eloise, Bannack, and Sibyl, and stealing glances at her. Amid the laughter about Luke's dogs, chatter about events at the Compound, and Sibyl's animated stories about her trip up the mountain with Diana, Luke progressively lost his composure.

Gratefully, Luke was dying a slow death. He longed to run his thumb across her dimples that appeared whenever she smiled. The perfume she wore – a slight berry undertone with powerful punches of lemon – had to be wonderful to everyone else too, right? He could smell her across the room, but then again, perhaps not. He could hear her heartbeat, or was that his, slamming primally against the inside of his chest?

She made him want to write ballads and hymns and epics, detailing his adventures across the seas of her mind, the vast oceans he wanted to consume whole as if stopping would mean his death. Perhaps conquer a kingdom or two.

Luke watched Sibyl lean against Eloise as they giggled over something, and he went all funny. Tingly. Warmer than the fire at his back. He just wanted to consume and consume and never share an ounce of her. Even watching her with her best friend made the irrational gremlins inside his head scream, "mine!"

Eloise left for a bit and came back with a tattered board game box. "Wanna play?" she asked.

Everyone gathered around the table and dove into Rummikub, picking their tiles to hide from each other. The game went on without issue, until Sibyl won and she leapt to her feet to dance, and bumped her hip into Luke's upper arm.

He froze, hands tightening on his knees. For hours, he'd been fine; managed the chaos in his head about Sibyl well, but the moment she touched him, Luke's entire body lit on fire.

"Oh!" She gripped his shoulder out of surprise. "I'm sorry. Are you okay?"

Sibyl spoke with a laugh in her voice smiling with that damn mouth again –he *ate* up her joy – and Luke stared at his Rummikub board, one move away from annihilating everyone.

"Yeah."

"You sure?" she asked and Luke wished that she'd sit back down so he could calm his trembling nerves.

He nodded. "Positive."

Oh my God, my voice just cracked.

When the base of his skull ached, Luke stood to leave. "I need to head back. Got a long day tomorrow."

Everyone said their goodbyes, Luke thanked Eloise and Bannack for a fun evening, and he called to his dogs. Awkwardly, Luke waved to Sibyl and closed the door behind him as fast as he could without - hopefully – making them think he was trying to run away. Because they'd be right. Once again, attraction to Sibyl and wanting more scared him off. He had to leave before his feelings overwhelmed him. Better to slowly inch toward progress than slam full speed into it.

Luke shivered in the biting cold, Levin and Boatswain trotting beside him as he started down the driveway.

"Luke!" Sibyl called.

He closed his eyes and considered pretending not to hear her, but all steps were progress toward who Sibyl deserved, so he stopped, paused to gather his bearings, and turned to see her running toward him.

She paused in front of him, hair wild, cheeks pink from the cold, round eyes hopeful, and hand gripping the front of her coat. God, she was damn, fucking delicious.

"I hope you didn't leave because of me."

"I didn't."

"Oh." She blinked as if trying to think of something else to say and a short period of agonizing silence spanned between them.

Please leave. Wait. Don't leave.

His mind formed images, dirty, filthy images of what he desperately wanted but wouldn't allow himself to make a reality, and if that meant avoiding her at all costs so he wouldn't hurt her again, then so be it.

"Well, you seemed a bit uncomfortable in there, so I thought I'd come check on you."

"I'm fine."

Her eyebrows knit together. "Are you?"

Don't lie to her. Don't lie. "You may have picked up on my exhaustion from traveling." Shit.

"Oh yeah. Your accident." She stepped closer and leaned forward a bit. "How are you healing?"

"It's been slow, but I'm on the tail end of things." He gave her a quick smile. "Thanks to you."

"You're welcome." Sibyl chewed on her lower lip. "Luke? Did I say something?"

He took in a deep breath. Honesty. "No. You didn't."

With his pause that lasted a bit longer than he intended, Sibyl launched into speaking before he had the chance to expand on his words.

"Don't do this to me again, Luke. Don't shut me out."

"I promise, Sibyl, I'm not shutting you out."

"Then why are you giving me these short answers as if you are?"

Sibyl looked at him, her chin quivering, brow furrowed, hands clenched in a fist, and his entire being ached to take the past few minutes all back. How could he even begin to prove to her that he wasn't shutting her out but rather trying to be better.

"I promise," Luke closed his eyes so he didn't have to see her cry, "I'm not trying to shut you out. I don't know the first thing about romance or relationships or friends. I don't know how to speak or how to share my feelings. I don't know any of it." He opened his eyes. "You don't deserve a person w...w-who'll hurt you again and I'm so fucking—" he couldn't stop the realization that fell from his mouth, "terrified that'll be me."

Sibyl's frown split him in half. "Then you *try*, Luke. You make mistakes, you tell me when you're scared, we work it out."

He shook his head. "I can't do that."

Her eyes flashed with barely contained anger. "Then why even speak to me? Why even come here if you were just planning on walking away and avoiding me?" She stepped into his space and put her fist on his chest, staring into his eyes. "I'm not going to waste my time."

Luke reached out and covered Sibyl's fist with his palm. "The minute you feel like I'm wasting your time, you need to go and never look back. I'm going to figure this out, but if I don't and you're tired of waiting, you can't let the possibility of us hold you back from living your life."

Her bottom lip quivered and her deep brown, beautiful eyes flicked down to his mouth. She inhaled softly. "I can feel you."

Luke tilted his head a bit. "Feel me?"

"Your heart..." Sibyl looked up at him and she leaned forward, her forearm flat against his chest now. "It's beating so fast."

"Because I'm terrified."

She gave a tiny, disbelieving chuckle, paused, processed his words, and leaned forward while saying, "I know." Then her ear pressed against his chest. "Terrified is good, though. Terrified means you care."

Luke lifted his head to the sky and slowly, tentatively, wrapped his arm around her, wrapped in her furs and shawl, and held on. "Does it now?" After her quiet hum, he whispered into her furred hood, "My heartbeat is yours."

Sibyl softened against him and he hoped to God he wouldn't fuck everything up again.

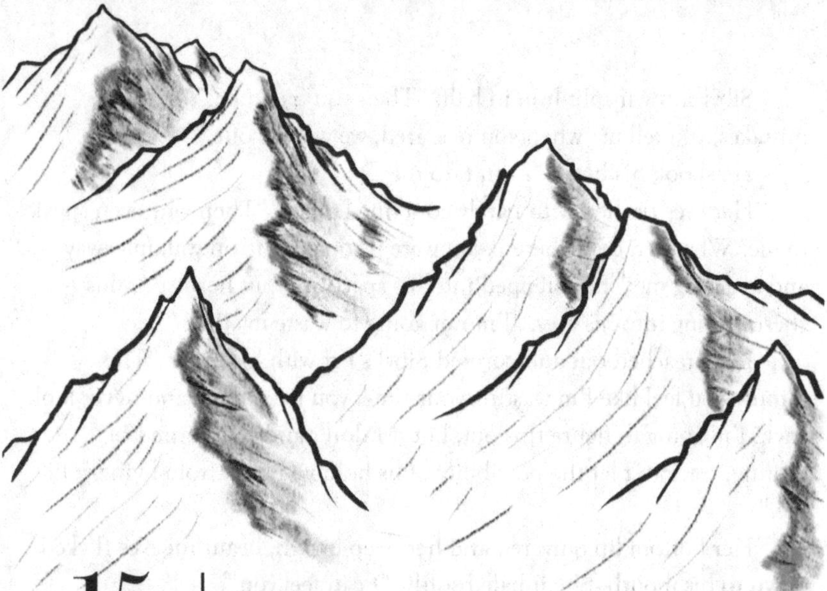

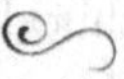

15 | SIBYL

I would rather live a single lifetime with you,
then a thousand without you.

A few days after hanging out with Eloise, Bannack, and Luke, Sibyl sat at a café table in her madrone wood-heated shop, scraping the pith from orange peels with the broad side of a fork, and dropped them into a medium bowl. Her shop sat silent, Hunter not due to arrive for another several minutes, so she enjoyed the peace.

Her hanging plants, nestled in macrame nets, loved the large front window. Sibyl glanced around the shop, eyeing the whimsical mix of unmatched glass containers and attached greenhouse beyond the archway, and smiled. There was a pride that came with building everything she had from the ground up.

It was all hers and she was glad to be back in its walls.

Her mind drifted to Luke, as it had all morning and throughout the night, barely getting any sleep.

"*My heartbeat is yours,*" he'd said and while she'd loved hearing those words come out of his mouth, she couldn't help but worry. Would he make good on his promise? Would he follow through? Would he fall into old habits? She trusted Luke, knew he was honorable and kind, but...would that cost her?

"I'm so stupid," she whispered into the silent shop. She let the fork clatter onto the tabletop and rubbed the bridge of her nose.

Shoppers passed by the window as the day brightened, visiting shops and vendors despite the overcast sky that signaled more snow. Their breath, unless bundled over by scarves, created personalized clouds about their faces.

Sibyl waved through the large window at Lillian, the grey-haired, plump woman whose shop carried textiles and offered tailoring and seamstress services. The woman quickly returned the gesture and scuttled down the road toward her supplier.

The bell hanging from the doorjamb jingled, announcing Sibyl's first customer, but when Sibyl turned, she only saw Hunter arriving for work. He rubbed his eyes and yawned before sliding into the second chair at the table where Sibyl had set up her peels.

"Late night?" Sibyl asked, smiling sideways as she lowered into the chair and continued working.

"Yeah. Professor Church is grinding us into the dirt." Hunter scratched the end of his forearm, where an elbow should have been, and started filling the jars at Sibyl's feet with the orange peels. "I officially hate calculus."

Sibyl chuckled and glanced up as the bell rang a second time. "Hello, Mr. Ikeda."

Her shop neighbor, Ikeda Aito, owned a book shop, its high popularity due to the secret book nooks around his store; ladders leading to fully furnished mattresses only visible if a customer walked down a certain isle, a fake bookshelf that slid open to reveal a reading room complete with overstuffed cushions and thick blankets to snuggle up in, but his most popular attraction was the book tree.

Before Sibyl had moved in next door, Aito's bookshop had been partially ruined by a falling tree. He righted the dead tree, fixed it up, and restored the shop around the trunk. It stood as tall as his ceiling, with shelves carved out of its hollow center. Over time, the tree became known as "The Kissing Tree" and couples often slipped inside to catch some private time, carving their name into the wood before they left.

She'd never been herself, Peter preferring to avoid those public displays of affection. The incurable romantic inside her shriveled up and died with those words, a raisin of nothing, discarded on the floor.

Aito smiled. "Neighbor. I've come for my package."

She motioned for him to follow her and walked to a back closet where she kept orders for pick-up. "I finished the latest batch of lavender oil late last night, so it's fresh and ready for Juliette."

"Good," Aito nodded as he waited by the door, his Japanese accent light. "I appreciate this."

"It's my pleasure, Aito." Sibyl inspected a package, determined the name wasn't Aito's, and put it away. "She can't sleep well again?"

"No. It's the children, mostly. They keep her up then the next night, she's too tired to fall asleep." Aito took his package from Sibyl once she found it, bowed, and walked back to the front door. "I'm not sure how much this oil helps, but if it gives her peace of mind, I'll buy your entire stock."

Sibyl laughed and accepted the money as it clinked into her palm. "You're a good man."

"Ah." Aito waved dismissively. "I'll be back."

He left the shop, wrapped his coat around his body and walked out into the snowfall.

The flakes were small and light, swirling through the air as it breezed through Market Town. Some continued on without a care, others tried to catch the snow in their mouths or ran through the street, laughing. The ambiance transformed into one of excitement and magic. People smiled. They snuggled together as they walked. Kids laughed and darted around the crowds. Snow stuck, a fine sheet of white muting the greens, yellows, oranges, and reds of Fall.

The scene saddened her, for she knew what lay outside her small world. Nowadays, Market Town masked Winter's vengeance, and she knew people visited the Town to escape their reality.

"More snow?" Hunter asked as he returned to the orange peels. "Last week's hasn't even melted yet."

Sibyl hesitated. "Do you think it'll stay?"

Hunter glanced at her. "Are you concerned about something in particular?"

"Just a bit. I mean," she left the shop window and sat back with Hunter, "when is it going to end?"

"You don't think it'll get worse?"

"I do, actually. And as someone who lost a toe to frostbite because I had no roof over my head, it's very hard not to worry."

"Jesus," Hunter said and puffed his cheeks out as he looked out the window. "You really lost a toe?"

Sibyl nodded. "My pinky toe. Zero out of ten would not recommend."

Hunter chuckled. "Well, I can think of one thing that improves all moods." He wiggled a jar of powdered roasted barley. "A warm drink. Maybe we can mourn the loss of your pinky toe while we're at it."

Sibyl smiled. "Great idea."

For the rest of the day, the snow fell. Customers came and went, some lingering for the fireplace and barley water, a depressing but adequate substitute for coffee. Everyone who entered La Parfana came in with snow dusted over their heads and shoulders. She sold more product than any other day in the month so far.

Around the time the snow let up, leaving one inch of powder in its wake, Sibyl said goodbye to her last customer. She cleared the leftover foliage she had used to make some displays into the garbage can.

All day and no sign of Luke. He was probably busy and since she couldn't send an immediate message, she refused to allow herself to judge him for not coming to see her. Still, she needed to talk to him and had hoped he'd show up.

She tossed the garbage into the compost bin out back, a familiar anxiety stuck in her chest as she stared at the compost, telling herself she must have done something to make him stay away. Sibyl pinched the bridge of her nose.

He just needs more time.

But how much time? How long until she decided their relationship was a lost cause?

Movement down the road caught her attention and she turned to see Luke standing there, staring at her. He ruffled his hair, wavy strands brushing across his brow and in front of his eyes, and her heart leapt. Every molecule in her body lit up at once. She nearly ran and jumped into his arms and kissed him until the sun came up.

He lifted his hand and gave a tiny wave. He then started a slow walk toward her.

Fear hit her in the gut, slammed right into her stomach and twisted an ugly, thick knife until her hands trembled.

This is just like before.

It had been raining then, his hair hanging in front of his eyes and around his ears, when he'd said nothing after she asked him to love her. Back then, they didn't know how to communicate properly, so she knew she'd been unfair to ask him. Still, seeing him do that little nervous wave and tentative walk brought back all the feelings from that night.

"Sibyl, I tried to come see you earlier – I know you probably got w...w-worried – but my parents had a crisis and I couldn't get away."

He let the words tumble from his mouth as he held onto her hips. She recognized the guilt and concern in his voice and the way he looked at her and she knew he meant it.

She'd been stupid to think he wanted to avoid her.

In her relief, Sibyl leaned forward and kissed Luke, his stubble rasping against her face, and she smiled as he sighed and his arms slid around her back. Wrapped around her, giving all of himself when he kissed her, solidified a piece of her that had been lost for so long, she desperately wanted it to fit amid the accumulative dust and clutter.

"What happened at your parent's?" Sibyl asked when they broke apart.

Luke reached up and pressed his thumb against her bottom lip before answering, "Someone rifled through their house. I'd left looking for a new home and Mom and Dad w...w-were out on their rounds. It rattled Mom a lot."

"Oh my God. Do they have any idea who did it?"

"No, unfortunately. We—"

Luke immediately pulled her against him and side-stepped behind the wooden compost bin. He peered out into the forest. Sibyl grunted when his grip on her wrist painfully tightened. Thankfully, he released her.

"Luke?" Sibyl whispered, wary and looking into the tree line as well. "What did you—"

The glint of a knife caught her eye. Someone clad in black moved through the trees, weapon in hand, their movements slow and deliberate. As she stared, Luke slunk toward the figure, and for a moment, Sibyl thought he'd forgotten about her or chose to ignore her, but he paused several feet away and turned. Luke reached for her, opened his hand, and waited until she joined him.

The wind bit her skin and her lungs constricted from the cold as she slipped through the forest with Luke. She struggled to track the person in the darkness, restricted to her ears and limited eyesight, and after nearly half an hour of walking, they caught up to the figure. Luke crouched beside her and they quietly watched and waited.

She didn't recognize the person, nor why they were meeting with another in the dark forest, but she couldn't just walk away. What if it put Luke in danger and she could've been there to help?

Whispers rose into the darkness. At first, she struggled to make out their words but when her hearing cleared up, one sentence froze her body.

"Fade will rise from the ashes."

She stared into the darkness, lost in fear. Luke, when she could move again to look at him, had a similar deer-in-the-headlights look.

Fade. The Fade. The organization that kidnapped the last and final POTUS and used the launch codes to target the six biggest fault lines in the country. Their leader was later caught and killed, but the Fate's thread had been cut for the United States. The faults had already shifted, creating massive earthquakes, tsunamis, and fires, devastating the entire continent. After a unfathomable amount of people died, groups of civilians, hardened by raids, civil war, and cold-blooded murders, banded together to methodically take down Fade. That was almost fifteen years ago. Sibyl thought they'd succeeded.

How are they back? Why here, of all places?

Cold blood ran through her veins at the thought of Fade's return, yet she pushed her mind to focus, the whirling, fumbling thing it was at the moment, and listened for something, anything that would clue her in on more details.

"Does she know you're close to finding her?" asked a lithe woman dressed in dark clothes.

"She suspects but she doesn't have enough information to act. I've thrown her off the scent for now but we have limited time. She'll figure it out soon."

"Good," the second person said, a man dressed in black and navy blue with a glittering white handle of a short sword at his hip. "I'll relay this to the next acolyte. If she tries to stop you, you have permission to take her down. We don't need our plans ruined."

The two operatives split off, the man disappearing into the forest, and Sibyl stared at the ground. Her chest tightened.

"Luke..." Sibyl whispered, searching for his arm. "Luke, we have to tell your mom."

"I know."

His tone, distant and distracted, made her turn toward him. His eyes darted back and forth as if he were thinking, and a thought occurred to her. She'd been suspicious before, but had written it off as her being paranoid. Now, with the excitement of seeing Luke gone, and the very real threat facing everyone close to her, Sibyl's control faltered.

"Why did you come to see me?" she asked, her stomach in knots over his possible answer.

He didn't answer for a few moments and she tried so hard not to read into it, but her fear reared and she closed her eyes at his response. "I missed you."

"*I missed you.*" Peter's voice echoed in her head and she clenched her teeth. Nausea rose in her stomach.

Sibyl stood and backed away. "It wasn't because you were following that Fade scout?"

"Huh? No. That was a coincidence."

Tears collected at the corners of her eyes and her nose burned. "I...I can't believe you. Not right now at least."

"W...W-Why?"

"Because—"

Luke jumped at the sound of bushes rustling, glanced around quickly, and reached for Sibyl. His hand on her mouth cut off more words before they left her. He pressed her body against the tree with his hips, his breath hot on her cheek and ear, and she bristled at the thrill that went through her body.

"Shh!" Luke peered around the tree. "Shit. He's coming. You have to hide."

"Me?" Sibyl hissed as he pulled his hand away.

The man collided with Luke which knocked him into Sibyl and she tumbled into the bushes before she could catch her balance. A long blackberry bramble scraped over her arm. Dots of blood immediately rose to the surface.

Sibyl carefully pulled at the vine to go help Luke, but the pain from trying to get it off her radiated into her neck and just like the night she'd pulled him from the ruins of his cabin, helplessness took hold. It twisted and knotted her stomach into a crumpled mess.

Luke took a blow to the face. Sibyl's eyes widened as she watched him nearly crumble. Sharp, thin branches burrowed into her skin, trapping her. Luke barely recovered when the scout advanced, feigning a high punch. Instead, he slammed his fist into Luke's stomach.

Sibyl panted. Her eyes dilated. It was only a matter of time before the scout pulled the knife Sibyl had seen earlier. At that thought, she lost all care about the thorns that would rip deep and grabbed the entire vine. Pain shot through her hand.

The scout pulled back an arm and slammed their elbow into Luke's newly healed ribs. He cried out and doubled over.

With Luke holding his torso and groaning, the scout ran at Sibyl. She yelped, ripped the bramble from the earth, and slashed it through the air. The scout's body took the blow and he screamed in anger.

"You bitch!"

With unexpected speed, the scout's arm flashed out. Sibyl's head knocked sideways as his fist made contact. She stumbled, panting from the pain. Several more punches landed on her chin and stomach, forcing her against a tree trunk. She tried to retaliate, but the fear of seeing Luke attacked and the possibility the scout still had his knife overwhelmed her. She barely fought back. The scout ducked, blocked, and spun as he avoided her blackberry vine whip and kicks. Wet blood trickled down her chin and tears mixed with them.

A dark form swelled behind the scout, consuming the moonlight. The form's arm raised and struck the back of the scout's head. He collapsed, recovered quickly, and scrambled back. Sibyl wiped at her mouth, anger swelling in her chest.

Luke moved into the cool light. Together, shoulder to shoulder, they advanced on the scout, Sibyl armed with her whip of thorns and Luke with a rock in his fist. It felt good to be by his side like the early days, even though she was terribly out of practice, and he truly was a force, relying on brute strength and a terrifying Mountain Man-like aura.

Sibyl's whip sliced through the air and came around to slice at his face. He cried out and hit the ground, palm pressed against his eye.

"Tell us what you know!" Sibyl bellowed.

The scout raised his spare hand. "Nothing. I know nothing."

Luke scoffed. "Liar!"

After a short pause, the scout took off into the forest, his crashing, frantic strides easy to follow. Sibyl panted as they followed, weaving and ducking through the trees with Luke beside her. He pointed to his right. She darted away in an attempt to flank the scout. Branches whipped her face and arms, stinging.

A wail sounded and Sibyl stopped dead, worry in her gut that Luke may have been the source, but as she walked toward the sound, she found Luke crouched at the edge of a ravine. He glanced up at her when she stopped beside him.

Luke ran his hand through his hair and sighed. "Dead."

The scout lay at the bottom of the ravine, his back and leg twisted unnaturally and a broken off sapling stump protruding from his chest. Sibyl's stomach soured. She looked away.

"Sibyl."

Before she could ask what was wrong, he caught her arm, turned it over, and slid her sleeve up. Blood covered her palm and forearm, a clear line of deep cuts spiraling over her skin.

"Oh, yeah." She inhaled hitching breaths as she pulled away. The worst part of a fight – she'd forgotten – was coming down from the adrenaline. With its levels dropping off, she always felt like she'd been hit by a train.

"I don't w...w-want you to get wrapped up in all of this," Luke half-whispered.

Her throat constricted. "In all of what?"

She hurt. She was bleeding in multiple places, the worst from the blackberry thorns, and every gust of air or movement of her muscles upgraded the stinging on her hand and arms to a burn. She had no energy left to devote it to a fight, but he just stared at her in that stupid, surprised way and she lost it.

"God! You really have no idea, do you? How mad you make me. You're hot and cold. One second, you're all 'don't want me, Sibyl, I'm toxic,' and the next you want me to fight alongside you, then you discard me as if I'm a check mark in whatever agenda you've got going on in your head."

She knew it was irrational right down to her very bones. Peter had messed with her head and she didn't understand how Luke didn't yell back at her for blowing up on him.

"You're right," he muttered.

"What do you want?" She gestured to her chest, smearing blood on the fur of her coat and hadn't quite processed his words. Hot tears drained down her cheeks. To see Luke stand there and listen to her verbal assault made her nauseous. Why hadn't he blamed her yet? "You can't just—" What he'd said clicked and all her anger died. "What?"

His shoulders sagged a bit and his eyebrows drew together. "I'm yanking you around, making you confused where you stand. I can imagine it's disarming or scary."

That shut her up. Scary? She wasn't scared or anything close to that, but her throat closed, and tears pooled in her eyes, and her lips quivered and Luke gathered her in his arms, holding tight. She cried for a few moments there and Luke whispered to her.

"There isn't a moment in my life, not one, I don't w...w-want you to be in. I promise to be clearer moving forward. Please promise me something, okay?" Luke sighed, his lips pressed against her cold hair, and caressed her cheek with his large hand. Callouses gently rubbed against her skin. "Let me in, too, Sibyl. Let me see all of you."

What he promised sounded nice but how could she fulfill her side? How could someone ever look at her, a dumpster fire of a person, and still want her?

16 | SIBYL

She managed to convince Luke to follow her back to La Parfana, stocked with a generous collection of salves, herbs, and wrappings.

"There's an old camping cot I keep for Hunter when he's busy with school. You can use that for tonight."

He didn't answer right away and instead scanned the forest, leaning to one side then the other until satisfied, then looked to her. "Alright," he said and followed Sibyl.

Fourteen years ago, the road they walked on would have been filled with noisy cars and bright lights. Everything would be moving. Now, it all sat silent.

Sibyl shivered. Bumps rose on her body and she pulled on the sleeves of her knitted sweater to cover the top of her hand, forgetting about her injury. Her breath hung in the air.

A coat settled on her shoulders. Luke.

Sibyl jerked her attention to him, unable to understand for a split second why he sacrificed his warmth, then she grabbed the lapel and hugged it closer, enjoying his spiced scent wafting off it.

"Thank you," she whispered.

They walked through a glade, a thin layer of frost on the plants, and toward the pines on the other side. No wind passed through. Only their steps created movement in the thigh high grass.

As she watched him two paces ahead of her, she knew what went wrong between them. They'd separated on bad terms, both hurt and misunderstood by the other, yet had never fought or argued. Disagreements had happened, him chronically avoiding conflict, and she agreeing with him even if she had a different opinion.

"We fought," she said out loud. Luke turned and she explained, "We've been fighting. That's never happened before."

He watched her carefully. "No, it hasn't."

"I'm sorry I avoided issues that were right in front of my face."

Luke approached and gently held her arms. "You aren't the only one to blame. I played my part." He paused for a moment, took a deep breath, and said, "I ignored you. I didn't realize you needed more than what I gave you and when you told me, I thought you were forcing me and I got scared. I'm sorry I didn't understand."

She looked at him, smiling, with tears misting her eyes. "You were always good at staying calm. Guess that extends to me yelling at you."

He chuckled, the corners of his eyes crinkling. "Too calm at times. I should have cared more."

They watched each other for a small moment longer, a tiny weight lifting off Sibyl's chest, and continued back to her shop.

Luke followed Sibyl through the sleepy Market Town. Fog haunted the area, filtered through the tall grasses, and over the moss and ivy.

Sibyl let Luke inside. As he stood awkwardly by the door, rocking back and forth on his boot heels, Sibyl sifted through the ashes in the fireplace, found some still red coals, and tossed small pieces of kindling onto them. She then used the newborn fire to light a thin stick and lit all her candles and lanterns in the shop.

She set a triple-wicked candle on the checkout counter. "First aid's in the back. Hold on."

Luke followed her and she almost told him to go sit down and wait, but she was determined to push away the unhealthy habits Peter had influenced. Together they gathered a bag of salves, some bandages, a bowl of water with plenty of clean rags, and various needles and brought all their supplies back to the counter.

Luke removed items from the first aid bag, inspected the tiny jars as if he were a near-sighted librarian staring down at a book with her horn-rimmed glasses. He picked a couple then held out his hand and pointedly looked at her.

She set her hand in his and winced when he rolled up her sleeve to reveal the scabbed over cuts from the blackberry vine. Softly, Luke dabbed at the cuts spiraling around her arm. She couldn't help it. She stared at him. His hands, large and calloused with years of hunting, expertly performed a gentle act. His eyes, dark with lashes long and thick, fluttered as he focused on her injury, the world around him gone.

Sibyl bit the inside of her lip to keep the electrical charge from destroying her. Even though he had his own injuries, he took the time to take care of her first and Sibyl's heart burst.

When he looked up at her crying, his brow wrinkled slightly, and reached up to wipe away the escaped tears.

As Luke guided the long bandage around the middle of her hand, he grazed the sensitive skin on the inside of her wrist. She did everything in her power to avoid shuddering.

When he finished and released her, she held her arm to her body, lungs tight as if she'd just run a marathon.

"I tried to be careful," Luke said with his fingers through his hair.

"N-no. You were gentle." She glanced at his injuries, bruises and cuts on his face, and dug into her bag for her curly dock ointment.

Sibyl lifted his hands, admiring how square they looked compared to the soft lines of hers, and rubbed some ointment on his bruised knuckles.

"You punched him pretty hard," she observed and lightly brushed a spot where the skin had broken.

"I w...w-wanted to shatter his face."

She smiled a bit. "I'm honored." Sibyl dropped his hands and focused on his face, cleaning the small cuts along his cheekbone and to the right of his eyebrow, a partner to his scar. "Where'd you get your scar, by the way?" she asked.

"Someone hit me over the head with a glass b...b-bottle."

Imagining someone angry enough to do something like that wasn't hard because Luke often rubbed people the wrong way by just existing – something about the way he spoke, maybe? – but there had to be more to the story.

"What happened?"

Luke shrugged. "I stood up to him, so he grabbed the nearest thing he could find, and hit me over the head."

"Oh my God. Who was it?"

Luke glanced down, his jaw worked, and Sibyl waited patiently. The longer he avoided responding, the more suspicious Sibyl became that he didn't want to tell her.

"Luke? Remember, we're trying to be more honest with each other."

He flicked his eyes away. "Peter."

She blinked, not surprised, but confused why he'd never told her. "Peter did it?"

Luke nodded. "He bullied me as a kid. He's the reason I hid away in my cabin for so long."

"Oh my God." Her mind immediately went to Luke's reaction after he'd walked in on Peter abusing her. "Is that why you were so upset when you saw him hurting me?"

Even saying it made her nauseous.

"Yeah."

It all made sense. Sibyl took a few beats to process, then set her hand on his cheek to pull his attention toward her. "I'm glad you told me."

Luke smiled a little and turned his head to kiss her palm. "Me too," he whispered when he pulled away.

Sibyl finished up caring for Luke's minor injuries, wrapped his knuckles to let the ointment soak in, and put her supplies away. When she returned, Luke had doused the fire and was leaning against the counter, tentatively probing his nose. He hit a tender spot, winced through his teeth, and jerked his hand away, then caught sight of her. His gaze softened.

"It's late and I don't want you walking outside after what just happened." Sibyl walked over to the staircase tucked against the shop's back corner and gestured. "I was going to have you sleep on the cot, but I have two extra rooms upstairs. You can use one."

Luke nodded and followed her.

Sibyl showed him where he would be sleeping, the cot already set up by Hunter a few nights ago.

They parted ways, Sibyl wanting to ask him to stay with her, but didn't know how nor was she brave enough, so she left to her room and as her door closed behind her, she sighed. Pressing her back against the wood, Sibyl covered her face, mumbling over the embarrassment that she couldn't tell him goodnight.

Sibyl awoke sometime in the night and had laid awake for fifteen minutes listening to someone pacing downstairs, her efforts to investigate squashed by fear. Her tight stomach made her nearly puke.

I need my spear.

She did have other weapons for protection – she wasn't completely unprepared – and even carried extra spears, but she wasn't as accurate with them as she was with her original spear. At best, she'd nick an arm or leg.

Sibyl rolled over, groaning, hid her face in the pillow, then steeled herself and rose from bed. She slipped on a thick, knitted sweater, covered her feet with woolen socks for warmth, and grabbed the crossbow resting against the wall by her door. Silently – the socks served a dual purpose to muffle her footsteps – Sibyl exited the room.

The pacing increased in volume as she slunk down the stairs with a crossbow in her hands, hoping the weapon's rattling wasn't too loud.

A shadow passed over the floor in the dim light right before dawn, back and forth in the center of her shop. Sibyl couldn't make out much, but they were tall, wide shouldered, and stocky. The perfect combo to give her a hard time.

Great.

Unfortunately, the intruder definitely would've seen the stairs, so she couldn't leave them to hide behind something without being seen. She raised the crossbow, shaking so much that she couldn't aim. So, she did the next thing she could think of.

"Get out of my shop!" Sibyl called out, her voice wavering.

"Jesus!"

"Wha—Luke?" Sibyl unloaded the crossbow and set it on a table. "What the hell are you doing?"

"I don't have my dogs."

When Sibyl didn't respond, he plunged on, the nerves in his voice hanging heavy in the air.

"I need them to sleep. I didn't think I did, but I do, and it's infuriating and even though they're at my parent's and they're okay, I still w...w-worry about them."

"So...you're going to pace all night?"

"That's the plan, yes."

She lifted the lantern. First his pants, warm, striped ones he'd surely found in a drawer – she hadn't even thought to show him where he could get clothes – a bare torso—

That's where she stopped and stared hard. Something about the way his stomach curved out a bit and the dark hair covering his chest with a little line down to his belly button and...beyond, had Sibyl's fingers itching to touch. His pajamas hugged his hips perfectly. Her mouth ran dry and she took a step forward before remembering herself. Distance. Must keep a reasonable distance, but damn it, if she didn't want to climb on top of him, clasp his large hands at her hips, and ride him until he begged.

She wasn't tired anymore, but still needed to respect his space, so she said, "But it's..." one look out the window revealed a sky beginning to brighten, "really early. When did you start doing," she wagged her finger in a circle, "this?"

"All I know is the goddamn sun w...w-wasn't up." Luke stumbled backward, pressed the heel of his hand to his forehead, and shook his head.

Tiny strands of black hair brushed his cheek, waves thick and soft. She loved his hair up, but seeing it down? Now that was a treat.

He needed to sleep and he apparently couldn't without someone beside him.

Adorable.

Sibyl smiled. "Come on," she said, hiking the crossbow against her shoulder, and waving her hand in the air. "We're tucking you in."

"I'm not a child." Luke grumbled as he followed her up the stairs. "Does that mean I can start calling you Cici for short?"

"Where'd you hear that?"

"Those kids said it the day you pulled me from the cabin rubble."

She smiled, amazed he'd even heard anything in his state of semi-unconsciousness that day. "One of them couldn't say my name properly because of his struggles with speech, so they all started calling me Cici for solidarity.

"Thoughtful kids."

"They are." Sibyl stopped at the entrance to her room, set the weapon against the wall inside, and stood there, waiting. The cool, new rays of sun cast enough light in the hallway to show Luke's confused expression. She couldn't believe she was even considering letting him into her bed – knowing the possible events that may happen – but he couldn't keep pacing.

"You need your dogs next to you, right?" she asked, knowing the answer. Luke nodded. "Well, would me being next to you help?"

His eyebrows shot together, but she saw that tiny smile. "Huh?"

"Obviously, you can say no, but I figure that we're both tired, you need a warm body beside you, and I'm the closest thing you got. Unless you want to continue this all-nighter, miserable and on your feet."

Luke stood in front of her for several moments then brought his bottom lip into his mouth. In a flash of embarrassment, she deeply regretted suggesting anything at all. He was desperately attractive and she desperately tried to ignore her building desire. She expected him to say no, because why would he not, but she never expected him to say—

"Sure."

17 | LUKE

He was completely insane to even consider her offer, much less accept it, but his eyes were falling out of his head. Nothing would happen, right? He'd follow her to bed, finally have a warm body beside him, and fall asleep quick, but he'd be damned if he didn't think of...certain things.

They'd be fine. Completely.

Is sleeping next to her even going to work?

Luke didn't know, but he needed sleep if they were going to travel to his parent's. The trip wasn't long, two hours at most, and making Sibyl not only alter her plans after the Fade scout encounter but also deal with his zombie ass would be unfair to her.

Luke stared at her lips—her face, damnit—a wide-eyed, mouth-slightly-open stare. "Did I make you nervous?" he asked, wanting to avoid assumptions.

"You agreed so fast, I'm not sure what to do now."

"You can start by showing me to your room." Sibyl's snort shocked realization into his brain. "That came out different than I planned."

Damn it, she was gorgeous. Her braid had come out somewhat, the layers of her hair loose about her round face.

"Come on," Sibyl said through a yawn. "Room's this way." Before climbing the stairs, she paused and turned to him with a smile. "Think Hunter would appreciate walking in on a trail of clothes in a few hours?"

Luke watched as Sibyl removed her socks and cardigan and dropped the items on the stairs and banister, and walked the final distance, humming a happy tune.

He smiled. Finally, the Sibyl he remembered. The one who had a bit of devilish humor in her. Unfortunately, Luke had no items to remove.

Candlelight carried by Sibyl guided him and when he reached the final step, Luke's foot touched nothing. In a flash, his stomach shriveled. Worst part was, instead of stumbling, he crashed directly into Sibyl, taking her down. The candle landed top down and extinguished immediately, leaving Sibyl and Luke in the budding morning rays.

Sibyl released a surprised cackle that morphed into a full-on laugh, and his heart sped up. They were tangled together on the hard floor, Luke so shocked that he couldn't move and Sibyl laughing uncontrollably.

Her laugh faded but he wanted it back, to hear the tiny snort she made, see the wrinkle of her nose.

Then she was staring at him, and he realized he hadn't moved.

"Sorry," he mumbled. "I'll just—"

Sibyl grabbed his forearm before he could stand, the touch slamming an electrical shock into his heart. It beat slow and steady and completely for her.

They laid there, sharing air, Luke's thigh between her legs and his arms braced on either side of her head. She was close. Touching. Sibyl stared at him with her beautiful brown eyes.

"Let's not make it to the bedroom," he whispered in a voice unlike his own. Deep and tight. At the moment, he couldn't muster much more.

"I agree. Luke?"

"Mmm?"

"Just kiss me."

Desire rose in his chest. He leaned in and her breath slid across his skin. Luke flicked his attention to her mouth, and he pressed his thumb to her bottom lip – God, he loved what it did to him – gently coaxing her mouth to open, just enough to slide a gentle tongue flick into her mouth. Oh, God. The warmth of her. The feel of her tongue sliding along his.

Sibyl tensed.

He pulled away, searching her eyes. "Are you okay?"

She smiled, grabbed the back of his head, and brought him closer. Luke grunted in surprise. He watched her eyes and her mouth move, distracted by those mischievous dimples playing peekaboo on her cheeks as she spoke.

"Definitely okay."

Then she kissed him. He slid a hand underneath her, softening when she arched slightly toward him, and braced her against him as she ground her hips against his growing cock. He couldn't stop the deep rumble that rose in his throat. He wanted more, so much more. Luke lost his fingers within the thick, brown abyss of Sibyl's hair and her tiny sounds of begging lit him on fire.

Luke shuddered, and her fingers reached up and intertwined with his.

They explored with greedy touches and kisses. Luke grazed the inside of her mouth, her breasts, the little spot where her neck and shoulder met, hoping to hear her tiny moans of pleasure. Luke catalogued those places based on the severity of her moans and gasping breaths, committing them to memory of where she liked to be touched most.

Luke groaned and nipped her earlobe.

Something changed in her then, an intensity absent before and with a shift of her hip, she rolled him over.

Luke's back slammed against the floor, and he half laughed, half groaned. The look of darkness in her eyes stunned him. It aroused him in wicked ways. When he leaned in, she shoved him against the floor again and a crack of intoxication went through him.

"Don't move," she demanded, and a half smile grew on Luke's face.

He waited there, shivering with want, and let Sibyl explore him. Her fingers traveled across his torso, chest, and he heard a tiny, shaking exhale come from her.

"Shit, Sibyl. Your hands are heaven."

She paused, undertones of mischief in her voice. "Good."

Sibyl's hand settled on his chest and slid lower until she lingered just at the waistband of his pajama bottoms.

That wouldn't do. Not at all.

So, Luke grabbed her wrist, quickly checked in with her to make sure she wanted to touch, and guided her hand underneath the fabric. His head fell back, pleasure pulsing through him as she placed wandering kisses on his skin while stroking his length.

It was official; he had lost his mind, but Sibyl was so utterly irresistible that he didn't want to see sense. All he wanted was to kiss her and get her in bed. And let her dominate him into next Tuesday. Yes. He'd welcome that.

Sibyl pulled away, making him grunt quietly, then licked her lips and said, "I want to touch you with nothing between us."

"Lead the way," Luke whispered.

Sibyl pulled him to her room. He didn't care what waited within the four walls as long as he had something to fuck her on. A bed? Common. Couch? Getting there. A dresser? Phenomenal.

He fell back against the comforter, shoved there by Sibyl and watched wickedly as she straddled him, flicked her hair out of the way, and kissed him on the lips, below his ears, and down his neck. She ignited him with her dominance, making him hopelessly intoxicated. He'd get to have his way with her, but first, he'd bask in the pleasure she gave him.

"I want to see you," she whispered and brushed her lips across his to pull a shudder from his body. She played with him, whispering with her lips barely touching his own. "I want to memorize every bit of you so I can remember it in the dark, cold nights."

In response, Luke moved Sibyl, stood beside the bed, and undid the tie on the warm, cotton pajamas. He let them fall to the ground with a soft thump.

"Oh my God," Sibyl whispered reverently and stared at his dick, then slid her attention up to his mouth, lingered there and licked her lips, then to his eyes. "I can't wait to have you inside me."

This woman. This god damn, fucking woman.

With great pleasure, he watched Sibyl explore his skin, as if learning of the world for the first time, and did it with a smile upon her lips. Gooseflesh rose on his skin as she fluttered her fingers across the veins of his arm, up to his shoulders, and through his dusting of chest hair.

Luke slipped his hands up her thighs, and underneath her shirt. Good God, someone had wrapped her in silk. Her curves made his vision tumble. When his hands found her bralette, she jerked in surprise.

Then her glorious weight left, and he felt empty.

Had he done something?

He sat up, her erotic body alight in the morning sun, the curve of her ass particularly appealing. Naked, Luke crawled toward her on the bed, heart throbbing in time with his cock, and watched her remove her shirt and pants. Bathed in the cool early light filtering in through the curtains above her bed, Sibyl turned and froze, immediate redness shooting across her chest and cheeks.

"Luke..."

He pulled his attention to her feet and smiled. "You intend on doing this w...w-wearing only socks?"

"No. I was gonna—"

Luke crouched before her, hand whispering down her leg and put the slightest amount of pressure on her ankle. She adjusted her center of gravity and allowed him to lift her foot.

"You know," he said slowly, hooking a finger around the top of her sock. "You can push on me."

A pause, then Sibyl put pressure on his chest, arching her foot so Luke could remove her sock. She caught on by then and before he could grab her other ankle, Sibyl all but shoved Luke against the bed. He grunted at the contact, staring into her eyes as she peered down at him, foot keeping him in place.

"Remove it."

The command went straight to his cock as he cradled her calf with one hand while slowly removing her sock, dropped it carelessly on the floor, then immediately returned to her leg. He dragged his nose up her shin as far as he could in his position and titled his head up to stare at her. Eyes wide, Sibyl drew in her bottom lip.

"I'm all yours. Tell me what to do."

"My brain's mush."

"That's not an answer."

She hid a smile and glanced around the room for a moment. "I don't want to use anything right now." Sibyl knelt between his legs and slid her hands up his thighs with a firm pressure that had his fists clenching. "I just want to taste."

Luke shuddered. "How deep do you want it?"

He couldn't believe his eyes when she wrapped her hand around his dick and slid it down to the base. She peered at him, confidence personified. "All the way. As deep as you can get. I want to be gagging, eyes watering, and when you pull out, I want thick saliva to drip off my tongue. Then I want to swallow."

The way she said it, slow and sensual, made Luke see stars. He took a fistful of her hair and titled her head back so he could stare into her beautiful eyes catching the early sunlight. Luke grabbed his cock and guided it to her mouth to draw circles around the entrance to her open and waiting mouth.

"Squeeze me twice if I go too fast or you get uncomfortable."

In response, she let her pink tongue fall out of her mouth and he set his cock on it, slowly pressing forward until he felt resistance. He pulled back and went in again, farther and farther, until his cock ached for him to pick up speed. Still, he went slow, carefully eyeing the way her eyelashes fluttered each time he entered her mouth, cock sliding down her throat.

"You're gorgeous right here," Luke crooned. "I'm going to speed up now. Ready?"

Sibyl made a noise of acknowledgment and Luke increased his tempo, each thrust pulling a quiet noise from Sibyl. He watched his cock slip in and out of her mouth, his fist tightening in her hair. Occasionally, she'd squeeze twice, he'd pause, they'd readjust, and she'd demand more, driving his mind into a tailspin. Her chest soon dripped with saliva and he reached down to swipe some onto his finger, her eyes widening as he licked it clean while he drove deep into her throat. She moaned around his cock, paused to tell him she wanted to lay with her head hanging off the bed, and let her saliva drip down toward her forehead.

They switched quickly. Luke easily slid down her throat and he shuddered.

"Faster?" Luke asked breathlessly and when she nodded, he pounded down her tight throat, groaning and shaking and listening to her gag through it all. "Don't swallow." He panted, desperately trying to speak before he exploded. "I want to taste."

Sibyl's hand immediately drifted to her clit, Luke pounded into her, and he let his head fall back as he came into her. All at once, the world around him exploded in light and heat and pleasure, and it was all he could do to stay upright.

Once he'd recovered a bit, Luke leapt onto the bed, slid his hand underneath Sibyl's neck, and whispered, "Come here."

He kissed her, sliding his tongue into her waiting mouth and found the salty taste of his own cum inside. Luke moaned with Sibyl and pulled back to watch her swallow, enjoying the way her throat moved so much that he ducked and kissed all the way down to her breast. Sibyl folded her arms and legs around him. He was spent, but he couldn't leave her wanting, so he cleaned her chest and face off, and returned to cradle her in his arms.

"It's my turn," he crooned against her hair. "My turn to drive you to the heavens."

As he laid Sibyl down, her knees fell open, showing him her sensual tuft of hair he couldn't wait to part. He sat there, admiring her, and couldn't lift his hand to touch her; only stare.

"Luke," she whined and reached out, her fingers searching for him.

So, he leaned down between her legs and gave her his hair to hold onto. Luke licked and sucked, slipped his tongue inside her. He reached up to palm her breast. Sibyl arched and moaned. He squeezed her thighs then hoisted her legs onto his shoulders and continued sucking at her clit.

Slowly, Sibyl progressed toward climax, her skin warming, moans turning to whimpering, and knees tightening on either side of his head.

If she crushed him, he'd thank her.

What a way to die, between a woman's thighs.

He kept a steady rhythm and brought her to release, Sibyl releasing a loud, whimpering grunt that tightened every piece of her underneath his touch. With a jolt, she relaxed and lay sprawled on the bed.

Luke dragged his lips over her stomach, breasts, and shoulders, cuddling in close to her on the bed, and pressed his face into her hair.

"How can I take care of you?"

"Of me?" she chuckled. "You already did."

"That's not what I meant, smart ass. Do you need a warm bath, some tea, a snuggle? A snack? All four?"

Sibyl giggled. "A snack would be wonderful because I'm starving."

"Good," he teased and got up to grab something when he paused and turned. "Location of the snacks?"

Sibyl rose onto her elbows, her breasts tilting with gravity and his cock twitched a bit. "In the cupboard under the window over there," she said and pointed to the room's far end.

Luke walked carefully to the free-standing chest of drawers. He opened the top drawer, found cured meats, dried berries, crackers, wax wrapped cheeses, a few canned jars of pickled vegetables, and some crusty bread.

"Impressive collection," Luke said as he chose a few items and brought them over.

"Yeah," Sibyl said with a smile. She popped a dried blueberry in her mouth. "Snackies are a necessity when I need to hide up here and stress eat."

He smiled at the usage of 'snackies,' leaned forward, and kissed her. She giggled.

"God damn it, woman," he whispered, his voice hoarse from a combination of attraction and trying not to chuckle. "You're making it real hard not to take you again."

Sibyl leveled him with a devilish stare, leaned in close, let the tension in the air harden, then snatched the meat from his hand and stuffed it in her mouth. "I mean," her words were muffled by the food she moved into her cheek to speak, "we're here alone and have all night."

He smiled and crooned, "You're not exhausted?"

"Not in the slightest." She swallowed. "We just did oral. Hardly a way to tire someone out."

Luke chuckled, which turned into a sigh right before he wrapped his arm around her back, arched it toward him and kissed her chest. He felt it rise and fall before peering up at her. "Tell me your desires. Tell me how you'd like me because if you don't..." he dropped his gaze to her lips, then her breasts, and back up to her face, "I'm going to—"

Banging on a door downstairs interrupted his speech.

Luke ground his teeth together and glared at Sibyl's door. "Fucking hell."

Sibyl giggled, kissed his cheek with her hand on his chest, and slipped out from underneath him. "I'll go check who's out there."

He flopped back on the bed, hand tucked behind his head, and watched her dress into warm clothes.

The knocking turned frantic and Sibyl jerked her head toward her door as Luke sat up. "That sounds urgent."

"Yeah." Sibyl rushed from the room.

Luke remained as he searched for a robe to hide the tent at the front of his pajama pants.

Sibyl's shrill, fearful call carried upstairs and he spun around to go to her, heart racing. "Luke!"

18 | LUKE

The wildflower.
A child of Mother Earth.
Resilient. Strong.
Oh, to grow in the broken places.
Oh, to be, even a small part,
a wildflower like you.

When he reached the bottom stair landing, Sibyl supported a red-haired teen as she walked to a nearby chair, two more kids entered behind her, helped by some adults. One of them, a woman, cried as she sunk to the floor with a young boy she called Ian.

"My baby boy," she wept and tears streaked down her face.

Deep lacerations spread across the teens' extremities and torsos. Claw marks? Ian was in the worst condition, his cheek split completely open and an injury to his head bled into his hair. Right hand gone. Luke struggled to look at him for longer than a few seconds.

Sibyl turned to Luke, her eyebrows together and mouth turned down. "Get the emergency kit under the sink. It's different from the one we used." Sibyl pointed to the main counter where she performed transactions. "There!"

Raised by a clan Leader, Luke knew better than to ask questions, recognizing the signs of someone in charge during a crisis. He rushed to the counter, threw open the door, and rifled through the items until he found a transparent box labeled, 'emergency first aid' and brought it to Sibyl.

"Thank you," Sibyl said and grabbed the kit. "I need you to get a fire going."

Luke nodded and loaded kindling into the fireplace. His arms were dead tired from the exertion of producing fire by the time he added on the larger logs. With the fire crackling to life, Luke sat on a chair to avoid getting in the way and occasionally hopped up to grab pitchers of water when asked.

He watched Sibyl care for the three boys, getting tiny glimpses of her genuine love for others, like the way Sibyl reassured the teenagers through their pain, how she didn't forget to make sure the adults who brought the kids in were cared for and as comfortable as they could be, and how she tied off the bandages rather than secured them with pins to prevent sticking the boys.

Hunter entered for his morning shift and stopped, the door bumping into his shoulder. "What the..."

Without looking up at him, Sibyl said, "Either come in and help or stay out of the way. You're letting the cold in."

Luke shoved a chair out for him with his foot. "Join us."

"What happened?" Hunter asked.

Luke sunk lower in his seat, the adrenaline from the boy's care wearing off and sleepiness setting in. "Animal attack, we think."

I'm so damn tired.

Sibyl finished stitching up the final boy and settled them on cots Hunter brought in from the storage room. Luke spoke to the parents who brought them in, getting information on the teens' whereabouts prior to the attack, how long they were missing, where they were found, and some other devastating questions that needed to be asked. He finished up and returned to his seat, about to speak to Hunter sitting beside him when Sibyl approached. She crouched in front of Luke and to his utter shock, put her hand on his thigh. He couldn't move, the warmth and pressure of her hand paralyzing.

"There's an empty bed calling our names upstairs."

Her hand slid up—

Luke jerked awake, fell off the chair, and hit the ground. He stayed there, groaning with his hands on his face.

It was a dream. Holy hell, it was a dream.

"You good?" Hunter asked over the edge of Luke's empty chair.

"Yeah, just..." Luke sighed. "Give me a sec."

Luke and Hunter cleaned up what Sibyl had discarded and stayed out of her way for the most part, then both returned to their seats to wait until they were needed again.

He watched Sibyl flow through the room, exhausted but smiling and in charge, and Luke's heart fluttered. Every bit of her shown bright. Then there were her hands. Soft. Tiny cuts on the tips from gardening. Nimble. God damn it, they were so nimble.

He rubbed his eyes.

She's bright and happy and I'm...not. Why do we even think we'd be good together?

She looked at him and his brain deflated like a balloon full of air released to whirl around the room. He stopped thinking. He couldn't. He loved her smile and her laugh and her kindness toward others. She commanded the room when she needed to, either becoming a lioness or a gentle deer, both equally regal and show-stopping, but vastly different in their approach to life. There were times when she disappeared into the background and let others take the spotlight, quietly cheering them on from the side. Sibyl was...well, did he even have a word that fit her? They all missed the mark. Stalwart, loyal, brave, kind, commanding. None fit her exactly, but perfectly all the same.

With the boys settled down, the blood cleaned, and the adults who brought the kids in all taken care of, Sibyl sighed into a seat beside Luke.

"You guys good?" she asked after noticing Luke staring.

He awkwardly repeated something she had said to him not too long ago in an attempt to lighten the mood. "Just making sure chocolate cake isn't on your face."

She blinked, confused for a moment, then chuckled and her smile could move mountains. "Good. I got rid of all the evidence then."

Luke released a small smile and stood up. "And you didn't share with me? Do you know how long it's been since I ate chocolate cake?"

"Around fourteen years, probably."

Luke shook his head. "Wrong. I'm allergic."

"You're..." Her lips contorted into a frown. "I'm so sorry."

Hunter appeared as if materializing from thin air. "You're both adorable."

"What?" Luke and Sibyl said at the same time.

"See. Talking at the same time is only the first step."

"First step to what?" Sibyl asked.

Luke and Hunter stared at her. "I'm shocked that went over your head," Hunter said.

Someone called out for Sibyl, and she rushed over to a seizing Ian. Luke followed her.

"What can I do?" he asked.

"Once I get him off the cot, move it out of the way and I'll manage the rest."

He followed her commands and scooted the portable bed to the side of the room. Sibyl dug her knees into the floor and rolled Ian to his side until the seizure passed. His mother gathered him up in her arms and held him close as he whimpered. Luke returned the cot, helped Ian back to bed, and covered him with a crocheted blanket again.

Sibyl stood near the front door of La Parfana with Ian's mother and Luke padded over.

"Is he going to be okay?" the mother asked.

"It's too early to tell. I'll do my best to keep an eye on him." Sibyl put a hand on the mother's arm. "He's in good hands here. Promise."

Through wet tears, Ian's mother smiled and her shoulders relaxed. "Thank you."

Before she walked away, Sibyl reached out to get her attention. "I am so sorry to ask this, but I need to know more of what happened."

That's right. Luke wasn't able to get information out of her before, with how distraught she was.

"I...I don't know exactly," Ian's mother said through tears. "They were all out together on the forest's edge chatting and laughing and doing what teen boys do, when all of a sudden Ian's friend Hannah," she pointed to a blonde girl holding Gabe's limp, bandaged hand, silently crying, "came to me, screaming and crying about them being attacked."

The mother's chin quivered violently and Sibyl put her hand on her arm. "Am I right to assume you arrived first?"

She nodded. "The other parents showed up a bit later. It was awful. I can't speak on it anymore. I'm sorry."

"You've given more than enough," Sibyl said, let the mom leave, and approached the blonde girl. Luke went with.

"Hannah, is it?" Sibyl asked as she crouched in front of her.

The poor girl wiped at snot under her nose, her eyes bloodshot, and hair disheveled as if she'd been messing with it for hours.

"Yeah," the girl whispered. She thanked Luke when he handed her a handkerchief. "What's going to happen to them? Will they be okay?"

"It's too soon to tell, but I need you to help me."

"Anything."

"Did you see what attacked the boys?"

"Who," Hannah corrected.

Interest piqued, Luke knelt on the ground beside Sibyl. "You said, w…w-who?"

"That's right. I was bringing them…" she glanced around as if expecting to get in trouble, "don't tell my parents, okay?" Hannah sighed. "Beers. I brought them beers and found them all on the ground, bleeding." The girl's face contorted and fresh sobbing stopped her from talking for several moments. "I'm so sorry. I shouldn't have suggested we go out there, but I did, and now they're going to die."

"No. Not if I can help it." Sibyl grabbed her hand. "Try to clear your mind, take a breath, and tell me what happened. Would it help if I just ask questions?"

Hannah nodded and sniffed.

"Alright. Did you see who did it?"

Hannah nodded.

"Did you interrupt this person or did you see them running away shortly after?"

"I interrupted him. Aspen, he—" Hannah broke down again.

She referred to the second boy, a stocky kid with a nasty cut across his neck. He'd survive, but with a nasty scar.

Luke and Sibyl waited for as long as Hannah needed before Sibyl resumed her questions. "He survived because you walked in. A little deeper of a wound and he'd have bled out. You did good. Now, did you get a good look at this man?"

"I did." Hannah had calmed down enough to expand. "He crashed right into me. I still don't understand why he didn't hurt me, but I saw his face and his weapon. It had a white…hand holder. He had a bit of a beard, but not really, and he was wearing dark navy and black. I'm an artist, so I can tell the difference between the colors. It was a black jacket, like a zip up hoodie, and a navy-blue shirt underneath."

Exactly the same description as one of the Fade operatives the dead scout met with. Luke eyed Sibyl and realized she looked at him with the same expression of dread.

Sibyl placed her hand on Hannah's knee. "Thank you for your help, Hannah."

When Hannah left to sit by Gabe, grabbing his hand and leaning against the cot, Sibyl pulled Luke next to the bay window at the front of her store. "I think your mom's in danger."

Luke nodded. "I have to go."

"Go. I'll be safe here."

He hesitated at first, part of him wanting to avoid whatever awaited him with his mom, but knew he couldn't abandon her, so he kissed Sibyl and ran upstairs to get his coat and shoes.

The closer he got to his parent's house in the snow, the more he mulled over the tragic situation back at La Parfana, concerned about Sibyl's mental state during the event and after. He'd need to do something to help her decompress, but what?

When he reached the porch, he put away his thoughts of Sibyl and forced his mind to shift to checking on his mom.

The dogs mauled him with wet tongues, body slams, and tail whippings when he entered the house. Luke welcomed them with chest scratches for Lev and ear ones for Boatswain, both dogs battling for attention and love after missing him for so long. Boatswain was particularly drooly, so Isaac handed him a towel to wipe off his arms and face.

Luke launched directly into explaining what he'd discovered in the forest and the boys who were attacked and how everything pointed to a target painted on his mom's back. Isaac listened intently, his concern mounting with each new piece of information Luke mentioned.

Luke glanced around. "She here?" At first, he thought his mom would be in another room, but it had been too long since his arrival for her not to have surfaced.

"She's visiting with some struggling families."

Luke's body tightened and he all but yelled out, "And she went alone?"

"Hold on." Isaac put his hands out. "Since when does anyone 'let' your mom do anything? She went with Ray."

Ray was her bodyguard, a precaution she always took despite not needing him in their current time of peace. No one wanted to hurt her; the clan loved his mom. Now, as Luke stood frozen in place, he wondered if she'd been hiding something. Did she always know Fade would come after her?

"That doesn't make me feel any better, Dad," Luke said as he opened the front door. "I need to find her."

Isaac eyed Luke for a few moments, then nodded. He grabbed one of Clara's shirts and tossed a bow and quiver through the air for Luke to catch. "Okay. We'll bring the dogs. With Boatswain's searching and Levin's protection skills, we should have a good chance of finding Clara and keeping her safe."

Luke and Isaac ran to the only secluded location on the island, agreeing that if Fade were to attack, they'd make sure to steal her away when no one was watching. The Rhondian clan sat on an island with roughly a three-mile radius and only a few hundred people living on it, so it offered plenty of places to pounce. Thankfully, getting Clara off said island without being seen in broad daylight would be almost impossible. Fade would almost certainly attack at night, so if they hadn't found her yet, Luke had time to get her to safety.

"Where you heading so fast?" one person called out.

Luke skidded to a stop, hoping whomever had called to them knew where his mom had gone.

Isaac followed suit. He waved and said, "Ammon! We need your help."

"I'm looking for Clara," Luke breathed, his chest tight. "Know w...w-where she is?"

Ammon stroked his dark beard. "I saw her an hour ago crossing the bridge to the mainland."

Luke's heart and stomach turned to mush then dropped out of his body when he looked at his dad, who wore an expression of deep fear. The mainland. She had to pick the exact moment she was in danger to go to the mainland. He knew Ray by acquaintance and only met the guy twice. He'd never seen Ray fight. He couldn't trust the man's ability to protect his mom well enough. Prior to the Day of Ashes, she'd been a diplomat and a lawyer, and while gritty and brave, she lacked hand-to-hand combat skills. If a group like Fade hunted her, Luke couldn't trust anyone nor assume anything.

"Where?" Luke barked at the man, unwilling to be polite. He raised the volume of his voice. "Which way did they go?"

"They turned right." The man glared at him. "Headed toward the inlet." Before Luke and Isaac left, the man shook his finger as if he remembered something. "You know, you're the second person to ask me where she is. Must be a popular day for her."

Luke ran off without thanking the man, but he heard Isaac doing so. He didn't care.

His mom was in danger.

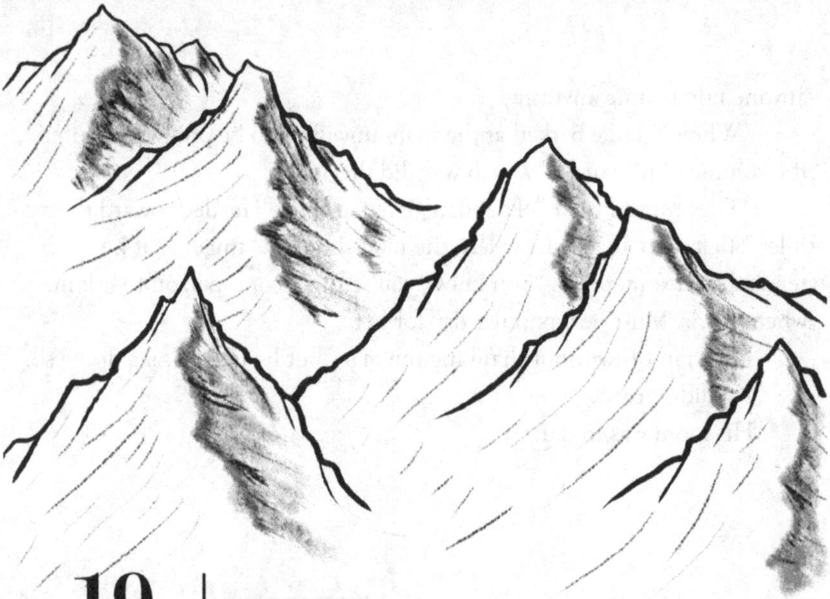

19 | SIBYL

When the universe began,
it looked upon your soul
and said, "This woman
shall be a warrior. She
shall banish the darkness.
And if she burns, she shall
fly home on scorched wings."

"Help him!"

Sibyl broke away from her conversation with Hunter, her cup of broth clattering on the counter top, and ran to Ian's side. He was thrashing again. The seizure lasted for seconds, yet they turned to minutes in her head as she tried to help him. It had only been three hours since Luke had left, and she used that as her gauge to count Ian's seizures.

They were up to four.

Ian's mother wept into her husband's shoulder as he stared at an empty space on the floor, pale.

After a minute, Ian calmed, and they were able to get him back onto the cot. Sibyl pulled the blanket over him, her hands trembling.

"I'm going to help you get better. We're going to fix you up."

He was unconscious, had been for over an hour, but she held onto the desperate hope that he'd get better. She rechecked his bandages, applied ointment, and settled down beside his cot opposite his parents. No one spoke.

Sibyl stared at Ian desperately hanging onto life. With his injuries and seizures, Sibyl doubted he'd survive the night and if he did, he'd be severely handicapped. She cried silent tears. The emotional toll hurt down into her soul, and she'd fallen too far into the pit of despair to claw her way out. Ian deserved more. Better care than what she could give. She'd normally take someone as injured as him to Soora, but in his condition and with the cold, she didn't dare. Instead, she closed her shop for the day, covered the windows to offer privacy for grieving and terrified loved ones, and made him as comfortable as possible.

The more she tried to understand the logic in attacking three innocent boys, the more she faded into a shell.

Hunter crouched beside Sibyl. "You're going to run yourself ragged if you don't take a break."

"No," she whispered. "I need to help him."

"It's okay to let him go."

Hunter gasped when Sibyl pulled him out of earshot. "I can't believe you would say something like that. He has just as much right to live as us."

"Yes, but..." Hunter glanced quickly from her to Ian then back again. "He's had four seizures in three hours, his fever is worse, his heart beat is weak, and he slipped into a coma an hour ago. You told me yourself that his prognosis isn't good. It's okay not to fix this."

"I have to."

"Why? There's nothing you can do."

Sibyl jerked her hands out to either side of her body. "I don't want him to hurt anymore."

With kind eyes, Hunter smiled. "Sibyl...he's already out of pain. You can't fix everything."

"Why not?"

"Because it's not possible. Because that's not how life works. And because you will lose yourself in the process."

She looked back at Ian and his parents beside him. The other two boys left an hour ago with their families. Was Ian in pain? Did his coma prevent that? Somehow, she had to stop him from dying, but she'd exhausted all remedies and now had to wait…for healing or death.

She smiled, the action a way to cope with the tornado inside her mind. "Look at you, all reflective and wise."

"I do study philosophy." Hunter shrugged. "Sibyl. I know you well enough to see through that smile. It won't work on me."

"I have to fix it, Hunter," Sibyl wept. "I told Ian's parent's he'd be okay. If he dies, it'll hurt forever."

"You can't control that. All you can control is how you respond."

Before Sibyl could say anything back, Ian's fifth – and final – seizure began.

Sibyl stared at Ian's cot, shaking. He wouldn't need it anymore. Outside, his mother cried, holding her son's clothes, folded and cleaned by Sibyl. It was the least she could do, after…

She spun away from the cot and hugged her body, crying. Why did I have to tell her it would all be okay? I should've kept my mouth shut.

The door opened, and Ian's mother walked in. Sibyl tensed, wiped her eyes, and stood her ground. She knew the look on the woman's face, the anger and mourning. Joy had the same one when she'd tried to kill Eloise several years ago.

Sibyl took a half-step back, her stomach hardening.

Ian's mother stopped and wrapped her arms around Sibyl. "Thank you for your kindness."

Sibyl broke. She cried big, ugly tears into Ian's mother's shoulder.

Ian's mother pulled away and smiled. "You did everything you could."

She had expected anger, resentment, and verbal attacks but not warmth. "Ian was lucky to have you as his mom," Sibyl whispered.

With a small, 'thank you,' the mourning mother left La Parfana. Sibyl stumbled into a chair and melted into it. She needed a stiff drink. Unfortunately, her choices were limited.

"After fourteen years," Sibyl mumbled as she poured half an inch of whiskey into a glass, "you'd think someone would have come out with champagne." She stared at the amber liquid. "Just once. I'd love to try it just once."

After she downed the less desired drink, Sibyl gathered up the bed clothes, treated them with her own stain remover concoction, and let them sit in the water to soak while she tended to her garden. She weeded the now dormant roses, watered the winter plants, and mixed a new batch of compost tea.

Once she cleaned off her hands, Sibyl sent Hunter home to study for his finals, and washed the blood from the bed sheets Ian had used, the water brown and sudsy. Sibyl sniffed as she worked, trying and failing to block the images of his final hours on earth. He only eighteen.

She wrung the sheets out and walked to her laundry shed to hang them inside.

Something stirred in the forest line.

Startled, Sibyl dropped the wet bundle in the dirt and reached for her spear behind her back...which wasn't there. Even a year and a half of being apart from it, she still hadn't gotten rid of the instinct.

In a fighting stance, Sibyl scanned the tree line and gritted her teeth. Someone appeared but remained in the shadows. They slumped to one side.

"Sibyl..."

Sibyl straightened. "God damn it, Luke. You made me drop my laundry in the dirt. I can't believe that you still insist on lurking—"

"Sibyl..."

"—in the shadows. I mean, come on! I'd think you'd be over that stage by now. There's no reason to hide because—"

"Sib—"

"What?" She turned on him with her hands on her hips. "I'm monologuing here. The least you could do is let me finish."

Luke emerged from the shadows, drenched in sweat. She blinked through the sun, her hand on her brow, and gasped. A bandage clung to his forehead.

In all the years that she'd known Luke, she'd never seen him cry. Tears covered his cheeks, his chin quivered, but in his eyes was a terrifying anger. Some, due to his size, feared him and she'd never understood why but now that she saw a glimpse of his seething, raw fury, she understood, and too terrified to move. If his eyes could change color, they'd be blood red. His fur lined jacket hung off his shoulders, his barrel chest heaved.

"What happened?"

The ends of Luke's trench coat slid across the knee-high bushes as he trudged forward until it fell and billowed around his ankles. Slow, methodical steps brought him to a stop several feet from her. Sibyl looked at him, forcing her body to stand still.

No matter how startling he looks, this is still Luke.

He bent forward and whispered, "They took her. They hurt Boatswain and I had to tell Levin to attack someone, something I swore I'd free him from." His face contorted from anger into sadness and Luke fell into Sibyl, a single sob leaving him. Luke burrowed his head onto her shoulder, trembling, and all she could do was stand there and listen to his whimpers and weeping.

"Wh-who?" Sibyl asked, her arms tight around him as questions swirled violently in her head. "What happened?"

On the outside, Sibyl remained calm, but on the inside, she was worn down. She'd barely cleaned up after Ian's death then Luke appeared at her doorstep, crying, with no context. Her mind numbed and she didn't even know if she was capable of emotion anymore.

"I w...w-was too late."

"Too late for what? Luke," she adjusted her hips, "they took your mom? Is Boatswain and Levin hurt? What happened?"

She felt him shake his head against her shoulder. Dread took hold and pulled her stomach in fifty different directions. "Okay..." she breathed out the words and hugged him tighter. "Are you ready to tell me what happened, at least?"

Again, Luke shook his head against her, but this time his shoulders trembled, and he took in several wheezing breaths.

Then he pulled her to the ground, grasping at her shoulders for support and she simply held him. He'd always been stalwart and strong, and emotionally even, although sometimes distant. Seeing him broken brought mist to her eyes.

"They took her. She's gone."

He'd already said that, but she kept her mouth shut and listened.

"I tried to stop them. Fade. Put up a good fight, too, but it wasn't enough, and I—I w...w-watched as they...kidnapped her." Luke groaned. "I'll never forgive myself."

Sibyl stiffened. "Luke," she cooed, hoping that her even, gentle tone would help. His mother was gone and she knew that hurt more than anything, so Sibyl didn't think changing her voice would even work. She still tried. "I'm so, so sorry. Come with me back to my shop."

Luke nodded and they stood together. She gathered up her laundry and when they got inside, she told Luke to wait while she deposited the laundry next to the wash basin to be cleaned again. When she returned, she found Luke sitting on the window seat at the storefront.

"Hey," she said as she sat beside him.

Luke glanced at her, his eyes wet, and looked away. She was used to emotionless reactions from him, but this was different. Broken.

"Hi."

"Tell me everything," Sibyl said gently.

Luke nodded. "Boatswain has a cut and a bump, but he's doing okay. Levin is fine...ish. I'm not sure if he'll relapse or not, but my dad's taking care of them. I couldn't be there anymore. Seeing B's injury and my mom's things without her there, knowing I could have protected them both," Luke linked his fingers together behind his head and shook, "it tears at me."

They sat together and for a while, neither spoke.

Within her shop, she found peace and solitude. Sibyl knew Luke preferred it as well, and didn't want to rob that from him, so she sat in silence.

"You can sit here as long as you like," she finally said and took a step to leave. "I'm going to—"

"Stay." Luke blurted out. "Please? It's just...I can't stand to be alone right now."

Surprised, she sat on the bench, surrounded by winter plants, and listened to him speak.

"There's something I have to tell you." Luke used the heel of his hand to wipe at his eyes. "My mom wasn't clear on it, but before she got...stolen...she said that Fade is searching for Joy, or at least, the reason Fade is here has something to do w...w-with Joy. But why would my mom even know Joy?"

"Oh my God."

Once again, the scientist that ruined Bannack's life, caused the death of Eloise's parents, and destroyed the minds and bodies of countless people in her horrid experiments trying to save her young teenaged son haunted the root cause of their problems.

"I couldn't find out more before we had to run. Sibyl," he peered at her for help. "I'm terrified they're going to kill her once they get what they want out of her."

She grabbed his shoulders and pulled him against her, his surprised inhale puffing against the fur of her collar. "You did everything you could to stop them."

"It w...w-wasn't enough," Luke whispered, his voice strung tight.

"Then," Sibyl pulled away and grabbed the side of his face, staring into his beautiful eyes, wet with tears, "what are you going to do about it?"

Luke blinked. "I..." he looked away, "I don't know."

She pressed her lips to his forehead and did her best to harden her voice so he could pick up on the seriousness of her words. "This is what you're going to do."

When Luke's eyes found her face, anguish within them, her voice faltered. Not from sadness, but from the anger swirling in her body. They hurt her Luke. She'd never been so protective of another human before but with him...he was hers and to hell with anyone who hurt him.

"You're going to bring her back," Sibyl said. "You're going to fight. Never give Fade the satisfaction of breaking you down. I know you and you are stronger than anything they could ever do to you."

Honestly, underneath her empathy for Luke lingered an anger that extended beyond Clara's kidnapping. It began as a child when Fade almost annihilated her country, and indirectly caused the separation of her from her family. They were to blame for every ounce of pain and trauma that came after the Day of Ashes, for every single death, and Luke's anguish.

"But w...w-what if she..." He couldn't finish. Didn't have to. Sibyl knew exactly what he meant.

"Then you will live like she wanted you to: with kindness and to the fullest."

"I don't w...w-want her to be—" Luke stopped and ducked his head, his jaw working.

"I know you won't give up trying to bring her back." She hugged him again. Into his mass of waves, she whispered, "if you want me to, I can come with you when you go back home."

"Thank you. I w...w-would like that."

20 | SIBYL

Isaac stared for a long time when Sibyl and Luke entered the house. He sat on the couch in the living room, Boatswain at his feet and Levin sprawled out, all legs, with his head on Boatswain's hip. Unwilling to get up from Isaac's side, Levin lazily wagged his tail and Boatswain released a whine of greeting.

Her heart sank.

It was beautiful to see the dogs offering Isaac emotional support, but the cost of it had been too great.

"Hey guys," Isaac finally announced once Sibyl had settled beside Luke. Then Isaac inhaled loudly, stood up, and walked to the window. When his fingers wrapped around the window jamb, the glass rattled slightly.

Sibyl glanced at Luke, wondering how to proceed. Luke put his hand on her knee, his eyes red-rimmed and chin quivering. He shook his head, unable to speak, and Sibyl knew he needed her to lead the discussion.

"Sir?" Sibyl asked. "I hate to ask...what do you know of Clara's past?"

Isaac flinched at the mention of his wife's name. "Not much." He turned and his eyes were dry of tears and dull, the look so uncharacteristic it hurt Sibyl's stomach. Isaac continued, "But I'll tell you what I know."

When he sat, leg crossed over his knee, Isaac spoke slowly. "Your mother was a lawyer before the Day of Ashes, tasked with representing the United States pharmaceutical companies in other countries. One such company, McCormick Regional Laboratories, was her newest client and they were making groundbreaking strides with their flagship drug, a serum meant to heal broken or damaged synapses in the brain." Isaac paused, closed his eyes, and swallowed. "The project was known as Project Nemosyne, named after the Greek goddess of memory."

Sibyl couldn't move for a moment, shocked that what connected Clara to Fade was the exact thing keeping Eloise alive. "Her past is directly related to Joy and Eloise's parents?"

Isaac looked to Luke. "She chose to hide this from you. I vowed to never tell you without her consent unless danger threatened her life. So, here we are."

Luke's hand tightened on Sibyl's knee painfully and she gave a quiet 'ow' only Luke could hear. He removed his hand.

"Do you know if they will harm her?" Sibyl asked.

Isaac shook his head. "I don't know what Fade wants, but I do know that it has something to do with Joy's son."

"Seth? But he's traveling the world. There's no way anyone could f—"

Oh. Had the reason they'd gone after Clara been because they couldn't find Seth? Something still didn't add up. "Sir?" Sibyl asked and Isaac met her gaze. "Why does Fade think she knows anything about Seth?"

Isaac sighed and took a step, wincing as if nursing an unseen injury. "Come with me."

Worried about Luke's emotional state with the revelation his mother had a secret life he knew nothing about, Sibyl followed Isaac downstairs, Luke not far behind.

Sibyl paused on the first landing and grabbed his hand. "Are you okay?"

"I...w...w-will be."

Isaac led them into Clara's office. Papers littered the floor and desk, some décor littered the floor and smashed, and her flower garden destroyed.

Luke picked up the handle of a shattered mug, the pieces painted with very young hands. His grip shook but when Sibyl's touched his shoulder, he calmed, and looked at his dad. "They were here again?"

Solemn, Isaac nodded. "I assume when we were out looking for Clara."

Luke groaned under his breath then said, "I'm going after her."

"Absolutely not!" Isaac's bark frightened the dogs. Boatswain jerked and lifted his head from the floor and Levin growled quietly.

"And w...w-why not?" Luke asked, his hand on Levin's shoulders until the dog relaxed.

Sibyl watched, refusing to step in and stop Luke from releasing energy she knew had been building. If words turned to insults or if she sensed a physical fight between them, she'd step in, but she had no intention of controlling the situation.

For the first time, Isaac's chin quivered. "I'm not—" His voice cracked. "I can't lose you, too."

"Dad..." Luke pulled his father into an embrace. "I'm not going anywhere," he whispered. "Promise."

"We'll figure out what to do, Mr. Blackwood," Sibyl said from her spot by the desk. She glanced again around the room. "I'll have Hunter get some people together to tidy her office up. You focus on you."

"Thank you, but Clara's very particular about things. Cleaning her office will give me something to do."

She sensed he wasn't completely honest, but couldn't be sure.

Isaac smiled at them both. "We will do something, just not half-assed and with more reinforcements." He looked at his son through the corner of his eyes. "You were too young to fully understand when Fade destroyed our country. If they are anything like what they were before, you do not want to go after your mother without a plan."

Luke folded his arms. "And w...w-what about the information about Seth?"

"I don't know what they want him for. Your mother is the only person, beside Seth, who knows where he went. Perhaps he never told her the whole truth, I don't know, but if Fade took her, then..." Isaac paused, closed his eyes and inhaled, "they might try to get the information out of her."

"Then let's form a search party and follow her."

Isaac paced. "We need to find out where they're heading, first."

Sibyl listened to the exchange, trying to figure out if they were missing anything. She thought of Isaac's brother, Mason, who ran the Compound. "Didn't your brother fight them during the wars that happened after the Day of Ashes?" Sibyl asked.

Isaac stopped. "He did."

"So, he'd know some of their hiding places and patterns, right?"

"That's true." Isaac wagged his finger lazily in the air, his eyes darting around as he thought. "This is what we're going to do. I'm going to pay a visit to Mason tomorrow. You," he pointed to Luke, "take a tracker out to the abduction spot and see if you can follow the trail."

Sibyl suspected that'd be her. Isaac didn't know she was one of the best trackers in the area or else he would've asked Sibyl directly.

"Alright," Luke said. "I'll see if I can find the best one."

He side-eyed Sibyl and his eyes sparkled.

Isaac shuffled around the room to pick up the strewn items and a broken chair. Luke and Sibyl helped.

When they'd finished organizing the room again, Isaac put his hand on Luke's shoulder. "We'll find her and bring her back."

Luke wrapped his fingers around his dad's wrist and gave a reassuring smile. "Yes."

Isaac turned to Sibyl. "Thank you for caring for my son."

She blushed and smiled. "You're welcome."

After Isaac left, Sibyl scanned the room then turned toward Luke. He sank into his mother's chair. "I'd like to know w...w-where the hell the person is that did this," he motioned to the ruined office, "and took my mom so I can—"

Sibyl laced her fingers between his. "You'll find your mom. You have Isaac, Boatswain, Levin, and a whole bunch of clan members to choose from. Focus on that." Sibyl's hand touched his cheek. "And you have me." She smiled, tears misting her eyes at the words. "Your anger is good. Use it to do whatever you can to find Fade and bring your mom back."

"I w...w-will."

To lighten the mood a bit, Sibyl questioned, "So, who are you going to ask?"

"The tracker?" He leaned back. "I have a few options I'm considering."

She leaned on his knees. "Can I do anything to help make that decision a bit easier?"

Luke absent mindedly brushed her cheek with his thumb. "My first pick might be a little busy at her shop right now, so I'll probably ask someone else."

Sibyl feigned insult then shrugged. "Yeah. You're probably right. Except, I seem to remember that this shop owner has an apprentice who would be more than happy to bring more pay home to his family."

"You think so?" Luke asked, straightening. "Think she'd help?"

"I'm sure if you ask nicely."

Luke suppressed a smile that tugged gently at the corner of his mouth. "I need your help, Sibyl." His eyes glistened. "I can't do this on my own."

"I'd love to. The shop's not open tomorrow, so that's covered. I just need to drop by Hunter's on the way to my shop and let him know I'm leaving. If we go now, we can get a head start before the trail runs cold or gets snowed on."

"I'll just leave the dogs with the neighbor."

"Are you sure?" Sibyl's concern made her eyebrows knit together. "You don't want them with you?"

Luke inhaled and closed his eyes. "No. I know they'll be stressed with me leaving, but I'd rather that than placing them in danger."

He still hadn't told her exactly what had happened out there with his dogs, and she didn't expect him to. She knew it hurt. Leaving them with someone, even though he trusted them, Sibyl knew would eat at him.

He cares more for those dogs than his own emotional comfort.

Sibyl's heart warmed.

You are a beautiful person, Luke Blackwood.

21 | LUKE

Luke waited in La Parfana for Sibyl, inspecting her items so he didn't have to think about his hands shaking and insides trembling. She hadn't been upstairs long, only minutes, but being left alone in a quiet shop without much to distract him from his eagerness to find his mom had him on edge. He adjusted and readjusted his arm guard, bow slung over his shoulder.

Footsteps came from the stairs, and Sibyl appeared, bundled in a thick coat, gloves, and boots. She adjusted a spear on her back. "Ready?"

"Where'd you get the spear?"

She chuckled. "You didn't see the two crossed over each other on my wall the other day?"

He thought back to the night they were interrupted by Ian and his parents, and honestly couldn't recall any spears.

Luke gave her an apologetic shrug. "Nope."

She laughed, the corners of her eyes crinkling, and gave him a quick peck on the cheek. "My sweet, dense man."

The heat of her kiss lingered on his skin, and he tentatively touched it, surrounded by everything Sibyl, wanting to stay in the shop so the cold wouldn't freeze her touch from his face. It had to be done, though, so Luke joined Sibyl outside.

Luke led the way to the abduction site, thankful no snow had fallen since. As they drew closer, his nerves and shoulders tightened.

Sparse memories flashed in his mind. The arrow through Ray's back as Luke tried to help him to safety. The rage in his blood when Boatswain had been injured. Watching his mother pulled away by her hair with Luke on the ground, arms forced to his sides by the ball and chain wrapped around his torso. Helplessness. Fury. Anguish.

"Luke?"

Sibyl touched his arm and he jerked away, inhaling sharply. She peered at him, worry settled in her brow and eyes. "If you need to take a pause, we can."

"I'm okay."

She nodded.

What would they find? Would Sibyl be able to track his mother and her abductors well enough? He didn't doubt her abilities, but the rational side of his brain fought with the irrational, trying to convince him bringing Sibyl along would put her in danger.

When they reached their destination, Luke's stomach was a nauseous mess and his muscles sore from being so tense. As if she knew, Sibyl rubbed his back.

"We'll find her."

She sounded so sure, so confident they would succeed, but they were losing daylight. Would they go back home when they couldn't see anymore? Would the trail even be there when they returned?

"Show me the exact spot where she was taken."

Luke brought her to the grove where they'd been attacked. His body ached in remembrance.

"She helped me up here, after I got hit with the chain. Then we ran this way."

Sibyl got to work, crouching and touching the indentations in the ground. Blood from the Fade members covered the leaf litter and sparse snow. She moved on, unphased by the signs of death, and mumbled to herself as she crouched a few feet from him, inspecting some crushed leaves.

"This way," she said.

There was no stopping her now. He followed, completely trusting Sibyl to lead him to his mother, and the anticipation neared painful levels. He was a grown man, but holding his mother was the only thing he wanted to do. The knowledge – or a hope? – that Fade kept her alive drove him to keep pushing through the anxiety and fear. Would he find her body in a river the next day? Or pieces of—

"No," Luke said abruptly, a cloud of air puffing around his face, and Sibyl turned around from inspecting a broken bush branch. He waved his hand at her. "Sorry. My nerves are fried."

She gave him a soft smile. "I understand. Would you like me to tell you what I'm looking for? Maybe that would help?"

He needed some distraction, so he nodded.

"I'm looking for here signs of breakage. Like this," she pointed to a branch. "Now, typically I would assume this is an animal, but I can see the boot prints, so I can safely assume that they took her this way."

She continued talking and Luke continued to listen, her voice slowly but surely smoothing out his worries. It was nice to listen with no expectations to speak or please someone. Frozen wind whipped through his hair and he pulled the hood up to block as much cold as he could.

Sibyl stopped abruptly and bent to pick something up. She handed a small bead to Luke. "Does this look familiar?"

It was the size of his index fingernail and blue. He rubbed the dirt from it and his fogged head cleared enough to remember. He looked at Sibyl. "It's from the bracelet she'd been w...w-wearing."

"Your mom's leaving us breadcrumbs."

Luke's heart sped up and he had to put in significant effort to reel in his excitement and hope.

They followed his mom's trail for almost an hour longer, Luke pocketing beads as Sibyl handed them to him.

Eventually, the trail stopped.

That didn't deter Sibyl. She crouched at the meadow's edge, squinting in the twilight.

"I can see the trail here in the grass but the forest is too dark to keep going through it." Her shoulders fell as she peered ahead. "We're going to have to try again tomorrow."

Luke scanned the forest, noting the darkness, and he shivered. He needed to hold something tangible, maybe then his growing fear could ease. It wasn't easy to stay calm when he just wanted to fold in on himself. How would he last? How could anyone stay afloat when their mind and soul were drowning?

"I know I've asked this a lot," Sibyl stood from her crouch and walked over, her touch on his face aggravating his need to be held, "but are you okay?"

"I'm fine." Luke moved his gaze from her and trembled against the cold.

She sighed. "No, you're not."

He looked at her and narrowed his eyes, his insides screaming. "You keep asking, yet you often can tell w...w-when I'm not. It's pointless to lie to you."

She blinked then smiled. He never could phase her with his words, no matter how grumpy or irritable he was, which infuriated him to no end.

And he was hopelessly attracted to it.

"Because," she leaned in, "you're easier to read than a book, honey."

He couldn't move. Honey? She never called him any pet names. It was nice. "I...I think there's a hunting cabin nearby."

Sibyl stepped back and he almost pulled her into him to stop her from leaving. "Good," she said, and chuckled. "Because I'm freezing."

They walked together, Sibyl keeping up with his long strides as he made his way through the forest. Their breath escaped in clouds and his thighs were beginning to register the cold through his double layer of pants.

After about thirty minutes and not too far from the trail, they arrived at the cabin sitting on the edge of a lake he'd used only a handful of times on his long hunting trips, an old remnant of before the Day of Ashes. The cabin probably hosted people as a vacation home, and wasn't big, but had two small bedrooms, a couch, wood burning stove, and adequate insulation.

"You find some blankets and I'll get the wood," Sibyl said and left.

Luke agreed, regretting not going with her. He didn't want to be alone, the need to be comforted by her presence overwhelming. In a daze, he rifled through the chests at the foot of each bed, eventually finding two blankets tucked away. A flint and steel, some pickled food items, and hard grain bars made with honey to bond the ingredients were in the cupboards.

Luke sat at the table, staring at the pickles, when Sibyl returned with some kindling and a bucket of lake water. He looked at her but she didn't seem to notice and set up the wood for a fire with the flint and steel Luke had placed on the stove. Then she poured the water into a pot and set it down to boil.

"Sibyl?" Luke asked when she'd built the fire up. He stood and walked over to her.

"Yes?"

Her hands were ungloved, and palms pointed toward the fire to warm them. He wanted them on his body. He needed her comfort or he would burst at the seams.

"Thank you for helping me."

She turned her body to him and put her hands on her thighs. "Always."

Slowly, Luke reached for her, vibrating with the need to be touched, comforted, and warmed from the inside out.

She welcomed his touch, her fingers slipping over the fleshy bump of his syndactyly scars. Sibyl paused and looked at the scar lines between his fingers.

"I forgot these were here," she muttered.

He should have kept his hands hidden better. Embarrassed, Luke tried to pull away but her grip tightened gently and he stopped short, a gasp on the tip of his tongue at the soft look she gave him.

"I wish you wouldn't hide them so much."

Luke stared, mouth open, and kicked himself for thinking she would be anything but receptive. His adoration for her swelled in his stomach. She was so beyond perfect, he wondered how in the hell he'd taken so long to realize it.

She accepted and loved with no conditions.

Bore her heart to the world.

Driven by a mad desire for Sibyl and for comfort, Luke kissed her.

She made a surprised noise in her throat then sighed. The air crackled and he immediately reached for her.

22 | SIBYL

In all my life, I shall never forget
your body against mine,
your whispers in my ear,
the touch of your love.
I love you.
I love you.
This truth is written in the stars.

Luke's large hands slipped into her hair, and she clung desperately to him as he explored her mouth, pulling moans from her at his touch. His hand gripped her waist, the other braced her head, and there, on the floor, he deepened the kiss.

"Let me love you," he whispered, humming through the words.

Sibyl's body shivered and sung in response. He pinned her wrists over her head, and with his free hand, cupped her breast through her shirt. She gasped, her back arched, and arousal warmed between her legs. She'd been hoping, silently begging, for Luke to initiate their intimacy.

Luke moaned and pressed against her. "God, damn it, Sibyl." He shuddered. "Do you know how much I need you?"

A wicked smile blossomed on her lips. "I can't miss it."

Luke smirked, thrust his hips gently, suspended himself above her on his knees and pulled off his coat and shirt. Those beautiful muscles, taut from the strain of hovering over her body while on his knees, called her hands to them, and she explored it all. His torso that dipped and curved. The veins of his arm. His shoulders. The hair of his chest. A riveting power rippled through Sibyl when Luke groaned deep in his chest in response to her greedy fingers.

They stood and tumbled into a bedroom. His touches grew feverish, taking and taking while Sibyl pleaded, helpless and flooding with need. When he slid his tongue into her mouth, her hips rolled of their own volition.

"Wait," Sibyl gasped.

He pulled away, searching her eyes with heavy lids.

"Pants off only."

The glorious sound of a belt buckle drew her eyes to his hands, and she watched as he did as she commanded, one side of her bottom lip pinched in her teeth as his cock slipped free. The girth of it had her nearly climbing him before she'd taken her clothes off.

To reward him, she slipped her own pants off, basking on the bed with her thick thighs and long legs. His eyes darkened and he took a step.

She lifted her hand. "No." Luke stopped immediately, his smile making his enjoyment obvious, and he slid his eyes to her mouth. She whispered, "If you stay there, I'll take my shirt off for you."

Luke stilled and watched, lazily stroking his cock, as Sibyl rolled her hips while removing her shirt. When she turned around to give him full view of her backside, a noise of pleasure rolled out of Luke, and she couldn't help but smile.

With everything except her bralette gone, she allowed him to approach, smiling and giggling beside herself as he closed the gap between them with startling speed and playfully grabbed at her.

"You intoxicate me," Luke whispered, his voice gravely and dark. "I desire every part of you. Every," he kissed her neck, "single," he dragged his teeth across her collar bone, "piece."

Luke's hands slid to her waist, and he jerked her against him, Sibyl chuckling. He smiled with one side of his mouth. Sibyl watched intently as he knelt and dragged his nose and lips across her belly, his fingers firm on her curved hips, intent on keeping her trapped for an eternity in a palace of pleasure.

She shuddered.

He looked at her. Those dark eyes and lashes, hair brushing over the bridge of his nose, and watched her with a reverence that made her tremble. When he opened his mouth, he spoke the words of angels.

"I w...w-want to w...w-worship you."

"I know," Sibyl caressed his cheek with the back of her finger. "The way your eyes darken, and you swell just for me. I see that look in your eyes, the one of torment at my touch. I've had my fun, now I want you to show me what you can do while you say my name."

He anchored her to him, twisted, and Sibyl landed with a bounce on her back, her hair falling in tendrils on the comforter. Luke bent over and played with the ache between her legs, with his fingers, his tongue, and light brushes of his teeth. She twitched and moaned. Her back arched.

"Shit," Sibyl moaned. "I want you in me. Now."

Luke leaned in, his breath puffing at her ear. "You made me wait. Now you must."

Sibyl laughed. "I hate you."

"I'm counting on it." He looked at her with a reverence she'd never seen before. "I'd like you to despise me so much that by the time I'm finished, you are annihilated. You're going to hate me as I haunt your dreams. And once at home," he licked a deviant, sizzling line up her thigh, "you'll take it out on me for days because you're so furious."

"I can think of no better way to punish you."

He pressed against her, slid his hand up her back, and Sibyl gasped when he tugged the last bit of clothing over her head and threw it across the room. No barriers stood between them now and he teased and teased, making her beg and whimper, retreating the moment climax drew near. She swore at him. He chuckled in his devious way, and came back to do it all over again.

"You...fucking bastard."

Luke hummed. "There's your dirty mouth."

He slipped into her, a possessive moan falling from his lips that morphed into her name. Over and over he whispered to her. His slow thrusts turned feverish and she held onto him as if she would fall if she let go.

Expletives tumbled from his mouth. Sibyl scratched at his back, growling, their bodies moving without thought, and tension built within her. Trembling and whimpering, Sibyl reached to her clit, circling and rubbing until her legs twitched.

"That's it," Luke breathed. "That's it. Let me see."

She increased the pressure and speed of her finger, whimpering underneath Luke as he kept a rhythm that sped up when she commanded. He left lingering kisses on her neck and mouth, his beard scratching her sizzling skin.

Moans of pleasure exploded from her. She rode the wave, jerking and gasping, all the way to her climax.

Luke was patient, gentle, his arms quivering as her body clenched around him. He pumped lazily into her, forehead pressed against hers, chest rubbing against her nipples.

Sibyl laid beneath him, lost in ecstasy, limbs heavy and tingling. Helpless. Luke pulled out and rubbed his cock with tight, hard strokes, and finished on her stomach. She glanced between their bodies to watch his cum land on her stomach. He shuddered, and groaned, back muscles gloriously tight beneath her touch. Powerful, and all hers.

Luke bent and kissed her gently upon the lips. She was slow to respond. Her fingers twitched first and she wanted to touch him again, but her body still rode the wave remnants.

"There," he breathed, "now you have no excuse not to despise me."

"...I loathe you."

"Good," Luke chuckled.

As Luke leaned back onto his heels, Sibyl met his eyes, swiped a bit of his cum onto her finger, and slowly licked it off. Luke's eyes widened; his chest heaved.

"Good God, Sibyl." Luke leaned down and smashed his lips to hers, pulling her mouth open with his thumb on her chin, and flicked his tongue inside. She curled around him, smiling and happy.

They cleaned up, and settled back in bed, their bodies warm and skin touching. Before she fell asleep pressed against him, he whispered a poem to her with his arm underneath her neck. She didn't know where the words came from, but she wouldn't complain.

"Rise like the sun. Claim your place in the clouds, paint your colors upon the canvas, light the world with who you are, and shout to the earth, 'I am here. I am power. I am Phoenix.'"

Sibyl awoke, buried in a nest of blankets and another human. She couldn't tell where he ended and she began. It made her smile.

Luke's face, in sleep, looked different. Typically, his eyes were intense and his mouth tight, but as he lay beside her, holding her with a familiar possessiveness she was only just getting acquainted with, those sharp lines were gone, replaced by gentle, soft curves. As she brushed the hair from his face, he opened his eyes.

"Hello," Sibyl said and smiled, pressing her cheek against the pillow.

He tightened his grip and brought her close with a single motion, and kissed her forehead. "Good morning. Breakfast?"

"Mmm. That sounds good."

Sibyl and Luke, wrapped in their furs again to protect against the cold cabin interior before a fire burned bright, ate the grain bars and pickled eggs from the cupboards, stealing tiny glances at each other. She saw Luke in an entirely new light. Their intimacy, in one single act, had brought new realizations. She loved the power he gave her without hesitation and most of all, perhaps they were finally figuring out how to make a relationship work.

Insecurity that she was wrong set in and she pulled her legs to her chest. She might be getting too ahead of herself. Luke stood and drank from the water bucket, some liquid trailing from the corner of his mouth down his neck. Sibyl swallowed.

I wonder what he'd say if I asked him to take me right here?

Now he'd gone and done it. He'd unlocked a part of her she kept hidden, even from herself, and now that he'd shown he wanted every bit of her, it no longer needed protecting. It was awake and so ready.

"So, how was it sleeping with a human instead of dogs?"

Luke swallowed and wiped his mouth. He didn't answer her, only dropped the ladle into the pot, walked to the table, grabbed the back of the chair she sat on, and bent over her. His arms, large and muscled, blocked her view of everything except him.

The pulse in his neck moved.

Sibyl held in a breath, the memory of his glorious mouth still fresh in her mind and waited for something to happen. He gave her a gentle kiss, inhaling her scent as he did so.

"Absolutely perfect."

Sibyl blushed. He pulled away and she grabbed him before he could go too far, her heart pounding in her ears as his gaze locked into her. She, selfishly but unashamedly, wanted him for as long as he wanted her, but they couldn't stay in the cabin much longer. So, she grabbed Luke's jaw with her long fingers, and smiled.

"Let's get out of here and find your mom, okay?"

It took a few minutes to dress for warmth and put out the fire, and soon they were back on the trail, the sunlight slowly warming the frozen dew. Sibyl quickly picked back up on the signs of Fade and Clara's travels, recognizing the tell-tale signs of a smaller human – Clara – digging their heels into the earth while the other, larger footed one – some Fade member – pulled her along. At some point, Clara had been struck or shoved to the ground, because the earth and sticks were indented where a body had fallen and rolled. She didn't tell Luke, though.

After a couple hours, the trail ran cold. They bounded across a creek, using the stones as steps only to find out some animal had lumbered through, shifting the footprints. She couldn't find anything. She even made Luke wait by the river as she walked the perimeter, trying to find something, anything, that would point them in the right direction. Nothing.

Stomach nauseous, Sibyl sat on a rock and put her forehead into her hands. "I can't go back and tell him. I can't."

She knew how much finding his mother meant to him and now she had to break the news.

"Sibyl?"

Shoot.

Bushes moved and Luke appeared. Why hadn't he waited?

"Find the trail?"

"Uh...no."

That's when his face turned from curiosity to dread. "It's gone cold. Hasn't it."

She nodded, worried about his reaction, but he simply sat on the nearest boulder, picked up a small rock, and hurled it into the river.

"I promise I looked," Sibyl knelt in front of him, his jaw working and face turned away, and fought with her voice to stay calm. Of course, he was angry. He'd put his trust in her and she'd let him down.

Luke looked at her and his expression softened. "You did your best. The fuckers know how to cover their markings."

"It wasn't even them. At least, not completely. Some animal destroyed it."

Despite his reassuring gaze, she still worried he was hiding his displeasure. Her voice, frantic and higher pitched than normal, didn't want to calm down.

She paced until Luke's hands were on her arms, stopping her.

"Sibyl. Pause. You're giving me an ulcer—"

"But the trail to your mom. It went cold and—"

"I don't blame you!"

Oh...Oh! She stared at him. That's when she realized she'd been completely stupid. They'd known each other for so long, and he'd more than proven she could trust him with her words.

"You looked so mad, though."

"I was. I am. Not at you, though. Never at you." He pulled her into him and caressed the back of her head. "Do you realize how perfect you are? You have done everything you possibly can to make sure everyone around you is safe, happy, and comfortable. You've neglected yourself a bit, but everyone's a work in progress."

Tears stung her nose as they formed in her eyes.

Luke continued, "The only time I have ever seen you take without first giving is last night." He pulled away and wiped a tear from her cheek, tilted her head up so she wasn't staring at her feet anymore, and gave her a kiss. "I want more of selfish Sibyl."

She released a wet chuckle and buried her face into his animal fur coat. "I'll try."

"Good. Now," Luke grabbed her hand, "let's head home and see if my dad has come back from the Compound." Luke paused abruptly, staring off into the distance as if he'd stepped on a landmine.

"Luke?"

"I..." A glistening sheen of tears caught the daylight and he blinked twice. "I can't move."

For a split second, she didn't understand, but then... "Because of what happened?"

He nodded.

Sibyl briefly squeezed his hand. "I'll be with you."

"Somehow, that doesn't help." He glanced at her apologetically. "Does that make me an asshole."

"No. You're scared. It makes sense."

"More than scared. I may have nightmares."

Even though she didn't think it'd help, Sibyl leaned against him.

"You can stay above my shop with the dogs, if it helps, until you're ready to go back home."

"No. Thank you." Luke reached around, grabbed the back of her head, and pulled her against his lips, kissing right above her eyebrow. "But, no. I need to go through this. My dad needs me right now and I can't think about just me."

Sibyl smiled and let out a single, breathy chuckle. "You've changed."

He watched her but his eyes didn't twinkle as he said, "Have I?"

Sibyl peered at him, her chest tight, but she kept smiling reassuringly. "I only wish it was better circumstances."

"Me too." He tried a step. "Oh good. Let's go."

As they walked, Sibyl hung behind him so she could think.

Am I expecting him to be too much like Peter? Even now, when he's shown me countless times he's not?

Luke pushed aside a branch and stepped under it.

He wants to see more of my selfish side?

Can I actually do that?

She jogged in the tall grass to catch up to him as he left the meadow near the cabin and entered the forest. Luke put his hand out behind him without looking back, completely trusting she would grab onto it. He knew her so well, didn't he?

"W...W-What happened between you and Peter?" Luke asked and rubbed his thumb on the top of her hand.

Sibyl stopped, her heartbeat trapped in her ears. "Oh. Uh...that feels like forever ago."

Luke turned around. "Your worry over me finding out that you lost the trail didn't sound like you are protecting me. You know I'm stronger than that. W...W-Will you tell me? Please?" He paused then added, "although, I've w...w-waited for you to be ready and can for longer if you need."

Could she? Even though Peter was long gone from her life, his effect remained, festering.

"It doesn't matter really anymore."

"Doesn't matter? Sibyl." He stepped closer and when she pulled back, he stopped. "You're still affected by w...w-what he did to you. It does matter."

She glanced away. The air changed, grew heavy, and Sibyl hugged her body.

He wants to know but my mouth won't move.

If she didn't figure out how to speak when she needed and wanted to, they didn't have a future together. The thought of that possibility made her nauseous.

Luke brought her face back to his with a light touch of a knuckle. Melting into him was a very good option; to just blow off everything he hoped she'd share, but this was Luke. He was proving to be a safe place. She wanted to trust him with her secrets, even though her body threatened to explode, her nerves the fuse, and words that would come from her mouth the detonator.

"...Okay." Sibyl sat on a nearby log, Luke sitting opposite her. "I can't do this with you looking at me."

Luke, without hesitation, flicked on his hood and turned so his back faced her. The pressure on Sibyl's chest lifted a bit, and in its place settled a ping of adoration for Luke.

"I tried so hard to keep us together. Every single part of our relationship was me trying to stay because I stupidly believed couples were supposed to support each other through even the hard days – he had a lot, by the way – and work through struggles the other had to make our bond stronger. The bad days were hard, but the good days were beautiful and made the hard days that much harder. Peter, he..." Sibyl sighed and rubbed her palms together, "made fun of me when I talked to my plants, refused to talk to me for days when Hunter first started working with me. I..." She eyed Luke's back, trying desperately to stop shaking by clenching her fists. "I think that he felt threatened by that. It was fine for a bit, but as we got further along in our relationship, if I did anything he didn't like he'd make me...feel small."

All the while she spoke, Luke stayed turned around, his shoulders tightening and the hands on his knees balling into tight fists.

"The worst part was the spear..." Sibyl tried to continue but her voice caught in her throat. She swallowed. "...he...I was so stupid! God! How could I have even thought he'd be a decent person. I knew he bullied people as a kid, but I thought he'd grown out of it."

Luke flinched as if he'd been punched but said nothing.

"Peter sold my spear without my knowledge, then lied, saying it had been stolen, and I believed him!" A hazy blur covered the world around her as tears dropped onto her thighs. "I didn't find out until I randomly ran into the merchant who bought it off him. Then Peter lied again, but by then, I was too frightened of him to say anything." Her hands shook and she shoved them underneath her thighs.

Luke cursed under his breath.

"I lost so much of my life being with him." She lost her composure. It felt good to cry, not for Peter but for the loss of herself. "I want myself back. Be like I was before Peter."

Luke turned, only his eyes visible over his high collar. "Can I hug you?"

She nodded and Luke pulled her into him, pressed his face into the top of her shoulder, and sighed. He held her, the trickling river over smooth stones the only sound around them.

"Peter deserved none of your kindness," Luke whispered into her hair. "He was a small boy who turned into a small man and abused you."

Sibyl nodded.

Luke's eyes sparkled, like they always did when he didn't smile, but that was the secret with him. He didn't show expressive joy like other people did; it was all in the eyes.

It's you and me against the world.

They stood and walked together in silence, listening to the cold ground and dead leaves crunch, and Luke held her close, occasionally pressing his mouth to the side of her head. A few birds sang, but mostly the forest stayed quiet.

Luke paused, listening.

"What is it?" Sibyl asked as he tensed beside her.

"Something's out there."

The hunter in him activated and, unfortunately, she couldn't pick out what he noticed. She knew how to search for past commotion, not future. That didn't stop her from flicking her spear forward, the tip of it slicing through the broad leaves of a nearby bush. Behind her came the creak of a bow draw and seconds later, Luke's back pressed against hers. They were one. A team. The action so effortless, she couldn't imagine them being anything else.

Her head swiveled and she stepped away for just a moment. A strange noise whispered in the air. Luke snatched her back and she collided with his chest right before a knife, handle wrapped in leather and a piece of paper tied to the hilt, thunked into the closest tree trunk.

Sibyl yelped.

Luke hissed, drew his bow, and jerked his head to the canopy.

"We want no trouble!" Sibyl called. When no sound came, she tightened her grip on the spear shaft and called into the boughs. "We're just passing through."

Tense seconds passed. Luke and Sibyl both shared glances.

"You're Clara's son," echoed a young woman's voice, someone barely over the threshold of adulthood.

Sibyl's vision tightened, and she whirled around to look at Luke, standing in the trail center, his teeth bared, and body crouched, arrow pointed up.

"W...W-Who's asking?" he bellowed.

"An ally. When you return home, show the photo wrapped on the hilt to your friend, Bannack. He'll understand."

It took a few moments for Luke to pick the knife up. When he did, a metal tin, much like the ones Sibyl used for her rouges, clattered through the branches and landed on the soft earth. She stared at the item as if it may explode at any moment.

"Why Bannack?" Sibyl whispered to Luke and he shook his head without looking at her, his attention still on the dark canopy of trees. Whoever hid up there knew how to hide. Sibyl glanced at the knife in the tree. A sting of realization hit her stomach hard: if the woman wanted to kill them, she probably would have with the knife.

"In three days," the woman called out and Sibyl snapped her attention back, "me and three other Fade operatives will move your mother over Silence Pass. If you want any chance of saving her, I suggest you gather your resources and follow her before that happens."

"How about you tell us w...w-where they are now so we don't lose more time," Luke ground out, close to exploding with his reddened face and wild eyes.

"The location is a closely guarded secret and thus will alert my colleagues something is amiss. The only alternative is a cabin where you can accidentally find them. They'll move her at night, so don't be late."

The imagery of Clara beaten along the trail weaseled into her mind. How safe is she with Fade? Sibyl bit her bottom lip.

"W...W-Why should I care? You're part of them and you kidnapped my mother. I should kill you right now!"

"If you do, there will be no one to protect her once she becomes expendable!" Silence. Then, "on the back of that photo, you will see a map to the cabin. Use it to find Fade and your mother before she disappears over the Pass."

Sibyl, her muscles aching from holding them so tight, walked over to Luke. Sure enough, a map had been scrawled with charcoal on the back of a family polaroid photo. Four people were in it: a husband, wife, and a three-year-old girl sitting pretty on a picnic blanket, smiling. Who were they? Who had taken the photo?

Luke cried out to the trees with his fists clenched, "How shall you keep your help from reaching Fade?"

"It's an old hunting cabin, open to anyone, just past an abandoned amusement park." She paused and her next words dripped with suggestive innocence. "Sometimes hunters happen to find it."

Sibyl bent suddenly to pick up the jar, which surprised Luke. He growled and whirled on her, his shoulders pulled together and fingers flexing on the grip of his bow. She stumbled back a few paces. Luke blinked and lowered his weapon.

He shook as he whispered, "I'm sorry. I..."

"No. I shouldn't have surprised you."

The dense fear infesting Luke's body leveled out a bit. His shoulders dropped to their natural position, and he let out a long, shaking breath. Sibyl then picked up the container and opened it. Inside was an opaque, semi-solid gel with a light purple shade to it.

"What's this?" Sibyl asked and tilted the container to Luke so he could see it.

The female voice answered, "That's an ointment made by Fade. It uses nanites as a base, developed by a scientist who your mother knew, to heal the brain. This ointment won't fix fatal injuries but will speed up healing of superficial ones, even if hope seems lost."

Sibyl's eyes widened. No. Way. "They have that technology?" Sibyl asked in a whisper and Luke shrugged.

"W...W-Why give this to us?" he asked the trees.

"Call it...a gift of good faith," the voice said and went quiet. Ahead, too far away to do any real damage if Luke were to release an arrow at her, the woman dropped to the ground and turned to face them. A black hood shrouded her eyes and a black mask covered her mouth and nose. She stood from her crouch, hands slack beside several knives glinting in the fractured sunlight, and disappeared into the forest.

They'd just spoken to an assassin and survived.

The bitter wind pressed against their bodies, flinging their hair about their faces as they waited.

Sibyl pressed against Luke, returned her spear to her shoulder.

"Let's get out of here," Luke said and yanked on the knife to free it.

23 | CLARA

The young woman wasn't back yet, so Clara waited. She was bound, yes, and sported a split lip from the last time she'd tried to fight her captors, but she hoped the beads from her bracelet were enough to lead someone to find her.

Two men paced while one sat off to the side, their large weapons forgotten at the metal stairs leading up to the world. They were holed up in a bunker - a fallout shelter, by the looks of it - the metal shelves with rations on them making space tighter than Clara liked.

She listened to the men whispering back and forth.

"If she ain't back in the next few minutes, I'm gonna fuckin' teach her a lesson."

The man who spoke was burly, large, had pale skin with a healed, red scar diagonally across his cheek and lips whom they called Banshee. He was quick to anger, Clara's throbbing lip proof of that. He'd been red faced when she refused to walk, oblivious that she'd paused to undo her bracelet and almost did more before the other two hadn't stopped him. Luckily, they didn't find out she'd dropped the beads in her entire bracelet.

"It's only her second, sacred mission," said a man called Ghost, one with a kind face and stocky build, his long, red hair pulled up into a messy bun. "Give her time."

Clara feared Ghost the most because if a gently-spoken person was a part of a group like Fade, only one of two possibilities were probable: Either he was forced to serve against his will or that kindness hid something much darker. When the burly man with jet black hair had hit her, she'd looked up to see Ghost watching intently with a small smile on his face and a shine of excitement in his eyes, proving the latter hypothesis correct.

"We don't have time, idiots."

This was the third man. He lounged in a stuffed chair pushed against the wall, tan skin bared by a sleeveless shirt, his full sleeve tattoos on full display, and short, black hair pushed back neatly. His nimble fingers twisted a knife with a blade so thin, it'd be hard to find the puncture wound in a victim.

"And what would you like us to do, Spectre?" Banshee asked the man with the knife. "Freeze to death in the Pass?"

Ghost nodded and pointed. "Banshee's got a point. We can't bring frozen cargo to Master."

Spectre sighed and stopped twisting his knife. That simple act made the faces of both Banshee and Ghost blanch. But why?

"Chances are, by the time we get there," Spectre started, "the snow on the Pass will have melted enough. She'll be back. She can't afford not to come back."

Clara didn't know what he meant, but she knew Spectre referred to the young woman who left the bunker yesterday. All three agreed she would be the one to brave the cold and scope out the Pass' condition. Clara never saw her face - she kept it hidden behind a mask - and she wondered if the men even knew what the missing young woman looked like. She had a small build, one perfect for fitting into tight spaces, with a flexibility Clara had only seen on circus performers.

"If you never would have convinced her she's God's gift," Banshee glared at Spectre, "she never would have done something so foolish."

Ghost turned a flushed face to Banshee, silently begging the man to stop talking. Clara watched, morbidly curious, as Spectre twitched, and his knife was gone.

"Please," Spectre drawled, his voice dripping with ice. "Tell me how wrong I am to mold an agent of the Master into perfection."

"She's not your pet to do as you will," Banshee snarled. "She belongs to him."

Clara watched the realization grow on his face. Ghost froze, stone still and wide-eyed, but it took Banshee, in his hot-headed anger, far too long to reach up to his nicked skin leaking thick, red blood.

Red blood covered his chest in the seconds he took to fall. Clara bit down a scream. With his chin high, Spectre glided to the collapsed Banshee, picked up his knife, and wiped the blood from it using Banshee's clean shoulder. He never looked twice at his victim.

She stared at the body, all his clothes crimson, and her world tilted. Someone spoke, the sound too garbled to make heads or tails of the words, and she had to shake her head slightly to clear her hearing.

"She is mine to do as I wish." Spectre turned to Ghost, skin white as the snow above them.

Ghost had been the one she'd been afraid of.

She was wrong.

If she wanted to escape and get home intact, she would have to cooperate. She could stall, hide information from them if they interrogated her, and even reveal just enough of what she knew to keep them satiated, but she couldn't act out. If she did, Spectre would kill her before she even realized what had happened.

Banshee was dead. They were down to three Fade operatives total, overkill considering that Clara had no intentions to attempt an escape until she was absolutely, unequivocally confident she could run without Spectre noticing or unable to catch her.

Ghost found a bit of his voice. "Y...you..."

"Yes, yes. Very sad." Spectre waved a hand in the air and sat in his chair. "You do remember how much of a headache he was getting here? If we're to cross the Pass, nothing can slow us down."

"What...do you want me to do with the body?"

Spectre shrugged and didn't speak.

Ghost dragged Banshee's body over to a corner, sat on the ground in the opposite one, and stared at the floor.

An hour later, two timid taps sounded before the hatch opened and Clara saw feet coming down the ladder. The young woman who Spectre had called Phantom stopped and stared for a moment at Banshee's body, then switched to Ghost huddled on the floor, and walked further into the bunker. Even though she kept her face covered, Clara noticed her eyes. They were lifeless, cold. She approached Spectre, let him caress her cheek, then stepped beside him.

"The Pass should be safe to cross in three days," Phantom said and paused when Spectre ran a possessive finger down the back of her arm. "The snowfall is too deep to safely walk through. I did find a cabin halfway to the Pass. We can wait there until the snow melts enough."

Spectre's calm face flashed with fury and his arm lashed out like a viper, wrapping around her neck, and pinning her against the wall. Clara cried out but Phantom did nothing. She didn't even flinch.

"This is your one mistake," Spectre snarled. "I will not inform the Master of this, but you will be punished for your poor preparations."

"Yes."

In an instant, he smiled and caressed her again. "You have a promising future. Don't destroy it."

"Yes. Thank you for the reminder," Phantom said, grabbed Spectre's wrist, and pressed the heel of his hand to her forehead, bowing slightly. "I shall do better, as you have suggested."

Clara's stomach clenched tighter when she saw the tears brimming in Phantom's eyes, hiding the effect Spectre's abuse had on her. Clara couldn't move. She watched Phantom carefully and saw no more sign of distress in her movements or demeanor after the tears. Her motherly instinct kicked in and a rage shot through her. Maybe it was the woman's youthful gait or her the way Spectre treated her, but Clara wanted to grab her and run, to protect her from the horrors she was going through.

Spectre knelt before Clara and her attention jerked to him. "Unfortunately," he said, and Clara wanted to shrink away, "the Master wants you alive and unharmed, so I can't enjoy hurting you. Yet."

She set her jaw and forced a glare, knowing that in a few days, she'd be over the mountain, away from any hope of rescue, and into the clutches of a madman who looked at her with bright eyes.

As if he saw her worry, Spectre let out an amused chuckle. "If you run, I will use your entrails to hang you from the highest tree the minute

Master has no more use for you."
  And she believed him down to her bones.

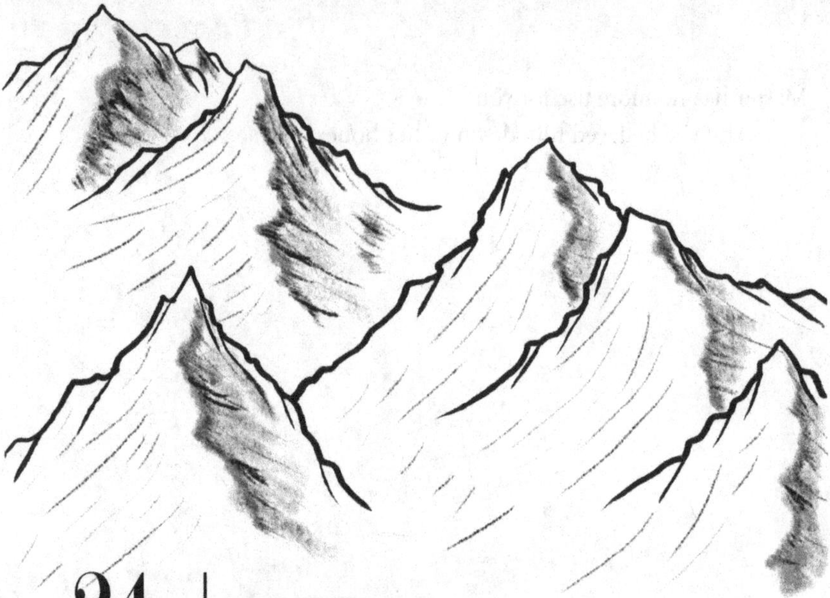

24 | LUKE

I heard your voice in the wind today.
It called to me to remind me
of your love; that you are not gone.
How can I listen to the windsong,
when my aching heart
only wants your whispers?

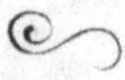

As they neared his parent's house, Luke slowly tensed. Sibyl rubbed the outside of his palm and index finger absently, as if she could sense his discomfort.

They had nothing to show for their efforts. Luke's mind had been on overdrive with all the things that could happen to his mom the longer they took to find her. They had to tell his dad and coming home empty handed would surely worry him.

"Come on," Sibyl said. She stood beside him and he realized he wasn't moving. "We need to talk to your dad about what happened."

Luke didn't move. "I'm so nervous."

She looked at him with her soft, beautiful eyes. "I'll be with you."

It was ridiculous being so nervous but his dad had counted on him to bring her home and Luke hadn't done that.

At least they had a lead.

Luke stuffed his hand in his pocket and grabbed the photo the assassin had given them, hugged his warm coat tighter, and walked toward the house.

"Dad?" he called once the front door closed behind him.

"We're in the kitchen."

The dogs bombarded them. Luke and Sibyl greeted the dogs, slipped their shoes and coats off, and entered the kitchen. Bannack and Mason were seated at the table, quietly talking with Isaac.

Every time he saw his uncle, he was reminded his dad had a twin. Isaac was the paler of the two, a red headed businessman who'd chosen the family life rather than serve his country, standing next to his fitter, militarized brother.

"Bannack!" Sibyl beamed and ran to give him a hug. She turned to Mason and lightly slapped his shoulder before saying to Bannack, "You didn't have to come all the way out here. I thought he'd just meet with you at the Compound."

"That was the plan, but wanted to avoid information getting muddled," Bannack said. He walked over to Luke and gently grabbed the side of his neck. "Sorry about your mom."

Luke nodded and put his hand on Bannack's forearm in a silent 'thank you.'

"I'm not staying long," Mason piped up and scratched his salt and pepper beard. "I only came to relay some intel."

Sibyl and Luke sat at the table and listened to Mason as he spoke. "When I was with the Fifty-Fifth Division, we were tasked with learning Fade's patterns and taking them down. This was after the Day of Ashes and after a huge effort and many losses, we managed to corner them at their home base. Turns out we didn't get them all." He paused and swallowed hard, then cleared his throat and continued. "Fade kept safe houses in hidden caves, underground bunkers, and basements of homes. They also used the underground subway tunnels, and never kept all their people in one place. They moved at night. They're much smaller now and we know we killed their leader, so I'm not sure how much they've changed tactics."

Luke listened with his fingers locked and pressed against his mouth, staring at a scratch in the table. Mason was right, after fourteen years, everything about Fade's operations could have changed drastically and they had no way of knowing anything about them. He appreciated Mason's information, but was it enough to get his mom back?

"I did do some digging the moment I learned of Clara's kidnapping," Mason said, and Luke flicked his eyes to him. "In the communication I kept from my time in the Fifty-Fifth, there is mention of a city over the Pass that acted as a first line of defense against Fade. The rumor is that they kept Fade contained so they didn't overwhelm the States, keeping them restricted inside a valley with one way in and one way out. There is no further mention if they are still around, so I highly doubt this city still exists."

Mason's hands shook the longer he spoke. This obviously bothered him and Luke was glad for Mason's help.

"So, we cross the Pass," Luke said. Both Mason and Isaac stared at him long enough for Luke to furrow his eyebrows. "The hell you looking at me like that for? Is there something I should know about?"

"You don't know what's out there?" Mason asked.

Luke folded his arms. "I w...w-wouldn't ask if I knew."

Sibyl kicked him underneath the table to let him know he was being rude again and he groaned quietly, poking her in retaliation. She squeaked. He didn't look at her, but he could feel the fire of her death glare on him.

"Skin Stealers."

Well, that name could put the fear of God in anyone. Luke blinked and cocked his head. "I'm sorry...Skin Stealers?"

Isaac explained. "They're the earliest victims of Joy's human experiments, their minds damaged by the serum to the point of becoming – how do I put this respectfully? – still human, but the animalistic side of the brain is causing impairment. There are only around twenty, but they do not like people invading their territory."

Bannack made a disapproving noise. "No one would enjoy invaders on their home turf either."

Luke glanced sideways at his friend, curious exactly what Bannack meant, but didn't say anything. He knew Bannack used to work for Joy, the muscle behind kidnapping innocent people to bring to Joy for experiments. Luke also knew that Bannack had spent years trying to undo the damage he'd caused. If the Stealers were victims of Joy's tests, it wasn't that far of a reach to assume the topic caused issues for Bannack.

"So," Luke shrugged, "w...w-walk around them."

Mason chuckled in a way that made Luke bristle, as if he were being mocked. Mason said, "You don't understand. Their territory is most of the Pass. Fade, somehow, has discovered a way around them, but until we know what and where that is, going over Silence Pass means death if you come across a Skin Stealer."

"And by Skin Stealer, you mean..."

"Yes." Mason's eyes darkened. "It's exactly what you're thinking. They will skin you and use your hide for anything they need."

Sibyl swore under her breath.

Luke sat back. "Jesus...Their minds can't be completely gone, though. You said they use human..." Luke swallowed, the mental picture too dark for his liking, "to create things, meaning they do have some level of self-awareness."

He was grasping at straws, but he refused to believe anyone could be so far disconnected from their humanity that they lacked any emotion at all. Luke looked at Bannack sitting very still, his fists balled. Something bothered him about the Skin Stealers.

Mason rubbed his face and Luke saw, for the first time since he'd arrived, how tired he looked. "Whatever they are like now, we have enough information, not only with our run-ins with them but also Joy's recovered notes of her experiments, to know that they are dangerous."

"So, w...w-we're going to assume they're dangerous only 'cause some notes from a dead woman told us? Cool."

Mason folded his arms and cocked an eyebrow at Luke. "You saw what Joy did to Eloise. How Bannack and countless others have been affected. You were there when Seth confronted his mom. I'd say if someone like her says a group of people are dangerous, it's wise to believe them."

He didn't like it. Something felt off about the Skin Stealers intel, but he also knew Mason had a point. If he went over the Pass and ran into the Stealers and they really were as dangerous as Mason thought...it wouldn't end well. Best to prepare for the worst.

Luke grunted. "Fair enough."

The tension in the room buzzed, annoying Luke, as he stared at Mason.

Bannack, who had been listening in on the conversation, spoke up, raising his voice on the first word, "Whatever the actions we take next, we all agree that Fade needs to be stopped and Clara returned. Yes?"

Both Luke and Mason nodded.

Then Sibyl, who'd been silent, squeezed Luke's hand and said, "We need to be cautious but there are ways around that. Fade's doing it, so why can't we?" Mason opened his mouth and she silenced him with a single glance. "It sounds to me like Fade is an emotionally charged group and possibly lacking in numbers and resources, which works for us because they're going to make mistakes. They're going to overlook things. I say we prepare for a fight. Bring a group of people, as small as we can, who move easily, have combat training, and if the Stealers are as dangerous as we think, we'll be ready."

Adoration for the woman leaning against him swelled in his chest. The original Sibyl was coming back.

"I agree," Mason said, nodding his approval.

"Great!" Sibyl wiggled her shoulders and pulled out the jar of ointment given to her and Luke by the voice in the forest. "Now we can talk about this juicy piece of tea."

Everyone stared at the jar. Isaac opened it first and looked inside. "Ointment?"

"It came with this," Sibyl said and placed the knife on the table, pausing for dramatic effect before she revealed the map, turning it over to show the photo. "The person who gave us the ointment, gave us this, too. She said she wanted to help us find Clara and that map points to where we can grab her. It takes us through an abandoned amusement park and the cabin marked here," Sibyl pointed, "is where they're staying. We only have a few days to make our move, though."

Mason shook his head. "I don't like it. Why would anyone from Fade want to help?"

"They could be a rogue agen—" Bannack started then stopped cold. He stared at the picture, eyes wide. Before Luke could ask, Bannack shoved the picture at Sibyl. "Where did you get this?"

"I...uh...the woman in the trees gave it to us." Sibyl cocked her head. "She said she knows you and gave us the photo. It's the only reason we decided to trust her, even after she said she was an assassin."

He swore and pressed the picture to his forehead. "You spoke to Nora Pemberton."

"Who?" Luke asked, trying to figure out if he'd mentioned the name before.

"Wait..." Sibyl said. "Eloise mentioned her before. Is...is she the girl you saved from Joy and took to Canada? The one who stopped the crowd in Kendal's village?"

Bannack nodded, hand pressed against his mouth as he stared down at the picture. "She had a brother, as well, but...she's with Fade?"

Luke wanted to ask about the brother and the ominous way Bannack's words fell off at the mention of him, but Sibyl spoke before he could.

"Unfortunately, yes. She's their assassin."

Bannack swore in Twi. "Then I failed."

"No, you didn't," Sibyl said and reached across the table to put her hand on his forearm. "She's still fighting. The picture and attempts to help us proof of that."

Luke smiled a bit and nodded when Bannack shifted his wet eyes to him. "We'll help her, if we can. Promise."

"I'm grateful," Bannack replied.

Sibyl rubbed Luke's knee, sitting so close to him that she basically sat in his lap. "We have three days to get reinforcements and I'm assuming we'll want to talk to the other clans, but there's no time to travel to them all."

"Then we talk to the clan closest to our island," Luke said.

Isaac grunted. "Mmm. That would be Thea's Equida clan. Luke," he turned to his son. "I need you to come with me. Clara worked closely with Thea when she made a bid for Equida Leader, so she could have good information for both of us as to why Fade wants my wife."

He couldn't argue with his dad's logic, and did need to get more information, but disliked his involuntary recruitment for a mission he knew meant being around strangers.

"W...W-Why talk with Thea? There are people here available."

"Rhondians with the skills to fight are gone gathering whatever they can carry to feed our clan members, and Thea's people have experience hunting and traveling in the hills and mountains of their territory, a much needed skill considering the terrain in the Pass."

A detail he, in his worry over his mom, completely forgot about. "I'll go," Luke said.

Bannack spoke up, and when he shifted, the sword at his waist tapped against his chair. "When you need me, I'll be available."

Luke watched his friend. He'd seen the man take down many of Joy's men in seconds and Luke knew Bannack would be an asset to their rescue. "Thank you. Remain close. We should be back in a day or so."

"He can sleep above my shop," Sibyl said. "Hunter and I will put him to work, too."

"Alright," Isaac gave a sharp nod and turned to hug Mason. "Thank you for your advice. I appreciate the help."

"Of course." Mason stood up and Bannack followed suit. "Bring her back safe, Isaac."

"We will."

Once Bannack and Mason left, Sibyl lingered in the doorway. He and his dad wouldn't be leaving for Thea's until the next morning, so Luke had a little reprieve of anxiety.

"I'll see you when you get back," she said.

Luke rubbed his face. "I'd do anything to save Mom. I'm just..." He glanced over her shoulder at Boatswain emerging from a hedge, "not looking forward to this trip at all."

A slow smile built on Sibyl's face, and she leaned in, making him severely aware of her close proximity. He studied her face, the dimples and the two freckles that had gotten lost from their companions and settled on her cheek and above her eyebrow. Then he recognized the slight droop to her eyes, knowing the wheels to her snark machine were turning.

"Well, find some cute poodle to hit on and you'll be fine." She scrubbed Boatswain's head when he knocked into her. "You could even play matchmaker to this guy."

"I...he can't..."

He didn't understand where her brain went, but knew better than to puzzle it out or he'd just get more lost, so Luke decided to continue on as if what she'd just said made perfect sense.

"Awe," Sibyl frowned, "poor guy." Then she looked at him. "So, what are you going to do about the awkwardness you're not looking forward to?"

Luke scoffed and folded his arms. "If I ignore it, it'll go away."

"Well, that's not going to work at all."

She placed her fingertips on his forearm, applying the slightest amount of pressure and Luke immediately lowered his hands. The tip of her shoes jutted against his bare feet, and her touch trailed up his arm.

"Do?" Luke couldn't form a complete thought with her body pressed up against his.

"Yeah. Can I give you a distraction to think about when you're gone?"

He nodded, now stripped fully of his ability to speak, and waited as Sibyl's hand found the back of his head and she pressed her lips to his. He opened for her and her tongue entered his mouth. Oh, God, she felt so good. His entire body hummed at her touch, from the scratch of her glorious, calloused fingers to the press of her hips into his. Desperate, Luke anchored her against him as he basked in her kiss. And she kissed him again and again. And again. Then he kissed her back.

Yes. This distraction would do nicely.

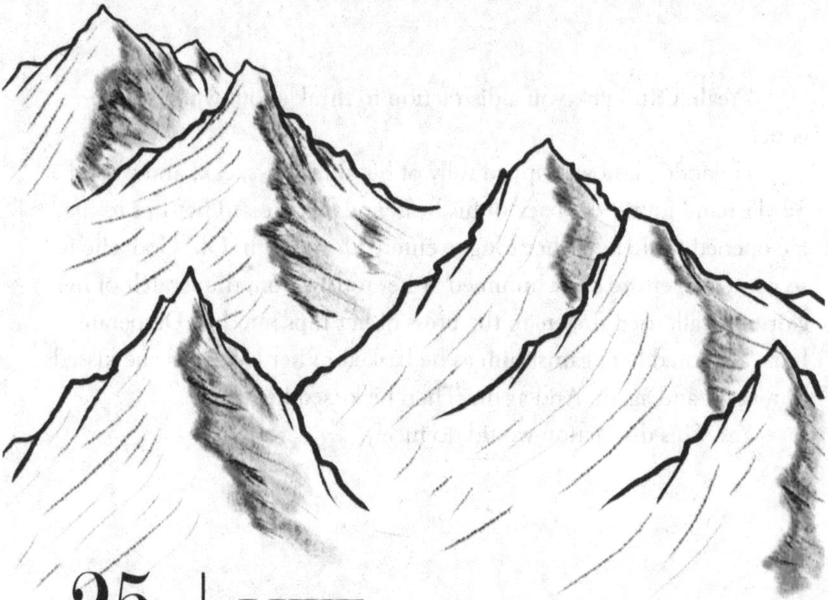

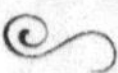

25 | LUKE

Love.
The greatest desire of mankind.
Love of things.
Love of the immaterial.
Love of vanity.
But to be loved?
That is the greatest desire of all.

The next day, someone woke Luke from a dream of Sibyl. He groaned, stiff from sleep, lifted his head from his pillow, and squinted.

Isaac stared at him, a tiny smile on his lips. "Get up. We have a meeting."

"W...W-With?" Luke mumbled as he righted the shirt thrown into his face, temporarily forgetting their conversation yesterday. He paused, his shirt covering one eye, and looked at his dad.

"Thea, Equida's clan leader," Isaac responded.

Now he remembered.

Isaac rubbed Boatswain's cheek while he waited for Luke to finish dressing, and the dog huffed, leaning into Isaac's affection. Levin trotted into the room, long ears flopping, and plopped down beside Isaac to stare at Luke. And boy, did he stare. The dog was an expert at it.

"You w...w-wanna go out?" Luke asked.

Levin smacked his tail on the floor, sharp thuds exploding up the wall. It wasn't until the sounds faded that Luke asked again, "Outside?" More tail smacks, these increased in intensity. Luke chuckled. "I'll get his leash."

He stopped by the kitchen, fruitlessly checking the cabinets. They'd rationed out half their food storage to families in need a couple days ago, and Luke and Isaac were trying to stretch the food shared between them and the dogs as far as they could. He could deal with a grumbling belly, but he worried for the dogs, especially Boatswain. Now that he had to cut his dog's food back, Boatswain was often tired without his steady diet of raw food for close to six years that gave him a youthful energy.

He knelt in front of Boatswain and scratched his ears. "I know you're tired but I can't leave you here. I need you to help me find my mom."

Before they left, Luke made sure Levin had a downy vest and boots on. Boatswain needed boots, but his thick double coat gave him the warmth he needed.

Levin's lead in hand, weapons loaded up, and everyone bundled, Luke pushed his worries away, and opened the door, blasted with a wall of ice-cold wind. He stumbled back, coughing, and looked at his dad with an eyebrow raised.

"Yes," Isaac said as he flung a thick scarf around his neck and put on gloves. "We're going out in that."

"So fun."

They rode the horses through the frozen wind, with the dogs trotting at Luke's side. Both he and his dad fought with the scarves around their mouths and noses. Luke's eyes struggled to focus by the time the wind died down.

Luke braced against a gust. "Tell me the exact plan after arrival."

Isaac's face shone bright red and he lifted his face out of his scarf to talk. "Equida clan is worse off than the others because of a recent surge of deaths, so I'm unsure how willing she will be to help us, but, because of her past with Clara, I'm hoping she'll at least consider it."

"Hold up." Luke motioned with his hand, the other on the reins. "Backpedal just a bit. Deaths?"

"Animal attacks."

Shock hit him in the stomach. "How?"

"That's what we're going to figure out. How these deaths occurred, what type of animal or animals killed them, and where they were attacked." Isaac adjusted his scarf. "Then we're going to ask Thea to help us rescue your mom."

The mid-afternoon sun accentuated the breath clouds in front of their faces by the time they reached the Equida clan gates. The weathered gate and fence were fortified by relatively new fortifications: spikes, both tied to the fence and sunk into the ground.

Someone tall and lanky ran up to them. "State your business."

"Luke and Isaac Blackwood here to request assistance from Thea," Isaac replied.

Luke nodded. He was completely frozen, past shivering, and irritable.

Recognition brightened his face. "Any relation to Clara Blackwood?"

"She's my mom," Luke replied.

"Understood." He put his hand out for it to be shaken. "I'm Marv. Come with me. Please leave your weapons there."

Marv motioned for someone to take the horses and Luke grabbed the machete his dad handed him and removed his own bow and arrows. They followed Marv past rows and rows of dead crops and through the streets of homes made of scrapped tin, siding, pallets, and more. The pathway, bare of most people, wound through the haphazardly built dwellings. The signs of life Luke did see ground his gut into a pulp. Huddled around pyres, shivering, sharing broth with some veggies, then hustling back inside for warmth. This was nothing like the Rhondian clan's houses, and Luke remained in shocked silence.

"Holy hell," Luke said, his voice low. "This happened w...w-when?"

"What you see is directly caused by the roofs of fifty homes collapsing in the early Winter's first month. We've gone through most of our food stores and struggle to find food to feed everyone since our gardens died. The mountain provides some resources, though." He pointed, snow glistening off the treetops. "But even that's proving difficult. Your mother made sure we were taken care of whenever she could." He paused and turned to look at Luke and Isaac. "She's a good woman."

The shacks turned into long, brick homes sunk into the ground a bit to allow for cooling in the summer. As he passed the homes, most held the warm glow of a fire.

"They don't leave the beginning of town and huddle into these houses here?" Luke asked, turning around to stare at the patchwork structures near the clan entrance.

"Many have already left for better living circumstances." Marv turned a corner and walked toward the largest home Luke had seen so far, so many people gathered inside, the house looked like it would burst. "Most victims of the collapse live in Thea's house and the others you saw at the front are prepping to leave soon. They've tried to stay, but..."

Luke hadn't even met with Thea and his mind and heart already weighed him down.

They made it to the house Marv spoke of. Four smooth, two-story columns held up a simple roof. Red brick and white siding lined the home's front. Luke followed Marv through the windowed double doors and into a foyer sporting a staircase that split at the top.

Enough people mingled within that Luke's throat tightened, but he followed Marv and his dad into the main living room to the right. Thea sat at a dining table, feeding a toddler some bread with butter. She was built strong and muscular, with brown, curly hair, and brown skin. She wore a trench coat of red, welding goggles beside her on the table. A child grabbed for them, but she pulled them away, her eyes gentle.

She glanced up and handed the child back to his mother. Thea motioned upstairs. "My office."

Luke wound his way through the crowd of people, the dogs right at his side. Levin panted and quietly whined as they walked. Luke knew he wasn't completely comfortable, but the busy house was good practice for Levin, and so far, he handled the experience well. Boatswain, on the other hand, meandered calmly, taking in the chaotic home.

People played board games around a table, read stories to their children, and shared hot bowls of food brought in from a room Luke assumed was the kitchen. Cots and nests of blankets peppered the floor, people sleeping wherever they could fit, while doing their best to leave pathways for walking.

"Doggie," said a child several feet away, holding the hand of a caretaker while pointing at Levin. "Pet?"

"Good job asking," said the woman.

Luke gave an apologetic smile as he stopped and put his hand on Levin. "He doesn't like pets. They make him scared. Do you ever get scared?"

The child nodded.

"Yeah. So does he. He loves food, though. Here." Luke handed the girl a piece of dried liver. "See if he'll take it."

Hesitating for a few moments with Levin watching her expectantly, the little girl inched forward and threw the treat. Levin caught it in his mouth and the little girl giggled.

Luke gave her a second piece to give to Boatswain. "He loves pets the most."

The little girl's eyes widened, and she gave Boatswain the treat. He took it with a tiny bite and pushed his nose into the girl's hand. She stared, then giggled, and Luke couldn't help but smile. Boatswain scooted forward on his bum, not crowding the girl but still giving her more real estate on his head to scratch. She squealed and hugged Boatswain's neck. After a few moments, the little girl broke away and gave Boatswain two pats on his head, bent at the waist, and looked into his big eyes.

"You pretty puppy."

"Thank you," the woman said as she gathered the girl in her arms. "Say thank you."

The little girl parroted her guardian and they walked away.

Luke scratched Levin's ears and handed him and Boatswain another liver piece. "Good boys," he said, then strode forward to follow his dad up the stairs.

Once at the top landing, Thea turned right, down a hallway lit by gas lights, a natural resource unfamiliar to Luke. He stopped at the first one, Isaac continuing into Thea's office, and stared. The dogs sat and leaned against his legs. The light flickered in its glass orb, happy to be dancing for a master who didn't have to slave to bring it to existence.

Thea's voice appeared over his shoulder. "Took us a bit to reconfigure the pipes."

"How?"

"Clara recommended a technician: Seth Ward."

Realization made Luke perk up. "He w...w-was here?"

"A few years ago, yes." She walked away and Luke followed her to continue listening to Thea's story. "He returned for a few months, looking for something to take his mind off his travels before heading out again. After Seth helped us and left, Clara expressed worry over protecting him on one of her many visits. I was the last person to see him, years ago, so she needed to make sure I truly didn't know where he went." She paused. "Odd though, now that I think about it."

"How so?"

"Clara was nervous. Way nervous. Almost as if me knowing his destination would be dangerous and when I told her I knew nothing, she fully relaxed. Now...she's been kidnapped."

Luke didn't like the implications of Thea's words, a reminder of what he already knew, and a sourness settled firmly in his stomach.

Thea motioned Luke into an office where his father waited. Luke sat next to his dad and Thea took a seat behind a large, maple wood desk, everything organized to pristine perfection.

"Do you know about mom intentionally hiding Seth's location from people?" Luke asked his dad.

"This is the first I'm hearing of it." Isaac shared an odd look with Thea, one Luke knew well as his 'I know but I'm not going to tell you,' look and Luke glanced at Thea to see if she would react.

Thea turned to Luke. "So, you're the reclusive only child, eh?"

Luke nodded and handed Levin a treat once he relaxed.

"Please don't nod. I need you to voice an answer." Thea said with her chin forward, her Portuguese accent faint.

Taken aback by the request, Luke cleared his throat. "I am."

"Thank you." She leaned back in her chair, and put her hands on the desk, keeping her eyes on him. "How are you holding up?" She turned to Isaac. "Both of you? And where's Clara?"

Luke's throat tightened and he glanced at his dad. If neither spoke, Luke would have to and he didn't want to stumble over his words in an important meeting.

Thankfully, Isaac spared him the grief of talking. "Your victims. Of the animal attacks. How are they?"

Thea narrowed her eyes but answered his question. "Stable, thank god. The wild animals are coming further into our perimeter, we think because the freeze is killing their food, so they're aggressive and hungry. For now, no one is allowed to leave, but a few still do."

"Do you know the animals that are doing this?" Luke asked.

Thea looked at Luke. "Sometimes black bear. Those victims don't survive long, if they make it back." Helplessness crossed her face, then flashed away. "Other times coyote or wolf. Feral dog. Puma."

Isaac folded his arms. "How many were attacked?"

"Ten so far."

"Do you have a location on where these attacks occurred?"

"The mountain." Thea chuckled dispassionately. "The very thing that's kept us thriving for so long is now birthing death."

"Can we help at all?" Isaac asked.

Thea shook her head. "It's an issue we're dealing with well enough. I appreciate your support, though." She leaned forward on her elbows. "But you never answered my question. Where's Clara?"

Isaac sighed. "She's been kidnapped."

"What?" Thea's voice boomed throughout the office before she collected herself in a micro-second switch to composed fury. "How?"

This woman took him on a roller coaster, and the up and down of her disposition reminded Luke why he struggled to be around people. His brain was already fogging up.

I need to push past this. I can't shrivel up.

He spent several minutes fighting with the strain and stared at his hands in his lap.

Slowly, Luke straightened and blinked, hoping he could force the growing exhaustion out.

Isaac spoke before Luke could process what to say in response to Thea's outburst. He explained the situation then said, "We are doing as well as we can."

"Good. Good." She looked at Luke. "And you?"

Remembering her request for speaking, Luke straightened. He didn't know if she wanted honesty or was asking but not really interested in the answer. "Uh, doing w...w-well."

He internally cringed. What an awkward and strange answer but Thea didn't appear phased by it because she nodded and brought no more attention to him.

Struggling to keep his mind on task, Luke's attention on Isaac's voice fell away and his attention focused on the office around him, background noise of a newborn wailing and muffled speech of the Equida clan filtering in through the bottom of the closed door.

Here and there, glimmers of pre-Day of Ashes remnants occupied the room in Thea's leather, high backed office chair, some abstract art in black, modern style frames, and built in shelves holding some old, worn books. Other than a few more knickknacks to give the office a homier feel, the rest of the space sat firmly in their post-apocalyptic reality. The walls needed tending to, vines of cords ran in swooping lines from one unknown location to another, a crudely drawn map of the area covered the wall, pin-pricked with notes and strands of yarn, and old pictures, horse tack sat atop barrels with a canvas tarp covering some square storage containers.

A foot tapped Luke and he jumped. His father stared at him, as did Thea, and he realized in a flush of heat, they'd asked a question he hadn't heard.

"Uh, yeah?"

Isaac nodded toward Thea while keeping eye contact with Luke.

Thea continued. "Clara was my greatest ally when I first became Leader. What do you need from me?"

"A small group willing to search for Clara with us. We don't need many. Five at the most and people who can leave their families for about a week." Apologetically, he glanced around. "We knew how dire the situation here was, but hoped, with you and Clara's shared history, you'd be willing to consider helping. Though, after seeing what you're going through with my own eyes, I do not expect you to agree."

"I'll help. God knows it'll repay only a small portion of my debt with Clara after she did so much." Thea moved to stand but before she could, the door knocked and opened.

Luke hadn't planned on turning, but the voice that came after Thea's, "what is it?" ran his blood cold and skin hot. He recognized the self-important tone.

Peter sauntered in, three goonies following him, and none of them bothered to close the office door. One had freckled skin and a great axe strapped against his back, while the other two were dark haired and pale. Luke bristled.

"I didn't expect to see you here." Peter smiled at Luke with just his lips.

Luke glared at him, failing to be cordial. "Peter."

He gave Luke's back a good thump. "Oh, don't be like that."

Luke surged to his feet and stopped inches from Peter's face. Thea and Isaac called out, but Luke ignored them and watched Peter's expression change from fake pleasantness to anger.

"You better listen to the boss, Fade spy," he whispered.

"Fuck you," Luke growled and held his dogs back with a gesture.

The man with the axe put his hand on Luke's chest. "Stay back."

He turned on the man and struggled to keep his voice in control over the rage and hurt bubbling just under his skin. "You are?"

"Kieran."

"Your ring leader's a cretin."

Peter's face reddened but he did nothing, and glanced warily over Luke's shoulder, probably at Thea.

"Yes," Kieran responded, obviously the mediator. "I won't let you hurt my friend."

Luke scoffed. "Your friend?"

Kieran narrowed his eyes. "Yes."

Peter didn't have friends. He had followers. Lackeys. Minions. And Luke highly doubted Kieran, or the two others with him, were any different. Either they joined in Peter's behavior or allowed it to happen.

The sound of a chair wheeling back came right before Thea's voice. "That's enough. You two are grown men. Act like it."

Luke turned around. Thea's leveled him with a hard stare, not quite a glare but close enough.

She folded her arms and said, "There's obviously a history between you two, but I will not stand for such conflict in my home. Am I clear?"

Luke nodded.

Isaac pulled Luke back, gave him a warning look, and turned his attention to Peter. "How is life here? Are they treating you well?"

Always the diplomat.

Peter softened his face, and the predator disappeared. "We're managing."

"And who are your friends?" Isaac motioned with his chin to the two other men with Peter and Kieran.

"Where are my manners?" Peter motioned to the three men beside him. "This is Preston, Kieran, and Guy."

Isaac extended his hand and shook their hands one after the other, encouraging Luke to do the same with a light shove of his elbow. Luke knew Thea would be even angrier with him if he rejected his father's command but also, if he had any hope at becoming a Leader, he needed to learn how to handle tense situations with pristine emotional control. So, Luke shook everyone's hands.

Luke sat back in his seat with a grunt. Thea fixed him with a warning stare, glanced at Peter talking with Isaac, and back again. She frowned.

Great. Not a good first impression.

Isaac took his seat, and Peter sat across from him, pulling out a letter for Thea and sliding it across the table.

Isaac tapped Luke's shin with the tip of his boot, and widened his eyes pointedly. Luke knew it was his dad's way of saying, "play nice." Reluctantly, Luke did as he wished.

Thea cleared her throat. "Now that you're here, Kieran, I'd like you to come with me to gather a few other people to help Isaac and Luke."

"What do they need help with?" Peter asked.

Oh my God. Stop talking.

"Clara has been kidnapped and they're asking for some help to rescue her."

"They need help for that?"

"Yes," Thea said, one eyebrow going up. "Fade is a formidable force, and they need all the help they can get."

"Fade hasn't been back for years. Are we sure it's them who kidnapped her?"

I'm gonna kill him.

Thea leveled Peter with an unamused gaze. "Thank you for the letter. I keep you on because we have too many jobs to fill and not enough people, but you're already on thin ice. Don't push your luck. I would like you to leave now. And close the door this time."

A flash of irritation went across Peter's face, but he left with his lackeys, Kieran staying behind.

Thea sighed and pressed her fingertips to her forehead. "Kieran, come with me."

Thea and Kieran left, returning in several minutes with three others.

"Got some for you," Kieran announced

Luke surveyed them. Two women and one man, plus Kieran, stood by the table, and Thea introduced them.

"This is Marie, Shinat, and Sam."

Luke looked at each person as Thea introduced them. Marie was shorter, stocky, with long blonde hair. Sam had a scar above his eyebrow that traveled three inches into his black cornrows, as if someone had slashed at his face with a blade. Shinat wore a khimar and a scimitar at her waist.

Isaac thanked Thea then looked at the group. "I assume you all have combat training."

They agreed.

"Good," Isaac said and nodded. "I know this is a lot to ask, so I'm grateful you're willing to help. Prep your bags and mounts and meet us at the front gates in about an hour."

Luke watched his dad command the room, asking all the right questions, and making sure everyone had their own tasks to work on, and he smiled a little.

Amid the hustle of Isaac giving orders, someone frantically banged on the door. Thea rushed to it, spoke in hushed tones with the terrified and wet-eyed visitor, then turned.

"I have to take care of this," Thea said. "We've discovered another group of victims. You have things handled, Isaac?"

"I do. Thank you for all your help."

"It's what I can do. I truly hope you can find her."

Thea left, followed a few moments later by Marie, Shinat, and Sam to prepare for travel.

Isaac turned to Luke. "Clara has gone to great lengths to keep Seth safe. I'd like to keep it that way and so Thea cannot know anything more. For now, we know Seth is safe. Unfortunately, with Joy missing or dead, your mother is the closest person to him."

"You told me Mom refused to speak to him."

"Yes. I did say that, and I apologize for not clarifying. The work Seth performed for Thea happened early in his travels. As soon as whisperings reached us of Fade possibly returning, Clara stopped all communication with him. One thing has always stayed constant, though: Clara made Seth promise to never, ever mention where he went or who he was. Told him to change his name."

Luke processed the information for a few moments, staring at his hands, and spoke slowly to hopefully juggle his stutter. "This all doesn't explain how they found Mom, or why she didn't relocate once she suspected Fade could come after her, or why her. Joy's out of the picture, but what about Sibyl's dad? He might have known Seth through Joy and he lives in the area, yet Fade didn't take him."

Isaac sighed. "Joy and Clara were best friends. Once Seth was born, Clara became his godmother."

Luke just about fell off his chair. "Excuse me?"

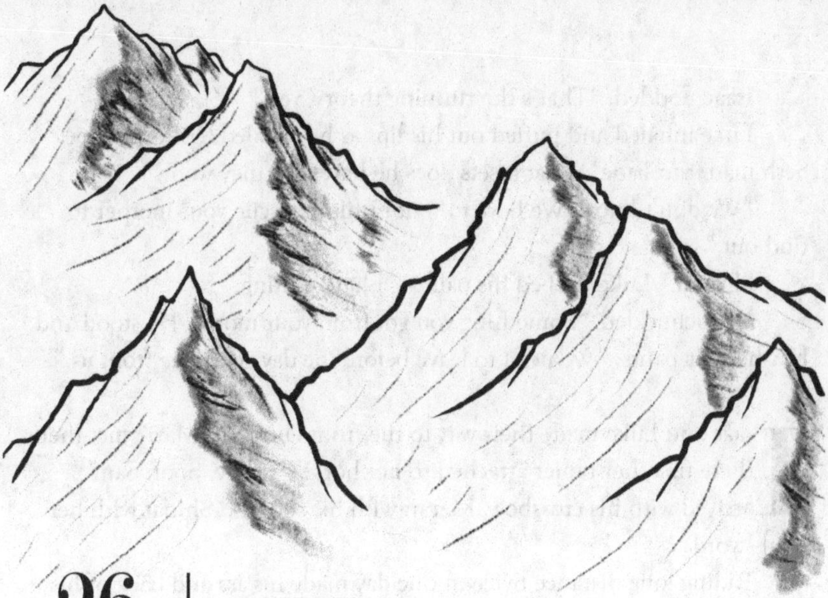

26 | LUKE

I have been empty for so long,
light was a delicacy.
The moment you smiled,
my world brightened
and you became the sun.

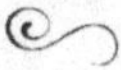

"You're joking," Luke said, his head in his hands.

"No."

Luke looked at his dad again. "And where do you fit in in all this?"

"Clara and Joy met in college and their friendship continued, even after Clara got a job through the government as a lawyer for the FDA. Seven years later, your mother began work with McCormick Regional Laboratories. Clara and I met a year later." Isaac smiled. "You know your mother. She has an incredible ability to separate her personal life from her work life, so balancing her friendship with Joy and acting as a lawyer was never an issue."

His mind reeled. "This...this is wild." Luke stood, took a few steps, and turned. "Alright. Mom and Joy were besties. Is that the reason Fade took her?"

Isaac nodded. "That's the running theory, yes."

Luke inhaled and puffed out his lips as he exhaled. "But why does Seth matter to Fade? What assets does he have that they want?"

"We don't know. We have to wait until we rescue your mother to find out."

"Damn." Luke rubbed his palms. "I hate waiting."

Isaac chuckled. "Something you got from your mom." He stood and brushed his pants. "We need to leave before the day gets away from us."

Isaac and Luke made their way to the front entrance. Marie met them there first, her rapier attached to her horse's saddle. Soon Sam arrived with his crossbow, Kieran with his axe, and Shinat with her dual swords.

Riding long distance twice in one day made his ass and back of his thighs sore. He shifted in the saddle several times, grunting and groaning when he couldn't find a comfortable seat, then eventually gave up.

Isaac smiled sideways at him, and Luke caught his eye. "W...W-What?" he asked and fidgeted again. "Your ass *doesn't* hurt?"

"Well, I do ride quite frequently. So, no. It doesn't."

To show off even more, Isaac tapped his heels on the horse's flank, clicked his tongue, and they galloped away, Levin and Boatswain following.

Luke grumbled underneath his breath then trotted forward to catch up with everyone, arrows clinking around in the quiver with every jarring bounce. He was shit at riding, but he managed well enough, even though at the end of a session his legs had aged fifty years. After a couple minutes of pounding his backside into minced meat, Luke caught up with the rest of the group.

Isaac turned to the new group members. "Thank you, everyone, for your willingness to assist us in finding my wife."

"You're welcome," Marie said. "We're glad to help."

Isaac fell into a conversation with the group about their life in Equida clan and Luke listened, growing grumpier by the minute about being stuck in the cold. He had no interest in making conversation, only how long it would take to get home so he could warm up.

In his grumblings over his stiff fingers trying to hold the reins, pinpricks of guilt aggravated his body. He should be able to do what came to his father so easily. He didn't want Sam or Shinat or Marie to think he was ignoring them or be confused why he wasn't more cordial or welcoming.

So, he steadied his breathing, and turned to Sam riding closest to him. Marie, Shinat, Kieran, and Isaac weren't too far ahead but just enough that when one of them belly laughed, the sound barely reached the ears.

"Thank you for helping us." Luke groaned internally at the robotic feel of his words as they left his mouth.

Sam took it in stride. "You need help from people with a certain skill set and I have it." He noticed Luke eyeing the crossbow at his back and smirked. "Wanna see something cool?"

Sam loaded his crossbow. "Yo, Marie!"

Without looking back, Marie slipped a ring from her finger and tossed it in the air. The bow's mechanism thudded and sent the bolt straight through the ring and into a tree trunk beyond. Marie pumped the air, Isaac spun his horse around, and Luke stared at the impaled tree.

"Remind me never to cross you," Luke said, half in awe, half terrified.

Kieran appeared at Luke's side, smiling. "Unless we come across some Stealers." Then underneath his breath, he added, "revolting creatures."

At Kieran's words Luke did a double take, convinced he hadn't heard him correctly and he glanced at Sam, wondering if he'd heard Kieran's comments as well. Sam's brow furrowed.

Did he really just say that?

Before Luke could call him out, Kieran sniffed and trotted away.

"He's still pretty sensitive," Sam explained. "Ah. I don't know if I should be telling you but," he scratched the back of his head, "you need to know in case it affects his performance. About a month ago, Kieran's fiancé took their newborn and left over the mountain. We can't find them."

Luke adjusted the reins, unsure what to say.

"You don't have to give your condolences." Sam put away his crossbow. "Kieran's skilled and strong, but he's an asshole. The search teams never found her, so I hope she found something better than him."

"Shit."

Sam nodded in agreement then gestured to Luke's recurve bow. "You prefer the old school ways, huh?"

Luke adjusted the bowstring across his chest. "It's served me decent so far."

"Hey," Sam chuckled, "if it works, it works."

When Luke and Sam caught up to their companions, Marie gave the bolt back and returned the ring to her finger.

"You and I both saw that shooting, right?" Isaac asked as he hung back from the main group with Luke. "No wonder Thea brought him to us."

For several hours they traveled in the cold, stopping to let the horses and dogs rest and drink from a nearby stream. The day waned, showering colors above them. They needed shelter for the night.

"Be on the lookout for a cave or old building we can hole up in." Isaac raised his voice to talk to the group, Sam beside him and Marie beside Luke with Kieran and Shinat taking up the rear.

Luke kept his eye out, concerned that he defaulted too much to his dad whenever they performed clan duties together. It was easiest but he wondered if he couldn't break away from that habit and take the mantle from his dad sometimes, maybe even when they found his mom, see if she knew of a job he could take over to help make hers easier.

Soon, Sam spotted a cave on a short ridge. Luke left his roan with the group and ran ahead to make sure no animals had moved in.

The body of the dark and damp cave curved around a narrow corner, providing some protection against the elements but was otherwise empty, and only big enough for a few people and a campfire. Small, but doable for the night.

He stepped out and signaled to the others. They tied the horses to a group of trees and string up a tarp to provide temporary shelter for the horses, and brought their saddles inside. Boatswain and Levin trotted into the cave with Luke, their snouts shoved against his legs to sniff at the horse sent. A puff of warm air invaded his ass crack and he jerked away and batted at a muzzle.

The soon flickering fire was the only source of heat in the cave, and everyone passed around a bread loaf, cheese, and warmed broth. Shinat contributed some biscuits made of cattail flour. The dogs enjoyed the chicken Luke gave them but only sniffed the cattail bread.

When Luke settled beside Shinat, she offered him an empty cup.

"Want some broth?"

It wasn't his favorite thing in the world, but he couldn't be choosy at the moment. "Sure."

Shinat poured him some and returned to her friendly argument with Kieran over whether bread made from cattail flour or wheat tasted better. "All I'm saying is cattail bread is a superfood," she said. "What does regular bread have? Carbs."

Kieran rolled his eyes then shoved a torn piece of bread at her. "Carbs are life."

"No thanks. I'll stick to my vegetables and meat."

Luke took a hesitant sip and his mouth exploded with flavor. Onion, carrots, chicken, and so many herbs he didn't know how to process them. "Wow."

"Good, isn't it?" Shinat smiled and pointed to Kieran. "He made it."

"It's great."

Kieran smiled. "Thanks."

Luke listened to Shinat and Kieran banter, the energy of the conversation reminding him of how he and his mother often spoke with each other. His throat tightened and he swallowed more broth, hoping the warm liquid would relax it. He glanced at his father.

Isaac sat on the log opposite him, swirling the broth in his cup absently, his leg bouncing, and Luke walked over to sit next to him.

"This broth tastes like what she used to make," Isaac said and handed his cup to Luke with a grimace.

"I miss her, too."

Honestly? Luke hadn't connected the broth's taste with his mother, but now even the smell made him nauseous, so he dug a collapsible bowl out of Boatswain and Levin's packs and poured the broth into each of them.

After dinner, Sam, Marie, Shinat, and Kieran hunkered down away from Isaac and Luke, consequently giving more room for them to talk. Isaac leaned against a rock and tossed the last bite of bread into his mouth. "I miss your mother's cooking."

Luke looked down at the leftover bread in his hands. It lacked the fluff he was used to but tasted decent, and he nodded. "Me too."

"That's how I knew I wanted to marry her."

The comment was so unexpected and odd coming from his dad, that Luke laughed. "Isn't that..."

"Clichéd? Mildly sexist? Yes. I know. But it's the truth." He shrugged. "You know I love food." Isaac split an egg, gave each piece to the dogs, and wiped his hands on his pants. "Although, it's not what you may be thinking. The key thing to remember about your mother is she puts love into everything. She cares, and her food is no different. I fell in love with her food because she poured her soul into it and every time I took a bite, I got to experience a part of her." Isaac chuckled. "You used to cry when I cooked because it wasn't hers, but I digress. When we met, she was teaching a college cooking class when on her off days."

Isaac put his hands behind his back and continued, "A friend brought me along to a class and when I tasted that food..." A far off look brightened Isaac's eyes and he smiled. "It wasn't right away that I knew she was the one, I'm not barbaric. But it did take me months of going to classes to work up the courage to talk to her."

Luke smiled. "That long?"

"Mason's the wild one between the two of us. He dragged me along to go free running and skydiving." A mischievous smile crossed Isaac's face. The fire crackled. "We spent our days skateboarding on anything and everything, women following us everywhere. He had plans to go big one day, already landed a sponsor, too, but when the injury happened, he shifted his goals to the military. Without him, skating lost its luster for me. Your mother's cooking brought that back."

Luke smiled, thinking of his dad flying through half-pipes, performing kick flips, and banging his way through towns. He struggled to imagine it.

Levin pressed his head into Luke's hand. As he petted the dog's neck, Luke asked, "After you started talking to her, what happened?"

"She blew me off."

He couldn't help it, Luke snorted.

Isaac tossed a small pebble at Luke, and said, "After one of her classes, we planned to meet for coffee, but she never arrived. I thought for sure that she'd changed her mind, so, like an idiot, I never checked up on her and moved on to focus on work at my own firm. I sold the company shortly after."

"Why?"

Isaac smiled and held his hands up to the fire. "I had a one-night stand with a lawyer from another firm and realized I was drowning in my job."

Luke's eyes widened. "Damn. W...W-Who?"

His dad's eyes flicked to Luke. "Your mom. Working as the CEO of a divorce law firm was stifling anyway. So, I sold the company, took the money, and we started a homestead."

Luke watched the fire and pulled his blanket further up on his shoulders, processing his dad's story, and smiled. His father was naturally very private and must've been feeling nostalgic because Luke had never heard his mother and father's story in full.

They sat together in silence for a while until Isaac announced he was going to bed. Luke nodded, still staring into the light. Could he chase after a girl without caring about the consequences? He sure as hell wanted to but his nature pushed against it. Maybe that worked for his dad, but he couldn't do that, especially when people were involved.

He needed to clear the worries from his mind, so he pulled out a few folded sheets of paper and a charcoal pencil he'd packed before they left and began writing.

At first, it was ramblings over his mother, how he missed her, and where he and Isaac were at the moment, then it morphed into a poem. He scratched out words and chose better alternatives, making sure each line conveyed exactly what he wanted to say. He had to do something, or he'd explode, and a poem was as good as anything.

When he'd finished, he read it multiple times, finally satisfied. It spoke of the universe's beginning and a warrior woman, and Luke would keep it a secret.

At least for the time being.

"Luke," Isaac said.

"Yeah?" Luke asked as he slipped the poem under his pillow and prepped his own bed.

"Your mother is the best thing to happen to me." His voice had a strained tone to it. "What I want, more than anything, is to hold her again. We aren't going to mess this up."

"No...Hey, Dad?" Luke listened for the quiet grunt he knew was coming, and when it came, Luke said, "Tomorrow there's only a day left. You ready?"

"...I am."

The next morning, Luke awoke frozen, but he got into the saddle anyway and ate a small breakfast as everyone trotted along an old highway. The horses parted the grass as they moved, and Levin and Boatswain chased after a bunny.

Thankfully, the sun warmed the air a bit and its rays touched Luke's back. They passed through a city, the buildings crumbling, and windows glassless. A herd of deer standing in a large fountain filled with grass, lifted their heads to stare, and darted away when the dogs ran at them.

He learned more about their new companions just through listening to Isaac make conversation. Marie was married with a deaf child at home, Kieran worked for Thea as a courier, Sam was a soon-to-be father, and Shinat was a combat instructor for the Equida clan. They were all willing to help despite their busy lives. Unfortunately, he now had to make sure no one got hurt so they could return to their families.

The weight of that responsibility weighed heavily on him and as he mulled it over, a sense of inconsistent information washed over him. Kieran's story had sounded slightly off. The lack of emotions and how he skirted around certain details made it clear he was hiding something, but Luke couldn't figure out if he omitted something due to privacy or something else, so he put his suspicion aside. He couldn't let his dislike of Peter affect his opinion of Kieran, nor could he overlook, that if he had been lying, Marie, Shinat, and Sam would've noticed and reacted.

Isaac reined in his horse and hopped off before she fully stopped. "Get down," he hissed.

Luke did so without question, heart thumping, and stashed his horse with the others inside an old building, closed the door, then slunk in a crouch to a nearby alleyway partially blocked by an overturned dumpster. Sam, Shinat, Kieran, and Marie joined them.

He whispered to his dad. "You saw something?"

"Skin Stealer."

Luke's body ran cold. "This far south? Aren't they supposed to be in the Pass?"

Isaac shrugged and peered around the corner. "I don't know. This isn't like them."

Luke followed his dad's line of sight. Five Stealers ambled along, hunched over, the only woman in the group holding a bundle of something in her arms. Of the other four, one held a baseball bat with nails through it and another held a spear and a shield covered in tanned skin, a black symbol on the surface Luke couldn't quite make it out. They seemed to be looking for something, sniffing the air, peering behind things. As the five walked closer, eyes and hair wild, Isaac made a noise and ducked behind the dumpster again.

"W...W-What is it?"

Isaac stared, pale and unblinking, hand covering his mouth. When Luke repeated himself, Isaac shook his head.

Luke went to look at the Stealers, but Isaac's hand shot out. "Don't move. They see you and they'll kill you. Tell your dog to be quiet."

Levin released a low growl that Luke knew would build into a bark if he didn't stop it. Luke tossed the opportunity to work with Levin's reactivity out the window and held the dog against his chest, stroking him.

After a few minutes of waiting for the Skin Stealers to leave, Isaac whispered, "We need to get out of here. Now."

"I don't understand." Still shaken by his dad's reaction to the group, Luke dreaded asking his next question. "You saw something, didn't you?"

Slowly, Isaac turned to Luke. "Chizu's right-hand man's tattoo on a shield."

"Meaning?"

Isaac swallowed, closed his eyes, and spoke low. "They didn't copy his tattoo. On that shield...is his tattoo."

27 | LUKE

"**H**ow?"

"Damn it! Do I have to spell it out for you? They skinned him. It wasn't some design they thought was pretty and wanted to decorate their shield with. That shield *is* him. Do you understand?"

Luke wasn't sure why he kept asking his dad for clarification when it was obvious what he meant from the beginning. Hearing about their actions was one thing. *Seeing* it for himself? Whole different ballgame. Luke shuddered to think about what Chizu's man had gone through.

He watched the Skin Stealers carefully, cautious about alerting them to their location.

"Could something have driven them down here?" Sam speculated. "Similar to the animals attacking our people."

"It's possible," Isaac replied. "We won't fully know unless we investigate, and we don't have time for that."

Marie shifted uneasily. "Best thing to do is move on."

"Agreed," Isaac said.

Luke couldn't let go of his shock. "If Chizu's right-hand man is dead, then is Chizu and the clan okay?"

Isaac scoffed, the sound more like a growl. "Damn! Okay, we have to keep going. Clara comes first then we can check on Chizu."

Luke glanced over at Kieran by chance and discovered his attention honed intently on the Skin Stealer woman.

"Something wrong?" Luke asked him.

Kieran flinched a bit. "Other than the Skin Stealers coming this way?"

Luke didn't press the issue. As far as he knew, Kieran disliked the Skin Stealers as much as everyone else and didn't hold back his disgust as well as the others. He still kept an eye on Kieran. Just in case.

They waited behind the dumpster for a while, the Stealers taking their sweet time to continue on. Even Boatswain struggled to keep quiet.

"We can't stay here much longer," Shinat whispered, eyeing the Stealer holding the shield as if it were a terrifying creature.

"For the moment, we stay," Isaac said and settled in.

"And if they don't go the other way?" Sam asked.

Everyone exchanged knowing glances. Luke rubbed his chin as if he were trying to wipe the stubble off. "Hopefully they do."

"You hope?" Kieran growled. He kept watching the woman, the energy around him winding so tight that Boatswain nudged Luke's knee, releasing a tiny whine.

"Calm," Luke whispered.

He made eye contact with Kieran before he flicked his gaze to the Stealer woman and man who had wandered away from their group. She picked flowers with him close by while the others rifled through a scrap metal pile. She smiled down at her bundle and a tiny arm moved from behind the ripped blanket. Of the group, the woman moved as if she'd never been affected by the experiments the others had been subjected to.

Kieran shifted and before Luke could do anything, there was a flash of metal and Kieran sprinted straight for the Stealer woman, great axe in hand.

"No!" Luke screamed.

The woman cried out and scrambled away, clutching the bundle close to her chest.

A Skin Stealer man, this one broad shouldered and his face hidden by a heavy mask with deer antlers, ran to save the woman. He struck the handle of Kieran's axe with his own and shoved, releasing a war cry as he did so. Kieran managed to stay on his feet.

"Stay." Luke snapped his fingers at his dogs and had to give Levin an extra poke in the shoulder to get his attention. They each reacted in their own way to the command but both laid back down, nervous energy tightening their bodies.

Luke flicked his bow over his shoulder and notched it within seconds, aiming at the Stealer man. His bow arm shook, knowing he might not get a shot off before the other Stealers overwhelmed him.

The woman fled into a nearby building. Kieran's attention shifted quickly her way before he barely blocked the Stealer's strike. A teeth chattering clash of thick wood vibrated through the air. Everyone behind the dumpster drew their weapons.

"Focus on Kieran," Isaac commanded. "I'll take the group and cut off the advancing Skin Stealers."

Luke nodded and returned his attention to Kieran and the Stealer man, knowing he had to shoot, but hated to attack someone defending one of their people. And selfishly, Luke needed Kieran.

What do I do?

The Stealer was only protecting the woman. Kieran was out of control. The three other Stealers were a ways off but Isaac's group would be on them in seconds. He had to make a decision, so he stalked toward the two men in a half-crouch, and realized late he'd hesitated too long. Kieran slammed his shoulder into the Stealer, knocking him to the ground, and swung.

"Kieran, no!"

Luke couldn't get a shot off fast enough.

Blood sprayed the ground, the man's gurgling cry halted when Kieran pulled his weapon out of his victim. A stab of disgust and shock choked Luke.

He ran toward Kieran standing over the mutilated Stealer body. Blood rushed in his ears. His breathing, labored from adrenaline and watching a murder so fresh, he couldn't think to do much more than run and try to subdue Kieran before he did more damage. Kieran didn't pay attention to Luke's cries to stand down, wasn't concerned with Luke's proximity to him. Instead, he glanced around with an expression of fury.

What's he looking for?

Weapons clashed up diagonally to his left and Luke briefly saw his dad, Sam, Shinat, and Marie holding their own against two Skin Stealers.

Where's the third?

A blow to Luke's shoulder sent him sprawling in the dirt. His arrows clattered from the quiver. When Luke found his bearings, a heavily built man, dark charcoal smeared across his face, and sharpened teeth stood over him. Luke scrambled for his bow. A heavy boot slammed down on his hand and Luke cried out, the ridged sole digging into his tendons.

The pressure lifted seconds later. Luke surged to his feet, pulled an arrow from the ground, notched it, and spun in one motion, dirt piling around his boots.

Sam jumped over the injured Stealer who'd attacked Luke, yanked two bolts from the man's thighs, and loaded one back into his crossbow.

Groaning at his throbbing shoulder, Luke gathered up the rest of his arrows and sprinted after Kieran disappearing into the same building the Stealer woman escaped to.

"Kieran!" Luke skidded to a halt inside. Crunching leaves and over a decade's worth of dirt flew into the air. He stood between two Grecian pillars in the foyer of an old hotel, rusted green paint peeling from the surface. Broken chairs and couches gathered around coffee tables and statues, or against walls.

He panted and listened. His head swiveled to search for movement or sound. A crash and terror laced scream jolted Luke up the stairs. He took each step three at a time, thighs burning by the time he reached the landing, and nearly fell over the iron banister as he turned the corner.

Another crash.

Down the hall, Luke could hear the crying.

"You should've died instead and taken it with you! Look at how pathetic you are. It's going to be exactly like them!"

A bead of sweat trailed down his nose as Luke, the bow aimed at a non-fatal location on Kieran, stalked into the room. His heart beat too loud to hear himself speak, but he did anyway, forcing his words to be firmer than he felt.

"Axe down. Now!"

Kieran didn't acknowledge Luke's presence, only launched a chair across the room, forcing Luke to step aside or risk getting hit.

Kieran screamed, "You ran to them, didn't you? And look what they did! Adopted you like an animal."

The woman, her face contorted in terror, held her child as if she were trying to shove the babe back into her body to protect it, and trembled. She yelped and tried to run but a bookshelf and a table blocked her path. The only way through was toward the man with the axe.

"Kieran!" Luke called out again. His anger festered, pain swelling in his gut and throat. "If I have to, I will shoot you."

"Give me the child and I will make your death swift."

What's wrong with him?

The Stealer woman shook her head, but said nothing, and Luke wondered if she could understand Kieran.

"Get away from her!" Luke screamed, his throat hoarse.

Kieran whirled on Luke, axe raised. "No! She deserves what's coming to her."

"Don't make me shoot you," Luke snarled in a low octave he didn't know could come out of him and anger roared right along with his words. "Leave her alone. She's done nothing to you."

"She's done everything to me!" He pounded his chest. "I loved her and she abandoned me. If she stays with those animals, our child will turn into a monster!"

"The hell you saying?" Luke's head spun but he kept his arrow aimed at Kieran's shoulder.

Kieran snarled and turned on Luke. "I gave her the world and the minute I snap *once*," he rolled up his sleeve, revealing a long, pink scar down his forearm, "she does this to me and scurries off!"

Luke stepped back, his body lead. "You're a...fucking bastard."

He glanced at the woman shivering and cowering in the far back. She kept her eyes closed and her head pressed against the baby's dark hair, humming something as she rocked back and forth.

Kieran advanced on mother and baby.

"Don't you dare touch them," Luke warned, and Kieran stopped, his furious gaze slowly training on Luke.

"The minute she picked their side, she became one of them. My child is going to grow up sick in the head and it's all her fault!"

"The hell? Can you blame them? The Pass is brutal and she has a baby!"

"I only want her to understand the consequences of her actions."

"Touch either of them..." Luke hissed and lifted his bow to send the message home.

If Kieran attacked the woman, Luke would shoot him, but could he make it count? His entire body quaked. He could miss, dooming them both.

Failing wasn't an option.

It took seconds for Kieran to raise his weapon and run at the woman. She closed her eyes, sighed, and stroked her baby's back.

Aim further ahead.

Take into account my shaking, Kieran's height.

And...

Kieran's axe crashed to the ground as the arrow hit him. To Luke's horror, Kieran ripped the arrow from his shoulder, growled, and advanced on Luke.

He'd calculated wrong.

Kieran, the woman ignored, continued his path toward Luke. "You first. Then her."

"Run!" Luke yelled at the woman as he loaded his bow again and retreated into the hallway. "Run now!"

Either too petrified to move or unable to understand, the woman ignored Luke and continued humming. Luke could distract Kieran enough for the woman to stay safe, he just had to get out before the other Stealers came looking for her, if any were left.

Damn it.

Luke gritted his teeth and aimed a second time. He refused to kill Kieran, no matter how much he wanted to, but he'd have to if—

Kieran lunged with the arrow in his fist. Luke sidestepped, taking the tip of his own arrow across his cheek, ducked, and sunk his loaded arrow into Kieran's stomach. The man let out a surprised grunt, his eyes wide.

"...Bastard."

A flash of Kieran's arm and before Luke could block, the arrow's sting hit him. Adrenaline prevented him from knowing exactly where Kieran had buried the tip. Still, Luke held position.

Kieran relaxed against him. His breathing faltered. Another stab hit Luke, some shallow place at his back, and Luke's body jolted. Sick to his stomach enough to struggle keeping his last meal down, Luke jerked the arrow from Kieran's midsection, took hold of it, and growled through pain as he aimed for Kieran's carotid artery, paused, then yanked it free.

Seconds later, Kieran wheezed and collapsed. Dead.

Luke stayed on the ground and waited for his adrenaline to calm before he inspected his wounds. He found two arrowhead sized cuts, one on the top of his shoulder and the other somewhere on his back – he had to feel for it. They twinged as he gingerly stood and looked for the woman.

She was still there.

Slowly, grunting as he did so, Luke approached. He unclipped his quiver, removed his cloak, and softened his posture. Training Levin, the epitome of a fear reactive dog, had given him the knowledge he hoped would aid him in helping the woman. He didn't want to scare her, so he entered her space slowly. Carefully.

Once he was several feet away, the woman's bright blue eyes flashed to him, her teeth bared, and she hissed. The sound came out hoarse.

Luke took several steps away and pointed to the door. "No, no. You're safe."

She glanced where Luke pointed, and he could see in her eyes that she took time to process his words. He didn't know how much she could with fear clouding her mind.

Luke pushed his luck to get closer and this time she allowed it. A silent understanding passed between them. She nodded slightly and Luke mimicked the gesture. The slightest smile tugged at her lips.

Up close, Luke could tell something was off. He'd seen the other Stealers, and they were rough, but this woman was almost emaciated. Had she not gotten enough food? Was that why they were down in the valley and not in their mountain? She licked her lips and her saliva was tinged pink.

"Did he hit you here?" Luke asked and touched his own mouth.

The Skin Stealer woman wiped at her lips. When the baby made an angry noise, the spell broke. She gasped and ran from the room.

Collapsing against the old bed, Luke closed his eyes, his head pounding from the tanking of his adrenaline.

Move. It's over. You can move.

He couldn't. He'd just saved a woman and her child from death. He'd earned a rest.

Someone's far off voice called out for him. It rang through the mist, muffled and garbled, and Luke opened his eyes to shadowed figures, one leaning close to him, and when he blinked, his father came into focus along with his dogs.

"Thank God," Isaac breathed, and ducked his head for a moment. "You're alive."

"Of course, I am." Luke straightened from his half-laying position, dull and stinging pain radiating from the arrow lacerations. He hated pain. It made him irrational and grumpy, but his dogs helped to alleviate some of that. "Did the woman get away okay?"

Isaac smiled, his worried expression softening. "She did."

"And the other Stealers?"

"Aside from the one Kieran killed," Sam said, Kieran's axe in his hand, "the others left with the woman. We thought it best to leave them alone."

Luke kept his eyes on the axe, not really hearing Sam, and tried to understand why Kieran had given it away. His brain took a few extra seconds to process Kieran's fate and his own hand in it.

"Shit." Everything in Luke's stomach came up. When his body stopped convulsing, he wiped his mouth and said, "I killed him."

"We figured that," Marie said. She grimaced, arms tight around her body. "Your arrow was still..." she swallowed, "in him."

Shinat was nowhere to be seen.

"What happened?" Isaac asked.

So, he told his dad about Kieran's attack on the woman, and pieced together why based on what Kieran had screamed at her.

A voice interrupted Luke. "You killed him."

Everyone turned to Shinat standing in the doorway, her face a greenish hue and balled fists trembling.

"I had no choice," Luke said as he stumbled to his feet. "He was going to kill an innocent woman and kidnap her baby."

"He's dead." Shinat swayed and Sam moved to catch her.

"She's in shock," Sam said when he pulled his hand away from her forehead. "She and Kieran grew up together, so they were close." Shinat slumped in Sam's arms, and he lowered her into a nearby chair. "We need to leave soon."

Isaac nodded his agreement and cut at a sheet he'd grabbed from somewhere. He ripped a few strips, folded them to absorb the bleeding, then wrapped more around Luke's shoulder and around his back.

"Let's get home," he said.

Sam spoke up. "Shinat and I will take Kieran's body back to the clan and meet you at the island."

Shinat leaned against him, wobbly on her feet, but recovering.

Sam paused and turned to Luke. "He didn't hurt her just once. It was years of abuse. When I return, I'll tell Thea his death was in self-defense. Hopefully that will satisfy her to not press charges, especially since she's seen marks on Harlowe – the woman you saved."

Isaac didn't waste time getting to business, but Luke saw the clenched fist and red creeping up his neck as his dad handed Luke's bow back to him. "We'll continue on back to Raft Island and wait for you at our house until we need to leave to get Clara tomorrow." Isaac barely kept his voice in check as he spoke to Sam, "Don't take too long at the Equida clan. We need to move before tomorrow afternoon to get to the cabin in time to save Clara."

"Alright, boss," Sam said and left with Shinat.

Luke groaned, pressing his fingertips to his forehead. "God, I hate w...w-waiting so much."

Isaac chuckled. "Come on. Let's get you home so your girlfriend can patch you up."

"She's not—" Then he paused. "Actually, that's undecided."

Isaac helped Sam gather equipment to make a makeshift, handheld sleigh while Luke and his dogs watched. Together, they attached it to Sam's horse, and Isaac helped him load the body onto it.

No other Skin Stealers surfaced as they traveled from the city. By the time they summited the ridge on the outskirts, Luke was completely irritated and sore from his injuries.

If Soora saw me now, she'd probably have an aneurysm.

"Where are we going?" Marie asked, trotting up next to Luke.

He glanced sideways at her, wincing when his horse crow hopped over a tall root. "Market Town. As my dad so delicately put it, my not-girlfriend, Sibyl Marchant, lives in one of the shops there." Luke motioned to his injuries. "She'll help."

PART THREE

POWER

28 | SIBYL

Sibyl leaned over, panting, sweat dripping onto the boxing ring floor. She'd discovered the hole-in-the-wall gym a few months ago and had quickly invited Eloise. They'd logged hours in the place, Sibyl too nervous to go against anyone else, but happy to watch Eloise take on whomever challenged her.

Today, the gym was empty except for a few older guys at the back taking turns on the heavy bag. Their punches reverberated off the gym walls, drowning out their conversation.

"Wow," Eloise said, locked in a hold Sibyl had locked her in. "I forgot how strong you are."

Sibyl chortled. "You're just slow."

Eloise slipped underneath Sibyl's arm. She slammed her shoulder into Sibyl's back, sending her stumbling forward, a move Bannack had shown her that she loved using.

"I fall for that one every single time."

"That's why it's so great." Eloise smirked and picked up her dueling sticks.

Sibyl smiled and swung her own stick in an over exaggerated show of fake anger. Their sticks clashed together.

"Awe, come on," Eloise laughed. "I still love you."

Coming in for a blow, Sibyl feigned, dropped her arm, and body slammed Eloise, sending her best friend tumbling into the ropes.

Sibyl pulled off her glove. "You okay?"

She rolled onto her back and put her hand into the air. "I'm good."

Sibyl couldn't help but laugh. She walked over to Eloise and laid down beside her. The boxing ring floor cooled her back off.

Eloise titled her head against Sibyl's shoulder and they laid there together for a long while in silence, listening to the quiet, save for clinking chains and landing punches.

Luke had been gone for two days and she missed his silence. Eloise's was nice but Luke's had an intimate depth to it that made her feel warm, comforted, and understood in a way she'd craved her whole life. He knew how to say so much with little words or a single look, and when his dark eyes settled upon her...they put the universe to shame.

Having her best friend close eased the worry in her gut over Luke's journey. Would they find the help they needed? Would Fade push to move Clara before they got there?

What happens if we can't rescue her?

"I have a gift for you."

Sibyl turned, broken out of her thoughts. "Oh?"

"And it's a good one. Took me ages to track down." Eloise hopped to her feet. "Come on!"

Sibyl followed Eloise, both bundled in thick coats they'd discarded when they got too hot during their sparring match. Sibyl waved at a few of her customers. Nowadays, with everything freezing and food scarce, her shop opened less and less, and now only available on the weekends. People just didn't have the mental energy or money to spend. A low customer count benefited her though, albeit in a small way. With less stock, she wouldn't have to close completely.

They entered Aito's book store, Sibyl shivering into her thick coat when the door behind her shut, hitting the bell above it a second time.

Aito's head popped out from behind the front desk and a smile of recognition broadened his face. "How's my favorite poison maker?" He looked at Eloise. "And friend."

Sibyl rolled her eyes good naturedly and approached. "This is Eloise. Eloise, this is Aito, our resident book hoarder." She smiled when Aito huffed through his nose. "It's funny you mention poison. I found the world's deadliest earlier today and just need someone to test it on."

"No unsuspecting humans available, I see, so you had to come here and ask for sacrifices."

"Unfortunately," Sibyl said. Eloise disappeared toward the back somewhere. "Got any villains hiding out back?"

Aito shook his head. "Only the paper kind."

"I come in here, asking for help, and you can't?" She quietly gasped and pressed her palm to her chest. "I thought we were friends."

Chuckling, Aito walked down an aisle and Sibyl followed, eyeing the rows of books. Adventures and romances and tragedies, their pages begging to be touched. She'd been in Aito's shop before, but she hadn't explored past the front desk, and the scent of books hung heavy in the air, musky with the slight after tone of vanilla. Immediately she missed Luke.

How had she never realized he smelled like this? All of a sudden, she wanted to devour every single volume, to understand why Luke loved books so much and to go on the adventures he'd experienced within the pages, to fall in love over and over again, experience heartbreak, learn how to use magic and ride dragons, and arrive at the end of a story either fulfilled or destroyed. Or both. All while curled up in his lap listening to his beautiful, deep voice read out loud.

"You have a beautiful collection," she mused.

Aito smiled, thanked her in Japanese, put a book away, and moved on. She meant to follow him into the depths of his shop, but she noticed the Tree in the store's center, its open archway beckoning to her.

As she stood between the non-fiction and romance, Sibyl couldn't deny the insatiable curiosity that begged to be fed. Would going in feel sacrilegious? Probably. Did she have anyone to kiss? No. Would anyone care? Also no. So, why not investigate?

Sibyl stepped up to the Tree and her eyes trailed its trunk, dark bark sporting rough canyons of texture. A lantern lit the confessions of love and adoration, and Sibyl leaned forward to peer inside. She recognized many familiar names carved into the interior bark and as Sibyl felt each with her fingertips, one inscription caught her eye:

Oh, to be near you and not kiss you.
To listen to the shell of the ocean
And within, hear your call.
My soul is stirring,
And I can contain it no longer.

Now invested, she searched for the unknown poet, guided only by their romantic swirls on the G's and the rigidity of the W's, as if the author couldn't decide which handwriting to use.

Tucked below a heart with initials inside, Sibyl found another poem.

You are worth it.
Every penny.
Every moment.
You rival the sun,
And you deserve to understand
just how precious you are.

"Who wrote these?" Sibyl whispered, the tickle of recognizing the handwriting in the back of her mind.

She *had* to know if there were more poems. Love poured from the words. It was there in the reverence of every single phrase, in the soft curves of each letter, in the spaces, empty yet overflowing with the promise of safe spaces, adoration, and acceptance. Whoever the author, they ached for their lover.

"Syb!" Eloise's voice from outside the Tree interrupted the silence inside. "Where'd you go?"

Aito responded first. "She's in the Tree."

Unable to get her voice working for a few moments, Sibyl listened to Eloise's chuckle.

"I remember when only couples went in here."

"Yes," Aito said and set something down on a counter. "Now, people wander in all the time. That local bookbinder visited a while ago, though his name escapes me."

Not wanting to leave, Sibyl read inscriptions from other people. Proclamations of love, announcements of broken love, and simple names, all adding to the beautiful, romantic memory of The Kissing Tree.

"Luke Blackwood?" Eloise asked and Sibyl's ears perked up. "Why remember him specifically?"

"Oh, only that I found it odd he entered without buying anything. I was under the impression that he's an avid reader, is he not?"

Sibyl took an excited half-step forward when she found a third inscription by the same poet as the last two.

> *Do you know what you are?*
> *Do you know what you do to me?*
> *You shine,*
> *And I am privileged enough to see it.*
> *My Light.*
> *My Cici.*

She stepped back, staring at the final word, and whispered. "That...that's me."

Her hand covered the smile that broke across her face. Those words she found all over the Tree – his – were written for her and she didn't care one lick that he hadn't voiced them directly. He didn't have to say anything, she already knew how much he cared. Tears misted her eyes.

Eloise appeared, carrying a long item wrapped in a piece of fabric. The sight was hilarious, seeing Eloise's five-foot-two frame up against the length of a six and a half foot long...something.

"What happened?" Eloise asked and stepped forward, hitting the item on the archway. "Oh, hell." She set it down and turned back to Sibyl. "Why are you crying?"

Sibyl released a wet chuckle. "He wrote me poetry."

Her mouth slowly dropped open as Eloise stared at Sibyl. "God, you're so sappy and I love you for it. If that's why you're crying, what I brought for you is sure going to get you going. You wanna see it?"

Aito appeared behind Eloise, curious.

"I do...Aito?" Sibyl glanced over Eloise's shoulder at him. "Prep the concrete. We're gonna need to build a dam."

Eloise cackled. "That's my girl!"

Still on a high from Luke's words, Sibyl stepped from the Tree and stood in front of Eloise holding the present, practically dancing.

"It took me ages to find it. Some guy was trying to pawn it off to someone who was going to take it far away. I had to clean it up a little but..."

Sibyl unwrapped the top first, revealing a leather-bound spear tip. "A spear?"

Eloise bit her lip with a smile and motioned for Sibyl to keep going.

The fabric unraveled as she undid the ties and they collected at her feet. Spear tip turned into spear shaft and upon it were carvings.

Her carvings.

Depictions of her early life as a way to connect with a family that had been ripped from her. Ballet slippers, flowers she wore in her hair, her mother's eyes, a little girl curled into a ball, weeping, mountains, horses, friends sitting on a log overlooking a lake, her favorite star constellations.

This spear wasn't just a spear, it was memories and experiences, some she would never have, memorialized into one spot that she carried always. Her heart and soul, desires, loves and losses, all in physical form.

"This..." Sibyl ran her fingers over the rich brown leather strings tied between the shaft and tip. "This is mine."

"It is." Eloise rocked forward and back on her toes. "I found it fo—"

Sibyl crashed into her, hiccupping from crying. "Thank you. Thank you!"

Her joy swam through her, filling every crevice of her body and warming whatever it touched. The spear that Peter sold under her nose then lied about, was finally home.

Sibyl laughed. She cried. She hugged Eloise. Tears coursed down her cheeks until Aito handed her a handkerchief to wipe them away.

"Thank you," Sibyl said to Aito and they both shared a smile. She rubbed her thumb along the carvings, sniffling. "I thought I'd never see this again." She looked at a beaming Eloise. "You...are the literal best. I can't believe you kept this a secret from me!"

"Ah, well, it was rough but I did it." Eloise shrugged. She handed Sibyl a leather shoulder strap used to keep the spear secured to the wearers back. "Made that special for you."

"Oh my gosh. It's beautiful." Sibyl glanced down at the spear again and slipped it onto her shoulder. The familiar weight made her eyes tear up again. "It feels so good."

"Well, what are you waiting for?" Eloise asked as she motioned to the front door. "Go try it out."

"You don't have to ask me twice!" Sibyl beamed, hugged both Eloise and Aito, and ran out the door.

She grabbed a sling bag from her shop and spent the evening out and about, exploring the beach and running trails above it. For a while, she spear hunted for fish or octopi, a rope tied on the shaft so she could reel in any catches without getting wet, then switched to gathering seaweed, crabs, and clams in the low tide. Her weapon stayed on her back, loyal and ever present, sea water dripping from the leather ties as she explored.

It's back. Sibyl smiled. *I finally have it back.*

Two years. The spear had been missing for two years. Simply put, Eloise finding it was nothing short of a miracle. Sibyl had run herself ragged trying to find it, thinking it lost forever.

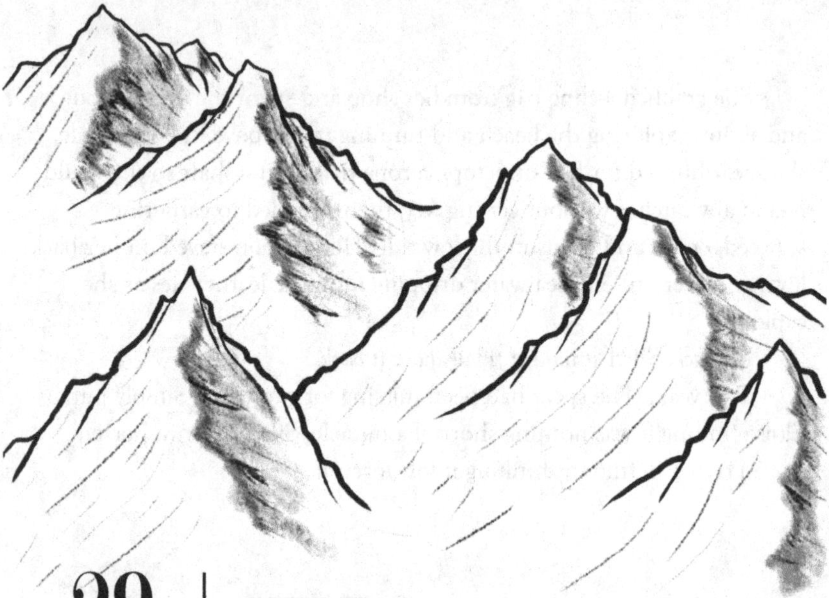

29 | SIBYL

One smile.
I desire one smile from you,
and I shall never want for anything more,
nor do I deserve it.
But your love tells me I am worthy of it.

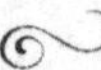

When she returned to La Parfana, Sibyl set the spear by the door and quickly prepped a saltwater bath for the clams and oysters she'd found attached to a dock column.

She shivered and struggled to get her stiff hands to move.

I really need to get that fire going.

Luckily, she had a metal fire starter that helped her avoid the manual labor of creating friction, so she knelt in front of her fireplace, piled on some dried moss and kindling, and scratched a blade down the metal rod, creating a shower of sparks. It wasn't long before a small fire began. She nursed it for the next several minutes and added larger pieces of wood as the fire grew.

"There," Sibyl said and smiled at the flickering light, then stood and walked over to a cabinet that held pots and pans. She mumbled to herself as she gathered supplies to make a seaweed and shellfish soup, setting the needed items out so they'd be ready when she returned from upstairs.

Sibyl took a quick sponge bath, too tired to fill up the tub, and washed her hair with homemade soap by leaning over the basin.

Clean but cold, Sibyl dressed, added two layers of socks, some thick pants, a long sleeve shirt, and grabbed her warmest sweater from its hanger. She padded downstairs as she maneuvered her long black hair free from the collar of the sweater then lit some candles and lanterns around the shop.

She dumped out her catch into a metal bowl to inspect it. Hand-sized clams, oysters, some smallish crabs, several handfuls of seaweed, and one bull kelp she had to snap into pieces to fit it in her beach bag when she first snagged it.

While the room warmed over the next half hour, Sibyl cleaned the clams and oysters, discarding any that remained open after a quick tap, then brought out her cutting board to prepare the seaweed and kelp. For good measure, Sibyl tossed in some onions, potatoes, and carrots she kept in the cold greenhouse.

She worked, humming and dancing to the tune in her head, and took an occasional opportunity to twirl or bounce, all the while stirring the boiling pot. The world fell away. Just her and the song in her head.

Someone knocked.

Sibyl screamed, the spoon flying. It clattered across the floor. Cold air slithered over the ground and invaded her socks as she lifted her gaze from the spoon to the person standing in the cold.

Luke leaned against the door jamb with a half-smile on his lips. Light from the lanterns inside La Parfana danced lazily across the planes of his face. She noticed a sliver of white underneath his traveling cloak, the hood of which lying flat on his shoulders and back.

Sibyl walked over to get the spoon and brandished it as if the thing was Excalibur and glared at him. "You scared me."

Boatswain and Levin ran over to get hello scritches.

There it was, the dark shine to his eyes, and Sibyl's face flushed with fire, but she kept her composure, still prickling from him scaring her half to death.

Luke tilted his head. "Can you blame me for enjoying your scream?"

"I screamed because you came in without warning!" Luke smiled wider before she realized what he meant and covered her face. "Oh. Oh my God."

The suspicious placement of the white underneath his cloak didn't click immediately in her brain as Luke sauntered toward her. The closer he got, the more she could smell those vanilla undertones and she really, really wished she could hold onto something for stability because she was going down like the Titanic, and Luke was the iceberg who brought her downfall.

"I can't believe you just let me walk into that." The smile tugging at her lips wouldn't be hidden.

He shrugged, now completely upon her, darkness personified. His chest touched hers and she released a tiny squeak.

"Welcome back."

"Nice to be back." Luke leaned in, his facial hair tickling her cheek, and when he opened his mouth, words she only heard in a deep rumble tumbled forth to awaken the primal desires in her mind. "I'd love for your smile to be the only thing you have on tonight."

Her skin. Her mind. Her legs. Everything weak and everything on fire, heightened – drugged – by his mere presence. Then his mouth found her neck and he used the tip of his tongue to stamp a brand onto her skin. She shuddered.

How could she be expected to breathe? How would she even touch him? She'd touched him everywhere, so it wasn't like she couldn't, but somehow this moment was different, and it sent her thoughts straight to heaven to be blessed by angels.

She stood there, staring like an idiot at him as he pulled back. At some point in his travels, he'd shaved, and it must have been right after he left because two-day old stubble made her stomach go all funny at the shape of his jaw. Angular. Masculine. Every single inch of her wanted all of him, to have that stubble brush against her thighs. How long had it been since she'd seen him? A day and a half? Longer? She couldn't think anymore.

"You've ruined me. I'm never, ever," Sibyl placed her hand on his chest and his muscles flexed underneath her palm, "going to enjoy any other coming home greeting ever again."

"I could up the stakes, if you desire. Maybe do a little—"

Sibyl blushed and whispered, "You're impossible." Then she realized no one was with him and peered around him to make sure she hadn't completely missed anyone coming in after him. "Where is everyone? Didn't you leave to go get people?"

His words fluttered across her neck. "They're coming soon."

"Wanted to get a little frisky with your girl first, huh?" Sibyl asked, a giggle rolling out of her but then it stopped short. Luke was looking at her but not smiling like she thought he would have. She put her hand on his face and asked, "What's wrong?"

Luke sat in the nearest chair, taking her with him, and pulled her onto his lap. "Tomorrow we're saving my mom. I'm nervous as hell." He leaned into her and sighed, and his words came out muffled. "I had to come see you before they arrived. You. Me. Nothing else."

"Will them being here make you worry more?"

Luke nodded against her, and when Sibyl innocently wrapped her arms around him, he grunted in pain.

She pulled away. "What did you do now?"

"I...uh," Luke looked at her apologetically, "got hurt."

"Yeah. I can tell." She sighed. "Come with me."

She plopped him on a chair in the back room and rifled through the closet to find her first aid. Again. "Take off your shirt."

Behind her, the chair squeaked as he shifted. Something warm and soft hit her at the back of her head. Luke's shirt and cloak. She closed her eyes so she wouldn't laugh, then turned around.

Luke sat slouched in the chair, bandages over his chest with two bloodied blotches on the fabric, his dark as night hair with a tiny curl at the bottom touching his shoulders. Both dogs laid at his feet.

"I need to see what's under the bandages, so I'm going to take them off."

Luke nodded.

Two, half-inch lacerations marred his back and shoulder. Yet another pair to add to his growing list of injuries that left white marks after healing.

"What happened?" Sibyl hissed through her teeth.

While guilt built on his face, Luke told Sibyl about his visit with Thea, the run in with the Skin Stealers, Kieran's history with Harlowe and his death, and his and Luke's fight. She listened, careful not to interrupt, but wanted so badly to give him a hug. Her eyes misted over.

"He almost killed them." Luke turned away, his jaw clenching.

Sibyl pulled out a numbing poultice made from cloves and dabbed the brown substance onto his skin. "You saved them."

"I know."

She knew by the way he glanced away from her that he didn't believe her, so she changed the subject. "I'm not as good as Soora and what I know about stitches is more like how to sew clothes, but I think they should look okay."

"That's still up in the air," Luke mumbled. Sibyl shot him an angry glare, though amused, and Luke tightened his lips. "Sorry. I meant, thank you."

She paused, her expression changing from playful annoyance to concern. "Hey," Sibyl touched his cheek, "what happened isn't your fault. Okay? Killing a man is traumatizing on its own, but what you went through is on another level. You did nothing wrong. In fact, you did the exact right thing."

Luke closed his eyes. His hand found the back of hers still on his cheek, and pressed her palm harder against his face.

As she continued working, she talked. "I saw your poems on the inside of The Kissing Tree today." She glanced at Luke. He didn't respond but she saw the tiny glimmer of amusement in the way his eyes dilated, and he pulled in his bottom lip. Sibyl smiled. "They were beautiful."

He shrugged, trying to let the compliment slip off his shoulders. That wouldn't fly. No way would he escape that easily.

"Luke," Sibyl said, stopping her stitches to spread her fingers on his neck. His dark eyes flicked to her. "Those words came from you and beautiful words like that could only come from a beautiful person." She whispered next, her voice threatening to crack. "You mean so much to me."

Crying was inevitable whenever she genuinely complimented someone, and Luke had tears in his eyes, too. They lingered there, not quite ready to fall over the edge of his lids, and he glanced down at his hands, ran his fingertips together, and clenched his fists. She placed her hands over them, leaned in, and left a long kiss upon his brow.

"You are...everything." Luke's whisper came out so soft and gentle, it fluttered, feather-light, through the air and settled upon her ears. There they would stay, immortal.

Sibyl smiled at him, leaned in or a kiss, and got back to work. She grabbed the ointment the assassin gave them and turned the container over in her hand.

Do we trust this woman enough to use this stuff?

Should we even test it?

"Thinking of testing it on me?"

"Oh no," Sibyl said and set it back down in the box. "Just thinking about bringing it in case it's needed."

He regarded the jar as if it were going to pounce on him. "Good."

"Do you think you'll grow things if we do?"

Luke pulled away. "I hope the fuck not." He relaxed when Sibyl laughed.

As she helped Luke into his shirt and closed the first-aid box, someone tapped on the glass insert on the door and Sibyl turned to see Isaac standing outside with a woman Sibyl didn't recognize.

"I'll get it," she said and let them in.

Luke stood with a grunt, and introduced her to the woman, his hand slipping around Sibyl's waist. "Sibyl, this is Marie."

"Hello," Marie said.

"Welcome to my shop." Then she motioned to the pot of soup. "Help yourself. There's plenty and I'm sure you're hungry."

Sibyl left Luke's side to go grab some food and joined Isaac and Marie with her own bowl.

"Thank you for feeding us." Marie filled the spoon with more broth. "It's so good to have something warm."

"You're welcome. Are the others planning to join us soon?"

Isaac swirled his food. "Luke filled you in, then. Good. We still have a full day left before we need to leave, so I'm hoping they can meet us at the house in time. If not," he shook his head with a frown, "we're going to have to continue without them."

Sibyl looked at her soup, a light shimmer of oil floating in the liquid. "Do you think we can rescue Clara without them?"

"I don't know. I hope."

Luke sat beside Sibyl and a quick rush of excitement ran through her. There was a delicate intimacy to how he touched her thigh with his pinky, then his entire hand, as if he needed to test the waters before diving headfirst.

She stole glances at him as they ate, Luke sneaking his dogs little snacks as if he were a young kid refusing to finish his dinner. She couldn't help but smile when their eyes met. He watched her, lifted the bowl to his mouth, and drank. Her vision honed in on his throat, skin working as he swallowed. She pressed her knees together.

"We'll meet you at the house, then?" Isaac asked after he placed his bowl in Marie's and took them to an empty counter. When Marie went to wait outside for him, Isaac gave Luke and Sibyl knowing glances then smiled mischievously. "Come to the house by tomorrow morning and don't be late."

He left and Sibyl stared at the empty window. "Did…did your dad just…"

"Make a sex joke? Yes, he did."

Sibyl leaned back and laughed. "I…don't know how I feel about that."

When she glanced at Luke, his expression calm. He slipped his hand into hers and turned to her, soft gaze upon her mouth. In the flickering lanterns, he said, "I'm going to take a kiss."

"Yes. God, yes. Please."

His thumb touched her lower lip and coaxed her mouth open just enough to slide a gentle tongue flick inside. The delicate exploration made her drunk on the liquor of him. Helpless. Sibyl's heart pounded on the inside of her sternum. Luke pulled away, then smiled. She wanted more, so much so that she whined deep in her throat and the breath of Luke's next words spread across her face.

"W…W-When the universe began, it looked upon your soul and said, 'This woman shall be a warrior. She shall banish the darkness. And if she burns, she shall fly shall fly home on scorched wings.'"

"Luke, I—" She started to say, 'tell me more,' because his poem weakened her knees the way he growled out the words and whispered them across her face, but then she was travelling with him. His hand touched her hip. He played with the hem of her shirt. Every move calculated.

And she was undone.

He graced her with another poem, the words falling upon her like the sun rays, seducing her into oblivion.

"She is the sun, and I the storm. Just as I crash upon the rocks, she rises."

It was official; she had lost her sense. But he was so utterly irresistible that she didn't want to see sense. All she wanted was to kiss him everywhere.

Sibyl pulled away, a quiet grunt revealing protest from Luke, and licked her lips where he left his mark.

"You are…" she had to actually take a break, her head spinning, "quite the surprise."

Luke grunted and kissed her again, adding a deep inhale as he did so, and slipped his fingers through her hair, exploring. Then he pulled her hips against him. She went willingly, prepared for whatever he wanted to do to her. She was his.

With his lips hovering over hers, Luke whispered, "I'm going to take you right here."

30 | LUKE

Luke stashed the dogs upstairs with some warm blankets and came back down to drapes closed over all the windows and their own nest of furs on the ground.

Sibyl was upon him, her hands on his stomach, leaving a suggestive lick on the side of his neck. Good Lord, this woman knew how to get right to the point. Luke stepped back, and took her with him while desperate calloused fingertips slipped underneath his shirt. An electric jolt hit his stomach. It was so powerful, he stood there for a few moments, re-learning how to breathe.

She didn't stop touching and touching.

"Cici," he muttered.

"Just to be clear," she muttered into his ear with a voice of warm honey. "I can touch everywhere?"

Words abandoned him, stolen by Sibyl's dark look, but he managed a single one. "Y-yes."

Clunky, but there it was.

"Like...here?" She ran her thumb across his inner thigh. His legs weakened and he nodded. "What about...here?" Two rough fingertips slipped underneath his shirt, found the trail of dark hair below his belly button and he stumbled. "And, can I touch..." she slipped her hand into his pants, "here?"

His head fell backward, he heard rustling, then she kissed his Adam's apple.

"Holy fucking hell, Cici." He continued to release a string of expletives because no conscious thought beyond swearing existed in his brain.

"What?" she asked with a mischievous grin, her eyes hiding desire that lingered underneath a veil of innocence.

"You—" he started but thought better of it, rallied his strength, and pushed her against the wall, careful not to open his stitches.

Her eyes danced with wild excitement as he smashed the palm of his hand next to her head, leaning into her. The furs were behind them but there was no time to get to them.

He wanted her.

Now.

They'd worry about the nest later.

"I want—"

Before he could finish his sentence, Sibyl grabbed his waist and moved his hips to her. She lifted her chin. "That answer your question?"

A laugh tumbled out of him as he spoke. "You are impossible. Alluring. I'm going to ravish you."

Sibyl nodded. "Okay."

Sibyl's fingers moved too slow for his liking, so before her pants hit the ground, Luke grabbed her ass and lifted as high as his injuries would let him. The wall became his leverage. She let out an erotic gasp and stood on her tiptoes as he played between her legs.

"I'm not going to go slow."

"I hope you don't."

He slipped a lustful tongue into her mouth. The scent of her arousal lingered upon his fingers when he brought them through her hair, listening to her weak moans. Soon, their clothes were lost.

"You're going to be mine."

"I'm counting on it," she breathed and responded to his caress of her breasts by tilting her chest for him so he could taste her nipples.

Her body was glorious - thick, feminine lines. Everything perfect, and he was the lucky bastard who she chose to share her most intimate parts with. In a silent plea, Sibyl thrust her hips toward him, and he entered her without hesitation, the world exploding around him at her wetness.

Luke continued to explore every surface he could reach with his tongue and teeth until he came up for air. "You poor, neglected soul."

"For the love of God, Luke, stop moving your mouth or I'm going to sit on it."

He chuckled and between thrusts said, "You dirty, foul-mouthed woman."

Their sex was rapid and dripping with desperate desire and unfulfilled fantasy. Sibyl bit the side of her lip. The look of her plump lips pinched between her teeth, her body moving with his plunges, made Luke wild.

Sibyl held him against her, arching and encouraging him to take and take. She moaned his name with every kiss and lick and tug. Her fingers were in his hair, pulling him to her breasts to steal and worship.

Death by Sibyl, Luke concluded, was the only desirable way to go, yet he wanted to remain locked in her arms and love so long, they became immortal. Then nothing could separate them. Not life, not the universe. Nothing. It would be just he and Sibyl, the woman who simultaneously brought his downfall and awakened him to life.

They slid into the nest of furs, soft textures against their sensitive skin.

Sibyl mounted him, her breasts bare, and he slid his fingers over her belly and chest, fascinated by the thick curves of her body.

After grinding against his aroused cock, pleasure flushing her face and chest, Sibyl guided him into her. Her hips, blessed by the angels above, rolled on top of him, and he lost control of his limbs.

Sibyl leaned down and whispered into his ear, "You are going to do nothing. You will lay there, unmoving, as I have my way with you."

"Hmm." He had to awaken his voice after it completely left him. "And if I don't comply?"

"Then I will make you pay."

But he laid there for her, despite the temptation not to, as she used her mouth to do horribly wicked things to his body. His fingers itched to touch but when he tried, she swatted them away. She was endlessly perfect, her dirty mouth and commands so different from her nature outside the bedroom. What would he do now that he knew this of her? How could he not look at her and remember that she dominated him? Nothing aroused him more than to hear pleasure tremble from her sweet, sweet lips.

"Look at me," he whispered and reached up to guide her face to his. Luke knew she loved his growls, so he dropped his voice low and purred. "Look at me as you come. I'd need to see you fall over the edge."

He was her captive, completely devoted and willing to let her do anything she pleased to him as she rode beyond the point of no return.

She rocked against him, faster and harder, and it took all his power to not move and watch her pleasure herself against his body. He'd wait for as long as she needed.

He loved her. Her mind, body, and soul. Sibyl was a rare and beautiful anomaly, powerful yet gentle, kind, fought for everyone, and gave without losing herself. With her, life flourished.

Then she reached her tipping point, shuddering and gasping, and in her orgasm, the most gorgeous creature on Earth. He watched until she let out one final audible shudder and laid against his chest.

Moments ticked by in where she did not move. He thought her asleep and would have rolled her over to cover her in furs, except she shifted and sighed and turned her head to peer at him from his chest.

"Your turn."

Luke's fingers instantly tightened on her thighs as she moved lazily, picking up speed and making his sensitive cock throb. She drew invisible letters with her hips. Luke saw stars. Warmth spread below his navel and he pressed the back of his head further into the pillow behind him.

"Cici," Luke groaned, his body tight and on the verge of—

A violent wave of pleasure hit him, and he groaned, digging his fingertips into her heated thighs, arms shaking, Sibyl sprawled across his lap, her own gasps pushing him further.

Sibyl stretched out beside him with the blanket covering the bottom half of her body, light tan skin flushed, and they took turns exploring each other's bodies for a long while. He languished underneath her touch, the way she ran her fingers over his chest, and fluttered kisses at his neck, stomach, and thighs. Then pinned her arms sleepily and took his time to show her how much he adored her.

Time didn't matter, but eventually, they broke free from their trance and melted into each other on the bed upstairs. A smile softened Sibyl's eyes, her long hair spread every which way.

When he kissed her afterward, his hand on her inner thigh and his lips coated with her scent, she spoke the two most beautiful words that he'd ever heard from her.

"I'm yours."

As he lingered in her space, admiring the dimples on her cheeks and her happy sighs, Luke determined that if she were gone from the world and he discovered that deals with demons existed, he'd ask to speak to the fucking manager.

He didn't want just this moment, he wanted them all.

And he was a greedy bastard.

He smiled, touched her cheek, and sat up. "It's amazing."

"What is?"

"You desiring me."

Sibyl chuckled and wrapped a bare leg around his. "Would you prefer if I hated you?"

Luke thought for a moment. "That is preferable."

She giggled and walloped him with a pillow.

He fell sideways. "Ow."

In the morning, he awoke with Sibyl in a soft fur blanket, and took a few minutes to admire her, his arm hooked behind his neck, and ran a finger over her cheek.

She smiled and gave a tiny moan as her eyes fluttered open. "Oh, hello," she said.

"I didn't mean to w...w-wake you. I w...w-was only admiring you."

Sibyl gave him a kiss and asked, "Breakfast?"

Luke nodded and they dressed, going downstairs to let the dogs out, heat rising from their furred bodies in the early morning air. He watched the dogs romp in the thin layer of snow. Boatswain sniffed, and Levin, all legs, collapsed on the ground to roll.

He heard Sibyl chuckle beside him, and she wrapped a gloved hand around his arm as they stood underneath the back porch awning. "They're adorable," she muttered. "Are you going to bring them to find your mom?"

A neighbor on Raft Island had volunteered to watch them several months ago and he planned on going back to ask her to watch them again, but he couldn't speak past the growing worry. They were going to finally get his mom. The only thing in his gut was a building dash of dread and a whole lot of concern.

"No. I'll ask a neighbor."

He ignored her hesitant gaze and walked back inside, feet nearly whipped out from underneath him by the clumsy Levin shouldering through.

They made some food with poached eggs and the leftover seafood dinner from last night.

Sibyl nearly spilled it from the cast iron pot as she brought it in from the greenhouse, stashed there so it would stay cold.

"Woah." He jumped at her to grab the pot before it tipped over. "You okay?"

She nodded, but as he watched, she fumbled with the stirring spoon and almost spilled it again when she dished it up.

The dogs waited patiently for breakfast. Luke set the bowls down, gave each dog a good scratch in their respective favorite spots – ears for Levin and chin for Boatswain – and walked over to a water bucket. He cracked the ice on the surface and used the water to fill up a container for the dogs.

Luke returned to Sibyl, and she motioned to join her. They ate mostly in silence, occasionally stopping to talk about random things: When the cold would leave, Aito and his bookshop, Sibyl's and Luke's families. All the while, Luke shoving away his nerves every time they wanted attention.

Once they finished eating, Luke let the dogs back in the main shop and washed out the dishes. He turned around to find Sibyl absently petting the dogs while staring at the floor. Normally she'd be smiling and talking to them. She'd been trying to stay positive – lift the mood a bit – all while hiding her own concern.

They busied themselves with various chores; Luke getting the dogs ready for boarding at his neighbor's and Sibyl packing things. She disappeared upstairs and returned a few minutes later, carrying a carved spear and smiling.

"Look," she said. The way she held the spear out to him, as if she were showing him her newborn babe, piqued his curiosity.

Luke walked over, not understanding completely. "What is it?" he asked.

Markings covered the wood, and he recognized a few from when he'd first met Bannack. Memories of a similar item strapped to her back and him with stars in his eyes as he spotted her on a foggy summer morning shortly afterward practicing with it bounced around in his head. That morning had been the first time he'd fallen for her, never to be the same again.

Before Luke figure out much more, Sibyl spoke with a voice edged in emotion, "It's my spear."

Memories clicked into place. "*The* spear?"

She took it back and secured it between her shoulder blades with a leather strap. "The one Peter sold."

He hadn't seen the weapon with its carvings before, and the last time he remembered her using it in their conflict with Joy three years ago. Then a burning anger hit him. Peter had stolen her weapon, her way of defending herself and connecting with what the bombs took from her.

He swallowed. "How did you find it?"

"I didn't. Eloise did. She gave it to me yesterday."

Luke looked at the spear with new understanding. He knew how much it meant to her and to see it in person again took his breath away.

"It's beautiful."

Sibyl beamed. "I feel like I have a part of myself back."

He kissed her.

They finished the last bit of packing and loaded their packs up with some extra first aid and weapons Sibyl kept stashed in her closet. When he'd asked, she smiled and mentioned they were a donation from Eloise. Boatswain and Levin were still staying with the neighbor, but he and Sibyl didn't have enough space to carry everything they needed, so the boys acted as pack mules until they could unload the supplies at Isaac's house.

Sibyl slipped the nanite ointment into a bag.

"Uh...I um..." Luke turned away, his neck warm.

What the hell's wrong with me? Now I decide to get nervous?

Sibyl tilted her head a bit. "What's this about?"

Just come out and say it.

"You found my poems..."

"I did." She smiled a bit and put a sewing kit into the bag without taking her gaze from him. "They were beautiful."

Sibyl leaned into him. He wanted to say so much more, but he feared his stutter would get in the way and when she kissed him, his uneven world fell into place.

31 | CLARA

Of all the places I lie,
it is your arms I love the most.
There, I am surrounded by you.
There, I am pressed closer to your soul.

They were moving her in a few hours. No one had come. Clara did her best to stay positive. She couldn't give into her dark thoughts.

Clara glared up at Spectre, his fingertips digging into the bones of her jaw. "Let go of me."

"The Master wants answers and you're going to give them to him."

"What makes you think I will?"

More pressure and pain. Clara closed her eyes, forcing her breathing to even out. Her mind raged with terror.

Spectre snarled at her. "I could snap your neck right now."

"What I'm hearing is you want to kill me. Is that correct?"

With a hiss, Spectre shoved her away and she fell harmlessly against the couch. "Fucking woman," he said.

She bit back tears and held her jaw, fingers coming away with a little blood on them. Moving her mouth hurt and so she curled up in a ball, her knees to her chest.

Someone touched her arm, so used to pain coming after a touch that she flinched. Phantom crouched in front of her, face hidden, but concern in her eyes.

"He's distracted right now. I can't talk to you long, but I want you to know that someone is coming." She pressed a wet rag, folded small enough to be hidden by her palm, into Clara's hand. "For your face."

A bark of a command came from behind Clara and Phantom scrambled back, morphing into a terrified animal, her hands up as Spectre pounced on her.

"Leave her alone!" Clara screamed and the back of Spectre's hand slammed into her face, the other around Phantom's neck. Her skin burned and as much as she wanted to fight back, she saw the warning in Phantom's gaze, so she stopped talking.

Phantom squeaked and clawed at Spectre's hand. He slammed her into the concrete bunker wall, and she went limp for a second, her eyes glossing over before they snapped back to reality.

"Know your place, little whore," Spectre whispered, the sound promising torture, his voice increasing in volume until he was screaming into her face. "Don't talk to the prisoner. Do not help her. If you do anything like that again, you are dead!"

Phantom stopped struggling and stared with wet eyes at Spectre. Clara's stomach rolled. The Master had hurt her before.

No! Tell him no!

But Clara knew that wouldn't be fair to Phantom. She was in an impossible situation. Simply telling her to fight back or get out would not be helpful, especially with an organization as formidable as Fade. So, as painful as it was to watch, Clara couldn't help her. Yet.

"Yes, sir."

Spectre released Phantom, scoffed with disgust, and wiped his hand on his pants. "Get off the floor."

The young woman, crying silently, stood and stumbled just a bit before tilting her chin up. She glanced at Clara as she walked past her to join Ghost and Spectre several feet away.

Clara couldn't make out most of what they were talking about, but she heard snippets, thankful for the slight acoustic amplification created by the concrete walls.

"Change...plans...going to...tonight. More...coming."

More? More of what? Then her eyes widened when she processed the rest of what he said. *We're leaving early?*

32 | LUKE

Luke was a different man when they left La Parfana and into the cold mid-afternoon sun. Sibyl walked with him, her long, dark hair braided high on her head and the fur of her collar caressing the soft curve of her face. He stared, unable and unwilling to look away.

His thumb whispered across the top of her hand. The soft curve of her jaw moved to accommodate a smile, and Sibyl buried her nose within the warmth of her fur collar but said nothing.

That was okay. Silence with Sibyl was comforting. She could say so much in that quiet and he knew how to listen.

They walked to the livery, chose a couple horses, and set off down the road to his parent's house. Soon, they'd have his mother back, his dad could hold her again, and they'd be done with the ridiculous game of cat and mouse Fade forced them into.

Sibyl trotted beside him, gave him a coy look, and kicked her bay into gear, leaning almost against the horse's neck as she galloped. He knew she could ride but seeing the skill in action made him smile.

She pulled the horse down a notch into a trot, spun him around, and returned, breathing hard and smiling.

Luke leaned over in the saddle and gave her a quick kiss.

They were the last to arrive at his parent's house after dropping the dogs off with the neighbor.

"Everyone here?" Sibyl called from the entryway and disappeared into the dining room connected to the kitchen.

As Luke took off his shoes, he noticed dirt lines tracked into the house. Odd. His parents never would have allowed that. The dried mud led into the dining room, so he followed it and stopped cold.

Peter stood by the table with two other men he didn't recognize. Immediately, Luke reached for Sibyl, who was standing, frozen, beside Eloise. Isaac, Sam, Shinat, and Bannack were there as well, all sitting at the dinner table or in various spots around the kitchen.

"What the hell?" Luke asked with a snarl to his voice. He couldn't take his eyes off Peter, not even when Sibyl squeezed his hand.

"Glad you could finally join us." An oily smirk grew on Peter's face as he pointed individually to the men who were with him. "This is Preston and Guy." He looked at Luke, "You may remember them from the day you met Kieran at Thea's house."

Luke remembered. They'd been silent then, too.

"Now that everyone's gathered here today," Peter said and clasped his hands together as if he were basking in the control he held over the entire room, "we can finally get down to business—"

"What business?" Sibyl asked.

Peter flicked his eyes to her, narrowed them for a split second before speaking. "Luke killed Kieran and he's going to answer for what he did."

Isaac slammed his palms on the table. "I allowed you into my house, put up with your complete disregard for my floor, and fed you, assuming that you were a man of your word when you told me you wanted to rectify your relationship with my son and Sibyl. No one will be taking anyone anywhere."

"A man is dead." Peter could barely contain his anger. "And you're standing up for him? A murderer?"

"Luke did nothing wrong," Sibyl cried out, stepping forward.

"Did he also tell you he was violent as a kid? Or that he slammed a kid's head so hard into the wall when we were teenagers that he has brain damage now?" Peter inhaled deep through his nose. "You got in bed with the wrong man, Sybie."

Luke trembled at those words. He remembered everything Peter put him through, including the brain damaged kid who had swung at him with a board filled with nails. Luke escaped with some bruising and a few scratches when he dodged the weapon, but in protecting himself, he almost caused the death of another. "It was an accident," Luke croaked.

"Point is," Peter said as he crossed the floor to stand directly in front of Luke. His gaze explored Sibyl's body before coming to rest on Luke. "You have a predisposition for violence. How easy would that leap be to murder?"

Peter's look of lustful ownership over Sibyl ran Luke's blood hot, and he stepped forward, baring his teeth. "Get out of my house."

"No." Peter stepped forward, their chests touching. "I hear you have a rescue party planned. Too bad you're not going."

"You *cannot* command me."

"I'm-m-m Thea-a-a's m-m-messenger. I h-h— How can you even *stand* talking? I have the authority here. I am acting in Thea's place."

At Peter's mocking of Luke's stutter, Sibyl stepped forward and shoved him, an action that shocked both Luke and Peter. She stepped in front of Peter.

"How dare you!" she screamed. "You pretentious, entitled, narcissistic bastard! Luke's not going anywhere with you, now get out of this house!"

Tension in the room shot through the ceiling. Everyone leapt to their feet, Eloise and Bannack both prepared to draw blood with their weapons in their hands. Luke watched Peter carefully, fully aware of what he was capable of, knowing that nothing would happen with an audience, but still waiting for that gleam in his eye: a gleam that promised future violence.

Peter adjusted his shirt and flicked his hair back to its preferred spot. "And I'm not leaving until he," Peter pointed aggressively at Luke, eliciting a growl from Bannack, "is in custody."

"You have no authority here." Isaac barked and he straightened to his full, intimidating height, advancing on Peter until one of the two silent lackeys stopped him. "This is the home of Clara Blackwood, Rhondian clan Leader. I am her husband and by default the acting Leader until she returns. If you are to arrest my son under false allegations, I better see some papers."

Grateful his dad stepped in but ashamed he couldn't bring himself to do much more than say a few words, Luke flicked his gaze to his father, fighting his desire to look down. He wouldn't give Peter the satisfaction of seeing how he affected Luke.

They shared a silent conversation, Luke trying to say, *"But I did kill that kid."*

His dad gave a tiny shake of his head, discernible to only Luke, which seemed to say, *"Don't say anything."*

Peter, smiling as if he'd just won the lottery, handed a letter to Isaac. As Luke watched Isaac read it, his heart thrumming in his ears, his dad's face turned from angry to confused to defeated. He tossed the paper onto the table and Luke picked it up.

By the authority of Thea Marques, Equida clan Leader,
I hereby order the containment of one Luke Noah Blackwood,
to be questioned on the matter of Kieran Minori's murder on the
15th of November in the year 2044.

He shall be detained until I, Thea Marques, can arrive at the
Rhondian clan for processing and interrogation.

Luke's stomach dropped out of his abdomen and he let the letter fall to his feet.

"There has to be some kind of mistake," Sibyl whispered with strained words. "Why would Thea allow this?"

"She wouldn't," Isaac said, his voice cold.

"See for yourself." Peter smiled. "Her handwriting and signature is right there."

Defeated, Luke slumped into a chair. Something was wrong. Peter had to be lying but he had no way of proving otherwise and they were wasting precious time arguing when they had to save his mom. He could handle being left behind as long as she came back to him.

"Leave without me," he said.

"What?" Isaac cried out.

"No," Sibyl said as she stepped toward him.

Luke shook his head and touched Sibyl's chin with a crooked finger. "Save my mom, and let's fix this later."

Sibyl glanced a wary eye at Peter. "You'll be stuck here with him."

"I'll be fine."

"No, you won't," Isaac said as pulled Luke aside, still in view of Peter, and clenched his hands into fists on the back of a living room chair. "I can leave some members of our group here. They'll protect you should something—"

"No, Dad." Luke eyed the group in the kitchen. "I don't w...w-want anyone to get hurt if something happens here. Myself, I can control. Others and w...w-what happens to them, I cannot. No. I can't do that."

"It's not like any of them aren't skilled enough to protect themselves. It's why they joined us. They can take care of themselves."

Luke did consider for a few moments, but then shook his head. "Mom needs all the help she can get."

Isaac worked his jaw. "Absolutely not. You have no choice. Someone is going to stay with you."

"I'll stay." Sibyl appeared at his side and smiled reassuringly.

"No," Luke whispered as he leaned toward her. "No."

She lifted her chin. "Tough. Someone has to protect you. Plus, I've memorized the map."

He eyed her, waiting for a small shift in her confidence, but she stared back, eyes hard and gaze unwavering.

Luke sighed. "Fine."

Luke took a seat at the table with her leaning against him while everyone gathered up the supplies and left.

"Please be careful," Isaac said as he lingered in the archway to the dining room.

Luke attempted a reassuring smile, and Isaac left.

"Stand up," Peter demanded.

Sibyl's hand tightened on Luke's thigh.

Not wanting to push the situation, Luke squeezed her wrist reassuringly and followed orders, even though his stomach had turned sour. Peter was in his home, sitting at his table, scaring his girl, and making demands. Nothing about this was right.

Peter's fist slammed into Luke's jaw, his teeth clattering together, and the force of the blow tilted Luke's chair backward but he managed to right it before it crashed to the ground.

Peter turned on Sibyl.

"No!" Luke yelled.

Sibyl jolted out of her chair and took a step back into Preston's chest. She tried to escape but the man's reflexes were too fast. He trapped her there with his huge arms, beaming.

Luke lunged to help. A chair cracked into his chest. The leg clipped his stitches and tore his skin open again. He collapsed in a dizzy heap as the world tipped sideways and fear clenched his stomach. He tried several times to stand.

"Get off me!" Sibyl screeched. She thrashed what she could: her head, legs, shoulders. Then she stopped and stared, wild-eyed, at Peter as he approached and stood in front of her.

"No!" Luke coughed. He used the table to stand, shook his head, and tried to run but the same chair that hit him in the chest connected with his back – he hadn't even seen Guy with his attention so focused on Sibyl – and Luke hit the ground. Hard. He groaned and rolled over, desperate to get to Sibyl to save her from Peter. "Cici!"

"Awe," Peter mocked. "Such a cute pet name, Sybie. So simple. Perfect for you both."

She kicked Peter in the gut, her face contorted with a mixture of rage and fear, dropped low to tilt Preston off balance, and slammed her elbow into his gut. He doubled over and hacked.

The chair hit Luke again. This time, he shifted his attention from Sibyl to Guy standing over him and, faster than Guy could react, aimed a kick to the side of his knee. It knocked sideways. Guy screamed. Luke grabbed the chair. He ground his teeth together and swung. The already weakened wood cracked over Guy's shoulder.

The unmistakable sound of a blade pulled from its sheath rang in the air. Luke whirled to witness Sibyl forced into a chair by knife point. She sat, chest heaving. She stared at the blade pointed at her then glared at Peter who held it.

Preston and Guy would recover soon, so Luke growled and leapt at Peter. He took a step back and forced Luke against a wall at knife point. He pressed the blade against Luke's throat.

"I am in control," Peter whispered.

Out of his peripheral vision, Luke watched Sibyl climb onto the table. She jumped onto Peter's back. He gasped and the knife clattered to the ground. Peter swung around, slammed Sibyl into the table, and grappled at her hands fisted in his hair. Still, she held on, crying out when all his weight pressed into her.

Luke moved to help her and punch the sorry bastard into a pulp, but Preston's elbow slammed into his sternum. His lungs seized. A fist hit him in the face.

On the ground, spitting out blood, Luke watched Sibyl land back first on the coffee table in the living room. She stilled for a moment. Rage jumped out of Luke's throat in a scream, but he was too weak to do much more than that. Preston easily shoved Luke's cheek into the rug.

Peter sighed as if satisfied the trash was taken out and reached up to adjust his hair. Luke tried to escape. Someone stepped on his hands and punched his ribs. After the third blow, Luke lost his ability to scream.

Sibyl groaned quietly and stirred. Peter's feet blocked Luke's view of her and he flicked his attention up as Peter crouched in front of him.

"You have no idea how long I've waited to see you on the ground again. Being a Fade spy is one thing, but stealing my girl? Unforgivable."

"You're a fucking bastard!" Sibyl screamed, slowly getting to her feet.

Peter winced. "You taught my Sybie how to swear?"

Luke growled and tried to move. The boots digging into the top of his hands and excruciating pain sapped all strength from him.

"I don't belong to you!" Sibyl yelled again, strain in her voice as it cracked.

He couldn't see her, didn't know if Guy kept her from moving or if Peter slamming her on the coffee table had significantly winded her. Either way, Peter was going to pay. Luke didn't know how with his strength nearly gone, but he would make Peter's life a living hell.

"You believe what you want, Sibyl." Peter looked back at Luke, yanked him into a sitting position and asked, "have you discovered her kink yet?"

Luke kept his face straight, but he wanted to smash Peter's smug smile in.

"You don't know, do you?" Peter laughed then he leaned forward and whispered, "She loves to masturbate after having sex. It's great. Dinner and a show."

He wanted grind Peter into the ground, but he couldn't stop laughing. A punch to his jaw knocked his head into the wall behind him.

Luke groaned, wiped at his lip, and smiled.

"It's not a kink, you idiot," Sibyl snarled. "You refused to find it, so I had to do it myself."

Peter's face reddened and he punched Luke again. Sibyl rage screamed. The skin on his lip tore.

Luke gasped as Peter grabbed his shirt collar and forced him forward and into his space.

Peter snarled. "You are a stuttering, scarred mess. No one wants you."

"I want him!" came Sibyl's cry and despite the situation, a thrill of love sang through Luke.

Peter put his hand on Luke's shoulder, his demeanor changing from fury to fake warmth. His fingers gouged into Luke's arrow tip wound.

Luke desperately tried to push against Peter's strength. Red hot pain covered his entire torso, arm, and neck, and Luke sank to the floor, screaming, with Peter still leached onto him. He stared into Peter's excited eyes, hate bubbling up from the depths of his soul.

Luke thrashed on the ground, his head banging into the wall and knees crashing into chair legs, all the while Peter held tight. His position allowed him a view of the living room Sibyl hadn't left. He needed to see her. Tears pricked at his nose as Peter's thumb sunk deeper into his flesh. Luke grappled with the little strength he had left and kept his gaze on her. Guy and Preston double teamed Sibyl but she held her own. Just seeing her, knowing she was afraid but wouldn't back down, brought comfort that eased the terror and pain overwhelming him.

He couldn't see now, knew his body was shutting down to protect itself. Final thoughts lulled through his head.

He hurt Sibyl.

He abused her.

And he feels no remorse.

Something snapped inside Luke, a long dormant part of him he'd kept locked away for too long. Luke inhaled through his clenched teeth, grabbed the nearest item his fingers found, and swung. It cracked against Peter's head, knocking him sideways, and the red-hot pain immediately released. Luke gasped as if he'd been drowning.

With Peter on the ground, Luke stumbled to his feet and Guy broke away from the fight with Sibyl to slam into him. They crashed into the foyer. Luke blocked a blow to his head with his forearm, stumbled back, and his hand found an old metal merry-go-round statuette.

Adrenaline now blocked his pain receptors, so Luke swung with his entire strength and hit the man upside the head. He dropped to the floor.

"Cici!" Luke cried out as he collapsed to his knees. His stomach curdled, but he managed to keep the contents where they should be. Hot blood trickled down his arm, staining his sleeve dark red. Sweat dripped onto the dark lines of the floor.

Luke's eyes struggled to focus but if he blinked, he could make out Sibyl standing on the coffee table, Preston unconscious below her. As she spun around, her eyes locked onto Peter coming for Luke and they lit with a bright inferno. She hit the ground with a heavy thump and instantly moved for her spear by the front door before Peter could even take a few steps.

"Go after him," Sibyl warned through gritted teeth, the spear in her fist, and slipped her foot slightly behind her other one. "I dare you."

Luke's arms threatened to collapse. He gasped out breaths and struggled to stand. Muscles creaked and ached. Luke could only manage to get halfway to his feet before he crashed to the ground, half blind.

Peter paused and slowly turned to Sibyl. "Oh, now you're going to grow a spine?"

A flash of brown tore Luke's attention from Peter to Sibyl. She spun the spear, blade covered by a leather sheath, and slammed the butt of the shaft into Peter's face. He cried out and hit the floor, still for several seconds before opening his eyes and scrambling away from an advancing Sibyl. Her eyes glistened, wild with long buried desire to hurt, and she seethed, hissing through her teeth.

"Look around you, Peter." Sibyl motioned with her free hand at both the unconscious guards. "There's no one to help you."

When Peter tried to escape, Sibyl stomped on his hand, pinning him to the wood floor.

What used to be the look of an abuser who'd won, was now of a mouse cornered by a lion. Peter stared up at her and whimpered once.

"You..." Sibyl said with white-hot menace. "You think that Luke is your only threat?" She raised her voice, practically screaming. "Do you think I wouldn't stop you if you came after the man I love?"

Hunched over Peter, Sibyl flicked the spear and the blade's leather cover flew across the room, knocking over a lamp. It shattered on the floor. Shards of glass flew everywhere. Sibyl wasted no time pressing the sharpened blade against Peter's throat.

"Luke may not be able to hurt you right now, but I will." She let the words sit for a moment, staring at Peter and pressed her blade into his neck just enough to form a small bead of blood. "Now, get over there and sit in the chair like a good little boy."

Sibyl tied up Peter, Preston, and Guy. The latter two awoke as Sibyl finalized Preston's ropes.

"You know," Peter said to Luke from the dining room he was tied up in, "you should really work on that stupid stutter of yours. No one's ever going to take you seriously."

Sibyl slapped a kitchen towel across his face and forced it into his mouth then tied another behind his head.

Luke recognized the hatred in Peter's words. He'd used that tone time and time again when they were kids and he hated it now more than he ever did. All the pent-up frustration and hurt over his mom's failed rescue, the early winter, the violence he couldn't seem to escape, and Peter being a grade-A asshole spilled over. He attempted to get up again, and found that even though he shook, he could move well enough. Luke slowly made his way over to Peter and used the back of Peter's chair as support in case he toppled over.

Fury contorted Luke's face and he ground out his next words. "I could w...w-work really hard on how I speak. But that w...w-wouldn't be normal for me. It sure as fuck w...w-would be normal for you."

Luke's voice built in intensity, his wide shoulders dwarfing Peter. He continued, "I have no intentions of 'fixing' myself. W...W-Why should I, or anyone else with a speech struggle or disability or physical limits, meet your unrealistic fucking standard of w...w-what is normal."

Peter's angry eyes flicked to Sibyl monitoring him, spear in hand and glaring down at him. He jerked but Luke refused to move.

"You w...w-want us to change so that it's easier for you." Luke poked Peter in the chest, making his face redden. "Do you realize how tiny you sound? How minuscule? I want you to get out of my house, bring your man child ass w...w-with you, and think about w...w-what you've just said to me, the man who will be the Leader of the *fucking* Rhondian clan someday."

Then Luke stood tall, inhaled, and spoke with darkness. "I have power that you w...w-will never have, and I'm the one with the stutter."

Satisfied with the look of enraged fear on Peter's face and having used his final ounce of strength, Luke stumbled back to a chair. Sibyl was instantly beside him, her softness replacing the fierce warrior from moments ago.

She looked to Peter. "If you so much as cough, I'm gonna knock you out, okay?"

Peter glared and jerked once against the ropes. He stayed quiet as Sibyl slid her hand over Luke's neck to move his hair away from one of his injuries. He couldn't help it. Luke stared at her, madly in love with the woman who'd just badassed her ex into submission.

"What?" she asked with her head cocked to the side, trying not to smile.

"I love you."

Then the world spun and went dark.

33 | SIBYL

He collapsed against her, limp, and they both tumbled to the floor. He was bruised and bloody. She had to get him stitched up before he lost too much blood, so Sibyl dragged him across the floor and onto the couch in the living room.

She leapt to her feet and walked away shaking. As she did so, memories flashed in her head of Peter hitting her, yelling at her, and making her feel less than human with his words. She couldn't, no matter how much she wanted to, stay by Luke's side; he needed help before they left but she couldn't do anything until she gained control of her hands.

She crouched in the living room and ran her hands through her hair, which had fallen out of its braid during the fight.

I need to get it together.

Underneath all the adrenaline and fear, was a warm relief that she'd finally worked up the courage to fight back.

When Sibyl returned to Luke, she was composed, but as soon as she looked at him; hair plastered to his face, body slumped, and skin sickly, her control threatened to break again.

She knelt beside him and put her hand on his thigh. "Where does your dad keep the first aid?"

For a moment, Luke didn't move, then he licked his lips, grunted, and fluttered his eyes open. "In...in the cupboard."

Sibyl found the box clearly labeled, grabbed a stack of rags, and filled a large bowl with cold water. She returned and cut away Luke's blood-soaked shirt. Her hands shook. The damage to his shoulder wound made her simmer and want to hug him. Peter had ripped it open further and even though it would heal, she worried about nerve damage.

"This is going to be cold, okay?"

The water pulled a strained groan from Luke, his body stiffened, and he smashed the cushion in his grip. She cleaned him quickly, trying to shorten the time the cold water touched his skin, and set to work on the stitches. The broken ones were removed, and new ones put in, Sibyl watching Luke carefully.

"You w...w-were incredible," he muttered.

If Sibyl hadn't been watching his face carefully for any sign of distress, she would have never known he'd spoken. Instead, she blushed and glanced away. "Thank you."

He put his hand on her thigh. "It was beautiful to see all that anger."

"Oh, I don't know about that." She sheepishly glanced around at the broken chairs and items scattered all over the floor in the kitchen and living room. "We ruined their house."

Luke shook his head, hair rubbing against her arm where he rested with eyes closed. "No. She'll celebrate you once she knows."

Sibyl smiled at that.

"Fucking goddess is what you are." And he went quiet.

After a few more stitches, Sibyl tied off the thread and put away her supplies. "All done." She looked at him, sweating and breathing heavily. "Hey, are you good?"

Luke slowly nodded. "...Yeah. Just...I need a sec."

Worry pinged in her stomach as she left to get him a fresh shirt. When she returned, she helped him into it and said, "Let's go get your mom, 'kay?" Then she double checked the ropes, making Peter's extra tight without cutting off the circulation.

She whispered in his ear before she left. "I'll cut off your favorite limb if you so much as touch me or Luke ever again."

Peter's face whitened in a flash as he stared at her.

They took the horses, Sibyl smiling when Luke asked for help onto Peter's horse and left.

Travel was slow at first, with Luke laying on the horse's neck and Sibyl leading her, but eventually, Luke recovered enough to wrestle control of the mare and encourage her forward. Little by little, they made their way toward the amusement park they had to get through to reach the cabin. When they reached the road that led to it, they stopped to cover her spear and Luke's bow and arrows in fabric so the weapons wouldn't clink together and alert Fade.

The top half of a leaning Ferris wheel covered in vines appeared over the tree line, and bit by bit, the small amusement park came into view. A partially disintegrated, wooden roller coaster traveled over the hill and disappeared behind it. Bumper cars, rusted and now home to a flock of doves roosting in the canopy, were covered in a layer of leaves and dirt.

Sibyl tightened her grip on the reins. She glanced to Luke, his face tilted downward, and gave him a nudge. He moved his hair out of the way and looked at her.

"You okay?" she asked.

Luke nodded but she could tell he wasn't completely. Their altercation with Peter, losing so much blood, and now riding bouncing horses through a spooky amusement park was enough to drain anyone.

"I don't remember w…w-what made him so angry." Luke sighed. "For years, if he saw me alone, he made sure to hurt me. Physically. Mentally. So, I hid in the cabin w…w-where he couldn't find me. I…stayed there for a long time until…"

The look of shame in his eyes was masked by physical pain but Sibyl knew him so well that she didn't have to look very hard to recognize it. "Until Eloise, Bannack, and I came along?"

Luke nodded and wiped sweat from his brow.

Something rustled in the bushes and Sibyl jerked her attention from Luke. Doves cooed as they exploded from their roost. The sudden burst of excitement startled the horses and Sibyl's horse crow hopped. She barely managed to stay in the saddle. Luke's horse was a bit more bomb proof than hers and it only shied away but that was enough to make Luke cry out in pain. He clutched his shoulder.

"You okay?" she called out after the horse calmed.

"Fine," Luke groaned.

They continued through the park. The fading painted eyes of a clown ride watched them as they walked the horses passed.

Eventually Luke and Sibyl left behind the park and remnants of human presence, and traveled up the hill, abandoned highway below.

She stole a glance at Luke and a tiny blink of attraction ran through her at his disheveled appearance of wild, dark hair. She knew it wasn't the right time, with them on the way to rescue his mom, but it happened nonetheless. Seeing him earlier lay into Peter despite being injured, had been an incredible sight.

Then the realization of what had happened at the house hit her and tears formed in her eyes. "What Peter did...he...I thought..."

"Hey," Luke tried a smile and touched her knee with a fingertip, "I'm okay."

"But can you fight? You're hurt, even worse than before." A hard sob shoved out of her. "You didn't see. You didn't see how much blood there was. And your *face*...you were so injured. I thought..." Sibyl buried her face in her elbow, the warm wool of her coat pressing against her skin, then whispered. "I thought he was going to kill you."

Luke pulled his horse around so the mare stood beside Sibyl's horse and their knees touched. He leaned over, grabbed the back of Sibyl's neck, and pulled her into a deep kiss. "You are the light of my life. I love you, Sibyl, even if it took me far too long to say it."

She chuckled and gave his nose a nudge with hers before Luke turned the mare around and they kept moving.

At the forested ridge peak, they found six horses tied in various spots around a collection of trees.

"That's their horses," Luke said.

Sibyl nodded. "The cabin isn't too far off."

They left the horses tied up in the shelter of a large shed. They could still get to them quickly if needed, but were too far from the cabin for any Fade operative to notice them.

The walk to the cabin was silent, Sibyl's nerves all over the place. They were so far behind the rest of the group. Would they make it in time?

We're going to fight Fade. I need to be ready. I can do this.

Beside her, Luke walked, his bow in hand.

Is he as nervous as I am?

She couldn't tell with him; he was so good at keeping a straight face when he wanted, but as they pushed through the bushes and grass growing in the forest, his face darkened.

"Are you ready?" she asked.

"Yes."

Luke's voice held an anger that startled Sibyl. She'd seen glimpses of this periodically over the past few months but here it was, at the forefront, reminding her that if someone put his loved ones in danger, they better watch their backs.

Sibyl knew that anger wasn't directed at her, but still she shied a bit from it, still on edge over what happened with Peter and let her mind wander to her own family.

It had been about a month – too long – since she'd visited and she wondered how her sister was doing, if her dad's cooking skills improved, and if her mom was still trying to breed her goats. She had to think about something other than the mission or else she'd explode. Luke was too in his head to hold conversation.

She didn't realize they were so close to the cabin until Luke pulled her behind a boulder. He pressed his fingers to his lips and flicked his eyes toward the building. The shadow of several people moved inside behind old drapes covering the windows. Sibyl counted six. They were there, but the movements – of what she could see – seemed off.

Luke pressed his forehead to the rock. Sibyl peered around it. Something banged inside.

She said, "We have to find out who exactly is in the cabin."

"I say we rush them."

She looked at Luke, her eyes wide. "And what if Fade's in there and has everyone tied up where we can't see? Us two against Fade with six hostages? It's madness."

"At least w...w-we'd learn who's in there."

"Yeah," she scoffed. "And die in the process. You gotta get your emotions under control."

Luke sighed, pressing his thumb and forefinger against the bridge of his nose. "Any ideas, then?"

She hated that she didn't have any, because that meant Luke would be reckless. He was already chomping at the bit, his fingers flexing and relaxing on his bow, and fidgeting. She looked at him and he caught her eye.

"Don't you dare," she warned.

Luke worked his jaw. "I need to do something."

"And we will. Safely." She craned her neck to look around the boulder, an idea forming. "Okay. We'll flank the cabin, cut off the entrances, but we need some way to get the attention of whomever is inside. Some way of getting them out."

Without missing a beat, Luke said, "I know. Come on."

"Luke!" she hissed after him, but he was already flanking right, hiding behind the bushes as much as he could, a cloud of cold breath following him before being absorbed into the air. "Damn it."

She went right, the butt of her spear tapping at her calf, and settled in the bushes behind the cabin, trying to see into the house.

A figure appeared in the small, square window.

They took a few steps, still not close enough for Sibyl to make out who they were except that they were tall.

She squinted.

One of Luke's arrows hit the front door, echoing a thunk through the forest and the figure burst away from the wall.

Of all the ways you could've gotten their attention, that's what you chose?

She'd scold him later, but for the time being, Sibyl slipped between two bushes, her spear ready, worried Luke was taking off in the opposite direction and had broken their entire operation, when a familiar voice called out from the porch.

"You look like shit!"

It was Bannack, his hand clasped around Luke's wrist, actively pulling him into a hug as Sibyl careened around the corner. She skidded to a halt, panting, and bent over.

"What happened?" she breathed, out of breath from the adrenaline spike. "You're here and Fade isn't."

Isaac spoke, angry. "They were missing when we got here."

Luke's eyes widened. "By how much did you miss them?"

"Not much," Eloise said. "Their fire was still warm." She held up her hand to stop Luke, who was opening his mouth to speak. "Before you get angry, no, we weren't sitting in the cabin waiting. You got here about twenty minutes after us."

"This doesn't make sense." Luke punched his bow through the air and spun on his heels. "They w...w-weren't supposed to leave before we got here."

"I'm gonna go look at the tracks and see if I can find a timeline." Sibyl didn't wait for anyone to say anything as she walked away, trying to discern which tracks were from her group and which ones were from Fade. She walked in a wide circle, knowing that Fade would be the only group leaving tracks from the cabin.

With the thin layer of snow on the ground, the footprints were easy to find. She examined them, noting the sharp edges and distance between each step to figure out if they were running or casually walking.

They're fairly fresh.

Sibyl glanced around at the snowfall. The flakes were tiny and extremely sparse, as if the weather hadn't decided if it would drop snow or not, and so the prints couldn't be more than a half an hour old.

This is good. We barely missed them.

She followed the tracks with her eyes which led her gaze straight to Silence Pass.

34 | CLARA

A dense fog had settled upon the charcoal grey and white Pass before her, a broken road dipping, rising, and winding until it reached a broken bridge at the base of the mountains. Clara stood between Spectre and Phantom with Ghost at the back.

There it is...

Standing on the brown grassy hill dusted with snow, staring at the monstrous Silence Pass split nose to navel and its rib cage snapped open by Mother Nature made Clara tremble.

How will they find me once I go through there?

Thus far, she'd managed to remain calm, but staring at the point of no return, the thing that could separate her from everyone she loved forever, threatened to turn calm to terror.

She hit the ground, her pants protecting her legs and knees from the frozen dirt. Her black ponytail spilled over the top of her head, blocking all view of the Pass, and cried.

A hand pulled on her collar, and she scrambled to her feet, glaring through tears at Spectre.

"I know you can walk," he growled. "So do it."

Clara jerked away from Spectre and smashed into Ghost. She flinched from him, spinning around to stare, but he stood there, still and blank faced, then after a few seconds, shoved past her.

Anger ran through her blood. It had taken fourteen long years for the survivors to heal enough to thrive, and Fade was once again threatening that. They'd killed billions of people during the Day of Ashes, both directly and indirectly, enough blood on their hands to turn pristine waters crimson.

As they walked, she stumbled occasionally, trying to land in places where the ground was softer, or she'd take a tumble down a hill, anything to stall their forward progression toward the Pass.

It now blocked the sunlight. Her feet ached. How far back were Luke and Isaac? Did they even know where she was? Clara exhaled, trying to keep from falling into despair, and a white cloud ghosted from her mouth.

They stopped at the end of a bridge too broken to cross, the beginning of Silence Pass on the other side, rapids from a roaring river below. She'd never been across.

"That's Skin Stealer land," Clara said, in a moment of bravery.

Spectre whirled on her. "You think I don't know that?"

"Boss," Ghost said and inclined his head toward the opposite side of the river. "They're here."

Twenty people waited at the bridge's end in military-style uniforms, black over their eyes to protect them from the sunlight reflected on the snow.

Clara froze.

Spectre stepped up to the ravine, pressed his closed fist to his forehead, and lifted it into the air. The people waiting parroted his action.

Fade. Or what's left of them.

Clara stared at those across the river, then reluctantly let Ghost grab her and lead her down the incline below the bridge. Wedged underneath was a boulder which Spectre moved effortlessly to reveal the opening of a concrete pipe. Small and tight, but could fit a human.

The closer she stepped to the pipe, the more her fear built, and when she was mere inches from the entrance, she stopped cold. Its maw threatened to consume.

Ghost pressed against her. "Go in."

Clara shook her head, hyperventilating.

"Do as I say," Ghost growled. "And I won't beat your ass."

She pried her gaze from the darkness and looked at Ghost. "I can't."

Spectre appeared from the shadows and sniffed. "You will, because you know what we are capable of. Those soldiers on the other side of this tunnel will find you if you escape us. There is no running from Fade." He lashed out and took hold of Clara's coat, the toes of her boots scraping on the ground, and brought her face right up to his. "Walk."

The concrete pipe was so small that even Clara had to crouch to walk through. Footsteps echoed inside, the musk of stale air surrounded her, and a death stench loomed. Thick darkness pushed on her body. Fear that they'd never reach the end built until she gasped for air again.

Phantom poked her from behind and whispered, "Show no fear."

The words, Clara knew, were a warning and comfort, so she hummed in her head, and slowly, the dark thinned out and she could breathe again.

A dull thunk sounded in front of her, then Spectre's voice came, loud and harsh. "Stairs."

Clara shuffled her feet awkwardly until the toe of her boots connected with something. She took a few stairs before something heavy moved and blinding white light slammed into her eyes. Clara flinched, her vision adjusted, and she walked into the sunlight. She glanced around to find herself intermingled with the Fade group Spectre had signaled to.

Spectre closed the fake rock "door" and placed several real stones around it.

Ghost grabbed Clara and, with kinder hands than Spectre, guided her to the grouping of soldiers that Spectre was greeting. Up close, the black on their faces was actually soot. A few gazes fell upon her, curiosity or hesitant excitement on their faces, but for the most part, they ignored her.

Spectre was locked in an angry conversation with a soldier. "You only brought two guns?"

The soldier, a woman with her hair in a tight ponytail said, "Supplies are so low, we couldn't risk bringing more."

"Are you *blind?*" Spectre gestured wildly to the trio of skeletons in iron cages hanging from a nearby tree. "We're entering Stealer country. How the hell did you get around them coming in?"

She glared at him. "Do not insult me. It was a command sent down directly from Master and you know what happens if we ignore his rulings."

Spectre lifted his arm to strike, but Phantom stepped between him and the woman. "Sir, please," she said with her palms facing him. "We have to keep moving if we're to stay ahead of the rescue party. The Stealers don't always frequent this specific area, so we may still be safe moving through undetected for at least several miles."

He considered her for a few moments, growled, and stomped up the trail. The soldiers glanced between each other before following Spectre.

Clara was left to her thoughts, winding through narrow trail after trail, and clambering over rocks. The further they traveled – slow due to the ice and falling snow – she wondered how long it would take them to come into contact with the Stealers. She'd never been in their territory, but she noticed signs of their presence as they walked. Painted skins with frightening images she avoided looking too hard at appeared in the bushes occasionally, animal skulls hung like demented Christmas tree garlands, and every so often, the loud rustling of a larger body in the brush tightened the ranks.

The Fade soldiers' heads swiveled around with their weapons at the ready, the two men with the only guns in the group bookending the procession. Clara stole a peak at the man behind them and saw him walking backward, caught the tight gaze of Ghost, and decided it was best to mind her own business.

She knew countless eyes watched her, so she wouldn't try anything.

A bird call sounded up ahead, strange in the snow-covered Pass where most animals hid away in their caves and dens, and immediately everyone halted. Clara glanced around, wondering what had happened.

Phantom scaled a tree and disappeared.

The hissing of an arrow through the silent air caught Clara's attention and the soldier at the front with the gun hit the forest floor, the woman in the high ponytail picking it up.

"Stealers!"

Bodies covered in white fur exploded from the bushes. Some Fade members dropped to the ground, dead instantly, while others ran for safety to regroup. Bullets from both rifles popped and Clara dropped to the ground, her hands over her ears. She dared to open her eyes, to right herself in the chaos, and watched a Fade soldier scoop up one of the rifles.

She was pulled and shoved, unable to make heads or tails of the violence and ended up huddled with Phantom behind a boulder.

"You ready?" the young woman asked, her eyes wild with fear but dead set on Clara.

She worried she had no breath left to say anything, but managed to whisper. "Let's go."

Phantom jumped forward and pulled Clara to the ground with her as a pair of stray bullets hit the opposite side of the rocks. She breathed into Clara's ear. "I can get you home, but you have to trust me."

It didn't take much thought – choosing to trust Phantom – because of all the little things she'd risked her life for.

"I trust you."

"Alright. Run to the right and I will find you."

Without another word, Phantom jumped into the fray. She snuck up on two Fade soldiers and delivered killing blows with a swift stab and flick of her knives.

Clara ducked when a hatchet came too close to her head. She scrambled to her feet and ran.

Survive. That's all that matters.

She sprinted through the forest until her already sore and tired feet doubled up on blisters, and Phantom joined her through the snowy forest. Clara never turned to see if they were safe.

After they'd run far enough that only whispers of the fight could be heard, Phantom stopped.

Clara glanced around, bent over, and panted. "Are we safe?"

"For now," Phantom said as she cleaned one of her knives, an eye trained on where they'd come from, barely out of breath. "Our footprints in the snow will lead them to us if we don't keep going."

"Thank you."

The young woman gave a short nod. "You're welcome. We—"

She jumped to her feet and Clara immediately moved, too, spinning around to face three angry Skin Stealers.

"Get behind me," Phantom commanded.

Clara followed orders and Phantom handed her a knife.

"You know how to use this?" she asked.

"Yes."

"Good."

The Stealers attacked, their movements erratic and unpredictable, and it took Clara a few moments to pull her brain back from shutting down so she could fight. Phantom had no problems using the forest around her to hide and move, but Clara wasn't so lucky. The Skin Stealer man she fought connected with her stomach and she tumbled away, her world spinning.

She lay on the ground for a moment, the soft snowflakes falling from the dark grey sky then remembered where she was, the danger if she didn't move, and rolled onto her feet.

He raised his club with a round stone tied to the end, and she bit down on her tongue to stop from screaming as she plunged the dagger into his stomach. The man grunted, gasped, and fell.

It had been over a decade since she'd killed someone, and flashes of last time ran through her mind. Two men and a woman. They'd invaded her home in the forest while Isaac was out hunting, and she was hiding with young Luke.

She used the memory to give her strength to stand. Phantom fought several feet away, dark brown hair buzzed short and mask over her nose, glaring at a Skin Stealer man as he advanced. She stood awkwardly.

What's she waiting for?

Clara rushed forward, jumped over the two dead Skin Stealers, and slammed into the third. They hit the ground, Clara on top, and she drove the knife into the Stealer's chest.

Phantom made a strange noise and Clara turned in time to see her collapse. She rushed to the young woman and knelt beside her in the dirt. Then she saw the blood. Phantom's dark clothes hid the color well, but up close, Clara could see the contrast. It was on her stomach and right thigh. Her left arm was most likely dislocated by the way it looked.

"Can you move?" Clara asked, heart beating hard against her chest.

"I...I don't know," Phantom groaned.

"I think your arm's dislocated. We need to get it back in place."

"Not now." Phantom stopped Clara with her good arm. "It's not safe out here."

Clara nodded and pulled her to her feet, pained noises coming from Phantom stabbing at her heart.

"By the way," Clara turned to Phantom as they walked together, "what's your real name?"

The young woman stayed silent for a few beats, then said, "Nora Pemberton."

Clara smiled. "Pleased to meet you, Nora."

She searched for a while, stopping periodically to allow Nora to rest, always checking behind her for any sign of the Fade soldiers. It irritated her slightly that they had walked for almost half an hour and hadn't even made it two miles, but Clara couldn't dwell on that. She had to get Nora to a safe place so she could tend to her wounds.

"There," Nora said and pointed to a small cave on the ridge.

"Can you make it up there?"

"I'll have to."

Together, they hiked to the top, Clara practically dragging Nora, and they collapsed against the cave wall, Clara panting and Nora sweating with an ashen face.

With a jolt of terror, Clara realized the bag that Nora had been carrying their entire trip wasn't around her waist. It had all the first aid in it.

"Your bag!"

Nora's eyes widened and her hand went to her hip. She closed her eyes. "Must've fallen off somewhere in the chaos." She groaned and looked at the blood on her body. "You have to leave."

"No! I'm not leaving you out here."

"You have to. Spectre's coming for us and I'm in no shape to be running or fighting, if it comes to that." She put her hand on Clara's shaking one. "I'll only slow you down."

Knowing she was right, Clara gritted her teeth, but refused to give up. "I'll sneak back and get your bag."

Nora released a strained chuckle. "God, you're stubborn. We both know that's not going to work."

No, she was right. Clara's shoulders fell and tears welled in her eyes. "I can't leave you."

"Yes, you...can."

That's when Clara noticed the weakening of Nora's body. How had she not seen it before? Terrified of what she'd find, Clara lifted Nora's shirt. She wasn't an expert at anatomy, but she did know that injuries to the stomach were bad news. The stab wound sat too close to the liver.

"Nora..."

"Yes," she answered, her voice weak. "I know. It's why you have to leave."

They had no first aid, no way of stitching her up, but Clara did have a shirt. She removed her thick coat, the icy cold air pricking at her skin, and pulled off her t-shirt.

Nora's eyes flickered half open. "Don't."

Clara fixed her with a hard, motherly stare. "You're not going to tell me I can't. This will buy you time. Once I find my son and husband, I'm coming back for you. Stay. Here."

She ripped a continuous strip of fabric out of her shirt. Nora allowed Clara to wrap the strips around her mid-section. Once finished, Clara squeezed Nora's arm.

"I'm coming back for you."

Nora stared for a moment, her clammy face blank, then nodded. Satisfied, Clara slipped her coat back on, peered from the cave entrance to search for danger, and when nothing came, she left, making sure to wipe away hers and Nora's footprints in the inch deep snow.

She slunk through the forest, watching her back to make sure no one snuck up on her. When she was almost to the path she'd come down on while with Fade, the one that would lead her home, a hand grabbed her hair.

Clara gasped, her hands flying up around the disembodied wrists, and dropped to the ground. She had to get away. Had to find some tactic to detach her hair from the stranger's grasp.

"Thought we wouldn't find you?" Spectre asked.

On the ground, Clara's eyes widened. She didn't dare turn around or else her eyes would confirm what her ears knew.

Spectre knelt in front of Clara and spoke again, the calm of his voice terrifying. "Where is Phantom?"

"Dead," Clara said without hesitation.

"How?"

"Skin Stealer attack."

Please believe me. Please.

Spectre inspected her injuries from when the Skin Stealers attacked.

One Fade soldier, a woman with close-cropped, blonde hair, put a hand on Spectre's arm. "We aren't going to look for her?"

"No," he said flatly. "If she's alive, she's more than capable of finding her way back. We move on without her." Then Spectre turned on Clara, gripping her chin in that vice grip of his. "Since you want to protect her so badly, you get front row tickets to my favorite little show."

Clara knew what Spectre meant. He'd spent days itching for it, and now that she'd given him a good reason, there was no escaping his desires. Her stomach dropped. She allowed the fear to sit for a moment, then she shoved it away.

I'm not going down without a fight.

Adrenaline pumped through her, and Clara smiled, locking her eyes straight onto Spectre's.

"You're not used to betrayal, are you?" She chuckled as Spectre stared in furious horror. "Honestly, it's quite impressive you managed to keep her under your control for so long."

The slap that Spectre delivered to Clara's cheek reverberated through her head, and a heavy silence spread among the remaining Fade soldiers. Clara hit the ground, her hip colliding with an exposed root, but she ignored the sharp pain and slowly got to her feet.

She licked her lips. "You can hit me all you want, tie me up, send me off to be tortured." Then she straightened, drew back her shoulders, and sucked in a deep breath. "But you will never control me."

Like the snake he was, Spectre hissed, grabbed her throat, and shoved her against a tree, simultaneously cutting off her air and forcing it from her lungs upon impact.

"I have your fear," he whispered low and venomous. "That is enough to control you."

Clara leveled him with her eyes, a growing tightness in her throat.

A Fade soldier appeared by Spectre and placed their hand on his arm. "Sir. Master wants her alive."

Tense moments passed where Clara was positive Spectre could feel her rapid heartbeat through his fingers, then she was shoved to the side. Once she landed, she knelt there for a few moments, taking in big gulps of precious air.

Before she had time to fully recover, someone pulled Clara to her feet, and a sharp weapon poked into her back.

She wasn't going to escape, but Nora was safe.

35 | LUKE

Luke followed Sibyl on horseback, worried she was pushing herself too hard. She refused to take breaks or eat, instead throwing herself into tracking.

Tensions within the group were high. They'd been chasing Fade through the Pass for what felt like ages, steadily growing closer but also more tired. Luke fought the urge to chew his cuticles until they ached.

Almost, Mom, he thought to himself, his thighs and face cold from the wind. *Hold on a bit longer. Please.*

At moments, there were glorious views of canyons, snow-capped pines, and herds of elk lifting their heads from the marshes to watch the procession of riders invading their home. At any other moment, Luke would've allowed himself to enjoy the sight, but he couldn't once he saw the great expanse before them, knowing his mother could be anywhere and they may never find her.

It wasn't long until they reached another forested area, and found the mutilated bodies of fifteen Fade soldiers and many Skin Stealers. Sibyl's horse balked. Luke's stomach slammed into his throat as he watched her almost fall from the gelding, but she got her mount under control, and covered her mouth as she stared at the dismembered bodies.

Luke walked his mare over to her. "Sibyl…"

"I can't look anymore." Sibyl jerked her gelding around and trotted away.

He eyed the carnage for a moment. The glade was empty and silent. *Where's everyone? Where's Mom?*

The emptiness made Luke uneasy. Too many unanswered questions hung in the air, and he couldn't push away the anger that was slowly building within him. He needed to channel it for the coming fight, so, for now, he forced it to stay under control.

Luke turned his mare around just in time to see Sibyl dismount and wander around the glade. She inspected the ground, bushes, and foliage, whispering to herself along the way. She returned a few minutes later.

"A lot of the trail is jumbled from the fight, but I believe Clara tried to get away with someone else."

"Tried?" Luke's stomach tumbled at the word.

Sibyl nodded and fiddled with the reins of her horse. "Yeah. The footprints that I think belong to her are paired with another set going east," she pointed to everyone's right, "and those are smaller, too. Then the rest of Fade seemed to realize she was missing, because there's a bunch of trampling going on all over, outside where the fight was. I can't really make heads or tails of it, it's so chaotic, but eventually, someone figures out where they both went and followed. If I'm right, they shouldn't be too far. The tracks are less than half an hour old."

Following the trail, they found their way to a cave, empty, with just enough blood on the ground to signal that whoever had rested there sustained a serious wound. Bannack, Sibyl, and Luke entered, everyone else outside the cave keeping watch and tending to the horses.

The horrid thought that the blood may be his mother's made his world tumble upside down and sideways, his stomach rolling right along with it, and he lost all understanding of which way was up and which was down. He crashed into Bannack, who instantly moved to hold him up.

"You can't tell if it's hers, can you?" he asked, to which Sibyl shook her head.

"All I know is that someone leaned against the wall here," she pointed to an impression in the dry dirt, "and someone knelt in front of them."

Sibyl stood up and followed something outside, Luke following. He watched her footsteps, so careful to avoid the trail of blood leading away from the cave.

"I'm not sure how far it goes," Isaac said as he stood beside Luke and Sibyl.

Luke eyed the red liquid, stark on the white frosted ground. "It's not Mom. She wouldn't run off when she knows someone's coming for her. And there's nothing that looks like she was dragged. Right?" He looked to Sibyl, and she nodded.

"Whoever this was," Sibyl adjusted her spear, "is long gone."

Everyone, except Sibyl, mounted their horses, walking them behind her as she followed the trail.

"Look," Sibyl said finally. She pointed to a pair of small boot prints.

Heart speeding up, Luke jumped from the saddle to look at them. "The track is smudged. What does that mean?"

"She's being dragged part of the way."

Luke gritted his teeth. "Let's go."

They led the horses to a safe area near a running river, secured their reins to the trees, and followed the tracks on foot. Luke's chest was about to explode with nervous anticipation. They were so close, so close to getting his mom back, and as they travelled, the minor tremors of his hands got worse. He couldn't have that. If he didn't manage to calm himself down before they met up with Fade, he wouldn't be able to shoot straight.

At the base of a hill, Luke heard casual talking, and he held his hand up. Ahead, two men foraged for berries. Careful not to be seen, he stashed his mare out of view and crouch-walked behind the mangled roots of a huge trunk lying on its side.

Sibyl took an empty spot beside him.

"The bitch Phantom wasn't there, man," The blond said. "We're gonna die if we tell Spectre we couldn't find her."

"Just tell him she's dead," said the other man.

The blond scoffed. "He's gonna want proof."

His companion pulled a bloodied strip of fabric out of his back pocket. "Proof."

Blond laughed and shoved his friend. "Brilliant!"

The other man turned as if he were suspicious of some noise in the woods and Luke ducked behind a rock to avoid being seen, his fast movement aggravating his stitches.

He looked to Sibyl, who was staring at the men as if she were preparing to pounce. Her hand went to her spear, and she inhaled.

"You with me?" she mouthed and flicked a nod in the two Fade soldiers' direction.

Luke's shoulders pulled back as he aimed. Sibyl and Luke synchronized their weapons, her spear flying from her grip at the same time Luke's arrow left his bow. Hit in the chest by Sibyl's spear and the neck by Luke's arrow, both men dropped without a sound.

Isaac appeared beside Luke. "What now?"

Luke pressed his palm to the injury Peter had made worse. "Go wide and flank them. Nab Mom before whoever has her can get too far."

His dad made a noise of agreement and made to go off by himself, but Sibyl stepped forward. "I'll go with you," she said.

"Sibyl?" Luke asked. He couldn't lose sight of her, not when chaos waited for them further up the trail, but in her eyes was determination and he had to let her go.

Sibyl ran with Isaac, who stooped to snag a sword from the dead, blond man, and the thick forest swallowed them whole.

Luke almost ran after, but he had a job to do, so he steeled himself and sprinted down the path to find nine people in the distance. Luke caught a glimpse of his mother, hands tied behind her back. A jolt of anger smacked into his gut when he watched a tall, lanky man hit her so hard, she spun as she fell.

Luke couldn't reach Lanky Man without being spotted early, so he fired into the group, doing his best to ignore the increasing level of pain radiating from his shoulder and back. Someone screamed, the arrow protruding from his body.

Fade scrambled to find where the arrow had come from. Three archers took the high ground and Lanky Man and two other Fade members dragged his mom off into the forest.

Damn it!

They'd have to fight their way through several soldiers before they could do anything about his mom.

Sam spun behind the boulder as an arrow clinked off the side of it. He returned fire.

"They're coming!" Sam yelled, his focus split between shooting at the trio of Fade archers on the hill diagonally from them and the Fade members heading straight for them.

Bannack, Marie, and Shinat each locked weapons with three Fade soldiers that arrived first, metal hissing and cracking together. Luke and Sam held off the rest with their long-range attacks.

Eventually, Luke would run out of arrows and he'd have to use the knife at his belt.

Bannack closed in on a Fade soldier retrieving their thrown weapon from the ground and swung his blade. In a spray of blood, the soldier fell with their head detached. Bannack stood over them, his signature emotionless expression upon his face. Eloise's knife brought another Fade member to his knees and Marie finished him off with a throat slash. Both women shared a grateful glance before returning to the fight.

Within a few moments, four people collapsed, including two archers, the others retreating further into the forest. Luke's chest heaved from the adrenaline and his fist tightened on his bow.

Marie's gut-wrenching scream made Luke jump. A Fade soldier had been hiding in the bushes and before anyone could react, he sent Marie sailing through the air. She slammed into a tree.

Luke frantically nocked his arrow, but he was too late.

Everyone was.

The man jumped from a rock with a heavy thump near her. Marie tried to scramble away.

Caught off guard, Luke took seconds longer than he should have aiming and just as the man flung his axe through the air, Sam's bolt and Luke's arrow shot the man through the forehead and neck at the same time. The axe, unburdened by human intervention, sunk into Marie's chest.

He gritted his teeth. Too slow. He'd been too slow stopping the man and now Marie was dead, but they had to keep pushing forward.

Luke ran and paused for a split second when he saw Marie's body on the ground, bent down to close her eyes, and remove the axe from her body.

We'll come back for you, he promised. Luke collected any good arrows from the fallen, several snapping as he pulled on them, and set off again.

As they chased after Lanky Man and his goons, hypervigilant of another surprise attack like the one that took down Marie, Luke stole glances at his comrades. Sam's arm was bleeding. Bannack had a bloody nose and a purple bruise on his chin. Shinat nursed cuts on her hand and cheek, and had a black eye. Eloise, due to the super healing of her nanites, had no visible signs of injury, but did have remnants of blood on the top of her hand. Luke knew the soldiers could hear them because the final archer turned on his heels and fired, his arrow zipping through the air to glance off a tree trunk beside Sam's head.

The cold air numbed Luke's lungs and injuries, making him slower than the others but not completely incapable of returning fire at the archer who'd tried to hit Sam. The four soldiers disappeared for a few moments as the trail dipped down.

Pieces of Luke were breaking, every fiber within him frayed. He dreaded what would come next. The past three days had snailed on, their careful preparations leading them to this one moment. They couldn't afford to mess it up.

Luke's throat burned from exertion by the time they summited the ridge, and there she was, his mother, tied and being forced into the thickest part of the forest by Lanky Man, two men following him. The very sight of her condition crashed fury through him.

Before Luke could stop himself, he screamed for her, his voice coming out desperate, ragged, and high pitched. "*Mama!*"

The Fade soldiers who had retreated earlier slunk up the hill, brandishing terrifying weapons. One flicked a long, razor chain whip and smirked.

Eloise snarled.

Luke drew an arrow, gritted his teeth past his injured shoulder, aimed, let it sing, and a soldier collapsed. Pain was inevitable and if experiencing it meant he could save his mom, he'd welcome it.

One down.

His crippling anger pulsed through him like a second heartbeat. Slow. Powerful. Heightening his senses and pushing him past the point of caring about the human lives he took.

Eloise downed the second soldier with her knives. Bannack appeared from the brush, catching the third Fade soldier off guard, and the ex-mercenary's sword slipped easily through the man's stomach. Bannack slammed the already dead man against a moss-covered boulder and his forward progression stopped with a jerk.

Blinking out of attack mode, Bannack yanked his sword from the man's middle and wiped off the blade as he followed Luke and the group down the hill.

I'm coming for you, bastard.

Only Lanky Man, his lackey, and a final Fade soldier stood in the way of his mother's freedom.

As Luke ran down the hill, Sibyl came into view, half-crouching with her spear behind her back. Hair previously trapped in a braid was now a swirl of black through the air as she twirled the spear, effortless in her manipulation of it.

The Fade soldier who had followed Lanky Man and his lackey had been caught in Sibyl's crosshairs and was now fighting for his life. He swung his axe in a desperate, poorly thought-out arc.

Luke skidded to a halt and drew his bow to fire.

In a movement Luke could only compare to smooth water flowing over a river stone, Sibyl sidestepped and locked her spear tip in the axe's curve closest to the wooden shaft. She released a short battle cry. Lanky Man's weapon tore from his grip so forcefully, he collided, head-first, with the blunt end of her spear twisting up to meet him. The soldier jerked backward in a spray of blood and landed hard on the ground.

It had been years since Luke had properly seen her with her spear. She was fluid and precise, years of practice obvious in her form. A brief jolt of pride poked at him. This, this was the true Sibyl. Strong and terrifying.

The bow creaked when he relaxed the string and watched Sibyl step over the man she'd just knocked out before taking off into the forest so dense, only small slivers of light could get through.

Luke followed her, catching small glimpses of the top of her head occasionally popping up from behind the tall bushes, while everyone else ran behind him. She wasn't waiting for them to follow. By now, his shoulder and back screamed in pain whenever he took a step, and he knew the sweat collecting upon his brow was from more than just physical exertion.

Beyond Sibyl, he saw his mother again. Dark hair. Hands bound. Climbing the treacherous trail, forced forward by the two men.

Where's Dad?

He hadn't seen Isaac in too long, and for a moment, he worried his father had been killed and they never noticed. His father was a smart man, though and Luke had no other choice but to trust that he'd show up soon. Luke forced his breathing to even out as he ran despite the noose of hatred tightening around his neck.

Fade had chosen well, using the brush and trees as cover, the soldiers and cold slowing Luke and his group down. He knew nothing of the Pass, but he knew forests. Judging by the density of it, this was an old growth stretching for miles and miles, and Fade had nowhere to hide.

Finally, panting and sweating when the dense trees thinned out to allow bright light through, Luke saw Isaac sprawled behind a log.

When his dad noticed everyone emerge on the ridge, his eyes widened. "Get back!"

A blade whistled and hit a tree beside Luke before he fully dropped to the ground. While there, he saw the flash of a soldier's uniform clad in many knives. He crawled to his dad.

"Mom? Is she—"

"Two Fade operatives and your mother continued on foot into the forest. Sibyl ran past me about a minute ago."

Another blade hit the trunk Luke and Isaac were hiding behind and Luke flinched. He ran his hands through his hair and glanced to everyone else, mouthing, 'flank them,' and gestured to his left and right. They nodded, using the thick underbrush for cover as they fanned out.

Luke ignored Isaac's command to stay down, took his bow and slipped behind a tree, the silken feathers gliding through his fingers until they stopped at the bowstring. His shoulders tightened, grunting when the pain hit him.

"Let us through!" he yelled, attempting to distract the knife thrower.

The only response he got was the blade of a knife zipping through the air and cutting across his thigh. The metal burned. Strength left his leg and he nearly toppled over, managing to stay upright but on his knees.

A bird whistle rang out, sung by Bannack, and Luke knew they were in position. It was now or never. Once they got through this lone attacker, his Mom was next.

36 | LUKE

Cutting off a groan, Luke stood, and closed his eyes, listening for any movement. The bushes shifted in the wind. A pinecone bounced off branches on its way to the forest floor. Squirrels argued and scrambled overhead.

Footsteps.

Rapid ones.

Starting and stopping as the owner shifted positions.

Luke's fingers touched the arrow's feathers notched on the bow string. He peaked out from his refuge, caught a glimpse of a body, and lifted the bow to his cheek.

Bannack knocked Luke's elbow. He jerked, the arrow whizzing into the brush.

Another shove sent Luke sideways into a tree, making him see stars from the pain, and Bannack narrowly blocked a second airborne knife with his sword. At first, Luke nearly shoved Bannack off, until he saw the knife underneath the bush where he'd been standing moments ago, and realized Bannack's quick action had saved his life.

"Thank you," Luke said to Bannack and his friend nodded. "You and Eloise draw his attention," Luke pulled an arrow from his quiver. The action made him groan. "I'll fire."

Bannack eyed Luke's shoulder, then nodded once, and bird whistled. This tone was different, musical, and Eloise appeared at his side. Together, they took off, and Luke waited. Quickly, the lone knife thrower honed in the couple, dodging Bannack's blade to toss his knives into the brush, narrowly missing Eloise.

Luke saw his opportunity when the man turned his back. Luke fired. The arrow sunk deep into the man's spine and the target fell.

Limping, Luke trudged with the group through the forest again, irritation and nerves building from the constant up and down of the battle. He hated that they couldn't just take her back, instead forced into a game of cat and mouse.

"There." Eloise pointed to a meadow of pansies and white heather with looming, rusted, and deformed metal skeletons of transmission towers.

Before a drop-off, stood Sibyl, coatless and sweating, battling the Lanky Man with Isaac. Clara sat on the ground, secured to the metal of a tower. She stared, wide-eyed, at Sibyl and Isaac, tears falling down her cheeks. She looked unharmed from Luke's vantage point, but he couldn't determine her condition underneath the layers of clothes and dirt.

Everyone fanned out. He stood behind a tall bush, bearing most of his weight on his good leg, and tried to aim. He pulled back several times fruitlessly, only able to force his shoulder to work halfway, if that. His head pounded, vision fuzzy at the edges. Underneath his coat, he was sure blood soaked his shirt. All in all, terrible timing to succumb to injury.

Luke panted, standing and falling, as he stumbled to his feet.

He ran – or rather limped – toward Sibyl, past the soldier locked in a power struggle with Bannack, their angry huffing fading into silence as he trudged on. He nocked the bow with his final arrow to do something. Anything. His shoulder burned, but he still managed to draw the string.

There you are.

Luke aimed.

Putting all his strength into pulling back the bow string, Luke aimed for Lanky Man's eye.

Lanky Man advanced on Sibyl and she danced away, her spear a blur within her hands.

Only one shot. One.

He exhaled.

Luke had seconds. He couldn't waste it.

The wind shifted to his favor.

Luke contorted his face as he nearly threw up, but he got the string taught.

Someone screamed his name, but he didn't register more than that, too focused on killing the man who'd taken his mother.

Lanky Man's eyes flicked to Luke for a split second, twisted, and placed his body on the other side of Sibyl just as Luke's fingers began to relax. That action forced him to shoot wide and the arrow shot into the grasses.

"No!" Luke screamed and discarded the bow, opting to just run. He didn't know what he was doing, or thought much into the why of his actions, he only knew that the three most precious people to him were fighting or in danger. With no weapon, with Sibyl and Isaac distracting the Lanky Man at the cliffside edge, Luke decided to run for his mom. At least he could free her.

Through the field Luke stumbled as he ran past the bushes and brambles, closer, and closer to his mother. When her eyes found him running toward her, she struggled against her ropes.

There was no time.

He couldn't both save his mom, and help Isaac and Sibyl, and even though they were pushed dangerously close to the cliff edge, he had to trust that they could handle themselves. He had to choose his mom.

Lanky Man bent at the waist to avoid Sibyl's metal blade. He kicked Isaac in the stomach, subduing him just enough to pull out a knife. Before the man could do anything, though, Sibyl's spear forced him back. His expression switched from surprise to amusement, and as Sibyl stepped too close, he used the butt of his hand then elbow to knock Sibyl's spear from her hand.

Luke gasped, fear shooting adrenaline through his body, almost skidding to a stop, but he pushed forward, his leg burning.

Almost to his mother, a battle raging to his far left, Luke was spent. He moved on less than fumes. Dust. Coal powder.

Sibyl screamed and the sound of terror he'd never heard from her jerked his attention away from his mom. Lanky Man sliced Sibyl's spear across her front, the weapon so sharp, it cut through her shirt and coat as if it were butter. A wet slashing noise followed by a guttural, primal scream of pain came from Sibyl.

Luke matched the sound.

He stood there, paralyzed by anguish, clawing at his chest and knees weakening as he watched her hit the ground. "No...No!"

He wasn't fast enough.

If he hadn't been injured, he could've reached them.

But he didn't. And helplessly he watched Lanky Man launch Sibyl's bloodied spear through the air and deep into Isaac's chest. He wrapped his hands around the shaft, fell, and moved no more.

The world shattered.

Luke went deaf. He screamed, his throat burning, and heard in the back of his mind his mother wailing with him as Lanky Man dragged her into the forest.

Covered in leaves, dirt, and icy water from the snowfall, Luke fell to his knees, silent. Or was his throat so torn up, noise couldn't materialize?

Luke's body snapped up, moving of its own accord, body weak from injury, and curled up beside Sibyl. "Listen. Listen. Okay?"

She grappled for him while blood soaked the ground around her.

He kept talking to her, trying to keep his voice even. The fear in her eyes...It hurt to swallow the bile rising from his stomach.

"We'll get you fixed up. Alright?" He forced a smile but it felt too stiff, so he shoved it away. Her bloody hand touched his facial hair. "I got you."

The wet gasping. The terror in her eyes. Whimpering. "Luke...I'm sc...scared."

"I know. I know." He managed to brush her dark hair away from her face. "I love you," he whispered through tears. "I love you. Please. Stay with me. Stay...stay."

Sibyl whimpered. "Y-your mom."

"Shh," Luke pressed his forehead to hers and felt her tremble underneath him.

She talked to him again, her mouth moving, every word muffled and unintelligible. Luke couldn't understand, no matter how hard he tried.

Someone pulled on Luke to stand, but he fought them. "Get the fuck *off* me, you *fucking bastard*. Cici! Let me go! I need to save her! She promised me she'd never leave!"

Weak, yet pumped full of adrenaline and grief, Luke swung at the nearest body. Bannack blocked him, swung Luke around, and wrapped Luke's arms around his chest, like a straight jacket. Rage poured into Luke. How dare Bannack stop him! How dare he pull Luke away from Sibyl and his dad!

"Enemy!" his mind screamed, and Luke snapped his head back, knocking Bannack to the ground with Luke on top. How Bannack held on was enough to push Luke fully into blind fury, and he snarled out profanities and threats with tears dripping down his dirtied face and over his ears.

"Get *off* me!"

"No," Bannack groaned. "Not until you calm down."

Luke thrashed. His chest ached, injuries screamed. "She's dying," Luke cried and jerked and kicked. "She's dying and you won't let me help her!"

Bannack remained quiet, grunting and hissing with each kick of his heels and blow of the back of his head that landed.

Eloise rushed over, dropped to her knees, and slapped Luke hard in the cheek.

Shocked, Luke stopped immediately and gasped when she grabbed the front of his jacket. "Stop being a jackass and *think*! You're hurting him."

His struggling faded, or rather, he watched it fade. His body accepted his consciousness back and Luke had control once more. Luke slowly stood, took steps as if floating, and slumped onto a log.

"Everyone will take care of her," Bannack said, and sat with him.

"What happened?" Luke asked because he truly couldn't remember. His arms wouldn't move the way he wanted, and his mind blanked. Strange. Hadn't he just seen something? What was it?

Bannack wiped at his nose, top of his hand coming away with blood.

"I'm sorry," Luke whispered.

"It'll pass. Now," Bannack set Luke's bow on his lap, "we save your mom."

Reality rushed back to him when he saw her crying on the ground, blood all around her, and with it, rage. He wasn't a man anymore; he was the personification of anger pushing him into the forest after his mom.

No matter how much he hurt, Luke had to be strong enough to save her. He couldn't let the grief take over. Not yet. Maan needed him. He could cry later.

Someone followed behind and he twisted to look over his shoulder at Bannack.

"I'm with you," Bannack said and handed Luke a bolt.

Luke and Bannack caught up to Clara and Lanky Man in an abandoned settlement of ten or so homes built from weathered, cracked bricks. Some were missing walls, with vines spread out over the leftover surfaces like giant, green blankets. And they were in the way.

"Luke!" his mom called out.

It was the first time he'd heard her voice in weeks. He nearly called out for her, eyes glistening with tears, but knew if he used his voice, he'd ruin their chances of saving her.

Clara collapsed into the mud, shoved there by Lanky Man, and Luke growled out of frustration.

"No." Bannack's hand on Luke's shoulder stopped him from making a mistake and Luke relented. "We must stop them, but we cannot be careless."

Luke swallowed down the knot in his throat, and both he and Bannack split off to cut off Clara and Lanky man. He wound through the broken homes. Cobblestones covered with moss and grasses muffled his limping footsteps, glad that the shallow injury to his thigh didn't prevent him from moving. He caught sight of Bannack stalking toward Lanky Man and Clara from the opposite direction, his sword drawn.

Clara's desperate screams stopped him for just a moment. The sound would haunt him for a long time.

Damn. His entire body ached, and he struggled to move, a consequence from his injuries and lack of sleep, but adrenaline and anguish kept him going.

Clara pulled and fought against Lanky Man holding her.

She turned her body into dead weight, fell back, and Lanky Man went with her, landing hard on the ground. Clara scrambled away.

She was close.

So close.

In Clara's hand, as Lanky Man got to his feet, was a dark, solid object. He moved away before she could hit him with it, and the rock cracked into the side of his shoulder. Lanky Man recovered quickly and snarled, grabbed the front of Clara's shirt, and pulled back his arm to strike.

"No, you don't." Luke nocked his bow. Lanky Man had taken his dad from him, he'd tried to murder the woman he loved, and Luke would rather have his liver eaten by an eagle for the rest of eternity before he allowed the man to take his mother from him, too.

Luke couldn't aim well, so he got to his feet to shoot Lanky Man straight through the forehead. He had a clear shot. The bow released a single, light creak, and the string snapped, whipping him across the cheek.

The shattering bow and clacking arrow on an exposed section of cobblestone made Lanky Man turn.

Luke sprinted toward his mother, desperation and fear stronger than the pain in his leg.

Lanky Man drew a thin blade with his good hand and flicked his wrist.

The weapon sliced across Luke's neck.

"No!" Clara screamed.

Luke stumbled back, his boot heel catching on a vine, and collapsed to the ground. Hot blood trickled from the cut. Bannack appeared, his tall frame casting a shadow on the crouched Lanky Man, swung his sword, and Lanky Man barely managed to duck.

While Luke registered he was alive, Bannack forced Lanky Man away from Clara and toward Luke. He gathered up the remnants of his broken bow. Bannack collapsed with Lanky Man's knife in his shoulder, alive and groaning.

Luke stood with all the strength he had left and swung his broken bow. At first, Lanky Man ducked, forced away from finishing off Bannack, but Luke faked a swing from above, shifted, and hit Lanky Man directly in the chest. The man skidded backward.

Everything hurt from stab wounds, cuts, and bruises. He couldn't see well, and sweat froze to his face. The only thing keeping him going was his terrified, crying mother watching Luke from behind Lanky Man.

He growled and advanced on Lanky Man again, swinging wildly as grief and rage coursed through him at unmanageable levels. This man killed his dad. He kidnapped his mom. He hurt Sibyl and stabbed

Bannack. His best friend, love of his life, and parents, all the people he cared about, had been hurt by this one man.

Using the last of his strength, Luke scrambled back to Bannack, knife still in his shoulder, and grabbed his friend's sword. He didn't know how to use one, but he had to try, so he swung blindly. Lanky Man ducked and dodged, cackling.

"You think you can best me?"

Luke didn't give him the satisfaction of a response. He kept pushing and pushing through pain, past the point of numbness. Bannack approached Lanky Man from behind and pinned his arms to his side in a hug.

"Now!" Bannack jerked his head away as Lanky Man tried to attack it.

Fury drove the sword true, slicing through the middle of Lanky Man. He screeched, blood gurgling in his throat, and Luke released the weapon.

Something whistled through the air and Bannack dropped the dead man when an arrow landed at his feet. Luke turned to see a group of Skin Stealers, one lowering a bow. Harlowe, leading the group with her baby slung to her back, outstretched her hand and called out something unintelligible.

Bannack cut Clara's ropes and she jumped to her feet. Luke was too weak to move, so she fell into his arms. She smelled of body odor and dirt, but she was alive, warm, and safe. Tears welled in his eyes and his entire body trembled.

"Mama," Luke cried and buried his face against her neck.

She whispered relief to him and he listened, basking in the sound of her voice, and the feel of her small frame in his arms.

He had her. Finally.

Luke wept into her embrace, the adrenaline he'd previously relied on to stay conscious left, and he sunk into her. The last thing he remembered was his mother's soft fingers brushing his hair from his eyes.

"It's over."

Part Four

Aftermath

37 | SIBYL

*This one moment shall
sustain me on cold, sleepless nights.
With it, I shall be immortal,
carried on the wings of our love.
Do not despair, love of my heart,
for I shall always return to thy bed.*

Reds, oranges, and yellows floated above Sibyl's head, a swirl of color without discernible form.

She blinked again.

Blankets? Scarves?

Blink.

Whatever they were, they hung from a round wooden beam, curved downward in the middle, and connected to all four walls. A fire crackled in a glass front fireplace. When she tried to move, her chest burned.

Sibyl remembered the injury. *How am I alive?*

The blade of her own spear had ripped open her body but now laid in a bed wrapped in clean bandages. As Sibyl glanced around the room, scared to move in case she was actually dead, she noticed Bannack. He lounged in a cot beside her, reading a book.

That's when the pain came, a fire in a searing line from her chest to her stomach, and she let out a shaking groan. She dared not move again in case the flare up continued and Bannack appeared in her vision.

"Wait here and I'll grab the ointment."

The pain built, her eyes watering, as she waited for him to return. Within seconds, he did, a jar in his hand.

"I need to unwrap your bandages," Bannack unscrewed the lid and placed it out of sight, "but I'll be careful not to see anything. Okay?"

"I don't care...if you see anything," Sibyl groaned, her brain in a jumbled mess. "I just need the pain to stop."

She laid there as Bannack worked. He kept her decent when he pulled away the bandages, revealing an injury she didn't have the stomach to look at quite yet, and the minute whatever he had in his hand spread across her skin, the pain eased. She could breathe again.

Sibyl labored into a sitting position.

Sheets of warm colors hung in a patchwork of fabric over six beds in the building. It was a cabin with concrete floors, two windows, and exposed, round logs.

"Where are we?"

"In the Skin Stealer village," Bannack said. He placed the jar on the side table between their cots, picked up his book again, winced slightly, and sat back down.

"Skin Stealers?" Sibyl squeaked. "How? Why? Who— What's going on? And why are you here?"

Bannack cleared his throat and told her everything that happened after she took a spear to the chest, and the appearance of Harlowe with the Stealers.

Worry poked at her stomach. Luke had been asked to do horrible things in the recent weeks, and to be forced to kill as the only way to save his mom made her nauseous.

"Why didn't they kill us on sight?"

"Harlowe, the woman who cares for the Stealers, showed up and was able to manage them, but they also recognized me," Bannack said before continuing. "Remember my work trips?"

Sibyl nodded.

"Well," Bannack continued, "for the past three years, I've been visiting them, bringing food, clothing, blankets. I tried language but they didn't understand beyond a few single syllable words. This is my first visit in months since the weather prevented me from traveling. It's what I can do after..." he lowered his gaze, "I'm the reason they aren't fully there in the first place."

She remembered Eloise telling her he went on a trip several times a year, but she never knew it was to the Stealer village. As Bannack spoke, she saw the deep regret that probably would never leave him after everything he did while working for Joy.

Sibyl reached out and put her hand on his knee. "I'm proud of you for holding yourself accountable." After they shared a smile, Sibyl asked again, "So, why are you in here?"

Bannack motioned to the bandages peeking out from his shirt collar. She hadn't noticed them before. "Stabbed."

Before Bannack could continue, the door opened with a creak and Eloise walked in, a steaming bowl of something in her hands. She gave a relieved gasp, placed the food on a half-circle side table by the door, and rushed to Sibyl's side. "You're finally awake!"

"Finally?"

Eloise sat gently on Sibyl's bed. "Yeah. You've been out for a week. Sam and Shinat left yesterday."

"A week!" Sibyl grabbed Eloise's wrist. "Where's Luke?" She glanced down at her chest, remembering with a shudder the hanging skin before she had passed out. "How am I alive?" She looked at Bannack. "Why didn't you use it?"

Bannack opened his mouth to answer but Eloise beat him to it. "Mr. Suspicious of Everything over there refused the ointment." She shot him a glare that looked halfway like teasing. "He insists he's okay, but I stitched him up, so I know how bad it is."

A smirk grew on Bannack's lips, and he opened his book to read. His wariness of the nanite-based ointment was probably because he'd been Joy's mercenary, tasked with kidnapping people to be experimented on with the same nanites that were in the cream.

Sibyl looked to Eloise. "Where is Luke?"

"I'm not sure. He hung around here – he was pretty banged up – then started coming and goin' a lot. What do you last remember?"

"Uh..." she began, but stopped. What did she remember? "Well, I remember the spear and that's it."

Eloise looked down at her hands. "When you got hurt, Spectre used your spear to...kill Isaac."

"No..." Sibyl's hand covered her mouth and threatening tears stung her nose. "Oh, no. No, no. I have to check on Luke." She tossed the covers off and a stab of pain tightened across her chest. "Ow."

"You still have to go slow, dummy," Eloise teased.

"Thanks for the warning." Sibyl lightly rubbed the pain. "I really need to find Luke."

Eloise stood. "At least eat something first." She brought over a savory, wheat-based porridge with some smoked meat and root vegetables.

After satisfying the grumblings of her belly, Sibyl stood gingerly and found her jacket and shoes waiting for her on a nearby chair. She winced when her skin pulled and accepted help from Eloise to slide her arms through the sleeves.

Sibyl stepped outside. She'd grown used to the warmth inside the cabin, so when her skin first touched the freezing air, she instinctively pulled her arms in to hug her body.

"Holy cow," she said and shivered then winced.

The village wasn't a bustling thoroughfare like Market Town or a well-oiled machine like the Compound, but rather sleepy and melancholic. There weren't many Stealers wandering outside, an experience she didn't think she'd ever have, but the ones that were out meandered as if their bodies weren't originally meant for two-legged travel. They were hunched, similar to an ape, and they eyed her with fearful curiosity.

This experience had to be as new and strange for them as it was for her, maybe more so. Here she was, walking amid them as if she were a guest, when – judging by Bannack's information and her small knowledge of their history – they probably didn't even understand completely. She also noticed, as she walked past the third house built with river rock and a thatched roof, no children wandered about. Why?

A trio of Stealers, dressed in white animal fur to blend in with the snow, paused to watch Sibyl. She smiled and waved, and they gestured with their hands to each other, expressions of worry on their faces.

"I know this is probably strange for you," Sibyl said, more for her sake than theirs. "Thank you for letting us stay here."

Something ticked in the back of her mind as she watched them...communicate? Is that what they were doing? She took a half-step closer, curiosity getting the better of her, and stared at their hands. The movements were familiar.

Frightened, the trio jumped away and two ran off. One stayed, though, afraid but his head cocked. Sibyl tried a wave again. He returned it awkwardly.

Sibyl beamed. The Stealer man began gesturing again with slow and precise movements. So many memories pushed at her mind. She knew these gestures and he kept repeating the same ones over and over. It wasn't until he tried for the fifth time that she finally recognized a variation of the American Sign Language alphabet. Crude, but there.

"Oh!" Sibyl got too excited, and she took several steps forward, scaring off the already skittish man. Her shoulders drooped as she watched him leave. Reed. His name was Reed. And she didn't even get to tell him her name.

"Reed's one of the braver ones," a voice from behind Sibyl said.

She half-turned to see a woman dressed in the same white fur as the Stealers, carrying a bundled infant at her breast.

"Are they all like that?" Sibyl asked the woman.

"Like what?" the woman asked. She lowered her hood, revealing platinum blonde hair done up in several braids and a Roman nose.

"Frightened."

The woman nodded. "Yes. They've suffered a lot and are wary of humans and prone to anger." She held out a gloved hand. "I'm Harlowe, by the way, and this little guy is Gauge. Your partner saved us."

Luke...

Sibyl leaned closer when Harlowe turned her body to show off the chubby face of a sleeping infant in a crocheted cap. "He's adorable."

"Thank you."

"I hear you're the one who got us to safety."

Harlowe nodded. "After what Luke did for me and Gauge, I had to help. If it wasn't for Bannack's involvement with your group, I'd never have gotten the villagers to accept you being here either."

She and Harlowe chatted for a while, walking past some shacks built from more rocks. Slowly, Harlowe revealed her story.

"After I ran from my abusive ex, I found refuge in an abandoned shack and stayed there for a few weeks until my body stopped producing as much milk for Gauge due to my own hunger. An older woman found me I guess took pity and brought us here. I planned to leave a month later, but when that time came, they were too attached to the baby. I remember," Harlowe chuckled, "trying to leave and seeing so many crying faces. I had nowhere to go that I just...stayed. Tried to teach them what little sign language I knew – my cousin was deaf – and some basic cooking and farming skills. It's been slow, but we're getting there." Anger flashed across her face. "After what Joy did to them – modified innocent people to save her son – it's the least I could do. They may never be the same, but..." She shrugged.

Her story was incredible. Surviving alone in the mountains while caring for a newborn. Running from an abusive situation into the unknown. Not only welcoming the hospitality of a non-verbal village but also fully accepting her place in the group.

Harlowe continued to share, telling Sibyl how she discovered they could communicate a little bit, and how they earned their name.

"It's a cruel name, really." Harlowe accepted a cooked potato from an older woman, showed thanks by pressing her forehead to the woman's and took a bite. "They *are* dangerous, especially if someone walks into their territory uninvited, and definitely now that Gauge is with me, but their name isn't completely unfounded because they do...do that to people. I try my best to keep people away, though, with frightening images and signs, but some get through the cracks. They don't see people as people. Think of it like...half ape. There, but not fully sentient."

"Because of what happened to them?" Sibyl questioned.

Harlowe nodded. "Unfortunately, outsiders don't see them as human, so they do what they can to strip the bits of humanity the villagers have left."

"Do you call them anything different?"

Harlowe took off her son's hat to readjust it, looked down at Gauge's head, and brushed his hair. It sprung back into place when she removed her hand and Harlowe smiled. "The Forgotten. I'm not very inventive, but I couldn't call them Skin Stealers."

When she looked at Sibyl, happiness fell. "I feel awful about that man with the tattoo. He tried to help me, thinking I was lost, and wouldn't listen when I begged him to leave. He thought I was being abused. An Forgotten with me attacked him and after that...I couldn't do anything. They've gotten better, though. I hope to steer them away from that practice completely but it's slow."

Sibyl pinched Harlowe's sleeve and smiled. "You did your best."

"Thank you."

"I'm really sorry about the group they attacked a few days ago. We were coming back from a hunt without food. They were angry, protective, and lost it when they saw the guns Fade had with them. I couldn't do anything to stop them." She hung her head. "I'm sorry."

"Don't be. Without your villagers attacking Fade, I don't think we would've gotten out alive."

Harlowe smiled and rubbed Gauge's cheek.

"You don't have any family, then?" Sibyl asked.

"No. Died when the bombs dropped."

"Oh no. I'm so sorry."

Harlowe stopped walking, stared at something ahead, and when Sibyl followed her line of sight, she saw Luke. He stood there, backlit by the light filtering through the pine trees. He haunted the spot, staring.

"I'll go," Harlowe whispered, giving Sibyl's hand a squeeze. "Stay as long as you need."

Then it was just her and Luke's shell.

"I'm—" Sibyl began as she walked toward him, unsure he could hear her.

"So, you're awake, then?" Luke asked when she stopped several feet from him.

His calloused words shocked her, and she half wanted to clap back, but something was terribly wrong. This was not the Luke she knew. This was something darker. Sinister. He glared at Sibyl, fists balled, his chin quivering. Sibyl had never seen his reaction to grief and pain, so witnessing the darkness looming in Luke's eyes made her take a half-step back.

"Yes. I'm awake."

"I don't fucking believe you," Luke growled.

What could she say? 'Believe me or not, I'm alive,' was an option but not a kind one and Sibyl knew that Luke needed as many people by his side as he could get to help him navigate the roller coaster of grief.

She opted for a different approach. Sibyl stepped toward him. He didn't move. As she came closer, the anger flowing off him slammed into her gut and chest, threatening to infect her. His eyes shifted to the floor, nostrils flaring.

"There's nothing I can say that'll make this better," Sibyl whispered.

Luke took in a deep, shaking breath. "Then don't."

"I won't."

And she hugged him.

He stiffened as if he were made of stone but felt of glass. Fragile and breakable.

Then Luke melted into her, sobbing. What began as only shaking of his shoulders morphed into wailing and she tightened her grip on him, caressing the back of his head, and waited until he stopped. Through it all, she stayed her own tears. She knew the horrid experience of mourning the loss of a family member, but she'd never watched the sudden death of a loved one while the other bled onto the frozen ground. She'd never diminish that experience, never turn his mourning onto herself.

"I w...w-want this to be over." Luke's voice cracked. "It hurts. It hurts so much."

"I know...I know."

So, she held him and waited until he calmed, then put her palm on his cheek. "I know this hurts beyond anything imaginable." Luke closed his eyes and she wiped away his tears, then asked. "Will you come with me?"

He nodded and followed her into an empty cabin.

When Sibyl closed the door, her body heavy, she released a breath. Her hands shook. She turned to see Luke curled up in a spare bed, hugging a pillow and walked around to see if his eyes were open. They were, so she crouched in front of him. He didn't focus on her.

"What do you need?" Sibyl asked.

He mumbled something, cleared his throat, then said, "Stay."

After a small caress of his cheek, his dark stubble poking at her palm, Sibyl walked around the foot of the bed and slipped behind him.

"Can you come closer?"

Sibyl did so, pressing her body against his, feeling the small tremors of his body, and he sniffled.

"Cici?"

She pressed her face into his shoulder blade. "Yes?"

"Can you put your arm around me?"

She did what he asked and felt his entire body deflate. "Luke, if I could take your pain away, I would. I am so, so sorry, and I will be here whenever you need and for however long. I love you. I love you so much, it hurts."

Between sobs, he thanked her.

38 | SIBYL

Sibyl awoke from her nap while the sun still sat in the sky and stretched gingerly, but didn't get too far before her chest burned. Her hands went to her chest then relaxed when the sharp pain left. She looked over at Luke, who had turned in his sleep and now faced her, the hard lines and angry eyes gone in favor of sleepy softness, dark waves of hair surrounding his face. She pressed her fingertips to the thin layer of facial hair, admiring the roughness of it, then struggled to her feet.

It took her a while with her injury as she slipped her shoes back on. She went as fast as she could, worried that he would wake alone, but she really needed to pee.

When she finished, Sibyl caught sight of Clara sitting on a bench beneath a tree. Even though the kidnapping had only been several weeks ago, with all the chaos it felt like years. Which, Sibyl realized in a sudden flood of relief and grief, was over, but came at a grave cost.

If I go say hi, how is she going to react? Would she rather be alone?

Sibyl swallowed her nerves and walked over. "Hello," she said.

Clara turned. She wore a fur coat and pants, an urn beside her on the bench. Sibyl's chest clenched.

Isaac...

"I'm sorry for your loss," Sibyl said.

"Thank you."

"May I?" Sibyl gestured to an empty spot beside Clara, who moved the urn to the ground and secured it between her legs.

They sat in silence for a while, listening to the birds and wind through the trees. Clara broke the silence first.

"We were wrong about these people," Clara said, her voice deeper than Sibyl remembered. "They are not brutes or mindless killers. We can't let the name continue."

Sibyl glanced around at the snow topped homes, built by the villager's own hands and how they'd welcomed Harlowe and learned to communicate. "I agree. Harlowe calls them The Forgotten."

"Perfect. We'll spread it to the clans and hopefully they can regain some respect."

Again, they sat in silence, Sibyl waiting for Clara to speak first, content to let the woman beside her take the lead.

Eventually, Clara spoke, her voice quiet and reflective. "Isaac always joked Luke would find someone opposite of him. He used to say, 'Clarie, that boy is gonna grow up, find his person, and they are going to be the happiest, warmest person he could find. Like the sun.' And you know what?" She looked at Sibyl, her dark eyes flashing with an intensity that reminded Sibyl of Luke. "I'm glad it was you...Isaac would be, too."

Clara patted Sibyl's knee. A few tears ran down Clara's cheeks and Sibyl quietly cried with her.

Sibyl said goodbye to Clara and wandered back to the cabin where she and Luke had slept. Inside, Luke still slept, so she set to work on building a fire. He stirred halfway through as if about to wake, but never did, so she finished up and closed the fireplace's iron door.

As the room slowly heated, Sibyl grabbed a fur blanket from the hope chest and laid it over the bed. Before she could climb in, Luke grabbed her wrist, and sat up.

He settled his hands on her hips and gently pressed his forehead against her stomach. When Luke slid his thumbs underneath her shirt, they grazed her bandages, and he pulled away as if he were afraid of hurting her.

"Does it hurt still?"

"A little…"

Sadness hung in the air as they settled into bed. Luke rolled onto his side, but Sibyl stayed on her back, the most comfortable position. She watched the shadow of a tree by the window dance in the sunlight.

A long while passed before she heard Luke's small voice. "I thought you were going to leave me alone in this world."

She turned. He watched her, eyes wet, and brushed his hand across her cheek. Not knowing what to say, she leaned forward and kissed him, his lips trembling underneath her touch.

"I'm here to stay," Sibyl said and ran her fingers through his thick hair. After a few moments, she asked as she gestured to her chest, "Do you want to help me look at it?"

Luke hesitated, then nodded.

Sibyl sat up and unbound the bandages. At first, they both stared at each other, a fear over what they might find underneath the white fabric between them. It wasn't until she walked from the bed into the firelight that she gathered the courage to be the first to look.

A fresh scar went from the far left of her clavicle, between her breasts, and diagonally toward her right hip, making her realize just how close to death she'd been, and it was her turn to cry. She cupped her hands over her nose and mouth, and tears fell through her fingers.

Then Luke's arms wrapped around her, giving chaste kisses to her brow. "You are my everything, Sibyl. You are the one I desire to awaken in the morning to, the one who breathes life into me every, single day. W…W-Without you, I'd still be in that cabin, scared of life, never truly living." He wiped her tears. "I know how to live properly now because of you."

Sibyl smiled and her cheeks heated. "I love you. I…" she took hold of his head, her thumb brushing across his cheek, "love you. You have my heart. Completely."

He blinked slowly with his mouth ajar. She closed it gently and he grabbed her hand, kissing the tender skin of her wrist.

Luke glanced at her through his eyelashes, his lips lingering on her pulse, and gently touched her collarbone. His thumb asked to touch her pink scar. In answer, she pressed his palm flat on her chest and nodded.

His finger trailed the line of her newly fused skin, the nanites in the ointment having done the job of a highly skilled surgeon. Sibyl gasped quietly. It was more sensitive to touch than the rest of her. Luke lingered on her sternum before continuing lower and gave her a deep, tragic kiss.

"Bed?" he asked.

They held each other until she fell asleep.

38 | LUKE

Harlowe gave them what she could for food and warmth and thanked Luke for saving her from Kieran, and allowed him to hold Gauge. The tiny child felt foreign in hands that dwarfed the baby's head, but Gauge's eyes watched Luke with a fascinating intensity. He returned the baby to Harlowe and left with Sibyl, Eloise, Bannack, and Clara.

His mother. They'd saved her. He wanted desperately to be happy about it, that they finally had saved her from Fade, but the cost of his dad's life had been so great, Luke didn't know if he could ever be the same again. Didn't know if his father's words of, 'What I want, more than anything, is to hold her again,' would never stop haunting him.

Luke worried about his mom, too. Would she take the time she needed to grieve, or would she throw herself into work as soon as she got home? He'd stay at the house just in case.

Luke didn't remember much of the journey home. Sibyl collected the dogs from the neighbor and returned muddy, reporting that they'd knocked her over in their frantic excitement. He couldn't even smile about it, so he grabbed a pillow that smelled like his dad and snuggled on his bed with the dogs in a warm pile around him. They seemed to sense his anguish. Levin was the most in-tune and he slipped underneath Luke's arm, sighing contentedly. Both dogs stunk like they had rolled in liquid sunshine, but Luke didn't care. They were a comfort when Sibyl couldn't be there.

Days blended together. The bushy and overgrown state of his beard told him long it had been. Some nights, when he couldn't shake the dreams of watching his dad die over and over again, he'd sit in the living room and watch the sunrise. Occasionally, his mother would join in his insomnia activities, bringing him a warm cup of tea wordlessly. Then she'd sit beside him and he'd drape his blanket across her lap. They didn't speak much on those nights.

Sibyl left the house for long periods of time and returned at random. Mostly, she would chat with Clara or clean or bring homemade teas and food.

"You need to eat something," she whispered one day when she arrived with vegetable and barley soup, and fresh, crusty bread. "It's been weeks with next to nothing."

He still wasn't hungry but he accepted the food so she wouldn't worry about him and kept the fact that his pants were loosening a secret. She probably knew anyway, thus the dual purpose of the beard. It hid any facial changes.

The second the soup hit Luke's stomach, nausea reared its head. Had it really been so long since he'd eaten that he couldn't keep food down?

"Where's my mom?"

Sibyl glanced at the bowl he held but didn't finish. "She's meeting with the other Leaders. And once you're done, you're coming with me."

"Where are we going?"

"I need help chopping wood. My stock's running low."

Luke lifted the bread to his mouth and took a bite. His taste buds returned in a rush, awakening his stomach, and Luke shifted from reluctantly eating to devouring his food.

Only then did he realize that she'd been doing so much with a fresh injury. He vowed then that he'd help more so she wouldn't over exert herself. Already, as Luke watched her wander around the living room, he could see the signs of strain around her eyes.

Sibyl took his bowl once he finished. "I'll take care of this while you get cleaned up." She reached over and rubbed his beard. "I kinda like this."

He grunted and once she left, set about trimming his facial hair and prepped the dogs. Once he emerged from the room, he found Sibyl waiting beside the front door in tall boots, a thick coat, and an elbow-length shawl. "Ready?"

They walked together in the cold, the dogs trotting alongside them, and a small ember of life awakened inside Luke. He could feel it there, warming him, and he held Sibyl's hand tighter, knowing she stood beside him.

Hunter had already opened the shop when they arrived and Luke hesitated at the threshold, people on the other side.

"They're distracted," Sibyl whispered. "I'll be here, okay?"

A tiny prickle of insecurity poked at him for a split second before he walked into the shop. He waited at the back for Sibyl to grab her axe, the familiarity of La Parfana more relaxing than he'd expected.

In the late morning, only a few visitors lingered in the shop. Hunter joined Luke as he restocked a shelf.

"Welcome back."

Luke glanced briefly at him. "Thank you."

"And I'm really sorry for your loss."

All of a sudden, he wanted out. He didn't want a reminder of his dad's death, didn't want to hear 'sorry for your loss.' He just wanted to chop some damn wood for Sibyl and go home. But he knew Hunter was being kind, so Luke tried a small smile, odd on his lips, and nodded once. "Thank you."

"You're welcome." He moved on.

Sibyl emerged from the back with an axe in her hand. "Would you believe it? A bird made her nest in the greenhouse." A smile brightened her face. "I spent so long trying to get her out, thinking she'd flown in by accident before I realized she made a home here. Maybe that means Winter's finally over."

Now that she mentioned it, the cold had been a bit less biting on their long walk to La Parfana.

"Hope so," Luke said, taking the axe from Sibyl and giving her a quick peck before leaving. He spent the next hour splitting wood. The activity was unexpectedly therapeutic.

Spring: Four months later.

He waited for her in his front yard in a light cardigan. Food grew in abundance, the town's folk of Market Square and Compounders voicing their excitement in amiable conversation whenever he passed by. He and Bannack even had made plans to travel to The Forgotten in a couple weeks to bring vegetables, fresh breads, and seeds, a few wooden toys for Gauge, and some clothes and flowers for Harlowe.

His dogs lay curled on either side of him, keeping him warm even though he didn't need it. Levin laid on his legs and Boatswain, as always, took his place at Luke's side. He was, quite literally, in a dog pile.

The cool wind blew. They had been trapped in a forever winter since early August. It was now almost May. They all deserved a break from snow and ice.

Grass tickled his cheek as the wind blew and the swaying branches caught his eye. He stared at them for a moment, book open but upside down on his chest, and the budded boughs danced together, as if the wind picked them up and tossed them about to silent music.

He smiled.

With one practiced hand, Luke turned the page of 'The Count of Monte Cristo' and dove straight into Edmund's escape from Chateau Dif. He'd read it over and over and never tired of the story, making a point to revisit Dumas' beautiful revenge story once or twice a year.

"Hullo! Whatcha doing?"

Luke flinched, snatched from the fictional world in his head to the world around him. He blinked, wondering for a split second where his sun disappeared to, then realized someone blocked it. He hadn't even realized his dogs had alerted him to her presence.

Sibyl.

She stood at his head, bent at the waist. Her dark hair spilled in front of her face. She smiled in that wonderful way, dimples deep and Luke had a fleeting thought to pull her down with him.

"Hi," Luke said in a slow drawl. "You're blocking my sun."

"Am I?" Her cheeks and nose shown red, and the white fur of her hood brushed against her face. She crouched on her haunches. Now that she was closer, and he could better make out the color of her eyes. Dark. Rich. He loved them.

"Last I checked, the sun can't shine on the words unless your book is turned the other way," Sibyl said.

She grabbed his book and turned it. He should have been mad at her for taking his entertainment but liked Sibyl's fingertips at the back of his hand too much to care and stared at her moving mouth, calculating how best to kiss it. He stared, unable to do anything as his chest swelled

He cleared his throat. "I'm reading."

"Oh. I know." Sibyl sat beside his head, returning his sun.

Luke shifted closer to her and snagged his book. "Then why did you ask w...w-what I'm reading?"

"I don't really know." Sibyl chuckled, the sound catching and intoxicating all at the same time. "I mostly said it to tease you."

"You do that a lot."

"Cause I like to see you smile."

Luke lowered the book and tilted his head to look at her, hiding the smile that played at his lips. "Do I have to smile for you?"

"Gosh, no." Sibyl shook her head. Her eyes widened, and she frantically waved her hands in the air. "I don't want you to smile for me, not ever, if it means that you're putting on a performance. I just like making you happy, is all. Always have."

Always have.

Those words bounded around in his head like a young buck. She always liked making him happy? Is that what her teasing and joking was all this time? Is that why she insisted on walking with him on grumpy days? Or why she interrupted a perfectly good moment of reading to sit beside him?

"You have an odd way of showing it."

"Well," she said with a tone that sounded like her voice rolled its eyes at him. "You've never been one to share. It took me for*ever* to get anything out of you."

He paused, realizing she was right.

Sibyl's long fingers wound absently through his hair, scraping his scalp. Shivers tickled down his back and limbs. His eyes closed.

For a long while, Luke stayed there on the warm blanket, her fingers scratching and rubbing. Then he reached up, grabbed her hand, and kissed the delicate heartbeat on the inside of her wrist. He felt it speed up underneath his lips.

"Do you w...w-wanna, uh, know w...w-what I'm reading?"

"Yes."

He smiled and put her hand back on his head, grazing the wedding band on her finger, then settled into reading a passage from his book out loud. "'I have seen the man I loved preparing to become the murderer of my son!' She said these w...w-words w...w-with such overwhelming grief, in such a desperate voice, that when he heard it, a sob rose in the count's throat. The lion w...w-was tamed, the avenging angel overcome.'"

He continued reading, her silence his signal to continue, and they lay there, his head in her lap, she stroking his hair, both listening to the birds. They were together, he and Sibyl, and all seemed right with the world. No worries of what he would do in the coming months as his settlement prepared to plant. No concerns over how Sibyl would balance the responsibilities given to them both as shop owner and Woodbrook Leader. Just he and Sibyl against the world.

But he had one more thing to give her. A book. One that he'd commissioned Maxwell to work on. It waited in his bag and had taken a good six months to perfect, just so he could see the joy blossom on her face.

"I have a gift for you." He sat up and fished the book from the bag, wrapped in a small blanket. "Here."

"A present just for me?"

"Open it."

Luke waited in anticipation as she opened the gift and gave him coy glances as she snailed on her task. He wouldn't give her the satisfaction, so he almost burst an eye trying to contain his composure.

Sibyl's amused laughter died down once she saw the leather work. A sun, embossed in gold glistened in the light of day, with leather stitching decorating the front and spine. She quietly ran her fingers over the front and touched the gold metal plate on the cover.

"'Her.' That's the title?"

Luke nodded. "Open it."

She did so and saw beautiful drawings of places they'd been, memories they'd created. Set at the front was the very same art piece of Sibyl he'd seen in Maxwell's folio. He'd recreated the drawing in exchange for more folios bound.

"Oh, Luke..." Sibyl touched her lips. "I...these are your poems, aren't they?"

"Yes. The ones in the Kissing Tree but also others you haven't read or heard."

"'This,'" Sibyl read, "'This one moment shall sustain me on cold, sleepless nights. With it, I shall be immortal, carried on the wings of our love. Do not despair, love of my heart, for I shall always return to thy bed.'" She chuckled and shook her head with a smile. "You are such a hopeless romantic."

Luke's love and adoration for her soared and he caressed her neck. She responded to him, sighing with her eyes closed, and leaned against his touch.

"I often w...w-wonder, love of my life," Luke whispered, "w...w-what is it like to be you. To dance in the rain, coo at your plants as they grow flowers, and smile at nothing at all. W...W-What is it like to awaken every day and see the earth as if you're seeing it for the first time?" He leaned in for a kiss, letting it linger upon her lips until she moaned underneath him, then he pulled away and asked, "Can you show me how?"

"Only if you take me to bed."

He pulled away. "So, we're negotiating now?"

Sibyl shrugged. "Of course," she said with mischief in her voice. "What else would I be doing?"

Luke laughed and pulled her to her feet, happy to give her what she asked and more.

The End

Don't miss Tristan and Nora's romance in...

Deception Isles

A Post-Apocalyptic Pirate Assassin Romance

Coming 2025

Turn the page to read the first chapter.

1 | TRISTAN

SPRING

He stalked up the stairs of the brothel, shedding his double-breasted coat as he went, and waved away the woman who tried to stop him.

"Kameron!" Tristan yelled when he left the stairwell and entered the hallway. "Kam, you fucker! Get out here and explain yourself."

Tristan threw open the first door, then a second, and a third, until he'd interrupted every threesome, forbidden hookup, and orgy in the place. Kam was in the final room, buried underneath a nest of blankets and three women, and only lifted his platinum blond head lazily when one of the girls squeaked in surprise.

"Huh?" He peered at Tristan with one hazel eye, the other still closed, and smiled. "Oh, hey, Tristan!"

"Leave," Tristan snarled.

"If you insist." Kam started to move, his shoulders drooping dramatically. "I mean, you could just ask nicely."

Tristan leveled Kam with a glare. "Not you and you know it."

The women went, gathering up their clothes and dressing before they filed out. Kam protested the entire time, now fully awake, and it wasn't until the final girl closed the door quietly that Kam gave up.

"What's going on now?" Kam asked.

Tristan grabbed Kam's boxers off the cushioned bench at the foot of the bed, tossed them into his best friend's face, and sat. He groaned in relief, stretching his stiff legs out. "The shipment is late."

"And what's that got to do with me?" Kam asked as his black hair and light tan skin popped out from his shirt collar.

Tristan fixed him with an unamused glare and Kam stared right back, shaking his head slightly. "You're the shipper!"

Kam nodded. "Ah. That."

"Damn it, Kam." Tristan stood slowly and opened the door. He leaned out into the hallway, catching the attention of the woman who followed him up the stairs, and gestured for a water basin. Then Tristan sat back down. "He relies on you to get things done and when you don't, it messes up the entire operation."

Finally dressed, Kam adjusted his trench coat and played with the ring piercing at the corner of his mouth. "What makes you think I don't have it handled? It's one shipment and it's late by a few hours. Pretty sure the Plague Doctor can wait."

"If it were textiles or grain, he wouldn't even care, but this is medicine we've been hunting down for months. Without it, people will die."

Kam's jaw worked as he stared at Tristan. "I'm not trying to minimize the situation but seeing as we have no way of communicating with the ship, which by the way is running on literal air power, there's no sense in working yourself up into a frenzy over something I have no control over. The ship will come and when it does, we'll deal with the issue. Alright?"

They stood facing each other, Tristan's anger boiling in his stomach, and only turned away when the woman entered with the fresh water.

"Where would you like this, sir?"

Kam and Tristan responded at the same time and pointed to two different locations. "Right there," they both said.

The woman stared, unsure what to do, when Kam lifted his hand to silently tell Tristan he could take over. Tristan cleared his throat.

"Just on the dresser is fine. Thank you." When the woman left, Tristan grunted as he stood, the braces against his skin pinching, and ignored the slight concern in Kam's face. "Wash up and meet me outside."

"Aye, Majesty."

Tristan paused with his hand on the doorknob, nostrils flaring, and had a fleeting curiosity if punching Kam would restart his brain that was still firmly in sex brain mode. The last bruise on Kam's face had finally healed from when someone mistook him for their woman's secret lover, and Tristan wasn't too keen on giving him more so soon, so he rolled his eyes and left, making sure to stop by Rysella's office first to apologize for tormenting her customers and workers. He only hoped she'd look past his carelessness once he offered to mop her floors for a week.

Old Marcus pushed his cart of fresh bread past Tristan as he waited for Kam and waved. "Good day, Detective."

Tristan dipped the edge of his worn flat cap in greeting. The older man mosied along toward the low hum of the farmer's market set up in the open courtyard beyond the brothel. Sea air blew through Tristan's brown curls as he listened to the mixed voices of bartering, hawking their wares, and children laughing as they ran along the bridges that connected the islands together. For fifteen years, Northshore had progressively gotten bigger as the people used plastic bottles and anything else that floated to build the foundation of the islands. What began as one single island had morphed into six that took up so much of the bay that the islands moved little.

Tristan glanced up at the mast of The Gull, a ship that had run aground during the pirate-citizen conflict and sighed. How could Kam roll around with the brothel women when he'd lost a fucking ship? It wasn't totally his fault, though, because Katrina's Lament was at the mercy of wind, and Kam had never once lost a ship in the six years they'd been working together.

The door behind Tristan opened and he pushed off the wall with his foot. Kam shook out his hands to adjust the sleeves of his black leather jacket then laid his arm across Tristan's shoulders, his beaded necklaces clashing with the metal on Kam's bracelet.

"Where to now?" Kam asked.

Tristan sighed, most of his anger from fifteen minutes ago faded. "Food, then we'll figure out this ship issue."

Their footsteps clunked on the wooden bridge connected to Courtyard Isle. Tristan popped the collar of his coat and stuffed his hands into his pockets, Kam a step behind him as calls from the vendors about breads, fruits, vegetables, furs, and cured meats fought to be heard by the shoppers.

It really was impressive, how Northshore had been built to stay afloat and while the Plague Doctor had expanded much of the bay, turning it from a degenerative, lawless place with no regards to the integrity of Northshore's foundation, to a place of order. Chaos still reigned, especially at night, but there was accountability.

Kam paid for ten meat pies while Tristan waited. "Your appetite never ceases to amaze," Tristan marveled.

"And what's that?" Kam raised his eyebrow at the bag of cured bacon, five rolls, and several carrots that Tristan held.

Tristan pivoted away so Kam couldn't judge his lunch fit for three people. "Eat your pies and leave mine alone."

Kam grinned wide and took a generous bite of pie.

They walked for a bit longer, taking in the ambiance around them. Ivy and clematis, left to travel as it desired, covered the front of the mix-and-match built buildings sitting on the outside edge of Courtyard Isle. Yellow scotch broom some idiot thought would be fun to bring from the Key Peninsula grew happily along the line of stakes tied to rope which separated the walking paths from the greenery.

Many of the items the vendors were selling; glass blown vases so tiny, they could only fit one or two dandelions a child gave their mother, shiny wooden bowls, knitted and crocheted clothing and blankets, distracted Tristan temporarily before he was able to wrestle his mind back to the current issue. The ship.

"Hey," Kam nudged Tristan, "these are from where you grew up."

He knew. He'd seen the 'Made in Gig Harbor' tag before he got distracted by the lace petals of the on-sale tulips, wanting to touch them so bad his fingers itched, and hoped he never had to be reminded of that place ever again.

"Wanna get one?" Kam asked.

"No," Tristan grumbled, stalked off, and Kam had to jog to catch up.

Several women stared as they watched Tristan and Kam pass, blushing and whispering to each other. He couldn't take Kam anywhere without that being the typical reaction to his presence. The guy had slept with almost every human in town who wasn't attached to another.

"Hello, ladies," Kam said as he flirted from behind Tristan. "How are we doing today?"

Before Kam could stop and speak to them further, Tristan turned, slightly tweaking his knee, and snagged Kam's shirt collar, pulling him along.

"Another time then!" He called and then fell in line with Tristan. "What's gotten you so grumpy?"

Tristan rolled his eyes and did his best to hide the limp. "You lost track of a ship, so of course I'm grumpy and I'll stay that way until it comes into harbor."

"Alright," Kam relented as they walked out into the open space of the long pier. "We'll have a chat with the Harbor Master and see what we can do."

"Good."

They walked along the bridge that stretched to the farthest island which lounged closest to the desolate mainland. Workers tossed bags of flour and potatoes down from one of the four ships owned by the Plague Doctor to more workers waiting on the pier. They called to each other, communicating the need for more bags or if they were ready to toss something down. As they always did, those on Pier 56 parted for Tristan, gave courteous nods, and continued with their work.

He eyed the repairs finished two weeks ago after their latest conflict with Southland. A band of them had tried to break the wooden bridge to prevent Northshore from following them. In the end, Northshore had five injured, Southland had one dead, and half the grain storage was gone. It'd take them weeks to build what they lost back up.

The Harbor Master's office wasn't far but walking there may as well have lasted hours with how impatient he was. They needed the ship. It carried medicines and first aid supplies unavailable for years until the Plague Doctor had gotten wind of its existence and sent the fastest ship, Katrina's Lament, to acquire some. Yet another reason why losing her was so frustrating. The hospital was bogged down by yet another outbreak of sickness requiring antibiotics and with Southland attacking, the injured were forced to lie in pain waiting for relief to arrive.

Marina turned to Tristan and Kam when the bell above the office door rang. Her blonde hair cascaded down her back in an intricate show of braids and she smiled easily.

"Boys!" Marina exclaimed and pulled each of them into a hug. "What brings you to this stuffy alcove?"

"We're down one ship," Tristan began as he sat.

Marina put the book she'd been holding down and sat at her desk to consult her ledger. After a few moments, she slowly closed her eyes. "The medicine ship."

"Yes." Tristan sat forward, listening to Kam pace behind him. "Have any of the other captains mentioned seeing it at all?"

"Possibly." She consulted another record, this one used for compiling all the captain's logs into one location. Her ringed index finger slid down several pages and stopped at the fifth page. "Here. Two days ago, Lorenzo caught sight of the blue and white flag of Katrina's Lament. That the ship you're looking for?"

Hopefulness fluttering through his gut, Tristan replied, "Yes. Does it say anything else?"

"Not much. Lorenzo did note that she was anchored near Southland in Baker Bay, which he thought was strange."

That was strange. When Tristan delivered Margaret's papers before she set sail on the Lament, there had been no orders to pick up in Baker Bay. There were never orders to visit their enemies, so why was Margaret even there?

He determined to ask her about it then asked, "Anything else?"

Marina shook her head. "No. Oh wait."

Tristan couldn't help but rub his knees.

Marina glanced at Kam. "You sent out eleven crewmen on Katrina's Lament with Margaret, correct?"

Kam finally sat. "No. I sent ten."

"Well, Lorenzo documented he saw eleven as they passed each other and we all know how meticulous that man is. He's rarely wrong."

Tristan and Kam glanced at each other.

"Congratulations, boys. Looks like you have a stowaway."

Afterword

And that concludes the second book in this four book series (the fourth one is currently deciding if it wants to be a short book or a novella when it grows up).

Luke and Sibyl were, by far, the easiest characters to develop and write through. Their banter, dialogue, and story just flew onto the page. I wrote the entirety of this book in less than six months while pregnant with my second child (who is now, at the time of me writing this, nine years old). I still don't know why they were so easy, but compared to the *years* it took me to nail down and understand Eloise (the female main character of *Metallic Heart*), that time frame was very much welcomed. Still haven't figured out how to repeat it, though. Ha!

Sibyl and Luke's spotlight is shifting to shine on the next couple and even knowing they'll have cameos in subsequent books, it's a bit sad to be leaving them, but I'm really, really excited to introduce my readers to Tristan and Nora in the next book, *Deception Isles*. It expands the world of The Fade Series and dive into a Waterworld-esque (if you've seen the 1995 Kevin Kostner movie) environment full of pirates, a reluctant assassin, a masked pirate king, manipulation and deception, and some major revelations on the terrorist group that catapulted this entire series into existence years ago: Fade. It's quite a ride, so be sure to return!

Silence Pass is the one that changed the writing game for me and it feels like it's been ages since. Originally, it was supposed to be written immediately after *Metallic Heart* and even though it was, my writing style and knowledge of the indie publishing trade had changed so drastically, I knew I had to rewrite *Metallic Heart* to match it's counterpart, a decision encouraged by the writing group I found.

I may end up talking about my writing group in each book. They changed the game for me, this small group of four women. What began as a fun way to share stories together and give feedback, turned into a deep, special friendship that went beyond writing. I wouldn't be the writer I am today without them.

Even though this book is done, I hope you will stay for more adventure and romance. Thank you for reading. It means so much to me!

And, as always, don't forget to leave a review.

Until next time!

About the Author

Liahona West spent her entire teenage years either glued to a book or wandering the forests surrounding her home. Whether it was escaping the dreaded high school lunch room in favor of reading in the library or exploring the forest barefoot with her younger siblings in the PNW, Liahona found countless ways to fall in love with the simple magic of life. When Liahona isn't writing in every location possible, she is raising three boys, tending to two dogs, and somehow managing to pursue a college degree.

Silence Pass is her second novel.

CONNECT BELOW

9 781736 820667